THEIR ICELANDIC MARRIAGE REUNION

SOPHIE PEMBROKE

SNOWED IN WITH THE BILLIONAIRE

CARA COLTER

MILLS & BOON

First published in Great Britain 2022
by Mills & Boon, an imprint of HarperCollins*Publishers* Ltd,
1 London Bridge Street, London, SE1 9GF

www.harpercollins.co.uk

HarperCollins*Publishers*
1st Floor, Watermarque Building,
Ringsend Road, Dublin 4, Ireland

Their Icelandic Marriage Reunion © 2022 Sophie Pembroke

Snowed In with the Billionaire © 2022 Cara Colter

ISBN: 978-0-263-30231-8

12/22

MIX
Paper | Supporting
responsible forestry
FSC™ C007454

THEIR ICELANDIC MARRIAGE REUNION

SOPHIE PEMBROKE

MILLS & BOON

To the people of that land of fire and ice
where I set this book.

And most especially to Sigurður Hjartarson,
for founding The Icelandic Phallological Museum.

CHAPTER ONE

Rumours are swirling that Hollywood's favourite fairy tale ex-couple, Winter de Holland and Josh Abraham, could be looking at a second chance at a happy ending, as both of them will be heading to the most unexpected destination of the year, Iceland, for the opening of Liam Delaney's new geothermal spa retreat hotel. After the tragic ending to their happy-ever-after last time, we here at Livingthe-FairyTale.com had to know more. So we caught up with Winter at a press conference for her nomination for Best Director to find out the truth behind the rumours...

THE CAMERA LIGHTS flashed as Winter stepped out onto the stage, then took her seat behind the table, ready for the press conference to begin. She made sure to smile and turn her best side towards the most prominent lenses, even as she ran through what she wanted to say in her head.

She knew how to do this. Even if she'd never done exactly *this* before.

Winter's assistant, Jenny, leaned over her shoulder to place a file folder in front of her, and she knew without looking that it would contain any answers she couldn't remember off the top of her head. Figures about representation in film, statistics about parts for women over forty, the number of female directors on awards shortlists, that sort of thing.

The important stuff. The things that she'd come here today to discuss.

Things that her first ever big award nomination, as Best Director for *Another Time and Place*, had given her a platform to say.

Winter took a deep breath, smiled her thanks up at Jenny, then laid her palms flat on the surface of the table in front of her.

She was ready.

The first questions were easy—the ones she'd prepared for long before the shortlists were even announced. How did it feel to be nominated? What was it about the film she thought had resonated with the board? Who did she give thanks to? What was the cast like to work with? Especially Melody Witnall, the fifty-year-old star of the movie.

'Melody was a dream,' Winter said, gesturing to where the actress sat to one side of the podium. 'A consummate professional, of course. But more than that, she brought such *life* to the part of Beatrix. She showcased perfectly what I was trying to show audiences—that age is just a number, and that women can find love and success and fulfilment at any age. That we, as women, get to set our own criteria for success, that we can choose our own futures, and a few grey hairs isn't going to stop us!'

That line got a laugh, as she'd hoped. Of course Melody's perfectly groomed ice-blonde hair wouldn't show a grey anyway, although Winter was hyper-conscious of the silver strands appearing in her own black bob. Maybe she'd stop dyeing it. Go grey gracefully, if she wanted.

Or maybe she'd dye it purple. It wasn't as if she had to ask anyone's permission.

'Do you believe in second chances in love then, Winter?' Another reporter shouted the question out as the laughter died down.

Bring it back to the film.

That was the mantra for this press conference. Whatever they asked her about, she just needed to bring it back to the film. The film was what mattered, not her thoughts on love. Or her own experiences of it, for that matter.

She'd had her life hijacked by love before. Now, she was focused on other things, out of the long shadow that love had cast.

'One of the things I loved about the script for *Another Time and Place* when I first read it was the emphasis on the idea that you don't have to be young and fresh to find love. That second chances—and third chances and fourth chances, for that matter—can come our way too, and it's up to us to grab them. In fact, I find those romances—the ones that come *after* a heartbreak—more believable, don't you?'

The reporter shrugged, not used to having his own questions turned on him, it seemed. 'I don't know. How do you mean?'

'Well, in a romance like *Another Time and Place,* the characters are not just older, they're more mature. They know themselves better, and have a stronger understanding of the world, other people, and what they want from both. That makes them more capable of building a real relationship—and that's how Beatrix and Harry are able to find their happy ending. You see?'

The reporter nodded, but the glazed look in his eyes suggested he'd tuned out halfway through. Winter held back a sigh.

If she ever loved again, it would be different this time around. It would be like Beatrix and Harry—real and private and, most of all, equal.

Or maybe *she* would just be different. Heaven knew she wasn't the same person she'd been the first time she'd fallen in love, eight years ago.

Winter shook her head and brought her focus back to the press conference. She didn't want to be talking about love, anyway. She wanted to be talking about female representation and power in Hollywood—in front of and behind the camera.

Melody fielded a couple of questions next, followed by Sarah, the writer. But it wasn't long before the cameras swung back Winter's way at another question about love.

'You've said that you believe in second chance love—but what about a second chance at *first* love?'

Winter blinked, trying to keep her expression blank even as her heart started to race at the memories of her own first love. 'How do you mean?'

This is not what we're meant to be talking about today.

'Well, your ex-husband, Josh Abraham, said recently that he thinks there's nothing more powerful than first love, or love at first sight. Would you agree?' The reporter raised her eyebrows, awaiting the response Winter just *knew* would be the only thing anyone took away from this press conference. Damn it—and damn Josh and his ridiculous romantic notions. Not to mention his unerring ability to take anything she thought was about her and make it about him.

When they were married, all anyone had ever wanted to talk about was their fairy tale romance—not the films she was making, or her acting or directorial dreams. All anyone cared about was her relationship with Josh. And, in the case of producers, how they could use it to sell more movie tickets. She'd lost count of the number of romcoms they'd been pitched by producers to star in together over those first couple of years, before—

Why was she thinking about this? She needed to focus.

This was her press conference, for heaven's sake! Why were they asking about him? They'd been divorced for five years—twice as long as they were married in the first place. Wasn't that enough water under the bridge to move on?

Apparently not, since the whole room was still awaiting her answer with bated breath.

'I think… I think that all love is first love when it's new. And what *Another Time and Place* shows is that the excitement of love is always fresh and new, whatever your age.' She gave a stock smile, one she knew barely reached her cheeks, let alone her eyes, and glanced up to give Jenny the signal to bring things to a close.

'Last question,' Jenny said, picking on a friendly reporter in the front row who could be trusted to ask something *sensible* about the movie, not the vagaries of love.

But the woman at the back—from some entertainment website or another—who'd asked the previous question, got in first. 'Actually, I had a follow-up. I just wondered if the fact you and your ex-husband will be spending the week together at a luxury Icelandic spa hotel owned by your mutual friend, Liam Delaney, might make any difference to your answer on second chance love?'

Winter gripped tight to the table in front of her and fought to keep her smile in place. 'I don't see why that should make any difference to my views, no. Now, thank you all for coming.' She stood, hoping she wasn't trembling too obviously.

Jenny, bless her, took control in a second, stepping in

front of Winter to draw everything to a close, so she could slink off to the sidelines and fall apart in peace and quiet.

'Are you all right?' Melody had followed her, Winter realised, and now stood at her elbow, shielding her from the glare of the cameras, as if they were just having a nice catch-up. God bless other women, Winter thought, as she looked up at her star.

'I'll be fine. Thank you.' It wasn't a lie. It couldn't be a lie. She'd be fine, just like she'd been fine last time. She'd pick herself up again and keep living her life. A life *without* Josh in it.

Everything was absolutely fine.

Or at least it would be, once she'd ripped Liam Delaney apart with her bare hands for inviting her ex-husband to what was supposed to be a quiet week of rest and relaxation at an Icelandic spa hotel.

Then things would be just fine.

'You didn't tell her I was coming. Did you?' Josh turned away from the computer screen in front of him to raise his eyebrows accusingly at his friend as he asked the question. He hoped the twisting turmoil that had taken over his stomach didn't show in his expression.

Liam merely shrugged, before replying in his usual drawling English tone, 'Course not. Didn't want to risk her saying no, did I? I mean, don't get me wrong. You're a big draw, mate. But Winter…she's in another league right now, especially with this nomination.'

And of course Winter *would* have said no if she'd known he would be here. Josh was just as sure of that as Liam was. She'd gone out of her way to avoid him for the past five years. Why would this trip be any different?

It wasn't even as if he could blame her. After everything that had happened between them…of course she didn't want to be around him. How could he be anything except a painful reminder of what they'd almost had and lost.

She probably didn't need him around to be reminded, though. God only knew *he* thought about it every day.

'Who's the blonde on the podium with her?' Liam gestured towards the computer screen they were watching the press conference on. 'She looks familiar.'

Josh squinted. Just on the edge of the screen he could see Winter deep in conversation with the star of her directorial debut. 'You mean Melody Witnall? Heck, you really are out of the business if you don't recognise her.'

'Not Mel.' Liam rolled his eyes and pointed—more accurately, this time. 'Her.'

'Oh, that's Jenny. Winter's assistant.' She was handling the crowd well, Josh judged, as he watched her manage the gaggle of gossip reporters all trying to get access to Winter. It was good to know that she had people like Jenny on her side, now he wasn't there.

She'd run to Jenny when she'd left him, he remembered. It had been Jenny who had helped her through those horrible months, not him. Who'd given her the support she needed. That he hadn't been able to provide.

'She's hot,' Liam said decisively. As if he were the arbitrator who decided such things. Which, actually, he might believe he was. Josh had never truly managed to fathom the man's confidence in himself.

Well, in most things. Not all.

There was, after all, a reason Liam had given up acting and retired to run luxury retreat hotels like this one.

Something else neither of them wanted to dwell on today. Josh let his gaze drift back across the screen again to where Winter and Melody stood. They'd shifted positions, giving him a better view of his ex-wife's face. She was smiling that smile she always put on when things were falling apart but she wanted to pretend they weren't.

Like the time she'd tried to make a homemade dinner for his brother and sister-in-law, going so far as to make the lasagne a week in advance, only for it not to defrost in time for them to eat. Every time she'd appeared in the doorway from the kitchen, unfamiliar apron knotted tightly around her waist, she'd been smiling that smile as she'd assured them it wouldn't be long now.

After three hours and two bottles of wine, they'd ordered takeaway.

'She looks good,' Liam said softly beside him.

'So you said.'

'Not the assistant. Winter. She looks…well.'

'She looks tired.' Josh resisted the urge to reach out and run a finger along her cheek on the screen. There were levels of pathetic that even his best friend shouldn't be made to witness. 'You really didn't tell her I was going to be here this week?'

'In my defence, she didn't ask.' There wasn't much by way of an apology in Liam's voice.

She'd looked blindsided by the question. God only knew how the reporters had got hold of the guest list before Winter did, but he supposed that was their actual job. And it wasn't as if Winter hadn't got other things on her mind.

She didn't ask.

Because she had assumed Liam wouldn't risk them both being in the same place for his fancy press week launch of the new hotel?

Or because she just didn't think of him at all these days?

Josh wasn't sure he wanted to know the answer to that one.

'Do you think she'll still come?' he asked instead.

'I bloody hope so.' Liam paced away from the computer screen and threw himself onto the black sofa that sat against the wall of his office. Josh followed, dropping into the armchair opposite him. Liam really had chosen the perfect place for his office. Through the window, Josh could see out across the rocky lava fields around the geothermal pools and to the snow-tipped mountains beyond.

This hotel was beyond any of the others that Liam had opened in his native Britain or his adopted country—the States. Josh wasn't sure what had drawn his friend to the spa retreat in Iceland, but once he'd snapped it up he'd spent a fortune turning it into the luxurious retreat—an escape from the real world.

Looking out over the landscape now, Josh could almost believe he was on another planet.

'This place has the potential to be really, really special.' Liam sat up, resting his forearms on his knees, and he leant forward to speak to Josh. 'I just need to get the word out. And this week…it's the key to everything. With you here, and Winter, and the press invitees and influencers…we can make the Ice House the name on everyone's lips.'

'As long as she still comes,' Josh said.

'Exactly.'

Josh studied his friend, taking in the new lines around his eyes and the sudden appearance of a few grey hairs at his temples. Liam was only thirty-eight, the same as him, but apparently this was what thirty-eight looked like. And felt like.

It felt old. But then, in other ways, it felt exactly the same as twenty-eight had. Except that when he was twenty-eight he hadn't even *met* Winter yet. And that didn't feel possible either—that there had ever been a time when she wasn't a feature of his life.

'I should leave,' Josh said, the right path suddenly obvious. 'It's not fair for me to blindside her here, when she clearly needs the break.'

'And you don't?' Liam asked, eyebrows raised. 'Besides, I invited you both here because I *want* both of you here. For publicity reasons, obviously.'

Something about his tone, or the way Liam didn't meet his gaze, gave Josh pause.

'Is that really the only reason you asked us both?' he asked, eyes narrowed. 'To get people talking?'

Liam shrugged. 'What do you think?'

'I think maybe you got bored without the rush of the Hollywood scene and decided to try meddling with your friends' lives instead.' Something he didn't appreciate.

Liam didn't rise to the bait. 'Look, if you two are happy, I am happy—especially if both of you can be happy here and raise interest in my new hotel.'

'But?' Because there was definitely a but coming.

'But you and Winter have always been unfinished business. The way she left, how things were before… there was no closure. For either of you.'

In an instant, Josh was transported to that moment, five years ago, when he'd arrived home from filming to their house in Los Angeles and found her gone. His heart dropped again now, the way it had when he'd read the note she'd left.

When he'd realised his marriage was over before he'd even had a chance to try and save it.

'It's been five years,' Josh pointed out, rather than admitting how close Liam's words hit on the truth.

'Five years in which you've claimed you've moved on, dated a selection of identikit blondes—but never for longer than a few months—and generally pined for your lost love.' Liam really wasn't pulling his punches today.

'I have not been pining.' Josh was almost certain he wasn't lying about that. 'It's not like I want Winter back, or that I think she's the only woman in the world for me or anything.'

'Except that you still talk about finding your forever love, the one you can grow old with. A love like your parents had.'

'Because that's what I want,' Josh broke in. He wanted to move on, find true love and his happy ever after, with a woman who would stay. It was just hard to do when he couldn't fully understand why Winter had left in the first place.

Her note had said that she couldn't do it any more—couldn't be married to him. And he'd put together plenty of reasons why that was in his head over the last five years, especially late at night when he couldn't sleep. But she'd never explained to him *exactly* what it was he'd done wrong. And, without that, how could he be sure he wouldn't do it again?

Not that he really wanted to say all that to Liam. So he cast around for another way to explain it. 'You never met my dad, but you've heard my mom and my brother talk about him, right?'

Liam nodded. 'Once or twice.' Liam was one of those rare actor friends who transcended that work-life barrier and became family, and he'd spent more than one holiday with Josh's family, especially after the accident. 'Your whole family is as American as apple pie, and about as sweet.'

'He and my mom had the real thing. True love. My brother, Graham, he found that too—you've seen how happy he and Ashley are, especially now the twins are here. They found the real deal. And I'm not settling for anything less either.'

Was that really so much to ask for?

Liam eyed him carefully. 'You thought Winter was your real thing once, remember.'

'And I was wrong.'

He remembered his mother's words, after Winter had moved out.

'I always knew she wasn't the one for you. Don't worry. She'll come along when you're ready.'

But he'd *been* ready, for years now. He wanted that settled feeling of home he saw on Graham's face when he smiled at his wife. He wanted that love and the laughter and the warmth he remembered from his childhood home, before his father passed away.

Maybe for a while he'd thought he'd found that with Winter. But he'd realised soon enough that he was wrong. Everything with Winter had been hard, and he'd felt himself failing from the start. And when everything went to hell…he hadn't been able to fix any of it. So she'd left, and he'd let her go without a fight, because he'd known then it wasn't meant to be between them.

Falling in love with Winter had been like a thunderbolt, knocking him out of his everyday life and into a fairy tale where the happy ending seemed inevitable. It had been powerful, overwhelming and life-changing, the way first love always was, according to the movies.

But first love wasn't the same thing as true love.

True love, he knew from watching his family, was easy. Comfortable. When something was right, when it was meant to be, the pieces just fell into place.

He just had to have faith that one day those pieces would do that for him.

'Just…if you're really ready to move on, mate, use

this week to prove it,' Liam said. 'Get some closure. Stop beating yourself up for what went wrong and start looking for things that are right. Yeah?'

'I don't beat myself up over what happened with Winter.' Okay, that one *was* a lie.

'Yeah. Yeah, you do.' Liam's smile was sad. 'I know what that looks like.'

It was the closest Liam had come in a long time to mentioning the mistakes he'd made in his own past, the ones that had led to the accident that woke him up and made him leave Hollywood behind. Josh wanted to push further, to see if he needed to say more, but before he could find the right way to do it, Liam was already jumping to his feet.

'Right. No rest for the wicked, as my grandpa used to say. I need to get back to work.' He opened the office door and raised his eyebrows expectantly at Josh.

Josh rolled his eyes and moved towards it.

'And mate…' Liam's blue eyes were bright under his dark hair, falling over his forehead. 'Think about what I said. About closure and all that.'

Closure. Josh imagined, for a moment, knowing exactly what he'd done wrong to make Winter leave, and felt a weight lift. Maybe theirs hadn't been true love or meant to be, or the fairy tale the gossip magazines had claimed after they'd fallen in love on the set of their first movie together and married within the year. But they *had* been in love.

And if Josh was going to risk his heart again one of these days, he wanted to give it the best chance of not getting broken. Which meant not making the same mistake twice.

True love might be easy and right when it came along, but it couldn't hurt to give it a helping hand. Understanding what went wrong with him and Winter...maybe Liam was right, and that *would* help him take that leap into love again.

'Yeah. All right.' Josh stepped through the door. 'I'll see you later. For dinner, yeah?'

Liam nodded and shut the door behind him.

And Josh took the corridor that would lead him back to his suite—the best in the place, Liam assured him.

At least he'd have a nice place to hang out, while he figured out what to say to his ex-wife when he saw her for the first time in almost five years tomorrow.

CHAPTER TWO

'I CANNOT BELIEVE Liam would do this.' The room they'd commandeered backstage at the press conference, a small meeting room belonging to the studio, wasn't really big enough for pacing, but Winter was giving it a good go. 'Why would he invite Josh if he also wanted me to be there?'

'Because you're both his friends? Because it will be fantastic publicity for that new hotel of his?' Jenny was sitting in the leather chair at the head of the oval meeting table, her long legs thrown up so her feet rested on the surface. The heels Jenny had been wearing for the press conference had been abandoned beside hers at the door, Winter noticed. They'd both clearly decided that this was not a moment for uncomfortable footwear.

She was going to have to spend a week in Iceland with her ex-husband. In the middle of winter.

This was a *terrible* idea.

Five years. In the five years since she'd walked out on her marriage, she'd managed to avoid Josh entirely. Their divorce had been conducted via lawyers and, apart from the occasional cold and clinical meeting on the particulars, she'd never had to have a conversation with her ex-husband since she'd written him that note telling him she was leaving.

And now she had to go to a hotel opening with him and make *small talk?*

How could she possibly do that, when everything that remained unsaid between them was so huge? It wasn't as if she could walk in there and say, *Sorry, my bad*, and make up for everything she'd got wrong. An apology couldn't wash away her guilt, and it couldn't change everything that hadn't worked between them by the end either.

'What was he thinking?' Winter reached the screen at the end of the room, pivoted on the ball of her foot and headed back in the opposite direction again.

'Liam? I've never met the guy, but I think I already covered his thought processes pretty succinctly,' Jenny replied. In her hands she held a stack of worn and dog-eared cards, rippling them into each other with nimble fingers to shuffle them. 'But if you want more insight, pick a card.'

Winter cast a dismissive glance at the intricately designed cards. 'You know I don't believe in that.'

'I've told you. Tarot doesn't care if you believe or not.' Swinging her legs down to sit up straight in the chair, Jenny gave the cards one last shuffle, then held the deck out to Winter.

Winter paced past her three more times before giving in and taking the damn cards and throwing herself into the chair beside her assistant. She shuffled the cards roughly as Jenny said, 'Now, think about what you want them to tell you.'

'How to get out of going to Iceland?' Winter suggested.

Jenny rolled her eyes. 'If that was all you wanted, it would be easy. A few phone calls, and suddenly you've got a can't-miss opportunity here and you're calling Liam to say you're sorry but you can't make it.'

Winter stopped shuffling the cards. She could just...not go. Couldn't she? 'That sounds great. Why can't we do that?'

'Because that's not what you really want,' Jenny replied sagely.

Winter considered. 'Are you sure? Because it sounds a *lot* like what I really want.' Not having to see Josh again, that was the main appeal of the plan. Not having to talk about everything that had happened between them. About the resentment she'd felt, and then the pain and the misery that had consumed the last months of their marriage.

About how she'd failed at the most important job she'd ever been given, and after that...just looking at the sadness in his eyes had broken her over and over again, until she'd had to leave and not look back.

Seeing Josh again, that would be looking back. And Winter had worked so hard over the last five years to only look *forward.*

'You've been looking forward to this trip for months,' Jenny pointed out. 'We *both* have. Remember? Ice yoga. Spa retreat. Geothermal pools. *Massage.* Relaxation and recharging, and other important things beginning with "re".'

Like *reunion.* With the ex-husband she'd never quite managed to fall out of love with, even after she left him.

Yeah, this was going to be a disaster.

Winter put the cards down on the table. 'I just don't see how I can go and spend a week in the same hotel as him.'

'Because you don't make life decisions based on the actions of your ex-husband,' Jenny said with a shrug. 'It's a big hotel, Winter. You don't have to see him if you don't want to. And if you do...well, that might not be the worst thing, anyway. Maybe it's time for you to get some closure.'

'Closure?'

Oh, God, what if that was what *Josh* wanted? What if he wanted to talk—really talk—about everything that happened five years ago?

Jenny had wanted her to go to therapy. To deal with everything healthily and move on. But Winter had always been more of a 'bury it deep and forget it ever happened' person, and it had served her well until now.

When there was a chance Josh was going to want to dig up all of her carefully buried history.

The history and the guilt she saw in the mirror every day when she met her own gaze. It was easy enough to look away from her own reflection. Less simple to ignore it when faced by the husband she had walked away from.

'Sure,' Jenny went on, oblivious to Winter's terrifying train of thought. 'I mean, you both work in the same incestuous film industry. You're going to bump into each other at events in the future—it's a miracle it hasn't happened already. Wouldn't you rather your first meeting be under your control, when you know it's going to happen? When you can get all the awkwardness out of the way and just move the hell on with your life?'

That did sound better than cowering in fear about ever seeing Josh again. Which, she admitted, she had been doing. And it wasn't as if Josh could *make* her have deep and meaningful conversations if she didn't want to. Jenny was right, the hotel was probably huge. She'd just hide in her room in between whatever events Liam had planned, and the rest of the time there'd be too many people around for Josh to try and get into anything too personal.

Winter's hand hovered over the deck of Tarot cards. 'Okay. So I want to know what's going to happen if I go to Iceland.'

'No good,' Jenny said. 'The cards can't actually tell the future, remember.'

Winter snatched her hand back. 'Then what good are they?'

'Think of them as starting points,' Jenny suggested. 'Each card is imbued with stories and meanings—ones that make you think. You draw a card, or a spread of them, and you look at all the thoughts and meanings there, and you make a story out of them. One that seems connected to your life right now. Basically, they help you direct your mind to the things you need to think about, to consider, to move forward.'

'So it's not really about the cards at all,' Winter said slowly.

'Nope. It's all about you,' Jenny agreed. 'Think of this as a tiny taster of all that therapy you never went to. So, have you got your question?'

'I think so.'

What do I need to consider about going to Iceland?

'What do I do next?'

'Cut the pack in half,' Jenny instructed her, and Winter did as she was told. 'We're keeping this dead simple for now. Just turn over the top card.'

Winter watched the image as it emerged. Naked people rising up from their coffins as an angel played a trumpet overhead. 'Zombies?' she guessed. 'If I go to Iceland I need to know there might be zombies?'

Jenny rolled her eyes again. 'Not zombies.' She tapped one short manicured oval nail against the card. 'This is Judgement. The card of consequences and reckoning, but also of rebirth and metamorphosis. If I had to guess, I'd say it's asking you if you're ready to face your past and move on to your future. Wouldn't you?'

Staring down at the card, Winter replied, 'I suppose

so.' The only thing was, she didn't have an answer for it. She'd spent so long avoiding even thinking about everything that had happened. She'd focused firmly on the here and now, on her career, her future, where she wanted to go next… She'd filled her life with so much else that the pain of the past was dulled by the weight of it.

Just *seeing* Josh was going to bring back some sharp edges, she knew that. Was she ready for that?

It had been five years.

Maybe Jenny was right. Maybe it was time.

'Judgement is also about figuring out what you're ready to leave behind, and what you want to take on the next part of your journey with you,' Jenny added, her voice softer than Winter was used to hearing it. 'Maybe that could be a good thing?'

Winter's gaze never left the image on the card.

Closure. That was what she was going to Iceland for. The chance to finally put everything that had happened behind her, rather than just burying it deep and hoping.

This could be her chance to *really* move on for good— to no longer be Josh Abraham's ex-wife, or the broken woman she'd left that marriage as. She'd failed as a wife, and more. She'd been faking it until she made it for the last five years and now, with a hit movie under her directorial belt and an award nomination to prove it, it was time to stop faking and start living it. Her new life.

She was going to put her past behind her in Iceland this week, and then she would move on.

'Come on,' Winter said, standing up. 'We need to pack.'

The first of Liam's guests were due to be arriving the following afternoon so, the next day, Josh found himself making any and all excuses to hang around the lobby. Now he'd decided to face things with Winter head-on, he found himself impatient to make it happen. Even if she told him in gruesome detail all the ways he'd failed as a husband, at least he'd know. And that had to be better than wondering, right?

So, he wasn't leaving the lobby until she arrived. However lame his excuses for being there got.

First, it was checking his schedule for the next few days. Liam had set up all sorts of experiences and adventures for his VIP guests that week, to showcase everything the hotel and the region had to offer, and Josh had somehow misplaced his.

Unfortunately, the extremely efficient receptionist was able to replace it in seconds, which took away that reason for loitering.

The Ice House hotel had a great coffee shop by the lobby, though, and some designer-looking transparent chairs placed by artfully arranged pot plants and marble tables, so Josh grabbed himself an Americano, a copy of *The New York Times* that Liam had obviously had shipped in and settled himself down in a secluded corner. From his clear chair, he could see everybody coming and going, but with the paper held in front of his face nobody could tell that it was him.

Perfect.

He sat and drank his coffee and watched three different taxis arriving, depositing two travel reporters, three social media influencers and another actor in dark glasses who nodded in Josh's direction.

But no Winter.

'She's not arriving until four, you realise.'

Josh lowered his newspaper to find Liam sitting in the chair opposite. Smirking.

'Who?' he asked, trying to sound uninterested. 'I'm just enjoying my coffee and the newspaper.'

'Winter,' Liam clarified. 'Apparently she and her assistant have just been collected at Reykjavik Airport and should be here in about an hour.'

'I'll probably have finished my coffee and gone back to my room by then,' Josh said. 'But we'll catch up at some point, for sure.'

Liam didn't look convinced. But he stood up and wandered over to the reception desk, welcoming another taxi-full of guests—more reporters, by the sound of the conversation—and Josh went back to his paper.

At least, until another cup of black coffee was placed on the marble table and Liam sat down opposite him again, his own cup in hand.

'This way, it looks like we're just catching up over a coffee, rather than you sitting here on your own, pathetically waiting for your ex-wife to arrive,' he said.

Josh didn't even bother trying to argue the point this time. 'I just want to get it over with. You know? The awkward first meeting.' After that, they could get down to the conversations he really wanted to have.

'I understand.' Liam blew across the surface of his coffee to cool it. 'I really can't believe that you haven't seen each other since the divorce, though. How the hell did you manage that?'

Josh shrugged. 'I've been busy. I guess she has too.'

In his case, it had been fully intentional. After the divorce he'd said yes to basically every project that crossed his agent's desk, until she told him he had to slow down. He hadn't wanted to slow down, though. He'd wanted to keep moving.

When he was moving, he wasn't thinking. And not thinking was the only way he knew to get through the pain that consumed him after Winter left.

But after two years or so that had led to a period of creative burnout, spent lounging around his mother's house in Ohio, watching his big brother lead the perfect married life until he couldn't bear it any longer—especially once he and Ashley announced that they were pregnant.

He'd called his agent and told her it was time for him to get back in the game.

The projects he'd taken over the last couple of years had been more strategically aimed at enhancing his portfolio and his career, showing his range as an actor. It wasn't just romcoms and action movies any more, which he was grateful for—not least because every romcom reminded him of *Fairy Tale of New England,* the movie he'd met Winter on.

But he'd kept busy. He'd sold the house in LA, found an apartment in New York instead and based himself out of Liam's retreat hotel in the Hollywood Hills when he absolutely needed to be in town.

Winter hadn't been there either. She'd dropped off the Hollywood radar for a while, before reappearing in some smaller, edgier films. The sort of thing she'd always grumbled about never being approached to do whenever they'd been sent another script for a romantic comedy someone hoped they'd star in together. Then she'd moved behind the camera with her directorial debut, *Another Time and Place.* After that award nomination, he suspected she'd find it harder to stay off the gossip radar. With his latest movie making waves too, he was already there.

Which meant the chances of them bumping into each other just went up.

Even if he didn't have other reasons to want to see her, Josh had to admit that it would be better to have that first meeting here, with only the travel press and Liam watching. He just hoped Winter agreed.

Another taxi pulled up outside, visible through the wide glass fronting of the hotel, and Josh jerked into sitting up straighter, eyes trained on the entrance over his paper. This time, the dark head appearing from inside the car was unmistakable—even if he hadn't recognised Jenny holding the car door open for her.

Winter.

She climbed out of the cab, glancing around her with a smile, and if she was as nervous about seeing him as he was about seeing her she sure as hell wasn't letting it show. Sunglasses hid her bright green eyes from him, but her wide mouth was just as he remembered. Luscious and loving and no longer his. Her black hair waved down to her chin now, rather than the shorter cut she'd favoured when they'd met, but it suited her.

'You're staring,' Liam murmured.

Josh ignored him and carried on drinking in the sight of his ex-wife.

He knew the moment she saw him too.

She was laughing at something Jenny said, brushing her hair away from her eyes as she looked up at her assistant as she turned towards the hotel. And then, of course, he realised that those glass walls worked both ways and that Liam was right, he *was* staring.

And she was staring right back at him.

The happy, carefree smile fell away, replaced with what he'd always thought of as her camera smile. The one she put on because it was expected, not because she felt it.

He was now only worthy of her camera smile.

Somehow, that made him feel even worse than everything else about this day.

Josh got up to leave, but Liam's hand on his arm stopped him. 'The stairs,' he murmured cryptically.

Josh looked towards the main staircase—a modern

glass and steel creation that occupied the central lobby, despite the glass elevator that sat just a few paces away. Three women were descending the stairs now, phones out, capturing everything about the hotel, the views, this moment.

He didn't want them to capture him running away from his ex-wife. He didn't particularly want them to witness him and Winter meeting again either, but it was the lesser of two evils.

Probably.

So Josh gritted his teeth, stood more slowly and followed behind Liam to go and greet his latest guests as they entered the hotel.

CHAPTER THREE

'HE'S THERE. In the lobby.' Winter squeezed the words out between closed, hopefully smiling lips.

'Great. Then we get this over and done with fast, and then we get on with enjoying our girls' week of relaxation. Right?' Jenny, holding the door for her, even though she had both their bags too, was still smiling. Damn her. Winter adored her assistant—considered her more of a best friend than an employee. But her friend's determination to always find a path forward, rather than sit and mope for just a little while, could sometimes be a bit much to take.

Still. She was right. So Winter straightened her shoulders and kept walking.

'And the reclusive entrepreneur has come to greet you personally,' Jenny said under her breath as Liam and Josh approached. 'You *must* be special.'

Winter smiled. She and Liam had been close once—before everything—and she was glad that friendship wasn't another thing she'd lost in the divorce.

Even if apparently she still had to share it with her ex-husband.

'You made it!' Liam stepped forward and wrapped her in one of his whole body hugs, the sort that made you feel like the centre of his world for a moment, and Winter let herself sink into it. 'I'm so glad you're here.'

'Thank you for inviting us,' Winter replied. 'I think... I think this might be just what I needed right now.'

She hadn't meant to be looking over his shoulder. Hadn't meant to be staring at Josh, and knowing he was staring back. Hadn't meant to catch and hold his gaze.

But she did.

And she knew in that moment that Jenny was right, and so were her damn Tarot cards. She needed closure if she wanted to move on. She'd rebuilt her life, her career, everything. But a part of her had never shifted from that past she'd run from. It had stayed in that house in LA the day she'd walked out on her marriage.

She'd been afraid, for the longest time, that it was her heart that she'd left behind. That she'd never be able to find love again, because she'd given up that ability when she'd walked out on Josh.

Now, she thought it might have been hope—hope for the future. And she was ready to claim that back.

Which meant facing him. Dealing with him as part of her history—someone who would always be a fundamental part of the person she'd grown into, but one who no longer had any impact or influence on who she became from here.

That was healthy. That was good.

And this was the best chance she was going to get to do that.

Winter pulled back from the hug and was about to take a step towards Josh when Liam said, 'And this must be the lovely Jenny I've heard so much about. I hope you know I'm at your service during your stay here.'

Since Winter had said basically nothing about her assistant to Liam, she raised her eyebrows at that, but he was already reaching for Jenny's hand and bringing it to his lips.

Oh. Oh, *no.* This was not going to be a thing.

Luckily, Jenny was more than a match for Liam's attempts at charm. 'Bag carrier and ticket booker extraordinaire at your service,' she said drily as she pulled her hand from his grasp. 'But it's great that you run such a full-service hotel.' She offloaded the bags on her shoulder onto him and pushed Winter's wheeled suitcase towards him. 'Why don't you show me where our rooms are?'

Liam looked slightly taken aback at his demotion to bellboy, but he took it in good part. 'This way, milady,' he said, flashing them all a cheeky grin as he set off for the elevators.

Winter would have followed, but the look Josh gave her held her in place just a moment too long, and Liam and Jenny were gone—replaced, she realised with dismay, by three young blonde women with camera phones.

'Oh, my gosh! I can't believe it's the *two* of you. Here!' One of the women darted into the space between Winter and Josh and stretched out her arm to take a selfie with the two of them. Startled, Winter let the stranger draw her in with her other arm, aware that Josh was leaning in on the other side.

Because this was what they did. They were celebrities, actors. Public property.

Never mind that they hadn't spoken in five years, that they had stuff they needed to process, in private. Someone wanted a selfie. That had to trump their needs, right?

And not just one person. Each of the woman's companions also needed a photo, and then the receptionist was drawn in to take a group shot. Winter forced herself to keep smiling throughout the whole ordeal, but she could tell from the set of Josh's jaw and the tension in his shoulders that he wasn't enjoying this any more than she was.

But this was the gig. So she—literally—had to grin and bear it.

It didn't stop the memories that bubbled up, though. The same feelings she'd had during her marriage, when it had started to feel as if the real Winter had disappeared behind a facade of the Celebrity Wife people wanted to see. She'd become almost invisible in the shadow of their fairy tale. All anyone cared about was the story— how their eyes had met across the film set, and Josh had turned to the actor standing next to him, who happened to be Liam, and said, 'I'm going to marry that woman.'

The fairy tale was a good story, Winter knew. From their whirlwind first date as soon as filming had ended that day, to their engagement six months later and their marriage just another four months after that. They'd been young and in love and at the time she'd barely noticed how closely the world was watching.

How nobody had asked *her* what she'd said when she'd met Josh's eyes for the first time. If she'd *wanted* to fall into a fairy tale instead of a normal relationship.

The expectations for their romance had been set so high from the start, was it any wonder they'd crashed and burned? That feeling of invisibility, of their fairy tale being more important than either of them were as people, hadn't been what broke them in the end. But it hadn't helped, Winter was sure of that.

How could they connect, become the people they needed each other to be to get through the hard times when they were both playing a part in a fairy tale?

'Can I just say how great it is to see you two together again?' said the first woman—who had introduced herself as 'Sarra—from SarraSeesTheWorld. The travel blog, you know? Two "r"s in Sarra when you're tagging…' as her friends edged towards the door that led to the spa area of the hotel. 'I mean, you two…you were my first couple goals crush, you know? I was *heartbroken* when you split up. And now…' She beamed at them both like a proud parent at a wedding. 'This is just the best! I can't wait to tell *everyone.*'

Winter's eyes widened, and she could see the panic settling in on Josh's face too. 'Oh, no, Sarra. We're not… we're both just old friends of Liam's so we're both here to support him this week. Separately.'

'Very separately,' Josh added, nodding enthusiastically. 'Because obviously we're still…friends.'

'Right. Friends.' Winter wasn't sure that was at all convincing, but what else was there to say?

Sorry, but you're interrupting our first awkward meeting in five years—please leave.

Jenny would probably have said that. Sometimes Winter wished she was more like her assistant.

Sarra's enthusiasm didn't seem in the least bit dimmed by their denials. If anything, she only seemed keener. 'Well, this is a very romantic place, don't you think? I hope you both enjoy it. We're off to try out the spa. Maybe we'll see you there later? I hear they do couples massages…'

With a last suggestive wiggle of her eyebrows, Sarra darted off to join her friends, and Winter took an instinctive step further away from her ex-husband, suddenly aware that they still hadn't actually said a word to each other.

She'd had so many plans. There'd been a whole speech, worked out in her head on the plane, intended for their first second meeting. About moving on and water under the bridge and closure and friendship and all those things.

She couldn't remember a word of it now. And even if she could, it was too late.

The chance to say it had already gone.

Josh met her gaze. 'Hi.'

Winter swallowed, her throat burning with all the words she'd never said—not just today, but five years ago. Everything that had been eating her up since long before then.

Suddenly she didn't want to say anything at all.

So she turned on her heel, walked towards the reception desk and hoped like hell that Liam had put decent sound-proofing on the suites in this place, because she was going to find her room and *scream*.

Josh watched Winter walk away, again, and willed his feet to follow her, his voice to call out after her, anything.

But he didn't. Instead, he stayed exactly where he was until Liam returned a few minutes later, without Jenny or any of the bags.

'That's the girls squared away in their suite, anyway,' he said, eyeing Josh carefully. 'I saw Winter on my way out. She looked...well. Everything go okay out here after I left?'

'There were some travel bloggers who wanted photos,' Josh said, his voice flat. 'One of them was really glad to see us back together again.'

Liam winced. 'Ah.'

'Yeah.' Josh shook his head, and finally stopped staring down the corridor Winter had left by. 'This was a mistake. Both of us being here. I shouldn't have come— or I should have left yesterday, when I realised you hadn't told her I'd be here.'

'No, no, you shouldn't.' Taking his elbow, Liam led

him back to the seats they'd occupied earlier. 'Come on. You knew that first meeting was going to be difficult.'

'And you left me here to deal with it alone, in public, while you chased after your latest hot blonde.' The accusation came out without thinking, and Josh regretted it the moment he'd said it, even before he saw the pain that flashed across Liam's face.

Because Liam *didn't* chase hot blondes any more. Oh, he flirted, he charmed, he sweet-talked. But then he left them at the door, went home alone and never, ever called them. And Josh knew that.

'That assistant of Winter's has a way of making you do things without even realising you've agreed,' Liam said mildly. 'I *am* sorry for leaving you, though. I didn't mean to.'

'It's okay. Jenny always was a force of nature.' That had been something of a comfort, actually, when Winter left. That at least she wasn't alone—she had Jenny on her side. And that was worth a lot. 'It was just unfortunate that those influencers happened to come down right then.'

'So maybe you need to make sure that your next meeting is more private?' Liam suggested. 'There's plenty of quiet, secluded corners around this place. Just drop her a line via Reception and ask her to meet you someplace, maybe?'

'Maybe.' It wasn't a *bad* idea—they did need to talk, after all, before their next public appearance, ideally. He just wasn't sure what he'd do if her answer was a flat no.

Liam clapped a hand against Josh's shoulder. 'Go on. Head back to your room. Go for a soak in that *stunning* private geothermal pool outside your suite. Relax a bit and think about it. Okay?'

The geothermal pool did sound nice. Liam had given

him one of the best suites in the place, and Josh certainly intended to make the most of it. And thinking…that was definitely something he needed to do.

'Yeah, okay.'

He managed to avoid any other guests as he made his way back to his room, but he couldn't avoid his own thoughts. He couldn't deny how seeing Winter again had affected him, not now there was no one else to distract him.

She was still so beautiful. When her eyes had met his, their gazes locked, he'd felt the same damn way he had on that film set eight years ago. The same rush of unnameable feelings running through him—some mix of excitement, anticipation, attraction, nerves and…home.

Except Winter wasn't his home any more. She wasn't his anything.

How was he supposed to find closure, to close the door on that part of his life and move on, when he still wanted her in his arms so badly?

Josh reached his door and let himself in with a sigh of relief when the key card worked first time.

His suite was on the ground floor, at the back of the hotel, and comprised of a bedroom, en suite bathroom and sitting room with sofa, coffee table, desk and a coffee machine. The Scandi-style design was soothing, with its pale grey walls, darker grey textiles and the warm wood of the furniture. Against the outside wall, there was even a wood-burning heater, to guard against the February chill.

Full-length glass doors looked out over the white tips of the mountains in the distance, the earthy colours of the rocky terrain around the hotel and the bright blue of the private geothermal lagoon just outside, surrounded by a wooden decked terrace with pale beanbag chairs around it.

He had to admire the attention to detail Liam had put into the place. It was the perfect place to relax and recharge.

Or it would be, if it wasn't for the screaming he could hear through the wall of the suite next door.

The screaming felt good, but it didn't really solve anything and Winter's throat was getting sore, so eventually she stopped, put her hands on her hips and stared out of the full-length glass doors at the view of the mountains and the private geothermal lagoon Liam had promised her to go with her suite when he'd been persuading her to come.

Jenny, sitting on the sofa of their two-bedroom suite, cautiously removed her earplugs. 'You're quiet. It's making me nervous.'

'I'm thinking.'

'That only makes it worse.' Jenny stood up and came to stand beside her, looking out of the window. 'Okay, so what are we thinking?'

'I'm thinking that the screaming hasn't helped, so I'm going to go try out the geothermal lagoon instead.'

'Good idea,' Jenny said. 'Your swimsuits are in the top drawer on the left of the dresser in your room.'

It was kind of sad how much she relied on Jenny these days, Winter mused as she changed into a black two-piece that was held up by a single strap and some hope. An assistant was meant to assist, but some days Winter wondered if she'd just fall apart without her.

She grabbed a fluffy ice-white towel from the stack in the oversized en suite bathroom and headed back out into the living area, surprised to see Jenny still fully dressed, with her laptop out, replying to a text on her phone. 'Aren't you coming?'

Her assistant shook her head and slipped her phone into her pocket. 'Actually, I'm going to go find a quiet spot with good coffee to catch up on some emails.'

'Work?' Winter frowned. 'Do you need me?'

'I got it. You go soak.' Packing up her laptop, Jenny headed for the door, leaving Winter alone.

Alone with a geothermal lagoon. That was the sort of alone she could get behind.

Slipping into the luxurious bathrobe provided for the purpose, along with the matching sliders for her feet, Winter stepped out through the glass doors and onto the decking. In the cold winter air her exposed skin puckered with goosebumps—but she could see steam rising from the small private lagoon. Its waters seemed absurdly blue, and a faintly sulphurous smell rose from them. Around her, a faint fog filled the air—the meeting of the warm water and the freezing atmosphere, she assumed.

It felt oddly otherworldly here, looking out over such unfamiliar terrain. She glanced back at the doors of her suite for reassurance that she hadn't suddenly been transported to another planet somehow—and spotted movement behind the doors of the adjoining suite.

Liam hadn't said she'd be sharing the private lagoon with anybody. Who could be in there?

The doors to the next-door suite slid open and she got her answer—even if she rather regretted asking the question.

'Hello, Winter,' Josh said, an apologetic smile on his face. He was still dressed in the clothes he'd had on earlier and held his hands out in a supplicant gesture.

She stared at him for a long moment, trying to find an answer, her anger at least keeping her warm. Not only had

Liam not told her that her ex-husband would be here this week, he'd actually put him in the adjoining suite to her.

'I'm going to kill Liam,' she muttered. Then, because it was bloody cold and this was *her* private lagoon, thank you, she shucked off her bathrobe and stepped into the water.

She thought for a second she heard a sharp intake of breath from him at the sight of her bikini. But if she did it was quickly lost behind the sound of her own gasp as she submerged herself in the water.

It was *warm*. Not just 'not freezing' swimming pool water, like she'd half expected. Properly warm. And wonderful. Like a bath. Her eyes fluttered closed as she settled herself against the smooth rock, her arms hooked back over the rim to support her as she floated.

It almost made her feel as if she could forget all about her ex-husband and soon-to-be-ex-friend if she could just stay in this water for ever.

'It's pretty incredible, huh?'

She opened her eyes at Josh's voice and found him perched on the edge of one of the recliners on the decking that surrounded the lagoon.

'You've been in already?' she asked.

Josh nodded. 'I've been here a few days. I... I'm sorry. I didn't realise Liam hadn't told you I'd be here until I saw your press conference yesterday.'

Winter started in surprise, almost losing her balance against the rock. 'You watched my press conference?' She'd already guessed that Liam wouldn't have told him. Josh had gone out of his way over the past five years to avoid her at all turns. But the press conference comment caught her off-guard.

He flashed her a quick smile—the one that graced movie posters across the world, and probably quite a few phone wallpapers. 'Of course I watched it. Best Director nomination? Winter, that's incredible. Of course I watched.'

The warmth that filled her chest was entirely due to the geothermal properties of the lagoon, she was certain. Just like the ache that matched it probably had something to do with the rocks.

Neither had anything to do with the man smiling at her, or the pride in his voice. His recognition of everything she'd worked so hard for since they'd parted. Or the fact that this was the first civil conversation they'd managed in years.

Almost as if he'd forgiven her for everything. Almost as if she'd forgotten everything that needed forgiving. Both things, of course, were impossible.

'So, what do you think Liam is playing at, then?' She'd meant it as an attempt to change the subject, to get away from all that heart-clenching feeling. But of course it only made things worse.

'Matchmaker, probably.' The twist of Josh's mouth told her he wasn't any happier about this than she was. 'God knows why. It's not exactly like him. But since the accident…'

'Yeah,' she agreed as he trailed off. 'Something like that changes a person, I guess.'

Another guilt to add to her list—not supporting Liam through his hard times. She was a bad friend, as well as a bad wife and a bad—well. Most things.

But she was a good director. She had the nomination to prove it. And Winter had always believed in building on her strengths rather than dwelling on her failings.

'So. How do you want to manage this?' Josh asked. 'I can always ask Liam for another room, if you'd like me to move? Although I think the hotel is pretty packed this week…'

Of course it was. This was Liam's big press week—one week of splashing out to put up stars and reporters and influencers, showing them everything there was to love about his new venture, then hoping their social proof of how great it was would bring the bookings rolling in.

Winter knew that she and Josh were here as the faces of the brand, every bit as much as Liam's friends. They'd both invested in his company from the start, so had their own interests in the hotel being a success.

Which meant supporting him. And, apparently, putting up with his matchmaking. However frustrating it was.

And she'd come here for closure, hadn't she? For the chance to move on.

Maybe the forgetting part was impossible. But could forgiveness be within their reach?

Winter knew she'd done plenty that she needed to ask forgiveness for, even if there were some things for which she'd never be able to forgive herself. And Josh…maybe he needed some closure too.

Maybe they could both find what they needed this weekend and be able to move on. If they were willing to face down the demons that had driven them apart five years ago.

Winter swallowed and made her decision.

CHAPTER FOUR

JOSH WAS ALL set to go pack his bags from the look on Winter's face, until her annoyance turned to something that looked more like frustration and she shook her head.

'No. There's no point.' She kicked her feet under the water, and Josh tried not to stare at the acres of bare skin her bikini showed off. It wasn't his skin to stare at any more, even if it was so incredibly close and tempting.

I want closure. I can't want her too.

'Liam would only have to move another guest into that suite to move you out, and then I'd have to share this beautiful lagoon with someone I don't even know.'

It was on the tip of his tongue to suggest that he could move into Liam's suite with him, even though he really didn't want to, when Winter spoke again, surprising him.

'And besides. Maybe this could be…good.'

'Good?' Josh concentrated hard on not just falling into the pool in shock at her calling anything to do with him 'good'. Almost as if she'd forgotten all the awfulness that had passed between them. How badly he'd failed her as a husband. How he'd driven her away. 'Good… how, exactly?'

Winter shrugged, the water rippling around her and her luscious body bobbing in the waves. Five years on, she was still the most beautiful woman he'd ever seen.

Still the woman he'd fallen head over heels for, so in love he hadn't been able to see straight.

'I guess…we're both here all week, right? And it has been suggested to me that our relationship ended without the sort of…' She pulled a face as she fumbled for the word she wanted.

'Closure?' Josh guessed, remembering his conversation with Liam.

'Exactly. Without the sort of closure we might need to move on effectively and healthily. Emotion-wise, I guess.' She shrugged again. 'Jenny wasn't entirely clear on that point.'

'Neither was Liam,' Josh admitted. 'But you're making me think that perhaps the room assignments weren't actually matchmaking. More…mending?'

'Match-mending? You know that's not a thing, right?' Winter laughed, and the sound echoed off the rocks around them like rainbow light in a prism. 'No, I get what you mean, though. You think he's trying to make us make up as friends?'

Josh nodded. 'I think so. He pointed out that things between us were left rather unresolved when you—' He broke off. He didn't want to cast blame around here. God knew, enough of it had landed on his shoulders anyway.

'When I walked out.' It was as though a cloud had crossed the sun, the way the laughter fell from her face. 'Yeah. He's right.'

'I think he was hoping we'd talk, at least,' Josh offered. 'Find some answers about what went wrong so that next time we can get it right.'

Winter's obvious surprise sent her eyebrows flying towards her hairline. 'Next time?'

'With whoever each of us falls in love with next,' he clarified hurriedly. 'I mean, as a way for us to move on

from each other. Because I don't know about you but…
the divorce left me a little wary of love.' To put it mildly.

He wanted to find the sort of love his parents had
shared, that his brother had found. But not knowing what
he'd got so wrong last time…it was hard to take the risk
of it all happening again.

It would hurt, Josh knew, to face everything that had
happened between him and Winter. Especially to relive
that terrifying, heartbreaking last few months they'd been
together.

But it would hurt more to never move on from it at all.

'So now you're ready to get back out there again? Find
Mrs Abraham number two?' She smiled as she said it, the
idea of him dropping the torch he'd kept gripping hold of
for her and moving onto someone new obviously a good
one in her mind.

As it should be in his. It was just easier to remember
that when she wasn't right in front of him. Wearing a
swimsuit that only highlighted those curves he'd once
loved. And held. And caressed…

'You kept your name,' he pointed out, looking away.
'So she'd have to be Mrs Abraham number one.' Except
that was his mother, or maybe his sister-in-law, Ashley.

'I suppose so,' Winter said with a brittle smile. 'The
point is, closure, right? We talk and we move on.'

'That seems to be Liam's plan.'

'In which case, it makes sense for us both to stay
here,' Winter said. 'It's probably the most private spot in
the whole place for us to talk and… I don't know about
you, but I'd rather not be overheard having these conversations. In case you haven't noticed, this whole hotel
is teeming with gossip journalists, travel reporters and
social media stars.'

'Who would happily broadcast our cosy conversations and lunch dates to the world.' Josh sighed. 'You're right. If we're going to do this, we want it to be private.'

He couldn't take all those stories again, speculating on his broken heart, or his prospects now he was single.

'Definitely,' Winter said with an enthusiastic nod. 'So…we keep them here?'

'And when we're out in public, with everyone watching, we…what?' Josh asked. 'Pretend like we hate each other?'

'I don't think we need to go that far.' Winter shifted in the water as she contemplated the question. Josh tried to think about it too, but found himself rather too distracted by her bikini again.

For once, he was grateful that Iceland in February was freezing, and he was wearing several layers of clothes. Otherwise his reaction to seeing his ex-wife lounging around in the warm water in a simple black two-piece would be far greater, and far more obvious to the woman in question.

As it was, he simply adjusted his position and waited for her answer.

'I guess it depends what we want the world to think about us, after this week,' she said thoughtfully. 'Don't you think?'

'Absolutely,' Josh replied, as if he'd been reaching the same conclusion as her all along, and not thinking about how the bikini looked a lot like the sports bra and shorts she used to wear to do yoga, on the balcony outside their bedroom in LA, and the way she'd fall back into bed with him afterwards, all warm from the sun and the exercise, and pliant and flexible in his arms…

'We want them to think that we're mature, emotionally healthy professionals,' Winter went on. 'Which means being friends—or at least civil and friendly acquaintances. Yes?'

'For sure.'

Closure not closeness. That had to be his motto now. It was just hard to remember now the memories were flooding back.

'That's settled, then.' Winter smiled up at him, and he tried to shake away the images of them in bed and focus on what they'd actually agreed.

'So we act like disinterested friends in public, polite but not close?' That he could manage.

'And then when we come back here we can, well, talk. Find that closure we apparently need.' The face Winter pulled at the word 'closure' told Josh she wasn't entirely convinced she needed it.

But he was, more and more. If the universe had given him another opportunity to spend some time with this woman, and maybe even understand exactly what he'd done wrong in their marriage—so he could get it right next time...well. He wasn't idiotic enough to turn that down.

Maybe Liam was right, and he really could find love again. The sort of love his parents had shared, that his brother and Ashley had now. True love, that was right from the start—and stayed right.

That was worth some difficult conversations. Wasn't it?

An hour or so later, skin still pink from the lagoon, Winter wound her way through the hotel corridors back to the main atrium, looking for her wayward assistant—and maybe a hot chocolate. Josh had left her to soak after their conversation, and she'd stayed in the lagoon longer than she'd meant to, lulled by the clear air, the warm water and the empty grey of the skies.

She was glad she'd come, despite her initial misgivings. Maybe Jenny was right, and some closure with Josh would be nice. But, even more than that, the chance to slow down, relax and let the water and the air chase away some of her worries—before the next round of whatever chaos came next hit—could only be good.

Winter had never been particularly good at slowing down, except when forced by circumstance. But she knew from past bitter experience that not giving her body what it needed when it needed it could never end well. So now she tried to take a break once in a while, give her physical self the time to catch up with her mile-a-minute mind.

She might not like it, but she knew now that it was necessary, if she didn't want her body to betray her again.

She came to the main atrium, with its wide open-plan space and huge glass walls, and smiled. Everything felt so…open here. As if anything was possible. She liked that.

Winter found Jenny sitting in the coffee shop area with Liam and raised her eyebrows at the sight.

'Does this place do a good hot chocolate?' she asked as she slipped into an empty chair at their table.

'The best.' Liam flashed her a smile and started to raise his hand to a staff member, but Jenny jumped to her feet first.

'I'll get it, boss,' she said, hurrying towards the counter.

'So, how did you find your suite? Jenny said you planned to try out the private lagoon. How was it?' Liam leaned back in his chair, long legs stretched out in front of him, arms folded over his chest and a familiar knowing smirk on his lips.

Winter resisted the urge to poke him in the ribs. 'Less private than advertised.'

'Ah.' The smirk turned into a smile. 'You met your neighbour, then?'

'You mean my ex-husband? Yes.'

'And?' Liam pressed.

Winter huffed a sigh. 'And what? What do you imagine happened? We suddenly and simultaneously realised the error of our ways and fell into each other's arms?'

'A guy can dream, can't he?'

'I seriously doubt that *your* dreams involve *my* love life,' Winter said caustically.

'Okay, fine. Is the best suite in the hotel still standing, or do I need to send the builders in?' Liam asked, then lowered his voice. 'Jenny told me about the screaming.'

Winter shot a glare at her assistant, where she was waiting for hot chocolate. 'Jenny should remember the non-disclosure contract she signed.'

Liam barked a laugh. 'I expect after five years she knows you too well to think you'd ever actually sue her. Besides, the way I see it, she knows where all the bodies are buried. You need to keep her close.'

'If you mean she knows where my plane tickets and passport are, my calendar for the next three years and the phone numbers of everyone who matters to me, you're right.' Jenny was the best damn assistant in Hollywood. Everyone knew that.

Winter's eyes narrowed. Suddenly, Liam and Jenny's coffee date made a lot more sense.

'You're trying to steal her from me,' she said.

Liam threw up his hands in mock innocence. 'I swear I have no idea what you're talking about.'

'Jenny. You know she's the best in the business and you want to hire her away from me.'

The innocent look slid away, and Liam shook his head.

'I promise you I'm not. I know how important she is to you, and I wouldn't do that.'

Somehow, that wasn't as reassuring as Winter had hoped. Because if Liam wasn't talking to Jenny for a job interview, that meant… 'Did you two conspire together on this?'

Jenny, returning with the drinks, slopped a little hot chocolate over the side as she placed them on the table. 'Winter, are you getting paranoid on me? Because all I did was go fetch hot chocolate.'

'No, you didn't. You sent me out into the geothermal lagoon outside our room but didn't want to come with me, when all you've been talking about for weeks was how much you were looking forward to sinking into it. You said you wouldn't come out of the water all week. And instead I find you here, talking to *him*.'

'Hey!' Liam protested. 'I resent whatever implication your tone there was making about my character.'

Winter waved an apologetic hand in his direction. 'Oh, you know what I mean. You two set me up.' Realising she was drawing more than a little attention from the group sitting at the next table, she lowered her voice as she accused Jenny, 'You knew Josh was staying next door. Didn't you?'

Jenny wiggled uncomfortably on her chair, then looked at Liam and shrugged. 'I told you I won't lie to her.' She turned back to Winter. 'I swear I didn't know until we got here this afternoon. Liam told me when he was showing me to our room.'

'So this is all your cunning plan, then,' Winter said to Liam. 'Dare I ask what you were hoping to achieve from this?'

A shadow fell across the table, and suddenly the fourth chair was being pulled out and Josh was sitting on it, claiming the second hot chocolate Jenny had brought but hadn't touched. This was definitely feeling more like a conspiracy than ever.

She wondered if she could blame the conspiracy for the warm feeling that started in her chest as she looked at her ex-husband, sitting at her side, looking for all the world as if the last five years had just been a nightmare she was now waking up from.

Winter looked away. Because it hadn't been a nightmare. Those five years had happened, and she had survived, and there was no way she could risk going backwards again now. Not when she'd worked so hard to get to where she was.

'Thanks for this, Jenny,' Josh said with a friendly smile. 'Sorry, got caught by a couple of autograph-hunters—I'd keep your head down, Winter, or they'll be after the full set.'

Winter scowled. Because, of course, people were only interested in her in relation to her ex-husband. As always. At least his comment was a timely reminder of one of the many reasons it was a good thing they were no longer together.

I'm my own person now. I went through hell to get there, and I'm not going back.

'Now, where were we?' Josh said lightly. 'Ah, yes. Liam. What exactly *were* you hoping to achieve by putting Winter and me in adjoining rooms?' He sipped his hot chocolate, raising his eyebrows over the rim of the mug, looking for all the world as if he was just asking about the weather, or what was for dinner.

Winter hid a smile as Liam squirmed a little under that friendly but unflinching gaze.

'I guess I just hoped the two of you would…find a way to be friends again,' he said eventually. 'I don't have many friends these days, you might have noticed. And with you two each pretending the other doesn't exist, it makes birthday parties and the like a tad difficult.'

Winter and Josh exchanged a quick glance. Liam had been through a lot these past few years, as much as they had. Even if they hadn't already decided to try to find some closure on the two of them, Winter knew that Liam's casual comment about birthday parties—and all the loss and pain she could hear beneath his words—would have convinced her.

'We are,' she said softly. 'Trying the friends thing, I mean.'

'Really?' Liam sat up straight with obvious surprise. '*Really*, really?'

Beside her, Josh rolled his eyes and slapped his friend lightly on the shoulder. 'Really, *really*, really, you idiot. Your plan worked. Soon you can throw all the birthday parties you want.'

Liam's smile turned devious. 'Only if Jenny comes too. Winter gave me the wonderful idea of trying to steal her away into my employ, but I think I'm going to need more than one week to manage that, so—'

'Hey!' Now it was Winter's turn to reach across and bat his other shoulder with the back of her hand, although she couldn't stop herself grinning. 'That was not an invitation.'

'No, those will need to have balloons on them,' Liam said, clearly delighting in the nonsense. 'Jenny, maybe you can help me with those?'

Jenny raised her eyebrows at him. 'You'd have to make it worth my while.'

'Ah, a woman who knows her worth. That's my kind of girl.'

As Liam leant across the table towards her assistant to begin his ridiculous negotiation over party invites for a birthday that Winter happened to know was at least six months away, she glanced over at Josh and found him already watching her, a soft smile on his face.

She returned it and watched his widen—then looked away fast as her treacherous heart skipped a beat.

This was how it had started last time. Secret smiles and knowing looks. Moments where the world disappeared and it was only them left in the universe.

Her heart skipping whenever he smiled at her.

Josh had told the world that when he'd met her gaze across that crowded film set, the day they'd met, he'd known that he was going to marry her. Nobody had asked Winter what she'd thought in that moment, but if they had she'd have told them.

She'd known that the man who looked at her that way, who smiled and made her heart skip, was the sort of man who could change the direction of her life.

She just hadn't known if that change would be for good or for bad. But she'd been young and hopeful, and she'd taken that risk.

Now, seeing that same smile, she knew she couldn't take that chance again. Not for anything.

Not when it had almost destroyed everything about her last time.

Friends. She could do friends. It was her suggestion, for heaven's sake.

But *just* friends.

Yes. This was fine. This was going to be fine. Probably not a disaster at all.

She chanced another look, and Josh flashed that smile

her way again, causing her certainty on that point to waver.

Probably fine, she reminded herself. *Just as long as I avoid that smile and don't throw myself at him over the next week, things will be absolutely, probably, fine. Probably.*

CHAPTER FIVE

LIAM HAD PLANNED a full programme of activities for the week, designed to show off the hotel and the surrounding area in their best possible light. Which was why Josh found himself, the following morning, queuing at the breakfast buffet far earlier than seemed reasonable, dressed in several more layers of clothing than he'd have needed if he'd just stayed in LA like a sensible person.

Outside the wide windows the sun wasn't even up yet, although Josh guessed that had more to do with the northern location than the actual hour. Still, from the yawns and demands for coffee, he suspected he wasn't the only one resenting the early start.

Their host, meanwhile, seemed in high spirits as he made his way around the breakfast room, with its glorious views over towards the icy mountains, clapping people on the back and making jokes. Shaking his head at his friend, Josh was about to go find a secluded table where he might escape Liam's early morning exuberance, when he spotted a familiar dark head of hair.

Winter. She was dressed like everyone else, in warm layers, ready for the day's adventures, and he could see a scarf and hat poking out of the bag slung over her shoulder. Josh hesitated. They hadn't spoken much after the hot chocolate with Liam and Jenny the day before, and when he'd headed out to enjoy the lagoon that evening she hadn't joined him. But if they were going to be friends—or even just act that way in public—shouldn't he ask her to join him now?

From the look on her face, he wasn't sure if the overture would be appreciated. So he watched a little longer instead.

Jenny stood beside her, yawning, her blonde hair twisted up into plaits on the back of her head. But while she had a full plate of food, Winter's remained empty. As she turned her head away from the buffet, he could make out the strain around her eyes, and the forced smile on her lips.

He let his gaze scan back over the breakfast buffet, and felt his breath catch as he hit on a probable reason for her discomfort.

Smoked fish.

Five years hadn't taken away the memories, it seemed. Even the small ones.

Decision made, he dashed forward, taking Jenny's arm and smiling broadly. 'Ladies! Just the breakfast companions I was waiting for. I've secured the *perfect* table, just over there.' He pointed vaguely at the last remaining window table and hoped no one else could steal it before they got there. 'Why don't you go sit down while I finish getting breakfast for us?'

Jenny was frowning at him in confusion. 'But Winter hasn't—'

'Don't worry!' he said, probably too loud. 'Leave it to me.'

'Come on, Jenny,' Winter said softly, and the two of them headed for the table he'd indicated.

Letting out a relieved breath, Josh quickly filled two plates with pastries, dark rye bread, jam and other inoffensive morning foods—choosing to leave most of the Icelandic specialities alone for now. While he'd be happy to try the *skyr*—a thick yogurt cheese—another time, he didn't want to tempt fate with Winter's stomach. And he couldn't remember ever seeing her eat oatmeal in the mornings, so he left the *hafragrautur* for now too.

The fish-based breakfast items were definitely off the menu.

Before he carried the plates over to the table, though, he collared one of the hotel staff and put in a special request—one he hoped they'd be able to fulfil before they left for the day's adventures. Then he headed over to join Winter and Jenny. Except Jenny had moved away to take a phone call, leaving him alone at the table with his ex-wife.

'How did you know?' Winter asked, looking down at her plate of bland, easy to eat foods.

Josh huffed a laugh. 'Trust me. You throwing up all down my tux at that charity ball is the sort of thing that stays with a man. It was the smoked fish again, right?'

She nodded. 'I can't believe it still bothers me. But even now, after all these years, my stomach still turns when I smell it.'

That night had been their first clue, Josh remembered, before the pregnancy test the next day had confirmed it. Winter had been feeling absolutely fine—maybe a little tired, but that wasn't unusual given how hard she'd been working. He'd pushed her to rest a little more, but she'd persuaded him to join her for a lie down, and neither of them had really rested very much after that.

They'd almost been late for the charity ball they'd agreed to attend, Winter still tying his bow tie in the cab there, both of them giggling at the reason for their lateness. Then, an hour or so later, after welcome drinks, the waiting staff had put a plate of smoked fish starters on the table in front of Winter, she'd taken one breath, turned to him and vomited. They'd had to reassure everyone else in the room that it wasn't a reaction to the food…but they hadn't known for sure what it was until she took the test.

But that night…that had been the start of everything, in his mind. The moment when the world had changed and the wonderful fairy tale he'd been living in had started to fracture. That afternoon in bed the last time anything had felt truly normal between them. God, he missed that.

'I'm sorry,' he said. She looked at him with surprise, and he wondered if maybe she felt that same longing for how things had been that he did. 'That it didn't go away, I mean.'

Except that wasn't really all he meant. He was sorry for so many things, he didn't think he'd ever be able to make up for them all. Not if he brought her breakfast every day for the rest of her life. Which she'd pretty much turned down the day she'd walked out on their marriage.

I'm sorry for everything I did that made you leave. Or everything I couldn't do. I'm sorry that you couldn't talk to me about any of it. That I couldn't fix it for you.

'Yeah,' she said. 'Me too.'

Before they could say anything else, Jenny returned, dropping into her seat, already talking a mile a minute to Winter about whoever had been on the other end of the call. Josh turned his attention to his own plate of food, and only smiled when the hotel worker he'd asked for a favour slipped a small packet into his hand when Liam gathered them all in the foyer, ready to leave on the day's adventure.

He couldn't fix things then. But maybe he could remind her that he cared.

As a friend, of course.

'Do you think we'll actually see some whales?' Jenny asked as they boarded the boat Liam had hired for them for the day.

'I think that's kind of the point of a whale-watching trip.' Winter eyed the boat with some trepidation. Her stomach was still a little unsure about everything after her encounter with the fish plates at breakfast, and she wasn't convinced that spending several hours out on the rolling waves was going to improve matters any.

'Yeah, but whales are freedom-loving creatures,' Jenny went on. 'I mean, how can anyone be sure exactly where they're going to be today?'

The boat was leaving from Reykjavik's Old Harbour, and Winter could see a number of other whale-watching tour boats being offered, although Liam had booked one out solely for their use.

She pointed to a poster. 'They seem to reckon a ninety-nine percent chance of seeing *something*.'

Jenny raised her eyebrows, arms folded across her chest with either scepticism or cold, it was hard to tell. 'I'll believe it when I see it.'

'It *is* a little harder to find them at this time of year.' Appearing behind them, Liam slung an arm over each of their shoulders as he guided them further onto the boat. 'But I'm assured of at least one small minke whale, and maybe a few harbour porpoises. Plus we get to enjoy all this fantastic scenery. Volcanoes to the south, maybe even a glimpse of the Snæfellsjökull Glacier if we head north.'

Winter leaned against the rail around the edge of the boat, the chill of it still biting through all the layers of clothes she'd put on. 'Are we going to freeze to death out there? Because I feel that wouldn't look good in your promotional brochure.'

Liam laughed. 'There are warm overalls over there that you can put on if you need.' He gestured towards the centre of the boat, where a staff member was handing out padded clothing. 'And if that isn't enough, the cabin at the centre there is heated too, so you can head inside to warm up. Just don't blame me if you miss a whale!'

With a final clap on their shoulders, he headed off to check on his other guests, and Winter and Jenny, in unspoken agreement, moved to grab some of the padded overalls.

Winter paused for a second when she realised Josh was already there. The conversation they'd had at breakfast, and all the words they hadn't said, weighed as heavily in her stomach as the pastries she was wishing she hadn't eaten. Neither of them had even said the word 'pregnant' or talked about—she swallowed before finishing the thought—the baby she'd lost. But, all the same, she knew it was the only thing she'd think about for the rest of the day.

Not that *that* was so unusual. There hadn't been a day in five years where she hadn't thought about it. Hadn't hated herself for not being enough, hated her body for letting her down.

A miscarriage sounded like such a small thing. Like a misstep, or at worse a mistake.

But it had shaped Winter's entire life ever since.

Jenny handed her a pair of overalls and Winter made herself step forward and stay in the present, not the past. Iceland in winter was nothing to be joking about and she wanted to be properly prepared.

Beside her, Josh yanked his overalls up over his shoulders and replaced his thick coat over the top, then fished something out of his pocket to hand to her. 'Just in case,' he said, and gave her a wink as he closed her fingers around a small packet before turning and walking away.

'What's that?' Jenny asked, watching her curiously.

Winter unfurled her fingers to find a small packet of ginger chews inside. 'Where on earth did he get these?'

'Ooh, are those for seasickness?' One of the influencer girls had appeared at Winter's side and was eyeing them covetously. 'Can I get one? I'm desperate to see the whales, but I just know my stomach's going to hate those waves.'

They all looked out at the choppy waters unhappily. 'Absolutely,' Winter said, and started handing them around.

By the time they were out at sea, the coastline around Reykjavik harbour retreating by the second, half of Winter's ginger chews were gone, but she hoped she was starting to find her sea legs. Maybe it was the brisk chill of the salty air against her face, or the excitement of watching for sea creatures, or just being somewhere so unlike anywhere she'd seen before. Whatever it was, it seemed enough to distract her from her rolling stomach—and even a little from the conversation over breakfast, and the memories it had stirred up.

They'd seen some seabirds circling, and Winter was still hoping for puffins when they came further in against the coast, but so far the dolphins and whales had eluded them. Jenny was looking increasingly sceptical about the whole venture, even after Liam's reassurances that the crew would have already been out to sea even earlier that morning, to discover where the whales were hiding today.

'It's pretty incredible here, isn't it?' Josh leaned against the railings beside her, looking out to sea the same way she was. He raised a hand to point northwards. 'Somewhere up there is some ice-topped mountain that Jules Verne said was the entrance to the inside of the planet.'

'*Journey to the Centre of the Earth*,' Winter murmured. 'Weren't you up for a part in a remake of that once?'

'Probably.'

They stood in companionable silence, staring out at the water for a long moment, until Josh said, 'It's not too awful, this friendship thing, is it?'

Hearing the hope in his voice, Winter smiled down at the water and thought about breakfast pastries and ginger chews. None of it erased all those painful memories, or even started to make up for them. But Josh knew her in a way that no one else in the world did. Had lived some of her very worst moments with her.

Having him back in her life, in some small way...it made her feel more like herself, somehow. Or, maybe, the woman she used to be.

But I decided I didn't want to be her any more. Didn't I?

Could there be a way to reclaim the parts of herself she'd liked back then, and add them to the woman she'd become? It was something to think about, anyway.

'Do I take this ominous silence as an *Actually, Joshua, it's horrible and I just don't know how to tell you*?'

She huffed a laugh. 'No. I was just...thinking. That maybe Liam was right, and friendship might be good for us.'

'God, don't tell him that,' Josh joked. 'His smugness will know no bounds.'

Suddenly a call went up from the raised platform

above the cabin, and the boat buzzed with excitement as everyone hurried to the starboard side of the vessel.

'What is it?' Winter asked, as they caught up to Liam and Jenny.

'A whale, of course! A minke, they think,' Liam said. 'Someone saw the spray of water from a blowhole so now we just wait and—ah!'

She saw it, then. The sleek, shining skin of a minke whale, water sluicing off it as it broke the surface, just a short way from their boat. Around her, she heard gasps and camera shutters on phones, but Winter just watched and let the moment fill her with wonder, stretching the seconds out as the whale crested and dived again, sending a spray of icy water towards the boat.

It was moments like this that had got her through the months and years after the miscarriage, and the collapse of her marriage. Small moments of wonder that made the world feel bright again, just for a little while. That gave hope.

It wasn't until the creature had disappeared fully under the waves that she realised she was holding Josh's hand. Worse, she didn't know if she'd grabbed him, or he'd grabbed her.

Winter had avoided him for the rest of the boat trip, staying far on the other side of the crowd as they'd spotted a pod of dolphins on their way back to shore. Josh tried not to take it personally. After all, they'd only just agreed to try friendship, and already the memories and emotions that had brought up had been intense. And if he was feeling that, he could only imagine how much worse it was for her.

In her eyes on the boat he'd seen a glimpse of the fractured woman she'd been after she lost their baby. The one he'd left behind when he'd gone to work on his latest movie—and returned two months later to find her gone.

This time, he wouldn't leave, not until they'd talked about everything that had happened between them—everything neither of them had felt able to discuss at the time.

But he would give her space. He ordered room service for dinner, and later heard her leaving for the restaurant with Jenny. So once he'd finished eating, he decided to take advantage of her absence and enjoy that private geo-thermal lagoon he'd been promised.

The evening air bit at his skin as he stepped outside in his swimming gear, towel draped over his arm, regret-ting leaving behind the fluffy bathrobe that came with the room. Still, it was only a few steps before he was sinking into the naturally warmed waters of the lagoon, the rocks smooth against his spine.

Josh let his head fall back until he was staring up at the night sky. It wasn't late, not by anyone's standards, but darkness dropped early and suddenly so far north. The last twenty-four hours had been…overwhelming, and to sit there in the dark and the silence was soothing.

He'd taken his watch off, and his phone was some-where inside, so he didn't know how long he'd been soak-ing there when he heard the glass doors behind him slide open. The water swirling around him, he turned to fold his arms over the rocks at the edge of the pool and rested his chin on them.

Winter stepped out onto the decking, wrapped in a fluffy bathrobe just like the one he'd neglected, and car-rying two white mugs.

'Hot chocolate,' she said, as if it were perfectly nor-mal for her to be bringing him hot drinks late at night.

'I can get out, if you want?' The thought of abandoning

the warmth of the water for the bitter air he could already feel, sharp against his bare back, was not a nice one. But he had been hogging the lagoon all evening. 'I've probably been in here long enough, anyway.'

After placing the two mugs on the decking, within arm's reach of the lagoon, Winter let the bathrobe fall from her shoulders, revealing a different swimsuit from yesterday's. This one was red, had only one shoulder strap, and a cut-out below it that showcased her trim waist. It also did things to Josh's blood that even the warmth of the geothermal springs couldn't match.

Closure not closeness, he reminded his rebellious body. It didn't listen.

'It's fine.' She slid into the water, a little way apart from him. 'It's plenty big enough, anyway.'

That much was definitely true. When Liam had first tried to sell him on this trip with the promise of a private lagoon, Josh had assumed he was just talking up what was basically a hot tub. But this pool was something else entirely. Large enough for a football team, it seemed positively decadent to have it to share between just the two of them—and Jenny, he supposed, although she seemed to have made herself scarce again.

Because of the way the rooms were angled, to one side at the back of the hotel, and with a rocky barrier between them and the suites around the next corner, lying submerged in the water together they could have been the last two people left on earth.

Josh reached behind him for his hot chocolate and took a sip. Already, the freezing air had cooled it to a comfortable drinking temperature.

'Is it okay?' Winter asked from across the pool. 'I could have made coffee, I suppose. Or found some wine, or something. But Jenny brought you a hot chocolate yesterday, so—'

'It's perfect,' he said, cutting her off. 'Thank you.'

'Okay. Good.'

'I mean, not as good as the stuff you used to make after a late-night shoot. You remember? With the cream and the marshmallows and the nutmeg grated on top?' Sometimes, he still dreamt about those hot chocolates. Especially after a really long night filming, when he started hallucinating his bed. The thought of Winter at home waiting for him, with one of her hot chocolates ready, had been the only thing to sustain him some nights.

'I remember,' she murmured, and they both lapsed back into silence.

These days, Josh reflected, he had to make do with hotel room service. And he was more likely to call for a whisky than a hot chocolate.

He took another sip and savoured the taste. He couldn't imagine he'd be experiencing it again after this week, however well their plan for friendship and closure worked. There was something intimate about late night drinks like this.

Maybe that was what he had missed most of all. Not the cream, or the marshmallows, or the nutmeg. Just coming home to Winter—or having her come home to him.

And that was something he couldn't get back. He'd failed at that once already. They'd tried, and they knew it didn't work between them. Better to learn the lessons now and try again with someone new.

Because losing Winter twice? No man could survive that.

'Thank you,' she said, her voice so quiet he had to strain to hear it. 'For breakfast and for the ginger chews.

That's why…why I brought the hot chocolate. To say thank you.'

'You're welcome.' It was such a small thing to thank him for. Nowhere near as much as he owed her.

He hadn't been able to fix all the things that had been wrong between them, in the end. Or the things that came from outside their control to destroy them.

He hadn't been able to save their baby.

Ginger chews were nothing.

'So,' he said, after he'd finished his hot chocolate. 'I figure we're getting pretty good at the friendship thing, right?'

Winter nodded. 'Which brings us to the second part of the plan. Closure.'

They hadn't admitted that part to Liam or Jenny, by mutual—if unarticulated—agreement. This part, this was just for them. To help them move on.

'How do we do that, exactly?'

Taking a deep breath, Winter placed her own mug beside his on the decking, and turned to face him, her eyes dark and serious under the subdued and unobtrusive lighting placed around the decking, and the pale light of the moon from overhead. 'I've been thinking about that. And I've got one idea.'

There was something in her voice. A warning, perhaps. Or maybe just a reluctance. Either way, Josh got the impression that whatever this idea was, he wasn't going to like it very much.

But it wasn't as if he had any better notions about how to find closure on their marriage. If he had, he'd have used them already, and let his failures go. It was this or nothing.

Josh braced himself against the rocks of the pool. 'Tell me.'

CHAPTER SIX

WINTER WAS PRETTY sure that this was a terrible idea. Why else had she been putting it off? Going for dinner with Jenny, then making hot chocolate, letting him talk about old times and night shoots?

She'd been half hoping that he'd have some ideas of his own. Or maybe decided to pack the whole thing in and head back to LA and leave her to her lagoon in peace.

But no. He sat there, half naked and gorgeous and distracting in the moonlight, and said, '*Tell me.*'

So she did.

'I think…there was a lot we left unsaid at the end. And I know a lot of that was my fault for the way I left. But I feel like…like the words are still sitting inside us, taking up space. And maybe we need to get them out.' She took a breath. 'So my suggestion is that we share a secret, each night we're here.'

'Get them all out,' Josh said contemplatively. 'Let them all go.'

'Exactly.' She was glad he'd got it so easily. She hadn't been sure.

When they'd first met, they'd talked all night sometimes. Genuinely forgotten to go to sleep because they were so wrapped up in hearing each other's thoughts on the world. But it seemed to Winter now that all that talking had been in the abstract, rather than anything useful.

Dreams for the future, favourite books, where they'd love to travel. Stories about growing up, from their fledgling careers, about family and friends. All important things to share.

But when it came to the problems that arose between them, she'd found herself suddenly mute. Weighed down by the romance of the fairy tale everyone told about them, admitting things weren't perfect had seemed impossible—especially when, for Josh, they obviously were. He loved to talk about 'his wife' or to find another film for them to appear in together, or to show up on those red carpets with her on his arm.

And she'd loved it too, to start with. Until the feeling that the person she was underneath all the trappings of their fame and their story was starting to blur, to disappear at the edges beneath the myth of who people said she was.

She'd tried to explain it to Josh once, but the lack of comprehension on his face told her he couldn't feel the same. Couldn't understand how she felt.

Then she'd fallen pregnant, and he'd been away filming, and the silence had gaped wide, seeming to push them further and further apart.

It was too late now to draw them back together, but having those hard conversations they'd avoided for so long might help with the closure they both so obviously needed.

'So. Do you want to go first?' The hope was clear in his voice.

'Not really,' she admitted. 'But I will.'

She should have planned this better. She hadn't thought beyond getting him to agree to her plan, to what secret she'd actually share first. There were so many of them swirling around her head, she didn't know where to start.

She sucked in a deep breath and decided to start small. 'The ginger chews, and breakfast.'

Josh frowned and shifted closer towards her under the water. 'What about them? They didn't really help? I could try something else—'

She cut him off with a shake of her head. 'They did help. And I appreciated both gestures—really I did. Just like I appreciated all the things you did to try and help me five years ago.'

The memories came rolling back in, the way she'd known they would. Because that incident Josh had joked about, her throwing up on his tux at that charity dinner, had only been the start.

She'd heard about morning sickness before, even expected it when she realised she was pregnant. But she'd never been prepared for what followed over the next few months.

It wasn't just that the sickness wasn't constrained to one part of the day or night. Or that foods she'd previously loved suddenly turned her stomach. She could have lived without coffee—quite happily, given the queasy feeling that came over her at the smell.

All of that was awful—but she would have suffered it stoically for her baby. Of course she would.

Josh had been on hand, when he could be, bringing her anything she thought she might be able to stomach that day, or making sure she napped and didn't worry about other things. And when he'd been away, filming or rehearsing, he'd sent constant emails and texts with links to articles and folk remedies. He'd shipped bottles of useless tablets and tonics directly to her, along with the endless packets of ginger chews which, at least, helped dim the nausea for the brief time she was chewing them.

None of it had helped for long.

The real problems had started when she'd been unable to keep any food down—even those damn ginger chews. Then it had progressed to any liquids. To even the feel of water touching her throat leaving her vomiting helplessly again.

Her doctors had been concerned. Samples taken, levels tested, and a diagnosis of *hyperemesis gravidarum* given. There were tablets to try, and an overnight stay in hospital to rehydrate her more than once.

Still none of it lasted long, and all the doctors could suggest was that she rest and try to get through it.

And still Josh kept sending new things to try, new ways to fix her.

And *that,* she'd realised later, was the problem with the ginger chews. Much later, as it happened—once the sickness was over, and the grieving that had followed had dulled a little too. Once she was miles away from her ex-husband, and her thoughts had started to make sense to her again.

'So? What was the secret about the ginger chews?' Josh asked, still looking baffled.

Winter tried to find the right words. She didn't want to sound ungrateful, or uncaring. And she didn't really want to make him feel bad for trying to do the right thing. But they'd agreed to share the secrets that had ended their marriage and, for her, this was where that ending had started.

'When I was so sick… I know you were trying to help me, and I appreciated that even then. But it also made me feel like, well, like you were trying to fix me. Like I was so broken you had to find a fast solution so I could be myself again, the woman you loved, that you'd married. So I could get back to my role in our story. And I knew then, even in my bones, that I'd never be that woman again.' She looked down at her moonlit reflection in the water and thought she could almost see the weight of the secret rising from it, with the steam from the geothermal lagoon. 'You were trying to fix me, and all I wanted was to see you. To have you with me. For you to *listen* to me, and empathise, without trying to make it all go away. Because then, when it did—'

She broke off, unable to find any words for that part. For when she'd lost that longed-for baby who had already made life so hard but was also already so loved. Her miscarriage had been a quirk of fate, she was assured by everyone from friends and family to medical professionals. She mustn't blame herself, there was nothing she could have done.

But she *had* blamed herself. Because she was the one who'd got out of bed, felt dizzy and fallen on the stairs. She was the one whose body hadn't been able to handle the trauma of the pregnancy and the fall. The one who had failed at motherhood before she'd even had the chance to try.

And worse still was the fear that followed. That Josh might be glad, because he thought he could have the old Winter back, even though she no longer existed.

More terrifying even was the idea that he might want to try again.

She knew Josh, knew he wanted the picket fence and two-point-four kids. And when she'd married him, she had too. But now she knew that was beyond her capabilities—physical, mental or emotional.

She could not risk getting pregnant again. Not after the fear and the pain and the loss of last time.

And that was when she'd known she had to move on and let him find that with someone else.

Across the pool, Josh looked poleaxed by her words, his mouth slightly open, his knuckles white as he clenched his fist against the decking. 'Winter. I—'

But she couldn't hear it. She couldn't bear it.

Water sluicing down her body, she hurriedly climbed out from the lagoon, grabbing blindly for her robe as she rushed towards her room.

That was all the secrets she could take for one night.

Josh didn't sleep. He dozed, but only to dream of those horrific days trying to care for Winter from thousands of miles away, seeing only her drawn and exhausted face on the other end of a phone screen.

Even when he woke, things weren't much better. Her pale face in the moonlight as she'd described how she'd felt during that time haunted him just as much.

I need to talk to her.

He had so many things still to say. To explain—if not excuse. To try and understand better what she'd been through. Because if he hadn't seen this—how his trying to fix things was only making her feel more broken— what else had he missed? How else had he screwed up without even knowing?

He'd thought she blamed him for not being there, but now he wondered how much more there was behind it. And he needed to know.

But he didn't imagine she'd appreciate him breaking into her room at three in the morning to discuss the matter further, so instead he turned his pillow over, settled down and tried to sleep.

He failed.

By the time seven a.m. rolled around and breakfast

was being served in the restaurant, he'd given up. To his surprise, Liam was already in the restaurant with a cup of coffee and a plate of food, so he joined him to find out his fate for the day.

'What is it today?' Josh slipped into the seat opposite his friend, his own cup of—very strong—coffee in hand. 'I mean, how are you going to top whale-watching? Is it a hike up a glacier? A trip to a volcano? Waterfalls? Ice caves? What?' Something active. Something to keep his body busy and his mind occupied with everything around him. That was what he needed today—a distraction. At least until Winter was ready to talk to him again.

Liam tutted at him over the rim of his coffee cup. 'Nothing so dramatic. Today, all my guests will be at their leisure to enjoy the incredible spa facilities here at the Ice House Hotel. In fact, I took the liberty of drawing up a schedule for you.' He fished a polished piece of card from the folder on the table, neatly printed with a list of treatments and timings for him to use the sauna, steam rooms and other spa facilities.

'I have to do all of this?' Josh asked, scanning down the list. 'It looks…excessive.'

'You've been working hard, these past few years,' Liam said blandly. 'You could do with a proper relaxing break.'

The schedule looked more like a route march through organised relaxation to Josh, but he didn't mention that to his friend. Maybe he could opt out when he got bored.

He stayed and shot the breeze with Liam over breakfast until his friend needed to get to work. Josh poured himself another coffee, reclaimed his table and watched the other guests filter down for their own morning meal.

Except two. There was no sign of Winter, or Jenny.

With a sigh, Josh resigned himself to the idea that they

must have asked for room service that morning. And he couldn't imagine that his ex-wife would be wandering out to the geothermal lagoon anytime soon, not after last night. Which meant if he wanted to talk to her, he needed to stick to Liam's schedule for the day and hope that his and Winter's coincided.

Knowing Liam, he suspected they would.

Thirty minutes later, Josh showed up as instructed at the entrance to the spa area of the hotel. Here, the glass walls and bright openness gave way to more warmth and wooden touches, leading him down a cocooning hallway to the reception desk.

He handed the smiling woman behind the desk his card, and was led to a locker room where he could change and prepare himself. Then he made his way to what was called the Lupina Suite. 'All our treatment rooms are named after native wildflowers,' his guide explained. 'Here you are. Enjoy your massage!' The door swung shut behind him, and he was committed to his fate.

Josh had experienced plenty of sports massages in his time, but he suspected this would be something different. A feeling that was confirmed by the soft panpipe music and natural world sounds being piped into the room, the dim, womb-like lighting and the fact that his ex-wife was sitting on one of the two massage tables in the space.

'Liam booked us a couples massage,' she said, holding the fluffy robe she wore a little tighter around her body, her fingers clenched around the fabric at her throat.

'Of course he did.'

At least they weren't alone in the room. Within moments, they'd been joined by their masseuses and were both lying on their fronts on their tables, towels just about covering their modesty.

Josh made a point of not peeking at Winter's table as she lay there. No point in making this any more awkward than it already was. But just knowing she was there, practically naked, covered in massage oil, just a few feet away…he had to admit it was bringing up memories she'd probably rather he wasn't thinking about right then.

His lack of sleep caught up with him on the table, though. As the talented and well-trained masseur worked his hands over his back, Josh felt some of the tension he'd been storing in his muscles all week start to dissipate. He couldn't forget the secrets Winter had shared the night before, but he could at least put them in the context of five years ago, and deal with them with a more distant eye.

He'd dozed off by the time his massage was finished and only realised the masseuses had left the room when Winter said, 'Apparently we're to lie here and relax for fifteen minutes before we get up.'

'When did they say that?' He hadn't seen it on the schedule.

'When you fell asleep.'

'I didn't—'

'I know your sleeping breathing, Josh,' she countered. 'You were dead to the world.'

He sighed into the towel pillow beneath his head. 'I didn't sleep well last night.'

Her breath hitched at that, before she said, 'Neither did I.'

For a moment the only sound between them was the waves crashing against the sand being piped through the sound system, backed by the odd gull, far away, and the start of another panpipe refrain.

Then they both spoke at once.

'I didn't mean to—' Winter started.

'I need to say—' Josh stopped and lifted his head enough to smile at her across the room. She rested with her head on one side, still lying on her front, looking back at him with wide eyes. The towel that covered her left her calves, her shoulders and her upper back bare, and they all gleamed with oil in the dim light.

God, I want to touch her.

There was so much he still didn't understand about how things had ended between them—more than he'd ever realised he didn't know. But he had to remember the reasons for finding out—to avoid making the same mistakes again. So he could move on and find love with someone who didn't break a little every time she looked at him. Whose presence didn't remind him of all his screwups.

Someone he could get things right with from the start.

He forced himself to swallow and focus on the conversation at hand. 'I need to say I'm sorry,' he said when it became clear she was waiting for him to speak first. 'I'm so sorry. Everything you said last night... I wasn't trying to *fix* you, because you never needed fixing. But I can understand why you felt that way and I'm sorry, so sorry, I couldn't be what you needed then.'

She dipped her chin, an accepting nod that looked strange in her lying position. 'What *were* you trying to do?'

Taking care to keep his towel in place, Josh turned on his side to face her as he thought about his answer. 'I guess I was trying to...be there, even when I wasn't. You were so miserable, and so ill, and I knew that there was nothing I could do to make it better, but that didn't make me stop trying. Because...'

'Because?' she prompted.

He sighed. 'Because I knew it was my fault. And I felt guilty as hell about that.'

Winter turned towards him in surprise, only remembering at the last minute to grab her towel to make sure it came with her.

'You thought my sickness was *your* fault?' All these years, she'd thought he'd been frustrated by her illness, disappointed by her inability to do pregnancy right, the same way she had. She'd always imagined, when she'd thought about it at all, being on Josh's arm at a premiere in a cute as hell maternity cocktail dress and improbably high heels, glowing for the cameras. She'd assumed that was what *he'd* imagined too.

Not her stuck in bed and stinking of sick.

Not losing the baby anyway, after everything she'd been through.

'I thought *all* of it was my fault,' Josh admitted. 'I still do. If I'd been more careful, you wouldn't have got pregnant then—I mean, it's not like we planned it, right? Because if we had, I'd have made sure I'd have been around more for when you needed me. But instead I was stuck filming on the other side of the world and you were too tired to even talk to me most nights, if our time zones even aligned, and all I could do was send you things to show that I was always, always thinking of you, even when I wasn't there with you.'

His words came out in a rush and she could hear the sincerity in them, could hear how badly he'd wanted to be there for her. How he, like she had been, had only been doing his best in a bad situation.

'I knew that,' she whispered. 'Deep down, I knew that you were trying. That we both were. But…those were such dark days. And I let that darkness overtake me sometimes.'

Josh's response was tentative. 'Like when…when we lost the baby.'

We. She'd never really thought of it as something that had happened to them as a couple, Winter realised. Only something *she* had done. *She* had lost their baby. She'd acknowledged the loss Josh felt, but still felt strangely separate from it.

'I blamed myself for that,' she admitted. 'Still do, most days. But back then… I thought that I'd spent so long wishing the sickness would go away that I'd made it happen somehow.' Because there were moments in that time, when the world wouldn't stop spinning, or when she couldn't lift her head without vomiting, that she'd have done almost *anything* to make it stop.

'No.' Josh reached out across the divide between their massage tables and grabbed her hand, squeezing it tight. 'I never thought it was your fault. Not for a moment. If anything, I blamed myself for not being there.'

The doctors at the start had tried to cheer her up, to tell her that the constant sickness was a *good* sign, that it meant a healthy baby.

Turned out they'd been wrong about that too.

For a long moment they lay there, hands clasped tight together. Winter gazed into his eyes and wondered how many other things they'd each been wrong about. That they'd blamed themselves for—and assumed the other blamed them for too.

Part of her wished they'd been able to talk like this back then, but a larger part knew that it was only the time and distance they now had between them and the events that made that possible. She was still too lost in the person the world wanted her to be, her real self shadowed by the stories the gossip websites told about her. The fairy tale romance they'd created, that had destroyed the very real love they'd shared in the end.

The woman she'd been then couldn't have managed this conversation. She was a little proud that she had now. That she'd rebuilt herself as a whole, real person again— as who she was, not who the world wanted to see. That had taken work.

But she didn't want to dwell either. She was about the future these days, not the past. They'd agreed to find closure this week, but also—she hoped—friendship. Time to get back to the more fun one of those.

'That's got to be our fifteen minutes, don't you think?' she said with an only slightly watery smile.

'Probably.' Josh gave her hand one last squeeze, then released it. 'So, what do we do now?'

Winter sat up, clasping the towel to her front. 'Why, Mr Abraham. Have you really never been on a spa day with a friend before?' She grinned, forcing a lighter tone to show him that it was okay for them to move on from the emotional conversation of earlier.

'Not exactly.'

Josh swung his legs around to sit on the edge of the table, and Winter pointedly did not look at how much skin he showed when his towel slipped. Even with it draped across his lap to protect his modesty, his bare chest— more muscled than she remembered, probably for his latest role—was distracting enough.

Friends. That's all.

'So, you'll have to be my guide. What do we do on a friends spa day?'

She grinned, glad he'd gone with her attempt to change the mood. Too much more serious conversation and she'd have been in a ball in the corner of the sauna.

'Well, first off, we need to go try out those heated stone recliners I saw outside, because they look amazing. And if we're lucky someone might bring us a glass of something cold and bubbly while we're there.'

'That does sound good,' Josh admitted. 'What else?'

'Basically, spa days are for sitting around gossiping, drinking champagne, enjoying the steam rooms, getting our nails done and generally relaxing,' Winter said with a shrug. 'Oh, and daring each other to jump in the ice pool, of course. But, most of all, definitely gossiping.'

He raised his eyebrows at her. 'Gossiping? Really?'

'Absolutely,' Winter said firmly. 'We've got five years of news to catch up on, remember?' And now she'd got the worst of her secrets out of the way, she wanted to hear it all.

CHAPTER SEVEN

Josh drew the line at getting his toenails painted pink, but he sat alongside Winter while she had hers done, and enjoyed a foot massage from another of Liam's very competent staff members. Winter's manicurist kept shooting glances between the two of them, although if she recognised them she made no comment on the two of them being there together.

Of course she didn't need to, because soon enough another trio of guests arrived for their appointment—three of Liam's influencers he was trying to seduce to the way of Iceland—and they had enough to say for everybody.

'So, are you two...you know?' One of the women—Josh thought she might be called Skylar, but he wasn't sure—waved a hand between them in a meaningful manner.

Not meaningful enough for her friend, Mo, who added, 'Together?'

'I always knew there was something special between the two of you,' the third member of their group—Sarra, maybe?—said wistfully.

'Oh, no. Like we told you the other day, we're just friends,' Winter said, a convincingly jolly smile on her face, even though her peaceful spa day was being interrupted. Josh had to admire that kind of dedication to the role.

Skylar leaned forward into Winter's personal space, and rather closer to Josh's bath robe gowned self than he was really comfortable with. 'You can tell us, you know. We wouldn't say anything.'

'We're the souls of discretion,' Sarra agreed, nodding.

Mo looked between them, bemused, which was the most honest reaction Josh could think of, really.

He exchanged a brief glance with Winter and knew already what she was thinking. There was no real way they were going to convince these three otherwise, if they'd decided they were back together. But the last thing they wanted was to give them anything they could use as confirmation—especially since it wasn't even true.

But truth, Josh had learned over the years, didn't tend to matter too much if it got in the way of a good story. And while these three might claim they wouldn't spread the word, Josh knew how that went too. It was too good a titbit not to at least hint at to friends, and then spill, while swearing the friend to secrecy. Then they'd do the same, and soon the buzz would be out there and someone— possibly a colleague of one of the travel journalists staying in this very hotel this very week—would be offering Skylar, Mo and Sarra cash to tell all, and provide photos.

The gossip magazines would have them married again before they'd even finished having enough conversations to find their closure, let alone their new friendship.

When Winter had said they needed to spend their spa break gossiping, he was pretty sure this wasn't what she'd meant.

'Well, I'm done here, anyway.' Josh got to his feet. 'Nice to meet you again, ladies. I'm off to whatever Liam has scheduled next on my agenda. I'll see you later, I'm sure, Winter.'

With a last meaningful look at his ex-wife, he sauntered off as casually as a man in a bathrobe could manage, and hoped she'd got the message.

Ten minutes later, he was relaxing in the steam room, letting the oils and sinus-opening scents fill his lungs, his head tipped back against the wall, eyes closed as sweat and steam ran down his torso. He smiled when he heard the door open, though, and someone enter very quietly.

'Josh?' Winter called softly.

He opened his eyes. 'Over here.'

She padded over towards him, her bare feet slapping against the wet tiled floor, and took a seat at his side. 'I was assuming you meant for me to meet you here. It was next on my schedule from Liam too.'

'I was hoping it would be,' Josh admitted. 'I thought we might want to continue our…gossiping in private?'

'Definitely,' Winter said with feeling.

Still, it felt almost the wrong place for conversation. They sat together in the darkened steam room, the colour-changing spotlights overhead barely enough to see each other by, and just breathed. Josh could hear Winter's breath pattern mirroring his own, and he realised suddenly this was the most at peace he'd been since she'd left him.

Winter had always meant peace to him. From the moment he'd spotted her across the set on their first day filming *Fairy Tale of New England,* he'd felt that calmness wash over him just looking at her—and known that she was meant to be in his life.

She still was. And as much as he told himself, and Liam, and anyone else who pressed him for answers, that he wanted to move on—to find that perfect romance, perfect relationship, that the other members of his family had, right now, he wondered.

Would he sacrifice all that if it meant ten more minutes just sitting here, breathing, with Winter?

No. He couldn't. Because losing her had almost broken him last time, and he couldn't put himself, or her, through that again. They just weren't meant to be. If they were, it wouldn't be this hard.

He shook his head instinctively, shaking away the vision and sending droplets of water flying from his hair in Winter's direction.

'Josh!' she squealed.

'Like you're not already soaked through,' he replied, forcing a smile.

Friendship. Closure. That was what he was here for.

Then he could move on and find that real love of his life he had to believe was out there waiting for him, somewhere.

Because the universe had already made very clear that it wasn't ever going to be Winter.

Spending the day at the spa with Josh was surprisingly fun. After their emotional conversation on the massage tables, and their escape from inquisitive influencers in the manicure room, they'd managed to enjoy the steam room, rainforest and ice walls, sauna, cold plunge pool and the heated stone beds Winter had so been looking forward to.

They ate salads for lunch in their white bathrobes, both of them red-faced and with hair pointing in all directions—a sad result of the massage oil, and constant water since—and the waiter in the spa restaurant even brought them over a carafe of white wine from 'the boss', which they decided it would be rude to waste.

Even reminiscing about their time as a couple didn't hurt as much as she'd thought it might. They'd been together almost from the moment they'd met on set—something the media and fans had made a big deal about. All those 'love at first sight' headlines were perfect for the romantic comedy they'd been filming, so Winter was pretty sure the marketing and publicity team had played them up too.

She and Josh had been too deeply absorbed in each other, and everything growing between them, to pay much attention to the outside world.

Back then, she'd felt everything so acutely—every lingering look from across the set, every smile, every kiss…she'd felt them in her soul.

She hadn't felt *anything* that deeply in five years now. Not even the award nomination she'd worked so damn hard for.

But now she could look back on those days with an outsider's eye, as if she were watching another younger, fresher, more naive girl make those choices, and fall in love. Which, in a way, she was, Winter supposed. Whoever that girl had been, it wasn't her any more.

'I thought we were supposed to be gossiping about the stuff we'd missed over the last few years,' Winter said after a while, when the memories started to sting a little. 'Not reminiscing about stuff we both already know.'

Josh gave her a smile and topped up both of their glasses with the last of the wine. 'Okay, then. Why don't you start by telling me all about how you came to make your latest *award-nominated* movie, Ms Director?'

Winter grinned. This was something she could talk

comfortably about. Something that had no connection to Josh, or the past, at all. At least, she thought it didn't.

Until she started talking to him about it.

'After…everything…' a useful shorthand that, to encompass all the things she didn't want to talk about again right now '… I guess I kind of threw myself into my career for a while. Much like you did, I think.' She gave him a knowing look, thinking of the half dozen movies he'd made in record time after their split.

'I guess I can understand that impulse,' he agreed wryly. His fingers twisted the fabric napkin in his hands and she knew that if this were a cheaper establishment, with paper napkins, he'd have shredded it to pieces by now. They were both trying so hard to act as if this was a perfectly normal conversation to be having, a normal situation, but underneath the strain was starting to show. 'For me, being busy stopped me thinking so much. Work was a distraction.'

'So what made you slow down again?' It was hard not to notice how, after that flurry of movies, he'd hardly been in anything new.

'Burnout,' Josh admitted with a shrug. 'I… I was just done. I went and stayed with my mom and spent time with Graham and Ashley and then the twins when they came along, and just, well, stopped.'

She felt the guilt rising again at that. Guilt that her actions had driven him so far past his limits. But pride in him too, that he'd realised that and taken the time to rest and recover.

'But I was asking about you,' Josh pointed out. 'What made you decide to move behind the camera for a change? I mean, it was obviously a great move—see nomination as noted above and all that. But I don't remember directing ever being something you talked much about. So I have to admit I was kind of surprised when I heard you were directing, not starring in, *Another Time and Place*.'

Winter leant back in her chair, staring out over his shoulder. The restaurant was the only place in the spa that had floor to ceiling windows and she looked out now at the pool beyond—another geothermal lagoon, this one much larger than the private one they shared. It was filled with other guests, all enjoying the warm water, views over the rocky landscape towards the snow-tipped mountains and the slightly sulphurous smell.

She wondered if any of them were watching them back, talking about the two of them having lunch together. Being together. Like the women in the manicure bar had done.

'If you don't want to talk about this, we don't have to.' Josh's brow was crinkled with faint confusion as he gave her the conversational out. Winter could understand why; they'd talked about far more personal, more difficult things without her bailing. Okay, without her bailing *much*.

But this cut to the heart of who she was these days so much more. This wasn't about the Winter she'd left behind. It was key to the Winter she was now. And somehow that made it harder to say out loud.

But she knew she needed to. So she shrugged nonchalantly and turned back to her dessert as if it were no big deal.

'Directing wasn't always a big dream of mine, no,' she admitted. 'But I spent so long having people only talk about me in relation to you—'

'Did they really do that?'

Winter stared at him. 'How could you not notice? I was always "wife of Josh Abraham" in every article for years.'

'Really? And that was...so bad?' The puzzled look

had faded into a stoic, blank mask, and Winter knew that meant her words had stung.

'Not the being married to you part,' she said. 'It wasn't like… I was ashamed of us or you or anything. It was just…'

'You wanted to be your own person,' Josh guessed. 'I can understand that. But, I mean, they talked about me as your husband too, you know.'

'I do know,' Winter said. 'Every article about either of us talked about our fairy tale romance, how we were living the true love dream.' She could hear the bitterness in her voice, and saw it reflected in the dismay that showed on Josh's face.

'I always thought that was…well. I liked it.' Josh gave a strange sort of half shrug. 'I liked that our love story was epic. That people saw it as a fairy tale.'

Of course he had. Because, for him, that was exactly what he'd always wanted—a love story to rival his parents' and his brother's.

But for her…

'It wasn't that I didn't love our story, and that it resonated with people,' she said carefully. 'I just didn't want it to be the only thing people thought of when they saw me.'

'So you took yourself off camera,' Josh said.

'I guess I figured that if no one was ever going to talk about my acting, I'd try something else.' Something where audiences weren't staring at her all the time, thinking about how she'd walked out on her true love. How she'd betrayed him.

How she'd lost their child.

Because of course that had been all over the papers too. Suddenly, she'd become a figure of pity, not one of envy, and it turned out she didn't like that any better either.

'You never said anything,' he said. 'Back then. You never told me you felt that way.'

'I didn't know how,' Winter admitted. 'You…you loved the fairy tale. It was everything you ever wanted. And saying that it wasn't what *I* wanted… It would have sounded like I didn't want *you,* and that was never the problem.'

She'd said too much, she realised, snapping her jaw closed. But she *had* always wanted him. That wasn't something that changed. It was just everything else that had.

Josh was studying her with a sudden heat in his eyes at her words, when in a flash his attention and gaze jerked away, to something over her shoulder. She turned too, and saw the women from earlier entering the restaurant.

'Time to move on?' Josh said, and she nodded, gathering up her things, even as she knew that this conversation wasn't fully over.

Josh leaned against the open doorway of Liam's office a few hours later, his hair still wet and his shirt sticking to his back from where he'd dressed too hurriedly after his time in the spa. But he'd wanted to speak to his friend, and urgently.

'How was the spa?' Liam asked, motioning him into the office.

Josh closed the door behind him and took his usual seat in the armchair by the window. 'Luxurious.'

'Relaxing?'

'In parts.'

'And the company?' The innocence in Liam's voice was definitely fake.

Josh gave him a look. 'We talked some,' he said. 'But not enough. Too many people watching.'

'I did give you a private lagoon for your conversations,' Liam pointed out. 'I mean, really, I got you both here in the first place. What more do you want from me?'

Just the question Josh had been pondering as he'd sat in the steam room and laughed at Winter jumping into the cold plunge pool afterwards.

The conversation they'd had at lunchtime wasn't the end of it, Josh was sure about that. Learning that she'd found the media interpretation of their story as a fairy tale, as true love, annoying had hurt. But at the same time he was beginning to understand her point of view at least. He could get how frustrating it must have been for her to only ever be seen in her relationship to him.

And that wouldn't change as long as they were both here, in full sight of all the journalists, bloggers and influencers Liam had invited to the Ice House for the week.

So, what did he want from Liam?

'I want your help getting Winter away from here for the night, somewhere we can hang out and talk in private. Somewhere fun.'

Liam's eyebrows leapt up at that. 'Because you're trying to *woo* her back to you again?'

'I knew that last period drama you did was a mistake,' Josh grumbled. 'I'm not *wooing* anybody.'

'Which is, I believe, part of the problem we're trying to fix here. Isn't it?' The eyebrows were still raised.

'Yes. Obviously.' Josh hoped he didn't sound as if he'd forgotten the objective for the week, even though he had.

He was here to find closure with Winter and move on so he could find true love again with someone else and stop obsessing over why his fairy tale romance hadn't ended in a happy ever after. And talking to Winter some more about how she'd felt when they were married was part of that.

That was all.

Nothing to do with wanting to see her let down her guard again and laugh with him. To see her smile across a table in candlelight like there was nowhere else in the world she wanted to be.

Nothing to do with any of that at all. Because that way lay heartbreak and burnout. Again.

'So you just want to take her out somewhere tonight on a friend date?'

'Yes. Exactly that. Except not a date at all. Just…we need to talk some more, away from watching eyes. And we've spent the whole day at the spa, so I think an evening in the lagoon is off the cards.'

Liam didn't ask why they couldn't just use one of their private suites, for which he was grateful. He didn't have much of an answer beyond needing to be on neutral territory.

And maybe somewhere neither of them could just run easily if the conversation grew hard.

Liam surveyed him across the desk, his gaze thoughtful. Josh wasn't sure exactly what his friend was looking for, but it seemed he found it because, after a long moment, he nodded.

'Okay, then. The pair of you meet me at the side entrance in an hour. I'll get you out of here.'

'You're not going to tell me where we're going?' Josh asked. Liam's idea of a perfect friends' night out was not necessarily the same as his. He'd have to warn Winter that wherever they ended up was all Liam's doing…

'It's a surprise.' Liam flashed him a grin and picked up his phone. 'Just trust me, okay. Don't worry. I'll tell Jenny the plan so she can help Winter choose an appropriate outfit.'

'What about *my* outfit?' Josh asked.

Liam rolled his eyes. 'My friend, you have been in Hollywood too long. Now, go figure out how you're going to woo your ex-wife back.'

'That's not what I'm doing.'

A knowing, slightly smug smile spread across Liam's face. 'Of course it isn't. Now, go!'

Josh was so busy denying Liam's accusations in his head he was almost back at his suite before he thought to wonder when Liam had got Jenny's phone number.

CHAPTER EIGHT

'WHY WILL NOBODY tell me where I'm going?' Winter asked the moment she opened the door of her suite to Josh that evening.

'Trust me, if I knew I'd tell you,' he replied with a shrug. 'I remember how much you hate surprises. But I'm afraid our gracious host hasn't seen fit to share his plans for our evening with me.'

Winter shot a glare back into the room at Jenny, who was trying to look innocent on the sofa. '*Jenny* knows.'

'Apparently our Liam is keener on sharing things with Jenny than either of us,' Josh said drily. Then he dropped his voice. 'You know we don't have to go, if you don't want to. I just thought it might be a good way to get away from here and finish our conversation from earlier.'

She couldn't deny that she liked the idea of getting away from all the people who seemed to be watching her every movement here at the hotel. Plus, she *had* got all dressed up now.'

'Oh, come on then.' She grabbed her coat and bag. 'Don't wait up!' Winter was pretty sure Jenny would hear the sarcasm in that one. If not, the way she slammed the door behind her probably did it.

Liam wasn't waiting for them at the side entrance, but a long black car with tinted windows was. The black-capped driver opened the rear doors for them, and they both slipped inside.

'I don't suppose you want to give us a clue where we're going tonight?' Winter asked him before he shut her door.

He gave her a not entirely reassuring amused smile in return.

'Liam really didn't tell you where he's sending us?' Winter asked as the car pulled away from the hotel.

'Not a clue,' Josh replied, looking a little concerned. 'But he said it would be somewhere we could talk in private, without worrying about being watched.'

'That's something, I suppose.' Winter settled back in her seat and watched the blackness of the Icelandic night passing by.

They were on the road back into Reykjavik, she realised. Maybe Liam had booked them a table at a private restaurant or something. That would be okay.

She and Josh tried to make small talk, but the apprehension that hung over both of them made it difficult and they soon lapsed into silence, long before they entered the city.

Then, eventually, the car came to a stop in front of a building. Except it didn't look like a restaurant. And the windows were mostly in darkness.

'Are you sure this is the right place?' Josh asked.

The driver was openly grinning now. 'Oh, for sure. Mr Delaney arranged for them to open this evening for you especially.'

Why did Winter have such a bad feeling about this?

She climbed out of the car, took Josh's arm, then looked up at the sign on the building in front of them.

The Icelandic Phallological Museum.

Of course.

Beside her, Josh was blinking very hard. 'Has Liam... has he sent us on a date to a museum full of...'

'Penises,' said a well-dressed woman who'd suddenly appeared in the doorway in front of them. 'That's right! We're probably the only museum in the world to include a specimen penis from every land and sea mammal found in our country. Please come in!'

The driver was already pulling away from the kerb, leaving them no escape route. Winter exchanged a slightly panicked look with Josh, who shrugged, making it clear it was her call.

'Well, okay then.' Winter pulled her faux-fur coat tighter around her. 'Let's take a look.'

Once they'd got over their initial embarrassment at Liam's choice of an appropriate date location—even if it wasn't really a date—Winter had to admit, the Icelandic Phallological Museum was genuinely interesting. Even if she and Josh couldn't help but snigger at a few of the exhibits.

'Did you see the size of the sperm whale?' Josh whispered to her, and Winter giggled as she nodded.

The museum was officially closed for the day, so they had the whole place to themselves, the museum worker who'd greeted them discreetly leaving them to browse the huge collection alone. For once, they didn't have to worry about anybody seeing them together or jumping to conclusions, but they were having too much fun to waste that opportunity on deep and meaningful conversations.

It felt...freeing. Fun.

By the time they'd taken in all the exhibits, Winter's stomach was starting to rumble. They wandered over to the abandoned café to find one table set out with a white tablecloth and candles she suspected didn't get much use in the museum day to day.

While Josh considered a pint of Moby Dick ale or a 'cockaccino' she surveyed the variety of penis-themed treats available in the nearby gift shop. Clearly this place had found a niche and really gone for it.

She kind of loved it.

Even if she was going to kill Liam for sending them there. The man was the opposite of subtle.

Except…it wasn't as if there was anything sexual about the museum at all, despite its premise. And actually, surveying the exhibits with Josh, giggling about animal genitalia…it had been *fun*. It had broken all the tension between them and given them a break from the difficult conversations they'd been having all week.

Maybe Liam had known what he was doing after all.

Not that she'd ever tell him that.

The museum café served them penis calzone followed by phallic-shaped waffles topped with berries and cream. While it wasn't exactly the gourmet dinner out Josh had been expecting when he'd asked Liam to arrange their date, he had to admit it was a lot more entertaining. And it had lightened the mood between them—something Josh hadn't been certain was possible after the conversations of the last few days, despite their best efforts in the spa.

They kept the small talk light and inconsequential over dinner, still giggling about their favourite exhibits, or the mug Winter had found in the gift shop.

It wasn't until they were sipping their coffees—with penis-shaped patterns in the foam, obviously—that he returned at all to their earlier unfinished conversation. And even that felt lighter. More…flirtatious, even—not that he'd admit that to Liam, or mention it to Winter, for fear of breaking the spell.

'So, you like directing?' he asked.

Winter nodded, placing her cup back in its saucer. 'I do. More than I thought I would. I mean… I think I was just challenging myself to try something new originally. And maybe…maybe hiding a little by being behind the camera instead of in front of it. But mostly it was, you know, throwing myself into my career because I'd been such a failure at the personal side of things, that old cliché.'

'Right.' It might be a cliché, but Josh's chest still tightened at the casual way she said it. *Such a failure.* As if it was an established, unarguable fact about her—the same way her black hair or green eyes were.

Except it wasn't true. *He* was the failure. Not her.

He was the one who hadn't been there when she'd needed him. Who she hadn't been able to talk to about how she was feeling. He'd failed as a husband, and it had cost him everything.

But Winter carried on, oblivious to his startled musings.

'But I really enjoyed it. I liked being able to tell a whole story, not just my part in it. I liked having that sort of control too—to put across things that mattered to me. Have you seen it? *Another Time and Place*, I mean.'

Josh started. 'Of course I've seen it. You think I wouldn't go see your first movie as a director?'

Was the pinkness in her cheeks just due to the coffee? He hoped not.

'What did you think?' Her voice was small, uncertain, and Josh couldn't help but smile at it.

'The award nomination wasn't enough for your ego?'

She shook her head. 'It's not… Awards aren't everything, you and I both know that. I want to know what *you* think.'

A warmth filled him at the idea that his opinion still mattered to her. That she thought about what *he* thought at all.

'I loved it,' he said honestly. 'I thought it was smart, and funny, and touching and *real*. And I could feel *you* in every frame of it.'

Her blush had gone from a faint tint to bright red now, and Josh realised he loved that too.

'Thank you,' she said softly. Her eyes looked a little wet.

'It must have been a hell of a lot of work, though,' he said, giving her a moment to recollect herself. 'I mean, it's such an…intense movie. So closely focused on your characters, and the setting. I know how demanding that kind of movie is to act in. I can't imagine *directing* one.'

Winter nodded. 'Yeah. I mean, I know we didn't have all the green screen effects or the action sequences or what have you. But making it powerful enough to stand without any of that stuff that audiences have come to expect…that was its own challenge. I was lucky with my cast, though. Melody especially—she really got what I was trying to say with the film, and she knocked it out of the park.'

'She did.' What she'd said about Melody, though… that had him thinking. 'The story you chose to tell… I heard the reporter at the press conference asking you about second chance love. Finding love again after loss, or divorce, or whatever. Was that… I mean…were you…' He trailed off, the words eluding him.

Winter seemed to know what he meant, though. She always had, until the end, when neither of them had enough words left to express all the terrible things they were feeling.

He'd thought that he'd understood her the same way. Apparently he'd been wrong.

'You mean was that a personal story to tell?' She raised her eyebrows at him with a smile. 'Am I searching for love again?'

'Yeah, I guess.' The idea of it made his heart hurt. But wasn't he doing exactly the same? Trying to find closure with Winter so he could move on for a second chance at love? He could hardly blame her for wanting exactly the same thing he did.

But Winter shook her head. 'No. I'm not…dating, or whatever. I'm focusing on my career and that's enough for me right now.'

'But one day?' Oh, God, why was he pushing it? Maybe so he could ignore the huge surge of relief that ran through him at her words.

'Perhaps,' she said with a light shrug, but she sounded unconvinced.

And that surge of relief turned into a tsunami, even as the guilt that came with it grew.

He should want her to move on. To find happiness again.

It was just…the thought of her falling for another guy the way she'd fallen for him. Of her experiencing all that heady emotion, the days where all they could see was each other, when other people and whole film sets disappeared and the world shrank to just the two of them. Those can't-keep-our-hands-off-each-other days, those share-all-our-secrets-in-whispers nights, and everything in between them.

He wanted that again. And he wanted her to have that again.

He just couldn't quite imagine either of them having it with anyone else.

And that…that was a problem.

Josh's gaze had turned glassy, as if he was occupying a world she wasn't part of. Lost inside his head, she supposed, now they were back on more dicey topics. Like her love life—or total lack of.

Was he disappointed she hadn't moved on? Had he hoped that she'd say she was out there on the dating scene and free him from any residual guilt about doing the same? That would be like Josh—a gentleman to the end, and not willing to move on from their fairy tale until she did.

Or…

No. She couldn't let herself think about that. The possibility that maybe he *didn't* want her to move on because he hadn't either.

She should change the subject. Talk about his next movie, or sperm whale penises, or *anything* that wasn't their love lives.

'What about you?' The words were out before she could stop them. 'Are you dating right now? I haven't seen many photos of you with anyone—not serious someone's anyway. But then, I haven't really been looking.'

'No, there's…no one.' He looked down at the remains of the foam in his coffee as he shook his head. 'First I was just working all the time, and then I was at Mom's, and since then…'

He looked up suddenly, his gaze catching hers like a hook, and the heat in it made her swallow, hard.

'There's no one,' he finished. But she heard all the words he didn't say—because she was thinking them too.

There's no one like you. There could never be anyone like you.

Oh, but she was screwed.

She couldn't do this. Couldn't risk falling again like this. She should have run the moment she'd realised her heart still skipped when she saw him.

She should never have come to Iceland at all.

'We should get going.' She pushed her chair out from the table and stumbled quickly to her feet. 'God only knows what Liam has planned for us tomorrow, but I doubt it will be as restful as today's spa activities.'

'Yeah, you're right.' Josh stood too, more gracefully than she'd managed. 'I just want to grab something from the gift shop first.'

When he'd paid for his purchases—a penis mug for her and a museum logo T-shirt for himself—plus a whole bag of gummy penises for Liam—they made their way back out front, thanking the museum employees who'd stayed late to give them their unusual evening together.

It was very late, she realised as the driver opened the car door for her. They must have talked for hours and, now they'd stopped, her tiredness was catching up with her. She dozed in the car back to the hotel, leaning on Josh's arm gratefully as he helped her out of the car at the other end.

They sneaked in through the side door and made their way through the dimly lit hallways of the hotel, towards their adjoining suites.

But when she reached her room she realised that, despite all her good intentions, she wasn't quite ready to say goodnight yet. Maybe she shouldn't have come to Iceland at all. But now she was here...she couldn't just ignore this moment.

It might be the last one she ever got with him.

'Thank you for tonight,' she said softly, leaning against the wood of her door.

'I think you have Liam to thank for the romantic location,' he joked. 'But thank *you* for your company. It was nice to have some time alone, just us.'

'Just us and over two hundred penises,' she pointed out, making him laugh.

'Yes. Can't forget the penises. Speaking of which…' He handed her the mug he'd bought at the gift shop. 'Can't forget this either.'

She pulled it from the bag and studied it with amusement. 'Ah, yes. Thank you for my…thoughtful gift.'

They shared another smile, and in it Winter could feel so many things that neither of them were saying. Or *could* say.

They were past all that. She'd walked out and left it five years ago and she couldn't honestly believe that there was a path back, even if she wanted to walk it.

This felt like goodbye. A real one this time.

But then he leaned in to place a kiss on her cheek, whispering, 'Goodnight, Winter,' against her skin.

'Goodnight,' she murmured back. And then, before she could stop herself, she turned her face and caught his lips with her own.

For a long moment she lost herself in the kiss—in the warmth of his mouth on hers, the way his free hand came to clutch at her hip as he met her kiss with his own, deepening it, sweeping his tongue across her lower lip in the way she'd always loved. She let the heat build between them, let him press her against the closed door, rejoiced in the length of him full against her, felt him harden against her stomach—

He pulled away.

'Winter.' Josh rested his arm above her head on

the door, looking down at her with darkened eyes. He looked…wrecked. 'I… We…'

'Right. Of course.' It *had* been goodbye. And she'd ruined it.

'I'm just saying—'

'No, you're right!' She spun out from under his arm, fishing in her clutch bag for her room key card, relieved when it slid into the lock and turned green first time. 'I need to sleep. I'll see you tomorrow.'

She opened the door only enough to slip through, then shut it fast and tight behind her, hoping it wasn't loud enough to wake Jenny.

Then she leaned against it and listened for Josh's footsteps walking away.

CHAPTER NINE

JOSH DIDN'T SLEEP MUCH.

How could he, after that kiss? After he'd held Winter in his arms again, even with that damn penis mug still dangling from her fingers.

He'd wanted to say so much, once he'd broken the kiss. But the words just wouldn't come. Maybe there *weren't* words for all the things he was feeling. But he had to find some that would do if he wanted Winter to understand.

The pain in her eyes when he'd pulled away…he'd known instantly that he'd done the wrong thing, again. That she'd misunderstood. That she'd thought he didn't want this when, in reality, it was the only thing he ever had wanted.

The last five years he'd thought he'd been moving on, but the whole time he'd been hanging on to the possibility of *this* and he hadn't even realised.

But giving in to it…

Josh wasn't sure he could handle the pain it might bring when he had to say goodbye again. Because they already knew they didn't work together.

As the clock ticked over towards morning, he gave up on even dozing a little longer and dragged himself from the comfort of bed. His shower woke him up a little at least, and he dressed quickly and headed for breakfast in search of coffee.

There was no sign of Winter or Jenny in the restaurant, which didn't really surprise him—he imagined they'd have room service again, especially after last night. But he'd only been sitting alone at his window table, nursing a black Americano with no foam to have penises drawn in, for a short time when Liam slid into the chair opposite him.

'How was your date last night?' he asked, a smile dancing around his lips.

Josh raised his eyebrows. 'You mean our guided tour of the penis museum?'

That drew a full-blown laugh from his friend. 'I'm sorry, I couldn't resist. And I thought it would be a good ice-breaker, at least.'

'It was,' Josh admitted. 'It definitely lightened the mood, anyway.'

'It's hard to be too serious when you're surrounded by two hundred plus animal penises,' Liam replied sagely. 'So, it went well?'

'Mostly.' He didn't want to get into how things had ended right now. 'Oh, and I bought you these.' Josh handed over the bag of gummy penises and earned himself another laugh.

'Just what I always wanted,' Liam said.

'So, what's on the agenda for today?' Josh half hoped that Liam would say that there was nothing planned, and they could have a free day. Maybe then he could drag Winter out to the private lagoon and they could talk some more about last night's kiss.

On the other hand, being around her in a two-piece swimsuit right now, trying to talk, might be a little more than his fragile sense of self-restraint could take.

'The Golden Circle,' Liam said with a grin. 'Geysers and waterfalls and iconic landmarks—oh, my!'

'Sounds great,' Josh said unconvincingly. At least it meant Winter would be wrapped up under plenty of layers of clothing for warmth. Maybe that would make it easier for him to concentrate while they talked.

'It will be,' Liam promised. 'Trust me, you haven't seen anything until you visit Gullfoss in full flow.'

Liam had arranged a coach to take them all around the Golden Circle, although a far fancier one than Josh suspected most people took this tour on. He'd taken his seat early, and used the free Wi-Fi to read up a bit on the tour on his phone. Not much of the information would be retained though, he suspected, since his attention kept drifting out of the window, looking for Winter.

But there was no sign.

As the coach filled up, his concern grew. Had she decided not to come at all? Was she that desperate to avoid him?

He was just about to disembark and go looking for her, when he spotted the multi-coloured pompom on the top of Winter's bobble hat, and Jenny's blonde head bobbing behind her.

There was an empty pair of seats in front of him, but Winter and Jenny bypassed them without looking at him, heading instead for seats towards the back. Josh watched them go, then glared at Liam when he took the empty seat beside him.

'Looks like last night might not have gone quite as well as you thought, mate,' Liam said.

Ignoring him, Josh hunkered down in his seat and began plotting his next moves.

'Are you absolutely certain nothing happened last night that you need to tell me about?' Jenny's eyebrows were raised but her voice was low, obviously conscious of all the other guests sitting around them.

'I told you,' Winter replied testily. 'We went to the penis museum. It was ridiculous. We came home. That was all.'

Jenny's sceptical gaze felt uncomfortable on her face, so Winter turned away to look out of the window at the passing landscape instead.

Snow had fallen again in the night and the rocky ground outside and its sparse grass covering was turned white. The roads were still clear, though—a testament to a good infrastructure that was used to the colder weather, she supposed.

She wondered what their lagoon would be like in the snow, if they met out there tonight. Whether the flakes would melt on impact with the warmer water. Whether she and Josh would cuddle closer to stay warm and watch it fall. Whether he'd put his arm around her. Whether he'd kiss her again...

No. She wasn't thinking about that. She was thinking about Iceland's Golden Circle and listening to Liam talk into the microphone at the front of the bus about the exciting sites they'd be visiting today.

She was not imagining kissing her ex-husband again.

Or more than just kissing...

Dammit! *Not thinking about this.*

She couldn't afford to. Giving in to her desires with Josh could only lead to her regressing into the person she'd been—losing all the change and growth she'd fought so hard for. Wouldn't it?

With a shake of her head, Winter forced herself to focus in again on Liam's tour guide patter until they reached their first destination—Þingvellir National Park. Although, as she couldn't remember a word of what she was supposed to look out for there when they arrived, she had to admit she might have drifted off a bit.

The others headed straight into the visitor centre, presumably to supplement Liam's talk with the official guide—and avoid freezing in the bitter air—but Winter stayed outside, staring out over the strange geology of the place.

Below her viewing point, the land seemed cracked in two deep fissures running through the rock and earth. Snowflakes fell either side of them, and deep down into the gaps. Across the other side of the canyon, behind a large lake, she could see a small white church, and a house the same colour, both almost invisible against the white-grey of the snow-laden sky.

'This is the point where two continents meet.' Josh's voice made her jump, and she turned quickly to find him a few paces away, watching her. 'A fault line between the Eurasian and North American plates.'

'A bit like you and me then,' Winter said, turning back to the incredible view. 'Your American versus my British heritage.' Their upbringing and nationality had never really seemed a rift between them before, but suddenly Winter found she needed to focus on all the things that separated them, rather than the things they had in common.

It was safer that way.

If she thought too much about the things that brought them together...well. She'd seen where that had ended last night. And she knew how *that* sort of thing had ended last time.

Better not to risk it again.

'There's constant earthquakes here,' Josh went on, his voice growing ever closer. 'But they're too minor to feel them.'

She didn't need to turn around to know he was right behind her now. In fact, if she did turn, she'd probably find herself in his arms.

Winter forced herself to stay put.

'And it was the site of Iceland's first general assembly—the start of a representative parliament, all the way back in the tenth century.' Was he just going to keep spouting facts about this place until she spoke to him? Probably.

'You were listening to Liam's talk on the coach,' she said. 'You know I was there for that too?'

'But were you listening?'

She shrugged, although the movement was probably completely hidden by the bulk of her warmest waterproof padded coat. 'It was hard to hear at the back of the bus.'

Or she'd just been too preoccupied to concentrate.

Josh sighed and moved beside her. Peeking sideways, she saw him fold his arms over his chest as he surveyed the view of the rift below. 'Well, it's no penis museum…'

'But it is pretty impressive,' Winter finished, flashing him a quick smile.

He reached out to grab her gloved hand. 'Winter. About last night—'

She pulled away before he could continue. 'We don't need to talk about that. In fact I'd rather forget it. And, anyway, it's cold out here. I want to see the visitor centre before Liam orders us all back on the bus.'

Without looking back, she strode away towards the visitor centre and its fascinating exhibitions on the geology and history of Iceland.

Because right now Josh and her relationship with him felt far too much like the landscape of this place. Fractured, unstable and drifting apart—but still so damn compelling she found it hard to look away.

Winter was definitely avoiding him. Or avoiding talking about the kiss. Or both.

And trying to talk to her without the whole bus watching—or eavesdropping—was growing impossible anyway.

Their next stop on the Golden Circle tour was Geysir, where they watched spouts of hot air burst from the ground into the snowy sky from the Strokkur Geysir. Then, once they were all shivering again and the joy of the water spurts had worn off, it was back on the coach towards Gullfoss.

The landscape of Iceland was unlike anything he'd ever seen before, outside of the movies and TV shows that had filmed there. Everything felt unfamiliar, unstable—and it wasn't helping him feel any more settled or centred in himself, or in the new friendship he was trying to build with Winter.

Friendship? Who was he kidding? Whatever Liam had hoped to achieve by bringing them both here, there could never be just friendship between Josh and Winter. They both felt too much—and had been hurt too badly—for that.

But what did that leave them?

Having found her again, Josh wasn't sure he could just let her go. Not when he'd felt more being with her in three days in Iceland than he had in the five years without her.

Not when her kiss could still light up his whole world the way it had last night.

They weren't meant for marriage. They couldn't do the whole fairy tale thing, they'd proven that.

Everything he'd thought he wanted his whole life—everything he'd thought he'd found with Winter before she'd left him…could he forget about that? Could he accept something else, something less, in its place?

He wasn't sure. But it looked as if he was going to have to decide. And fast. They only had limited time left in Iceland, then Winter would be walking away from him again. If he didn't want that to happen…well. He had to get her to talk to him, for a start.

The big question was, which would be worse? The lifelong regret if he didn't at least try to have *something* with her one last time, or the pain that would come when he inevitably had to watch her walk away again?

Josh wasn't sure there was a good answer to that one.

The final stop on the Golden Circle tour was the waterfall of Gullfoss. The coach pulled into the car park near the wooden-clad visitor centre, but this time nobody rushed inside. Everyone wanted to see the famous waterfall first.

Josh followed behind them, watching as Winter and Jenny picked their careful way along the wooden slatted path towards the viewing point, wary of any icy patches. The snow had settled on the ground around the waterfall and on any of the rocks that pushed through from the river bed, but the water flowed around it without disturbing it. On the far side of the falls, where even the weak winter sun didn't reach, ice had formed, a strange solid contrast to the rushing roar of the waterfalls. Steam rose up from the ravine where the racing, cascading falls hit the icy river water below.

As he moved to the wooden rail of the platform, jutting out over the very edge of the ravine itself, the roar became louder, so loud he couldn't make out the conversations of anyone around him.

And that gave him an idea.

Already, members of their group were starting to turn to head back to the warmth of the visitor centre. Josh watched them go until only a handful were left, then made his way towards where Winter stood alone at the rail.

Nobody watching would know or care who they were, not through the mist rising off the waterfall, and the bulky clothes and hats they both wore. And nobody would be able to hear a word he said.

It was the most privacy they were likely to get until

they were back at their rooms—and there he had no guarantee she'd talk to him at all.

'We need to talk.' He had to get close to Winter, his mouth almost at her ear, to be sure she'd hear him over the roar of the water, but apparently she'd been so distracted by the view she hadn't realised he was there, because she jumped at his voice.

'I can't hear you,' she lied. 'It'll have to wait.'

'Nobody is watching. Nobody can hear us. Trust me, this is the best chance we're going to get.'

He could see the indecision in her eyes, in the way her gaze darted over her shoulder to look who else was around.

'What if I'm just not ready for this conversation?'

He had to read her lips to catch her words, but they prompted an ironic smile, anyway.

'Winter. It's been five years. If not now, when?'

She didn't answer, so he took her silence as permission to plough on with what he had to say.

'I've been thinking about this all day. Since the moment I left you outside your room last night. From the second your lips left mine. And all I can think is... I can't bear the thought of a world where I never get to kiss you again.'

Her sharp intake of breath told him that, whatever she'd expected, it wasn't that.

'I know we failed at marriage.' *He* failed. 'I know we can't have the fairy tale. But maybe that isn't what I need any more,' he pressed on.

'Yes. It is.' More lip-reading, her words torn away by the wind and the water. 'You know it is. And I can't give that to you.'

She was right. He knew she was right. It just didn't seem to matter any more.

When he'd realised she'd gone, when he'd found that letter five years ago, the pain had been unbearable. He'd blocked a lot of it out, over the months and years that followed. But one thing had stuck with him.

I didn't know it was the last time.

The last time they'd kissed. The last time they'd made love. The last time she'd smiled at him. The last time she'd told him she loved him.

Some of them he couldn't even remember. And even those he did…he hadn't known.

Hadn't known that he'd never experience that again.

That it was the last time.

And if he *had* known…maybe he couldn't have changed anything. But he'd have paid better attention. Savoured the moment more. Committed every second to memory, so he'd always have a piece of it with him.

Winter leaving without warning had taken that from him. But now…

Now he wondered if he could get something of that back.

They had only a few days left in Iceland. Days in which he could relive those last times, if she let him. And after that…

Well. One step at a time. First he had to convince her.

'You can give me something else, though,' he said desperately. 'You can give me something more. Maybe that closure we were looking for wasn't a goodbye. That's not enough for me. I need you again.'

CHAPTER TEN

I NEED YOU AGAIN.

Josh's words were whipped away by the wind, but somehow they still echoed in her brain as she tried to make sense of them.

The confusion in his eyes told her that he didn't understand this pull between them any more than she did.

She'd walked away. She'd spent five years rebuilding her life without him. And now...

Now all she wanted was to kiss him again.

'Until we're able to say goodbye?' Winter's eyes must be wide, because she could feel the chill of the air against them as she stared at him. 'You mean...find a way to finish things properly?'

'One last time,' Josh whispered, so close to her ear that she could feel his breath against its shell, could hear him even over the roaring water.

It wouldn't be enough—she knew that instinctively. But if that was what he needed to move on...

'Real closure,' she murmured to herself.

This was what they'd been missing all along. She could see that now. What she'd robbed them of by running the way she had.

She hadn't been able to face him, or her feelings, back then. But this week...they'd done that, together.

They'd faced everything together. Said all the things they'd held back.

All that was left was to say goodbye.

'You're right,' she said, louder. 'Everything between us…it ended so abruptly. And those last months with the pregnancy and the sickness and the miscarriage and afterwards… Maybe what we need is to finish things properly.'

One last time for good luck…

He used to say that, before kissing her goodbye when he left for a shoot.

'I say we try it.' He smiled at her, the icy wind turning his cheeks red, and she returned it.

They could do this. *She* could do this. Otherwise, what had the last five years even been for?

'Then meet me in the lagoon tonight,' she said.

Winter had thought she'd have to wait until Jenny went to bed, or come up with some excuse why she wanted to go out to the lagoon alone that evening. But, to her surprise, her assistant disappeared after dinner without any explanation for her absence, and Winter was able to sneak outside in her bikini and towelling robe, two mugs of her famous hot chocolate in hand, unobserved.

Except for Josh. He was already waiting in the private lagoon, his bare torso mostly hidden by the dark and the water, but his arms outstretched over the rocks holding himself in place. Winter let her gaze run across the muscles of his arms and shoulders—God, she'd always loved those shoulders—before meeting his gaze and smiling at the heat already on display there.

She had no idea what she was doing, she freely admitted that. But she was damned if she could bring herself to stop.

'I brought hot chocolate,' she said, waving the mugs slightly before placing them on the side.

'Hot chocolate always helps,' Josh replied. 'Now, get in here before you freeze.'

She slipped the robe from her shoulders, wincing at the biting cold before she stepped into the water. The heat of the geothermal pool soon warmed her skin, but she found herself floating towards Josh all the same, the desire to share body heat impossible to ignore.

'How do you want to do this?' She looked up at him, his blue eyes so dark against the night sky—or maybe it was the lust covering them. And suddenly the double meaning of her words hit and her mind was filled with every sexual position they'd ever tried, every place they'd ever made love, every moment they'd ever been touching...

'Winter, I—' He broke off, clearly as unable to find the words as she was.

Maybe they didn't need words any more. Perhaps they'd said them all already.

She lurched towards his lips, trusting him to catch her, which he did, his strong arms wrapping tight around her waist in an instant. And then she was kissing him again, and she knew this couldn't be a bad idea because it felt... So. Damn. Right.

This time, Josh didn't break away—she did, and only because she needed to gulp more air into her lungs.

'Are you sure?' he whispered against the skin of her neck, as he kissed his way down towards her collarbone. 'This isn't what either of us came to Iceland for.'

'But it's what we need,' she finished for him.

His head jerked up and his gaze met hers, and she knew they were on the same page for the first time in years.

'It really, really is.'

She could feel how much he needed it, even in the water. Somehow, she'd ended up straddling his lap as they kissed, her knees knocking up against the rock wall of the lagoon. His hardness pressed up against the core of her, and she knew that wasn't going to be enough for her, not for long.

'Should we take this inside to your room?' The words came out breathy, and he smiled a slow, special smile—one she'd only ever seen him smile at her, usually in intimate moments like this. Even when she'd studied his sex scenes on film, that particular smile had never been on display.

It was hers.

And God, how she'd missed it.

'Not yet,' he murmured back, his mouth at her throat again. 'I've been having a lot of thoughts about this lagoon this week, you know. It seems a shame not to make some of them reality, while we're here.'

It was too cold for them to stay out there long, Winter knew. Unless he'd suddenly gained the ability to breathe underwater, his kisses were never going to make it below the straps of her bikini, and she definitely wanted his mouth on more of her than that. But he was right that this was a once in a lifetime opportunity...

She nodded, and instantly his hands went to the thin pieces of material holding her bikini top in place.

'I hope this place is as private as Liam promised,' she joked as he stripped the fabric away from her breasts.

'You're under the water anyway,' Josh reassured her. 'Besides, in a landscape like this, a lagoon like this, what could be more natural?'

His hands came up to cup her breasts as she adjusted her position, sitting on his knees to give him better access. The milky water hid everything lower than her waist from view, but she could see his fingers brushing against her nipples with perfect clarity in the moonlight.

'Turn around,' he whispered against her ear.

Swallowing, Winter obeyed.

He felt so hard against her, even through his swim shorts and her bikini bottoms, that she couldn't help but imagine how he'd feel inside her again after so long.

Josh moved his hands back to her bare breasts, thrumming his fingers against her nipples in the way she'd always loved. His mouth was back at her throat, kissing the sensitive skin between her neck and her shoulder, and Winter knew the heat building inside her now had nothing to do with any geothermal power.

It was all him.

It was *them.* The way it always had been.

How did I ever walk away from this?

No, she wasn't thinking about that now. This couldn't last for ever, so she intended to enjoy every second of it.

His right hand drifted lower, between her legs, and she let her head fall back against his shoulder as his touch worked to both relieve and build the heat and the want growing there. And soon there was nothing in the world except that tightness building inside her, her whole body reaching for something that felt just out of reach, straining and desperate, the muscles in her legs tense as she braced herself, hoping and wanting and—

She broke against his fingers, the swell of her orgasm overcoming her as she fell boneless against him.

Josh chuckled warmly against her ear. 'Okay. *Now* we can move this inside. Your bed or mine?'

Josh awoke in his own bed the next morning, knowing that the whole world had changed overnight. And even if that knowledge hadn't been innate, the dark head pillowed against his shoulder and the pale, smooth arm wrapped around his torso would have filled him in fast enough.

He'd slept with Winter. He'd taken his ex-wife back into his bed, five years after she'd broken his heart for good, and he had absolutely no regrets. Except, perhaps, that she was still asleep and he couldn't do it all over again.

Regrets were for later. He couldn't let himself go down that path now.

A knock at the door made him tense as Winter stirred in his arms, then settled down again. He waited, hoping whoever it was would go away, but then they knocked again. With a frustrated sigh, Josh gently disentangled himself from Winter, pulled on a pair of boxers and stalked across to the door.

'What?' he asked in a harsh whisper as he opened the door just a crack—and found Liam's smiling face on the other side.

'You realise you're missing a guided tour of Reykjavik right now? And you missed breakfast,' Liam said, too innocently. 'I thought I'd better check everything was okay.'

'Everything is fine.' The words came out through gritted teeth, as Josh tried not to wake Winter. It might only be Liam at the door this time, but she'd made her wish to keep whatever this was between them well under the radar.

'Are you sure?' Liam pressed, grinning. 'Only it turns out that *Winter* missed breakfast, and the tour too. And Jenny says she doesn't think she came back to their suite either. All. Night.'

Josh stepped into the corridor and pulled the handle of the door up so it wouldn't lock behind him. Luckily their rooms were on a secluded corridor away from the others, so the chances of being spotted in his boxers were slim, especially if the others were all off on today's tour.

'We're...trying something new,' Josh told his friend.

Liam raised an eyebrow. 'Sex? Honestly, Josh, it's really not that new. Unless you're doing something particularly innovative you want to tell me about...'

'That's not... God, just for once, can you be serious about this?'

'*Is* it serious? That's sort of what I'm here to ask,' Liam said, his smile vanishing. 'Jenny's worried about Winter. *I'm* worried about Winter. And yes, before you ask, I'm even worried about you. Do you know what you're doing here?'

Josh thought about how Winter had fallen apart in his arms last night. How he'd worshipped every inch of her body, committing it to memory in case it were whipped away from him again without warning.

Did he know what he was doing?

Saying goodbye.

'I'm taking a risk,' he said softly. 'Because honestly, Liam, I don't know what else to do. We've talked and talked this week. We've uncovered a lot of pain, a lot of history, and I think we understand each other better than ever.'

'So you're getting back together?' The astonishment in Liam's voice wasn't entirely encouraging.

'That's not...exactly the plan.' Josh winced as he realised how, in the cold light of day, last night's idea—born out of lust and need and desperation—didn't quite stand up to reality as well as he'd like.

'Then what is?'

'We figured that if talking it all out hadn't helped us move on, maybe we needed another sort of closure.'

Liam's eyebrows hit close to his hairline as he snorted a laugh. 'This is a "we'll just sleep together once and get it out of our system" plan? Haven't you been in enough romcoms to know that *never* works?'

Josh slumped against the wall. 'The idea was that because things ended so abruptly between us, and because those last six months were so…awful, this was what we hadn't had real closure on. Us being together like this. We hadn't had a chance to say goodbye to us.'

'And now?' Liam asked. 'Do you feel like you can move on now?'

An image of Winter lying in his bed, her black hair against the white sheets, her sated body relaxed and peaceful, burned against the back of his eyes. 'No.'

How could he ever move on from that? From what they were together?

From how in love with her he had always been—and would always be?

Had he just done the one thing that might actually destroy him this time?

He swore, quietly but vehemently, and Liam clapped a hand against his shoulder in sympathy. 'I guess you two have got some talking to do.'

'I guess.' Except Josh didn't want to talk any more. They'd done that, almost to death.

And he didn't want to say goodbye.

So what *did* he want?

He wanted to try again. He wanted to believe that things could be different this time around.

That things could be easy between them this time.

He wanted to remind her how good they'd been, before everything had gone wrong. How good they could be again. To show her that he'd listened, and he'd learned.

That they could get it right this time and everything would be plain sailing.

Love would be enough this time around.

Liam was watching him. 'What do you need? How can I help?'

Josh shook his head. 'I think this one needs to be all me.' Then an idea struck him. 'Actually, there is something you could do. Help me find the right place to talk to her.' Because he had a feeling Winter was going to need some convincing.

'Not the penis museum again?' Liam guessed.

'Definitely not the penis museum,' Josh said. 'I was thinking something rather more…romantic.'

'Such as?'

Josh smiled. 'Let me put on some pants and I'll tell you.'

'Where, exactly, are we going?' Winter asked as Josh bundled her into the car that was waiting for them at the side door the following evening.

'It's a surprise,' Josh said. 'Can't you just trust me?'

'Last time you took me on a surprise date we ended up at the Icelandic Phallological Museum,' Winter pointed out.

'Ah, but this time I didn't let *Liam* come up with the destination,' Josh said.

'I suppose that's something.'

They'd had a blissful couple of days together—mostly staying in Josh's suite or the lagoon, only venturing out for dinner with Liam and Jenny, during which they'd sat on opposite sides of the table and pretended not to be playing footsie underneath.

Winter had also pretended not to notice the scorching looks between Liam and her assistant, because if she started asking all the questions that raised, she was sure they'd have some of their own to ask her and Josh.

Questions she didn't have any answers to. Like what would happen when their Iceland trip was over in less than two days, and they had to return to the real world.

Questions like *What the hell am I doing?*

Objectively, it was hard to see a way that this would end well, when she studied the situation in the cold light of day. They'd already tried marriage once, and failed. She was focused on her career now, and had no interest in trying to live up to Josh's high ideals of what a perfect marriage should be. Plus, she did not want her burgeoning reputation as a director to be buried under other people's interest in her love life. She didn't want to lose herself that way again. So she needed privacy, not internet fame.

Something she'd had to remind Josh when he'd cornered her outside the bathrooms in the restaurant the night before and kissed her breathless. Of course, his solution to that had been to drag her into the unmanned cloakroom nearby and continue kissing her which, while a *lot* of fun, had resulted in them having to leave the space a few minutes apart, and a lot of knowing looks from their friends.

She just hoped the two influencers she'd passed on her way back to the table hadn't noticed her mussed hair and smudged lipstick. Or the dazed look on Josh's face when he'd followed her a couple of minutes later.

But now they were heading somewhere away from everyone else, somewhere Josh had chosen, and she had a feeling he was going to be looking for some of those answers once they arrived.

Maybe she could just distract him with sex. Because she was pretty sure she wasn't ready to deal with the real world again yet.

'This place is incredible.' Winter stared around her at the tiny glass cottage Josh had brought them to, awed by the sheer amount of window between the metal frames and walls. Thank goodness there were no other structures on the horizon, and not another soul around for miles now their driver had left, because a place like this didn't provide much in the way of privacy otherwise.

But as it was…they were in the middle of nowhere, in a glass house with a giant king-sized bed covered in furry blankets and rugs occupying the central space. And Winter was starting to think that maybe Josh hadn't brought her here to talk at all.

'It's the perfect place to view the Northern Lights.' Coming up behind her, Josh wrapped his arms around her middle, pulling her close against his chest. 'I told Liam I wanted something properly romantic this time, somewhere we could relax without worrying about anyone seeing us. And I said I wanted to see the Northern Lights. So he found us this place.'

'It's perfect.' From the wood-burning stove in the corner to the hamper of easy to prepare and eat food in the tiny kitchenette, Winter couldn't imagine a better place to spend their last night together in Iceland.

Even if the lights didn't show, or the clouds covered them, she had a feeling they'd make the most of this place anyway.

Josh had dumped their bags by the entranceway and Winter left them there for now, moving instead to the bed. Flopping down on her back, she propped herself up on her elbows, staring through the glass roof at the sky above.

A moment later Josh joined her—bringing with him a bottle of champagne from the hamper, two glasses and a box of chocolates.

'You really have thought of everything,' she said as he opened the bottle with a pop.

'That's the hope. Because I don't want either of us to

have to think about *anything* between now and when that car arrives to take us back to the Ice House Hotel tomorrow morning.' He poured her a glass of champagne and handed it to her, before pouring his own and placing the bottle on the bedside table. 'Sound good?'

'Sounds *perfect*.' Winter took a sip of champagne, letting the bubbles burst pleasurably on her tongue before raising her glass in a toast. 'Here's to escaping reality for a while.'

Josh clinked his glass, then made his own toast. 'Here's to new beginnings.'

Winter felt the first stirrings of doubt start in her stomach, but smiled anyway, drowning her worries in another gulp of champagne.

They were here together, for fun, in this most incredible place. Reality could wait.

CHAPTER ELEVEN

'I'VE NEVER SEEN anything like it,' Winter whispered beside his ear. 'It's so beautiful.'

It was later now, much later, and the Northern Lights had come out to play—something Josh was taking as a sign. This time of year was a good time to see them, but still nothing was guaranteed, and they could have easily disappeared behind cloud cover tonight.

But there they were, glowing and swirling green and white and purple through the glass roof of their tiny home for the night. They felt like a benediction from the universe, a sign that he'd done the right thing bringing Winter here.

That they were doing the right thing, reconnecting this way.

He pulled Winter closer into his arms as they snuggled under the furs and blankets on the bed, staring up through the glass ceiling at the incredible phenomenon overhead.

Not as beautiful as you, he thought, but didn't say.

It was a cliché, like something from one of his movies, and he knew she'd pull a face at the line.

But it was true anyway.

'Good date then?' he asked. 'Better than the penis museum?'

She snorted a laugh at that. 'Different,' she said after

a moment. 'The museum was fun. And… I think we needed it, to help us lighten up.'

'Plus you kissed me that night.' Josh smiled at the memory. 'So it can't have been all bad.'

'The waffles were pretty good.' He poked her in the side, and she laughed. 'No, it wasn't bad at all. I… I just liked spending time with you again.'

'Me too.'

They'd done a lot more than just spend time together now. More than just kiss too. In some ways it felt as if they'd fallen straight back into the fairy tale that had been derailed by Winter's miscarriage, and the collapse of their marriage that had followed.

And Josh had to admit he was starting to hope again. He knew what he'd done wrong now. Maybe he could get it right this time around.

If she let him.

If she didn't… His heart stung at the thought.

In the corner the wood-burning stove crackled and popped as it warmed the room, also providing the only light beside the glowing rivers in the sky. The remains of the picnic dinner they'd shared sat on the table beside it, along with the empty bottle of champagne.

Josh couldn't think of anywhere in the world he'd rather be.

'This is the perfect way to spend our last night in Iceland,' Winter said, snuggling closer again, and Josh felt the first pinprick in his dream.

He didn't want to ask. He wanted to just fall back into this life and have it all back again.

But he knew he couldn't just assume that was what happened next. Assuming that just because he was happy meant that she was too had been part of what had broken them last time.

He couldn't make that mistake again.

'What about when we leave Iceland?' he asked tentatively. 'Do you think we might have this again, somewhere else?'

She lifted her head from his chest and gave him a curious look. 'Well, there are other places you can see the Northern Lights, I suppose.'

'That's not what I meant.'

Her bare skin was pressed so closely to his that Josh felt the tension enter her body. 'What *did* you mean?'

'I mean…we're leaving Iceland tomorrow. We've talked, I think, about everything we needed to talk about to find some closure on everything that happened. And we've, well…'

'Found physical closure as well?' Winter suggested, with eyebrows arched.

'That's one way of putting it.' She moved against his body and he could feel it reacting to her closeness again, threatening to distract him away from the conversation they needed to have. But he couldn't bring himself to stop her.

'So, what's the problem?' She pressed a kiss to his collarbone and he shivered.

'I'm not ready to say goodbye again.'

It was, he'd realised, somewhere around the time the skies started dancing above them, as simple and as complicated as that. And he couldn't leave this place without knowing if she was on the same page.

Winter sat up, folding her legs underneath her and pulling a blanket around her—for warmth or because she didn't want to have this conversation naked, Josh wasn't entirely sure.

'What are you suggesting, exactly?'

He forced himself into a sitting position too, leaning against the wooden headboard with a pillow at his back.

'I don't know, exactly,' he said with a sigh. 'That depends where your head is with this too. I just… Being with you again this week has reminded me how great it was when we were together—'

'It wasn't all great,' Winter reminded him sharply. 'That's one of the reasons I left.'

'I know. I know that. But…we're older and wiser now, right? Don't you think there's a chance we could get it right this time?' There had to be, surely? Otherwise, what were they even doing here together?

Winter pulled back a little further. She couldn't go far on the bed, but Josh still felt the distance between them like an icy blast of Icelandic air.

'I can't go back to being the woman I was when I married you.' The words were stark, but the look of horror in Winter's eyes was even starker.

'I don't want that,' he reassured her. 'Neither of us are the people we were then, and that's *good*. We've grown. But I want more time with the Winter I've got to know here, this week. The woman you are *now*.'

Some of the tension disappeared from Winter's shoulders, bare above the blanket. But not all. The wariness around her eyes remained too.

'So you're thinking we…date?'

'Maybe? I mean, we're a bit past that in some ways. But in others…' He thought about their date at the penis museum, and how fun it had been to just hang out together. 'You know, dating could be fun.'

Winter's small smile made him think she was remembering the same things. 'I suppose it could.' Then the smile fell away. 'Except…we were able to do this, here, because we had Liam to help us sneak around, and book places out so we had total privacy. How are you expecting us to manage that back in the real world? Especially with us both working away so much.'

Josh slumped a little against the headboard. 'You don't want anyone to know about us.'

'I thought…' A frown line formed between her eyebrows. 'I thought we talked about that. I don't want the only thing anyone knows about me to be that I'm dating you—again. I don't want to be the subject of gossip and world expectations. Plus… I mean…it ended badly before. If that's going to happen again, I'd rather do it without an audience.'

'Privacy takes the pressure off,' Josh said, musing. 'I guess I can see that.'

'If we're really going to try this, it needs to be just between us,' Winter pressed. 'That's the only way I can handle it.'

He pushed aside his first, instinctive feeling—that she was ashamed or embarrassed by their relationship—and focused in on what she was really saying.

She was scared. He could see it now, in the shadows in her eyes. And he could understand it too—hell, he was petrified himself.

Last time around, they'd both been swept away by the romance of it all. By the fairy tale.

This time, they both knew exactly how badly they could hurt each other. How, if this fell apart again, it could destroy them. They'd be fools *not* to be afraid.

But all the same…he couldn't not try.

'Just between us,' he promised. 'We just…try. Okay?'

There was still some uncertainty in Winter's gaze as she nodded. 'Okay.'

He smiled, and hoped it was reassuring. Then he took

her into his arms and they lay back and watched the night sky dance above them until they fell asleep.

The plane back to London was packed, and Winter was glad of their first-class tickets. Not least because the Saga Lounge at Reykjavik-Keflavik Airport had given her and Josh the privacy they'd needed to say goodbye.

That had been harder than she'd anticipated. Yes, the last week had been special, and she'd loved being with him again in so many ways. But she'd built her own life away from him over the past five years. She wasn't his doting fairy tale princess any longer, and she wouldn't wither away during their separation.

She wasn't that woman any more. That young, naive, hopeful Winter. She couldn't be. It hurt too much when that hope was broken.

So on the drive back to Liam's hotel from their tiny glass cottage under the Northern Lights, they'd hammered out some rules for their fledging... Winter hesitated to call it a relationship.

Arrangement. That was what it was.

A mutually satisfying arrangement that gave them both the benefits of the relationship they used to have—basically sex and each other's company—without all the issues that had driven them apart. Like the way she lost herself, disappeared into his shadow the moment they were a couple, and how he wanted the picket fence perfect life, when that was *not* something she could give him.

Even the separations caused by work that had been a problem for their marriage were now just something factored into their arrangement.

It was all going to be fine.

And there was absolutely no reason for her to miss him before the plane had even left the runway.

Jenny, meanwhile, looked like there was definitely something she was regretting leaving behind. And she had been spending an awful lot of time with Liam…

'So,' Winter said, twisting slightly in her seat to face her assistant, who was staring out of the opposite window. 'How was *your* stay in Iceland? Anything…new and interesting happen there?'

Jenny turned to face her, eyebrows raised. 'Are we really going to talk about *my* sex life, when you just shared the most passionate goodbye kiss in the history of kisses in the airport lounge, with your *ex-husband*?'

'It wasn't *that* passionate,' Winter mumbled, hiding her smile by looking down at her hands.

'It really was,' Jenny assured her. 'Seriously, what's going on there? Liam and I came up with all sorts of theories, but—'

'Liam and you? Because you two were spending so much time together….?'

'Not talking about me right now.' Jenny's gaze turned serious, and Winter swallowed as she met it. 'Winter. As your friend—a friend who remembers what happened last time you and Josh were together, incidentally—I'm asking. What's going on, and are you sure about it?'

'We have an agreement,' Winter said. 'An arrangement. It's going to be fine.'

'An arrangement?'

'Yeah. We set ground rules and everything. Number one: nobody finds out.'

'Well, that sounds like a perfectly sound basis for a loving relationship.' The sarcasm rang out from Jenny's voice.

'Which is why it's an arrangement, not a relationship,' Winter shot back. 'We've done the whole fairy tale thing, and I have no interest in doing it again. We enjoyed spending time together this week, and we'd like to keep doing so, when our schedules permit. But that's it. No big romance, no public hand-holding, no promises I can't keep, or anything like that.'

'Promises you can't keep?' Jenny frowned. 'What do you mean?'

Frustrated, Winter turned to look out of the window. 'It doesn't matter. I didn't mean to say that.'

'But you *did* say it. Which means you're thinking it. What promises, Winter?' Jenny sighed. 'You know how this goes when you bottle stuff like this up. Neither of us wants to go back there, do we?'

Winter thought of those horrible days and weeks and months after she'd lost the baby. After she'd left Josh. When all she had was Jenny's spare room and the pain of her memories.

'No,' she admitted.

'Which is why I'm the person you tell,' Jenny said. 'No one else in the world needs to know, but you need to tell someone, and that person is me.'

'I don't pay you enough for this,' Winter stalled.

'I do my job for the money. This I do because you're family, and I know you'd do the same for me.'

That much was true, Winter supposed. Which meant she was going to have to ask a lot more questions about Liam later. But for now…

'He still wants that picket fence life,' she said with a sigh. 'He says he's moved on, but I *know* him, Jen. He wants the perfect romance, the perfect wife, the perfect kids…and I can't give him that. I just can't.'

Jenny's eyes were sympathetic. 'Well, there's *perfect* perfect, and then there's perfect for him. Maybe he's more interested in the second one these days?'

'I don't think so.' Josh's world view was ingrained in

him, by the perfect marriage his parents had shared before his father's death, not to mention his brother's own ideal relationship. 'He might *say* he doesn't need those things, but I know that the day will come when he'll realise he's not complete or happy without it. And I can't face losing him again then.'

'You've changed a lot in the last five years,' Jenny pointed out. 'Maybe Josh has too.'

Winter's heart lurched—was it with hope, or just turbulence?

But she shook her head. 'I can't risk that. Not again.'

Which was why they had to stick to the arrangement. It was the only way she could see she had of getting out of this with her heart intact.

The flat Josh had leased in LA, ready for his next shoot, seemed stark and empty which, considering the only other place he'd spent time recently was in a pared back, Scandi-style hotel room with only the bare essentials of his belongings with him, was ridiculous.

Except he knew what that feeling really meant was that Winter wasn't there with him.

Throwing his keys into the bowl on the kitchen counter, he hung up his jacket, grabbed his phone from his pocket and dropped onto the leather couch to call her.

The eight-hour time difference between LA and London, plus their differing work schedules, had made keeping in touch trickier than he'd like, but they'd managed so far. Over the week since they'd left Iceland, they'd spoken by video call most days, and at least messaged on the days where that wasn't possible.

'Hey,' he said when her face appeared on the screen. 'How're things there?'

'Mmm…fine,' she said. 'You're done early?'

Josh looked out of his window at the Californian afternoon. 'Started in the middle of the night,' he said. 'My call was stupid o'clock this morning, but at least it means I'm done in time to call you before you turn in for the night.'

'Only just.' On the screen, Winter's smile was tired. 'It's been a long day here too.'

'But you're still coming out here next weekend?' He didn't mean to sound quite as eager as he did but, well, he'd missed her.

Not that he planned on telling her that just yet. Winter still seemed skittish whenever they spoke about what happened next between them, so Josh was trying to learn to go with the flow and take each day as it came.

He supposed he could understand her reluctance to plan too far ahead. Last time they'd tried this they'd been engaged within six months, married in under a year, and with their whole lives together planned out over late-night conversations and whispered dreams.

And it had all gone to hell. This time, he was happy to move a little slower if it still got him where he wanted to be—with her.

'I'm still coming,' Winter assured him. 'I mean, I kind of need to be there for the awards ceremony anyway, right?'

The awards ceremony they would both be attending—separately. Another thing Josh was willing to live with as long as he got to take her home to bed afterwards, once the cameras and the press weren't watching.

It wouldn't be for ever, he reassured himself. They were just going under the radar for now so they could take the time to figure out things between themselves. That was all.

One day he'd be able to walk out there with Winter on his arm again, the proudest man in Hollywood.

Just not yet.

'I'm not ready,' Winter had said apologetically, when he'd asked about attending the awards together on one late-night phone call. *'You know that appearing at something like that together would be tantamount to announcing our second engagement. The gossip sites would have us married before the winners were announced. And that's not... I can't do that.'*

She was right, he knew. Going public would push them to define exactly what was happening between them before they'd had a chance to figure it out themselves.

It didn't mean he liked the idea of hiding their relationship away any better, though.

'You'll come here before the awards, though?' He needed time alone with her before he had to pretend to be nothing more than her ex-husband in public.

'I will,' she promised. 'You'll see me before the awards. I'm hoping I can come out a few days early and we'll have some time together first.'

The tight fist that had been forming around his heart loosened a bit. She wasn't pulling away, wasn't leaving him again now that they'd left the magical bubble Iceland had given them. She was just being cautious. Protecting their privacy.

He could live with that. For now.

'That would be nice,' he said, trying to keep things light. 'And we won't need to worry about bumping into any paparazzi types if we just stay in bed all week...'

Winter laughed at that, helping his spirits rise a little more. 'That's a plan I can live with,' she agreed. 'I'll let you know my travel plans as soon as I—' She broke off as a chime sounded from her computer.

'What is it?' Josh asked.

'Check your notifications.' Winter's voice was tight.

Josh swiped away from the active call and opened up his Instagram account, where his notifications were flashing. Since he kept them pared down to the bare minimum, that meant *something* had to have happened.

'Got it?' Winter asked.

His heart was racing in his chest, the terrible feeling of doom chasing him as he swiped through the app.

'Almost—' And then, there it was.

A photo of the two of them in the apparently not so private lagoon at Liam's hotel, their arms wrapped around each other, their faces clearly visible. And the next frame, showing them kissing. From the grainy nature of the shots, it looked as if the photographer had zoomed in a lot.

Just checking through my photos from my amazing trip to Iceland and look what I spotted in the background of these landscape shots? Are Hollywood's favourite fairy tale couple back on again?

CHAPTER TWELVE

WINTER COULD FEEL the panic rising inside her the longer she stared at the photo on her screen. She needed Jenny here to help make sense of this, to strategise and decide on their next moves. Her phone was beeping with another call coming through from her agent, but she couldn't take that yet. Not until she knew what she was going to say.

And not while Josh was still on the line, swearing like a sailor as he saw the same images she had.

There was no denying it was them in the photo. Their presence in Iceland had been well publicised by Liam's team at the hotel, and they had both posted their own social media photos of the trip too—taking care that none of the shots included each other. They'd been *so* careful the whole time. And now this.

Her hand shook as she banished the images and returned to Josh's face on the other end of the video call.

'What do you want to do?' His expression was more serious than she was used to seeing from him, especially recently. She knew he was putting the ball in her court, that he'd go along with whatever she needed, because that was the sort of man he was. And she loved him for it. Had loved him when she'd married him and loved him now. She wasn't even sure if she'd ever really stopped loving him at any time in between.

But love, as her failed marriage and broken body had proved, wasn't always enough.

Love hadn't kept her baby alive inside her. It hadn't protected her from the sickness that had racked her body before that. And it hadn't stopped her walking away when she knew that staying in that marriage would destroy her.

Worse still, she knew that love would be no protection at all against the camera flashes and the social media chaos that would follow now. Those photos were out there, and the world was watching—just when she'd hoped that they would avert their gaze.

She could already feel her sense of self slipping. Backsliding into the woman she'd been, rather than the one she'd worked so hard to become. She'd thought she'd finished that process—had rebuilt herself from the ground up into someone strong enough to hold her own in front of anything. That she could be her new self and keep Josh at the distance she needed, and have both the things her heart desired—Josh, and the new life she'd built for herself.

But she knew now that new life would buckle. It wasn't strong enough. *She* wasn't strong enough.

Already, the same feeling of panic she'd experienced so often in those months after she'd left Josh was rising again. Already she was starting to doubt herself.

What had she been thinking, imagining that things would be different this time? Even if Josh really had changed—if he'd reassessed what he wanted from life and from her, if he was willing to do things her way this time, to let her set the pace and keep their relationship in the dark…the world wasn't going to let this be enough.

Her love life was going to be thrust back into the spotlight whether she liked it or not. And whether she and Josh were back together again was the only thing people were going to be talking about across the country—heck, across the world!

The film she'd worked so hard for, the new career she'd built for herself, the whole *life* she'd recreated from the ashes of tragedy…they were going to be swept away. Because the only thing that mattered to the press was who she was sleeping with.

I'm not ready for this. I can't handle this.

She had to set her boundaries to ensure that *she* remembered what mattered about herself, even if no one else did.

She'd almost broken under the intense scrutiny the media had placed on her marriage, miscarriage and divorce. She couldn't go through all that again. And she knew that, if she tried, it would probably spell the end of any relationship she and Josh managed to salvage anyway.

But she also knew Josh would want to try. He'd need to believe that she didn't want this, didn't want any real relationship between them, if he were ever to step away.

'We need to deny it,' she said before her heart could overrule her head. 'We need to put out a statement making it categorically clear that while we remain friends after our divorce, that's all.'

Josh's usually mobile face stilled. 'But it's not.'

Winter shook her head. 'I'm not ready for that information to be out there yet.'

'But if it comes out later, everyone will know we lied,' Josh said. Winter winced, and he continued, 'Unless you're not planning to *ever* tell people we're back together.'

Back together.

Was that what they were? Already he'd made this into something more than she'd agreed to. She'd agreed to a fling in Iceland, to find that physical closure as well as the emotional one. And okay, she'd sort of said yes to carrying on when they could…but the arrangement she'd agreed to didn't add up to a relationship. It didn't mean 'back together'. Did it?

Clearly in Josh's head it did.

He'd promised he didn't want the things she couldn't give him—that picket fence life with the kids in the yard and her at home waiting for him. But he was already trying to make it happen.

She could feel the walls closing in on her again. The panic rising in her chest.

She'd told him all this. But it seemed it hadn't sunk in.

And now… She couldn't have this argument now. She needed to get off the phone, find a way to breathe again, and fix this.

'I can't talk about this right now,' Winter said. 'I just… It's so soon. And there's so much going on.' She cast around for an excuse that he'd buy. Something that would make him back off, for now, at least.

Something that wasn't *I can't be what you need me to be.* Because he still didn't seem to believe that, even though she'd proven it time and again. Was proving it right now, for that matter.

'I don't want news stories about you and me to overshadow the awards next weekend,' she said, hating herself even as she spoke. 'That wouldn't be fair to everyone who worked so hard on the movie, would it?'

'I… I guess not,' Josh said haltingly.

'So it's probably best if I don't come see you before the show, under the circumstances.' If she saw him she'd break. If he kissed her, held her, he'd know she was lying. That this wasn't about the film at all.

She loved him. She wanted him. But she couldn't be

what he needed. She'd fail him again and she wouldn't survive the heartbreak this time around. Maybe he wouldn't either.

They both loved too deeply to say goodbye.

'If that's what you really want.' His voice was cold now.

'It is,' she lied.

'Then I guess I'll see you on the red carpet.' He ended the call with a sharp tap and Winter stared at the blank screen for long minutes afterwards, but the tears just wouldn't come.

She'd done what she needed to do, to protect them both. What was the point of crying now?

Josh stared at his phone, wondering what the hell had just happened.

How had they gone from planning to spend three days in bed to not even seeing each other at all, in the space of a couple of minutes?

Blinking at the screen, he pulled up the fuzzy photos of them together in Iceland again. The comments were mounting up underneath them, some enthusiastic and hopeful, some disdainful, mostly accusing Winter of wanting her cake and eating it.

In fact, reading the vitriol some of his fans shot in his ex-wife's direction, he could completely understand why she might not want their reunion to be public knowledge yet. Hell, he *had* understood. That was why he'd agreed to all the secrecy in the first place.

But now the news was out there…

He'd known she wanted to protect their privacy while they figured out where things were going. But he'd never foreseen that she'd call the whole thing off if they got found out.

He was missing something here. And he had no idea what it was.

Unless…

A new comment on the post of the travel blogger who'd been with them in Iceland caught his eye.

She's just leading him on again. Just you watch. She'll be using this to promote that movie of hers before you know it.

Was that it? Was this *really* all about the movie nomination somehow? Except Winter had said she didn't want them to distract from that. And besides, he *knew* her. She wouldn't use him that way.

Another comment read:

I can't believe he's going to let her break his heart again. She was never good enough for him.

Except he knew the opposite was true, there. *He* hadn't been good enough for *her.*

He kept scanning down the comments, unable to stop himself, even though he knew that none of these people really knew anything about him or Winter, or what they'd shared in Iceland.

They'd all formed an opinion, though. Just like they had after Winter had left him, five years ago.

The comments in the media and online then had been vicious, especially before the news of the miscarriage had come out. Winter had wanted to keep everything private, of course—so had he, for that matter. But it hadn't made any difference. Someone always talked.

But the rumours that made it out there were given the same weighting as the facts, and their fans picked and chose the ones that best suited the narrative they wanted to tell. His fans painted Winter as a callous heartbreaker. Hers blamed him for not being supportive enough.

The worst of the commentary had definitely been pointed at Winter, though. He'd seen that, even then, through his anger and his pain after she'd left.

No wonder she didn't want to go through all that again.

She wouldn't have to if we just stayed together this time.

The thought nagged in his head. Was this reluctance to admit their relationship because she *didn't* see it lasting this time?

He hadn't seen the end coming last time, although she clearly had. Was history repeating itself?

There were dozens more comments already, and notifications pinging into his email about other mentions of the story across the internet. This was going to be everywhere, fast.

With a sigh, Josh tapped to read a message from his agent that read:

CALL ME!

He supposed he should do just that.

If Winter wanted damage limitation measures, that was what he'd give her. But he suspected the damage to his heart was already done.

Maybe she'd been right all along. They'd failed at marriage once. Why would they do any better this time, when they couldn't even make it two weeks into a new relationship without a crisis?

Better to end it now with a bruised heart than later with a smashed one.

Perhaps this was the closure he'd really been looking

for in Iceland. The final death knell of the fairy tale of Josh and Winter. The one that would let him move on and find the sort of relationship he'd always wanted. One like his parents had shared.

Really, this could be a good thing. In the end.

He just wished that closure didn't hurt so damn much.

'I just don't understand,' Jenny said, staring at the fuzzy photos on the computer screen.

'Neither do I,' Winter grumbled. 'Liam *said* that the lagoon was private.'

Jenny shot her a look Winter couldn't quite read. 'That's not what I meant.'

'So what *did* you mean?' She wasn't up to inference today.

'I thought you and Josh were happy again. You certainly looked it when you got back from your mysterious Northern Lights trip.'

'We were,' Winter said, mystified. What did happy have to do with anything here? 'I mean, we had a nice time together.'

'So why am I proofreading a press release denying that there's anything going on between the two of you?' Jenny put the paper in her hand down and met Winter's gaze across the desk.

Winter looked away. 'Because there isn't. There can't be.'

'Why not?'

Standing up, Winter paced across the lounge of her London flat towards the darkened window. It was so late already, but she couldn't sleep until they'd sorted this. 'I need to focus on the movie right now. And the next one—on my career. I don't have time for love.'

'Then what was Iceland?' Jenny pressed.

'A goodbye.' The lie stung even to speak it. She'd thought, just for a moment as the Northern Lights had danced overhead, that it could be a beginning. It had all seemed possible then.

It didn't now.

'Really? That's not what it looked like at the airport.' Jenny pulled a face. 'Well, it kind of did, because you *were* actually saying goodbye. But you know what I mean. It didn't look like goodbye *for ever.*'

'We both agreed we wanted closure on how our marriage ended,' Winter said, trying to sound pragmatic. 'For a while, I thought maybe we could carry on with something else. But these photos have made clear to me that is not possible.'

Jenny sighed, and reached across the desk to take Winter's hand. 'You're not talking to the press now, Winter. This is me. You know I understand how scary this must before for you. So tell me. What's going on in your head? Is this *really* all about the movie, or the award, or your career?'

'Why wouldn't it be?'

'Because I've never seen you look at another person the way you look at Josh. And I don't think you'll ever even want to, will you?'

Jenny's words slashed deep towards her heart, but they couldn't reach it. Winter had put back those walls that had defended her so well after her divorce, the ones that wouldn't let in the awful words and comments about her on the internet, or the prime-time gossip shows debating whether she had ever actually been pregnant at all.

She wasn't going to do any of that again. She wouldn't let it hurt her.

And if that meant keeping her friends out as well as her enemies, so be it.

Except apparently Jenny didn't get the memo.

'Winter. What are you doing?' Jenny's voice had dropped to a whisper. '*Why* are you doing it? I don't believe this is about a movie, or an award. I don't even really think it's about your career.'

'Why shouldn't it be?' Winter shot back. 'You know how horrific this job can be to women—you've lived it. You know how unfair they are when it comes to things like this. My whole life will be picked apart, and that's all anyone will care about. Not the work I've done, or all the other people who've invested so much of themselves in our movie. No one will even remember the *name* of the film, just that I tried to seduce my ex-husband in a geothermal lagoon!'

She was shouting, Winter realised. And standing up. She didn't remember doing either of those things.

Maybe she wasn't handling this as calmly as she'd hoped.

'You're not wrong,' Jenny said softly, and Winter knew she was remembering how she'd come to work for her in the first place, and regretted reminding her of it. 'I know all that better than almost anyone. But I don't think that would be enough to stop *you*. Not if this is love.'

'Love?' Winter shook her head. 'Do you really think that's enough? Even after everything you've seen in this place? Everything you've been through? You think love can fix it all?'

'Not fix it,' Jenny said, meeting her gaze steadily. 'But you know that the gossip sites will talk about you anyway—that's part of the gig. Love—being with someone who truly knows and understands you—I can only imagine that's what would make the rest of it bearable.'

The worst thing was, Winter knew that she was right. It just didn't change anything.

'I can't, Jenny. I can't love him again.'

'Why not?'

'Because…' Winter took a breath. 'He wants things I can't give him, remember? Marriage and kids and a perfect wife and I'm *not* perfect and he knows it.'

'You're scared of getting pregnant again,' Jenny guessed, and there was something that flashed behind her eyes that Winter couldn't quite read.

'I'm terrified of it all.' It felt good to admit it. 'Yes, the idea of getting pregnant and that sick again is awful, but nowhere near as horrific as the thought of losing another baby. And it's not just that! If I can't give Josh the family he wants, what *can* I give him? Eventually he'll want more and I'll lose him too, and I just can't take that again. I *can't*.'

'I get that. You're too scared to take a second chance on love,' Jenny said. 'Oh, Winter.'

'I can't do it, Jenny. I won't let him down that way. And I won't risk my heart that way either.'

Jenny's gaze was direct, demanding, and the grip on her hand had grown tighter. 'But what's the alternative?'

'I carry on the way I have been for the last five years.' Winter attempted a casual shrug and a watery smile. 'I focus on my career. I make great movies and maybe even win an award.'

'That's it?' Jenny asked. 'That's the plan?' She sounded disappointed. Like she'd thought there would be something more. Some great wisdom to make sense of it all.

'It's all I've got,' Winter told her.

And she hoped against all hope that it was going to be enough.

CHAPTER THIRTEEN

Josh didn't answer the first knock on the door of his house. Or the second.

In fact, it wasn't until Liam called him and said, 'Open the door and let me in, you tosser!' before hanging up that he dragged himself off the couch at all.

'What are you doing in LA?' Josh let Liam in and slammed the door behind him, hoping that no lingering paparazzi had caught the ex-Hollywood heartthrob showing up on his doorstep with a bottle of bourbon in the middle of the afternoon, just three days after his ex-wife had issued a statement categorically denying any rekindling of their relationship. It wouldn't take a genius to ferret out the subtext there.

'Just a stopover.' Liam headed straight for the kitchen and pulled out two cut glass tumblers. 'I'm on my way to Costa Rica to my latest hotel site. Thought I might drop in on an old friend.'

'Let me guess. Jenny was busy?' He'd seen the looks between the two of them and, as good a friend as Liam was, Josh couldn't believe he'd really come all this way to salve his broken heart.

Liam paused in pouring the bourbon. 'I didn't come to see Jenny. She's still in London with Winter anyway. I came here because... I feel like this is my fault.'

'You came here for absolution?'

'That's why I brought bourbon.' Liam handed him one of the glasses and took the other.

Josh dropped onto the couch at the far end of the kitchen, motioning for Liam to follow him.

'It's not your fault,' Josh told him. 'You brought us together again, sure. But that had to happen some time. You just gave us space to do it in private.'

'Apart from the Instagram snappers.' Liam sipped his drink. 'I *am* sorry about them. And I genuinely wasn't trying to get you two back together, you know.'

'Really?' Josh asked, sceptical. 'What *were* you trying to do then? Distract us so you could seduce Jenny without Winter objecting?'

Liam waved a hand at him. 'None of it had anything to do with Jenny, okay?'

'Then what?'

'Is it so hard to believe I just wanted the two of you to be friends again? To stop living with this huge tragedy hanging over you, and never moving on?' Liam leaned forward, his forearms resting on his knees, and surveyed Josh with serious eyes. 'Mate, I know what it's like to live in the past. I know I'm every bit as guilty of it as you. And I know how bloody hard it is to put the events that define who we are as a person behind us and move on. I'm trying—damned if I know if I'm succeeding, but I'm trying. But you…you wouldn't even admit you were stuck back there, mentally living in a fairy tale that ended years ago.'

'Believe me, I know my marriage ended,' Josh said caustically. 'And I knew it *before* my ex-wife took my heart and trampled on it again.'

Liam winced. 'Maybe you knew it, but you hadn't

moved on from it, had you? I mean, seriously. Have you had anything past a third date in five years?'

'I was working,' Josh pointed out. 'A lot. Hardly conducive to starting a new love affair.'

'Really?' Liam raised his eyebrows. 'Half the Hollywood relationships we know started on film sets. *Including* yours and Winter's.'

'And look how *that* worked out.' Josh sighed. 'I know what you were trying to do, Liam. Give us closure. Right?'

'I guess that's as good a word for it as any.' Liam sat back, sprawled against the soft sofa cushions, his eyes contemplative. 'It's hard to find that closure sometimes—especially when the person you need it from is gone. I figured at least you and Winter were both still alive to find it. I just didn't expect—' He broke off.

'What? That we'd fall into bed together again?' Josh asked bitterly. 'Trust me, neither did I.'

Liam gave a soft chuckle. 'Honestly? I wasn't counting on it or anything, but with you two…the way you fell for each other the first time, that was something else. And I've never seen two people look at each other with such love as you guys did on your wedding day. So, yeah, I guess I always figured there was a chance you two would get back together again.' He met Josh's gaze and held it with an intensity that was almost unsettling. 'I just didn't think you'd be such idiots as to throw away that kind of love a second time, when some of us would kill for a second chance like that.'

A shard of guilt stabbed Josh somewhere around his heart, as he remembered how much his friend had lost. But still he shook his head.

'I didn't throw it away. She did.'

'What do you mean?'

Josh explained, as best he could, everything that had led them to this moment. How he'd thought they were trying again, for real and for ever. But she'd chosen her career and her privacy over him.

'I guess she never really saw us going the distance,' he said. 'Or else she'd never have given up so easily on us. But really, it's probably for the best.'

'The best?' Liam asked. 'How do you figure that?'

Josh had spent the last few days, ever since that picture leaked, looking at the situation from every angle, and had finally landed on one he could live with.

'Love—real love—it's not meant to be this hard, right?'

Liam laughed. 'In my experience, love is the hardest thing of all.'

'But it *shouldn't* be, that's what I'm saying. True love is meant to be effortless. Like you couldn't imagine being apart. That's what it was like when Winter and I met. Falling in love with her was the easiest thing I ever did.'

'Until things got hard.'

'Exactly!'

'Do you really believe that?' Liam asked, looking amused. 'I mean, have you just made so many romcoms now that you've bought into the idea of the eternal happy ending? That once you reach the last frame it's all sunshine and strawberries from there on out?'

'It's not the movies that taught me that,' Josh hit back. 'I've seen it. Remember? My mom and dad, they had it. Graham and Ashley, they have the same. It's not *work* for them, being in love. It's not this…this pain and frustration and feeling of loss and lack of understanding. If anything, it's the opposite.'

Liam eyed him for a moment, then drained the rest of the bourbon from his glass before standing up. 'Well. If you're determined to give up on the love of your life just because things got hard, and you believe love is meant to be easy…' He shook his head and placed the empty glass on the kitchen counter. 'Then there's nothing more I can say. Except…call your brother.'

Josh frowned. 'What?'

'Call Graham and ask him to confirm your theory. That true love is easy. That's all I ask.' Liam grabbed his jacket from where he'd draped it over the back of a kitchen stool and shot Josh a grin. 'And let me know how it goes, yeah? I've got to move. Costa Rica beckons.'

He walked out of the door with a backward wave, leaving Josh wondering exactly what Liam thought Graham knew that he didn't.

Winter reached for the water glass on the table between her and Melody, the star of *Another Time and Place*, and tried to stifle a sigh. This pre-awards press junket seemed to be going on for ever, and the hotel suite they'd been given for meeting the journalists was stifling. Plus, apparently their next—and final—interviewer of the day was running late, interviewing someone else in another suite.

'Bored of talking about the movie already?' Melody asked, her perfect eyebrows arched.

'If only they'd *ask* about the movie,' Winter said. 'I'll talk about our film and its message all day long. But the first question everyone asks is always about—' She broke off, not wanting to say his name.

'Your ex-husband,' Melody finished for her. 'I read the stories, of course. But I have to admit, none of it really made any sense to me.'

'You and me both,' Winter said with a wry smile. 'I

issued a statement when the photos were released. I don't know why people are still going on about it.'

'Because you're the fairy tale, of course,' Melody said with an elegant shrug. 'Everyone loves a fairy tale.'

'We *were* the fairy tale, the better part of ten years ago,' Winter replied. 'And then we were just a failing married couple, then a pair of divorcees. Plenty of those to go around without talking about us.'

'I didn't mean back then, when you first met.' Melody waved a dismissive hand. 'I've seen the photos and all that. You were both very young and beautiful and in love. All very nice. But *now*. *Now* you're the real thing.'

Winter stared at her in astonishment. 'What on earth do you mean?'

She and Josh were nothing now, and never would be again. She'd seen to that. So why were people still talking about them?

'Young couples falling in love are ten a penny. But you two…finding your way back to each other after heartbreak, taking a second chance on love, even knowing the risks…now *that's* a story worth following.' Melody gave her a wolfish smile. 'You *literally* made the movie about this, Winter. Are you honestly surprised that people are fishing for the story that links your *award-nominated* movie with your real life?'

'I hadn't thought of it like that,' Winter admitted. 'And anyway it isn't really. Like I said, nothing is happening between me and Josh any more. We wanted closure on our relationship and we found it. Now we can move on.'

Melody's gaze was sceptical. 'I think that, if that were true, you wouldn't mind so many questions being asked about him.'

Jumping to her feet, Winter paced to the window, glass

of water still in hand. 'It didn't…it didn't end as cleanly as I'd like, that's all. It's an awkward situation.'

'Because he's still in love with you,' Melody guessed.

Winter scoffed. 'If he was, I dare say he isn't any more.' She'd burned that bridge. And she was living with it.

Everything was fine.

Apart from the way her chest ached every time someone said his name.

Melody didn't answer, and when Winter turned to look she found the older actress watching her with compassion in her eyes.

'What?'

Melody shook her head sadly. 'I just think it's a shame. When I made this movie, I hoped it would help *me* move on. To find closure on the love I let go, because I believed I couldn't have this career I wanted so badly *and* a healthy marriage and home. I thought I had to choose, so I did.'

'What happened?' Winter asked.

'I've regretted it every day since,' Melody answered simply. 'I let her go and she found love elsewhere, and I tried to be happy for her…but I never stopped regretting it.'

'I'm sorry.' Winter tried to imagine seeing Josh happy with someone else, but the pain in her chest got worse, so she shook the image away.

She'd seen a few photos of him on dates, or with co-stars, in the years since their divorce. But he'd never seemed to settle down with anyone longer than a few dates. She'd never really been confronted with the idea of him being happy with someone else, except in her imagination.

But that would change now, she realised suddenly. He'd found the closure on their relationship that he'd needed to move on. And while he might be hurt right now that she'd ended things again, he wouldn't take so long to recover this time, she was sure.

Josh still wanted that perfect love—marriage, family, home—the American ideal of a relationship that his parents and brother had. Now she'd made it completely clear that she couldn't give him that, he'd find it with someone else.

He'd fall in love again, with someone who wasn't her.

'You're imagining it, aren't you?' Melody said. 'Your Josh loving someone else.'

'No,' Winter lied. 'He's not my Josh.'

Melody laughed. 'Trust me. However much you're imagining it hurting right now, it's a thousand times worse when it happens in reality.'

Winter swallowed, desperately wishing the images away. But they wouldn't budge.

In her imagination, Josh's new love was tall, willowy, blonde—all the things she wasn't. And pregnant, of course. Of course.

'It doesn't make any difference.' Winter stared out of the window at the LA skyline rather than risk Melody's knowing eyes again. Her whole body felt wrung-out—exhausted and aching. She blamed it on the jet lag, even though she knew she'd felt like this long before she'd left London.

Jenny said she was heartsick. Winter kept ignoring her.

'Why? Why doesn't it make a difference?' Melody asked.

'Because...because I already broke things off. I told him I couldn't do this. I've broken his heart too many times already for him to risk it again on me.'

'Isn't that a decision for him to make?' There was a

rustle of fabric as Melody stood up and crossed to stand beside her at the window.

'He wouldn't make it,' Winter said softly. 'That's why I had to do it for him. I can't be what he needs.'

'One thing I've learned, growing older,' Melody said, 'is that we can't decide what matters for anyone other than ourselves. We can't choose for other people, that's not our right. If you want to be apart from Josh, if you want to watch him find love with someone else, then that's your choice to make. But if the idea makes you want to scream…well. You're choosing it for him, and that's *not* your job.'

Winter swallowed, blinking away the pinpricks behind her eyes as the tears formed.

'But what if it doesn't work? What if I'm not enough, again?'

And wasn't that what it all came down to? Jenny had told her she was afraid, and she was right.

She was terrified she wouldn't be enough for Josh. That she wouldn't be able to be what he needed. That she'd run again when things got too hard, rather than having those impossible conversations where nobody ever, ever won.

That her heart would break again, whatever decision she made.

'That's the risk you take with love,' Melody said softly, sadly even. 'I'm not saying it's not a big one. But Winter, isn't this the story you were trying to tell the world with our movie? That sometimes the bigger the risk the bigger the reward? That even if you've been hurt, if you've experienced more of life's ups and downs, if you know how bad things can be…you still have to get out there and live.'

'I suppose.' Winter knew Melody was right. But it was

so much easier to believe those things when the only heart that might get broken was a fictional one. 'But what if... Last time, it felt like I lost myself in that relationship. Like I only mattered in relation to him. I forgot who I was outside being his wife.'

And the mother of his unborn child. The pregnancy... the way that had taken over her body and mind, turned her into someone else, she *knew* that had affected her mindset too. Then losing the baby...

She'd felt out of control in her own life. As if nothing was her decision any longer. Everything that happened to her was caused by outside forces—Josh, the media, her body...everything and everyone except her own mind.

That was what she'd been searching for when she'd left. Autonomy. The chance to make her own decisions and decide who she wanted to be for herself.

And she'd done a pretty good job, as far as she was concerned.

But was it enough?

The hole in her heart that had started to fill when she'd reconnected with Josh in Iceland whispered perhaps not.

Melody seemed to understand. 'I know that when you've reached the point you have in life—you're successful on your own, you set your own rules, you've found your own self and you have your freedom to live however you want—it's hard to admit that you want something else. And even harder to take a risk on it when it might not turn out for the best. But all that means something else too, you realise.'

Winter blinked up at Melody. 'What? What does it mean?'

'It means you know you can survive.' Melody gripped Winter's shoulders and held her gaze. 'You've done it before, remember? You know you have the power to pick yourself up and start again and be *magnificent*. If you don't try again with Josh, you might always regret it. And if it falls apart, it will probably hurt like hell. But none of that changes a bit of who you are, you see. You're Winter de Holland, and you will be *amazing* with or without him. Nobody can take that away from you unless you let them.'

The words echoed in Winter's mind until they were the only thing she could hear. Not the traffic outside the window, or the rattling trolley going past outside the room.

Nobody can take that away from you unless you let them.

She'd found her true self now. She could cling onto that. She wouldn't give it up.

She wouldn't let them take it. Not this time.

She was stronger than that now.

'The only thing that matters is what will make you happier right now and has the potential for greater happiness in the future,' Melody said. 'Okay?'

Winter nodded, dazed by her revelations. 'Okay. I… yeah. Okay.'

There was a knock on the door and Jenny popped her head around to tell them that their last interview of the day was ready at last. Winter made her way back to her seat, hoping she could still remember enough of the talking points to get through the interview.

Because suddenly her mind was overflowing with *other* things to think about.

And a decision she had to make.

Graham sounded surprised to hear from him late on a weekday afternoon, Josh thought. Or perhaps just surprised to hear from him at all. He hadn't been the best at staying in touch lately. And he hadn't called at all since everything with Winter in Iceland hit the news.

'How're things going in Holly Wood?' Graham pronounced it as two words as always, a not-so-subtle reminder that the world Josh lived in wasn't the same as the rest of them.

'Same old, same old,' Josh replied.

'Heard you had a run-in with your ex.' His brother always had been one to get straight to the heart of the matter. 'That what you're calling about?'

'Partly,' Josh admitted. 'It's not…we're not…' He sighed. 'Liam told me to call you.'

Graham barked a laugh. 'Did he? Got tired of dealing with your shit and decided to palm you off on family at last?'

'Not exactly.' Josh frowned as he tried to figure out exactly why Liam *had* wanted him to talk to his brother. 'It was just…we were talking about love.'

'Drunk, were you?'

'One solitary glass of bourbon, I promise you.'

Graham groaned. 'Talking about love sober? This must be serious. Hang on.'

Josh heard his brother calling out to Ashley, telling her he was going to take the call outside. With beer. The screen door slammed and the creaking of wood and scrape of the runners told him Graham was sitting on the old swing seat on the porch, even though it couldn't be that warm out there yet, at this time of year.

'Okay, I'm listening,' Graham said. 'Tell me everything.'

'You don't have time for everything,' Josh hedged.

'I'm your big brother,' Graham replied. 'I'll make time.'

Josh hesitated for a moment. And then he started to talk.

The story came easier this time than it had with Liam,

perhaps because he was getting more used to telling it. Graham needed more background too. He'd been there for the fallout of Winter leaving the first time, so all of that was old news. But their trip to Iceland, how it had come about and his feelings about it, all weighed in to the story.

He finished up by recounting his conversation with Liam over bourbon the day before.

'And he told you to call me?' Graham said.

'Yep. Any idea why?'

Graham sighed. 'Because your friend knows you well enough to have realised that you're an idiot. And there are certain truths you're only ever going to believe from the horse's mouth.'

Josh ignored the idiot comment—that was just par for the course with brothers, right?

'What truths?'

'You think true love should be easy? That Mom and Dad had the perfect marriage? That me and Ashley do?' Incredulity coloured Graham's voice.

'Don't you?' Josh countered. 'I've seen you two together. You *are* a perfect match.'

'I don't deny it,' Graham said. 'There's no other woman in the world for me, just like I don't think there's ever going to be anyone for Mom now that Dad has gone.'

'So I'm right.' Josh couldn't explain the slight disappointment at realising his brother was agreeing with him.

'No. You're wrong.' Graham laughed. 'And the most ridiculous thing is, you can't even see why, can you?'

'I suppose you're going to enlighten me.' No way Josh was admitting to not knowing, though.

'You think perfect is the same thing as easy,' Graham said. '*That's* where you're wrong.'

Josh blinked, letting the words settle, but stayed silent.

'Just because we're a perfect match, it doesn't mean Ashley and me don't work on our marriage every single day,' Graham went on. 'And if you think we don't have fights or disagreements…well, you *clearly* weren't here for the Great Dishwasher Row of four Thanksgivings ago is all I'm saying. Or any of the other hundreds of things we've disagreed about over the years.'

'Disagreements are normal,' Josh said. 'Even I know that. But underneath them…' Surely, underneath the petty stuff, the surface stuff, there had to be something more solid. Something that told a person that everything would be all right. A certainty that took away the constant fear.

'Underneath them everything is even harder,' Graham said soberly. 'The thing is, Josh, every moment you're with another person is a choice. Marriage doesn't change that. Every single day you wake up married to someone you still have to decide to *choose* them. To keep loving them. To stay by their side. To work as a team. True love isn't everything suddenly going smoothly because you said some words in front of a priest. It's deciding every day to make it work. To stick it out. To keep trying. Because the day you give up is the day it's all over.'

It was as if Josh blinked and clarity flowed over him.

Winter had given up on them when she'd walked away. But he'd given up too.

She'd accused him of always trying to fix everything, but that was only because it was easier than trying to understand it. To be there and feel her pain with her. To realise that there were things he might need to change— about himself, his life, his expectations.

He'd bought into the lie of the happy ever after. That once he'd put that ring on her finger everything would be plain sailing. And when it wasn't he'd pulled away.

He'd *known* she was unhappy and because he didn't know how to fix it he'd pulled away.

Because it was easier to accept failure if he could blame it on something other than himself. On their schedules, or the miscarriage, or the press.

The truth was, he hadn't fought hard enough. He hadn't been the man she needed.

But now…now he needed to ask himself. Was he ready to be that man?

Because if he wasn't, then Winter was right to walk away again.

'Some days love is easy, some days it's hard,' Graham went on, unaware of Josh's sudden epiphany. 'The only thing I know for sure is that it's worth fighting for on *all* the days.'

'I think… I think I need to talk to Winter.'

He could almost hear Graham's smile down the phone. 'I think you're right, little brother.'

CHAPTER FOURTEEN

WINTER HAD SPENT a whole afternoon being primped, prodded, dressed and made up by the team Jenny had organised to get her ready for the awards ceremony that evening, and she hadn't even noticed half of it. Her mind was still focused on her conversation with Melody the day before. And what it meant for her future.

Josh would be at the awards tonight, even if they weren't going together any more. It would be her first time seeing him in person since Iceland, and she couldn't imagine making it through the whole evening without some sort of awkward conversation between them.

An awards ceremony red carpet was the last place she wanted to talk about her failure at a relationship with her ex, and she wasn't sure the afterparty would be a better location either. But they *did* need to talk.

She owed him some explanation. And a say in what happened next between them too.

And if he walked away… Melody was right. She'd survive. She'd *thrive*.

If she had to.

By the time the stylist was pushing a heavy emerald ring onto the finger of Winter's right hand, her hands were shaking with nerves.

I'm not ready for this.

But it was happening anyway.

At least she had the drive to the awards venue to get her nerves under control. Thanking everyone involved in making her look presentable for the night ahead, Winter took a quick glance in the mirror on her way to the door, still surprised to see herself looking so different to how she'd been when she'd dressed that morning. Then, with a last wave goodbye, she headed for the door.

The black limo waiting outside had the back door already open for her, a driver standing beside it as she climbed in. She thanked him, settled into her seat as the door shut behind her—and then screamed.

'What are you doing here?' She clutched a hand to her chest as she stared at Josh, sitting across the way from her.

'I needed to talk to you.' He shrugged. 'This seemed like the best way to get some privacy tonight.'

The old fears reared up again before Winter could stop them. 'Except now we're showing up at my awards ceremony together and—'

'I'll stay in the car,' Josh promised. 'We'll go round the block again and I'll get out later. Or I won't go at all. Whatever. I don't care. I just need to talk to you.'

'I… I wanted to talk to you too,' she admitted. 'So this isn't actually the worst idea in the world.'

'No, that remains sending two people on a date to a penis museum,' Josh joked, and Winter couldn't help but laugh.

'What did you want to say to me?' she asked.

Josh reached across and took her hand, the one with the heavy emerald ring, in his. He bit down on his lower lip, his gaze searching hers before he started to talk.

'I wanted to tell you…losing you again this last week or so has been hell. I tried to tell myself that it was for the best, that if something was this hard it just couldn't be meant to be. But I was wrong, I can see that now.' He sucked in a deep breath before continuing. 'I realised I was making the same mistakes I made when we were married. Every time things got hard then, especially with your pregnancy and everything that followed… I tried to fix it. To make things easy again. And when I couldn't… I pulled away, because I felt like a failure.'

'You didn't fail us,' Winter interjected. 'My body did.'

Josh shook his head. 'No. You needed me—not to fix things, but to just be there, to be your husband. To choose every day to stay by your side because I loved you and being with you was worth every bit of pain we went through. But I didn't. I took jobs I didn't need to take, I spent most of my time away from you, because I couldn't forgive myself for the pain I was putting you through.'

Winter swallowed, her throat tight and her eyes burning. 'Josh…'

He squeezed her hand. 'Let me…let me get through this first, yeah? I've been thinking about this for days, and I want to make sure I get it all out.'

Winter nodded, and he continued.

'When you left me…part of me knew I deserved it. That's why I never fought for you, never tried to win you back. I let you go because I deserved to be without you,' he said. 'I told myself that it wasn't meant to be. That we'd bought into the fairy tale because of the media and all the talk about us. That if it was *really* true love it wouldn't be so hard. But I realise now, love has nothing to do with easy or hard. It's both.'

'I think you're right,' Winter said.

He flashed her a smile, but then his face turned serious

again. 'I was using perfection as an excuse. A reason to stay away from you, so I didn't have to accept how badly I'd failed—last time, and this time, in Iceland.'

Winter frowned. 'How could you possibly have failed this time? *I* was the one who said we needed to deny the story. *I* gave up on us.'

'I failed because I never told you the truth,' Josh said. 'I went along with the idea that we were just trying a casual thing, to find closure, but that was never true for me. I didn't have the courage to tell you then what I need to tell you now. I love you. I never stopped loving you. I never *will* stop loving you. And I will wake up every morning for the rest of my life and choose you, no matter how hard it gets.'

Winter stared at him, the impossibility of it all battering against the optimism her conversation with Melody had given her.

'You can't mean that.'

'Why not?'

'Because…you want things! Things like marriage and kids and a picture-perfect life that I can't give you. That I don't think I even want these days!'

He shook his head. 'I don't need any of that. Our relationship won't be perfect, but it will be ours, and that's all that matters to me. If we—*we*—decide we want kids down the line, then we'll talk about that. About adopting or fostering or whatever works for us. But none of it is a dealbreaker for me. It never was.'

Her head was spinning too much to make sense of it all. And as much as she wanted to jump, to take the risk and be there with him, she had to be clear about everything first.

'Josh, I'm not the woman you fell in love with, remember? I'm harder and sadder and more independent and—'

'You're you,' Josh said simply. 'And I love you.'

And in that moment Winter knew exactly what she had to do.

It was as simple and as risky as that, Josh realised as he spoke the words. He'd put his heart on the line, and now all he could do was wait to see if she felt the same way.

Her green eyes were unreadable, her hand still in his. The limo came to a halt and he knew he was out of time.

Reluctantly, he let go of her hand. 'Go on. You go ahead. I'll go round the block a time or two and come back in a bit, once you're inside. We can talk more later, when we have some privacy.'

Winter stared at him for a long moment, those green eyes almost as bright as the emerald on her hand. 'I don't need privacy for what comes next,' she said finally. 'Come on.'

He blinked at her and opened his mouth, but before he could ask any more questions she'd swung her legs out of the open limo door, grabbed his hand and pulled him out behind her.

Josh had stood on a hundred or more red carpets in his career, but the flashing of bulbs and the shouted questions had never felt more intimidating than they did now, following Winter, unsure of what was going to happen next.

They hadn't agreed anything, had they? He'd put his heart on the line, but he still didn't know what was in hers. What she wanted.

'Josh! Winter! Are you two here together tonight?' one of the reporters called out as they made their way to the area where they'd pause for photos and answer a few questions.

Winter ignored him, so Josh did too.

Finally, she stopped in front of the crush of cameras,

turning and smiling and posing just like she was supposed to. Josh stood back and watched, wanting her to have this moment in the sun, basking in her achievement. This was *her* night, and he wouldn't do anything that would take that from her.

But when she beckoned for him to join her he went and stood at her side, beaming proudly as they had photos taken together.

'Winter, are you and Josh here tonight as a couple?' a different reporter asked.

Winter flashed Josh a small secret smile and his heart felt as if it stopped as he waited to hear her answer.

'I'm here tonight to celebrate my film, *Another Time and Place*,' Winter said, her voice strong and clear. 'To celebrate the achievements of every person who worked on it, who gave their heart and soul to it, and who will equally share in the glory if I win best director tonight—or even if I don't.'

'But you and—' someone started to interrupt.

Winter held up a hand to stop them. '*But*,' she said, 'it was brought to my attention recently by someone that I admire very much that, since the film is all about second chances in love, about taking chances even when you know how big the risk really is, and how bad the pain can be when things go wrong, it's only right to talk about my own journey to accepting the power of second chance love.'

She held them all in the palm of her hand now, each reporter hanging on her every word. Josh watched her proudly and tried to hold back any fears about what she was about to say.

'I've been asked often while working on this project, why showing second chance love matters in film. I talked about the importance of representation, about how the characters were more mature, how they knew themselves better, that sort of thing. And I stand by all of it. But one thing I've learned over the past few weeks is just how *brave* second chance love is. And that's the message of my movie, the message I'm sending out there to everyone watching tonight.

'Falling in love is scary. Giving your heart to someone else to hold is always, always a risk. And it's so easy not to take it. To hold back and protect ourselves from the heartache we know could come. Especially when we've been there before, we've already experienced the pain. We want to save ourselves from ever going through that again.

'But I'm here to tell you that it *is* worth the risk. Even if it hurts. Even if it goes wrong. Love is worth fighting for, every single day. It's worth every chance. Because sometimes you'll find your happily ever after—or even just a happily for now. And *that* is worth *everything*.'

A huge cheer went up from the surrounding crowd as she finished speaking and the camera flashbulbs went crazy. But Josh didn't notice any of it really.

All he could see was Winter. Winter smiling at him. Winter, beautiful in her gown. Winter, glowing with happiness and potential.

Winter, ready to take a second chance on love. On *him*.

She stepped closer and stretched up on her toes to kiss him, her arms wrapping around his neck. And Josh knew in that moment that she was completely right. Even if their love was never perfect, or easy, or anything else he'd thought it needed to be, it would always, always be worth fighting for.

EPILOGUE

CAMERA BULBS WERE flashing again as Winter sat down to another press conference, this time for her new movie— one she'd both directed *and* starred in for the first time. For a moment she felt as if she'd flashed back in time to two years ago, to that press conference after the award nominations had been announced. The one where she'd been blindsided by the fact she'd be spending a week in Iceland with her ex-husband.

Winter smiled, more to herself than for the cameras. If she'd only known then what she knew now...

A hand took hers as Josh sat down in the chair beside her and she turned her smile at him instead—knowing from the flashes that the cameras were going crazy at the signs of affection between the two of them.

She didn't care.

Something she'd learned over the last two years— and learned the hard way, through trial and error, she'd admit—was that the cameras and the people behind them would see what they wanted to see, whatever she did. She couldn't control that. Just like she couldn't decide what Josh wanted from their relationship. Or how her body reacted to certain things.

What she *could* do—and what she now worked hard to do—was focus inward.

She put boundaries in place around her time and energy with the press, with social media and with the fans. She showed them her true, authentic self—and stopped worrying about what they actually saw, and whether it was the same thing.

Josh had put the work in too—although with him it had less to do with the press and more to do with their relationship. That was where the real effort went, for both of them.

The night they'd agreed to try again—the night she'd taken home the award for best director for *Another Time and Place,* and they'd fallen into bed the moment they'd got home from the afterparty and not left it except for food and bathroom breaks for three days—they'd talked, in between everything else, and come up with…not rules but a new guide for their relationship. The fact that she'd agreed to call it a relationship was, she'd thought at the time, a pretty good start.

Now, every day, they took time out to talk—to check in on each other's thoughts and feelings before they built up too much. They communicated far more than they ever had the first time around, and so much more honestly. They stopped guessing what the other wanted and started telling each other what they needed.

It didn't solve every problem, and God knew they still got it wrong sometimes. But every day they kept their promise to each other.

They chose to be together. They chose to find a way to make it work.

As for her body… Winter wasn't sure she'd ever fully trust it again, after the way it had betrayed her. But she'd learned to appreciate all the things it could do, rather than focusing on what it couldn't. Taking care of it—rather than just training or dieting for a role, or to fit into a dress—in a loving, mindful way, seemed to make a difference. She rested when she needed to rest and ate ice cream when she needed to eat ice cream. It worked for her.

In fact, it all did. She controlled what she could, communicated where she needed and let the rest go.

It felt amazing.

'Winter! How did it feel to get to boss Josh around on set for this movie?' The first question from the gathered throng of reporters earned a laugh, and Winter smiled before answering it.

'Lucky for me, Josh is a professional,' she replied. 'And when you're making a movie that's what you need more than anything. It didn't take us too long to figure out a way to make it work—and keep our home life off set.' No need to mention the time they'd had an argument about *someone* not putting an appointment on the calendar, gone to work in a bad mood, then been caught making up in the props trailer later that afternoon...

'Josh, same question for you, really,' another reporter called out. 'How did it feel being directed by Winter?'

Josh squeezed her hand before letting go and answering. 'My life is always better when I listen to her,' he joked, earning a laugh from the gathered reporters. 'No, seriously. We approached this movie the same way we approach our relationship, every day. We start with a commitment to put the work in to make it the best we can and go from there.'

That got 'Aww's from the audience, and Winter ducked her head to hide what she suspected was a rather besotted smile.

The questions about the movie kept coming, finally shifting from their relationship to the actual film, and its chances come awards season. They took turns answering them, working in sync in a way she'd never imagined they could have again.

A way she'd never take for granted after all it had taken to get them there.

Finally the press conference started to wind down, and from the wings Winter's new assistant signalled the last question.

'What's next for you two?' the chosen reporter asked. 'Straight into another project? Together or separately? Or are you going to take some time off?'

Winter and Josh shared a glance. 'Definitely some time off,' Josh said, and she was sure that everyone in the room had to be able to hear the heat in his voice. 'Together.'

At least they didn't know all the things he'd promised to do to her during that time off, several of them involving her wearing her red bikini—and then not wearing it. Although if the heat in her cheeks was any indication, her blush might give some of them away.

She cleared her throat and smiled brightly at their audience, while lightly slapping Josh's thigh under the table.

'We're off to Costa Rica,' she said. 'We've got a wedding to go to.'

'Yours?' someone called eagerly, as a hum of speculation filled the room.

Josh laughed. 'Not this time, I'm afraid.' He reached for her hand again under the desk—her left hand—and Winter felt him run a finger across her ring finger, over the spot where her wedding ring used to sit.

Where, just last night, he'd placed another ring, a new one. One he'd had designed just for who they were now, not who they had been.

They'd agreed she wouldn't wear it today or it would be all anyone would ask about, so it hung on a chain under the high neck of her dress until the press conference was over and she could wear it again.

There was no rush. They'd tell the world when they were ready.

After all, they had the rest of their lives to look forward to.

Together.

* * * * *

SNOWED IN WITH THE BILLIONAIRE

CARA COLTER

MILLS & BOON

In memory of Avon
1956–2019

PROLOGUE

JACEY TREMBLAY SHUT the door of her apartment and looked down, with a frown, at the rectangular eight-by-ten cardboard envelope in her hand.

Registered.

In her experience, nothing good ever came by registered mail. Her divorce decree, of several months ago, being a case in point.

She turned the letter over in her hands. It was from a law firm she had never heard of, which made her dread worsen.

Obviously, she was being sued. By someone. For something.

She took a deep breath. Who sued a music tutor?

Johnny Jordan's parents, of course. They had entrusted her with their protégé. Given her firsthand experience, she should have known that was not going to work out!

Fourteen-year-old Johnny, musically brilliant, had not gained admission to the Canadian Academy for Betterment of the Arts. That was despite near perfection on that devilishly difficult Chopin piece they had rehearsed for his audition.

Really? Jacey should have warned his parents she was something of an expert on failed protégés!

No, it wasn't that, she told herself, but doubtfully.

While turning the envelope over in her hands, she scanned her mind for other possibilities.

What about that little fender bender on Bloor? Jacey had exchanged insurance information with a delightful geriatric, who had accepted all the blame and admitted she had pulled right out of her parking spot without shoulder checking or signaling. There had never been another word, and that had been at least three months ago.

But that didn't mean said granny hadn't died, or suffered an after-injury that she or her family were now suing for.

With her heart racing at the endless possibilities for catastrophe to visit her life, Jacey took the envelope and sat down on her love seat, which acted as the sofa in her tiny apartment. It was white with a backdrop print of large purple pansies. She had purchased the piece of furniture after the divorce, in a futile attempt to find the bright side in the failure of her marriage.

See? I don't have to consult anyone about what furniture I buy. Her ex, Bruce, who in retrospect she could see had been stingy with his approval, would have hated every single thing about the love seat: form, function and especially the flamboyant color.

She turned her attention, resolutely, back to the envelope.

"Not this week," Jacey told it firmly. "It's a bad time."

So bad, she had taken the week off and canceled on all of her students. Given her failure with Johnny, her most promising student ever, she was not sure she should go back to teaching music. The local supermarket around the corner always had a help-wanted sign up...

But a new career was for next week. This week she had laid into an extra-large bucket of Neapolitan ice cream and bought new comfy pajamas. The pajamas, covered in adorable cartoon kittens, were, like the sofa, a statement about not needing to care what anyone thought.

Jacey had also made a list of movies she planned to watch. It was a shorter list than what she had hoped for, as she had crossed anything romantic, and anything sad, off her list.

"Open it," she commanded herself, turning her attention, again, to the envelope.

For some reason they made these kinds of official-looking packets extremely hard to get into. But finally, Jacey wrestled a single slip of paper and a bulkier brown envelope from the now mangled packaging.

Surprise!

She felt the blood drain from her face as she continued reading the familiar handwriting.

...and I know nobody hates a surprise more than you.

CHAPTER ONE

"Go away," Trevor Cooper called, annoyed, from his prone position on the couch. "Unless you have pizza. Then you can just drop it on the doorstep."

Not that he'd ordered pizza, though come to think of it, that wasn't a bad idea. He tilted his head, looking away from the three side-by-side wall-mounted TV sets, where he was, thanks to the miracle of modern electronics, keeping a close eye on several sporting events simultaneously.

And keeping his mind off what day this was.

Maybe ordering pizza was not such a great idea. His huge open-concept living room, dining area and kitchen was already littered with greasy empty boxes, begging the question: *Could man live on pizza alone?*

Apparently, he could.

Even when he didn't want to. Live, that was. Because two years ago today, his reason for living had gone.

The knock came again, persistent. Trevor thought, crankily, he shouldn't be paying exorbitant gated community fees to be fielding unannounced solicitors at the door, because, Lord knew, he was not expecting company.

When the knock came the third time, he unfolded himself from the couch, glanced down at his naked chest and low-hanging pajama bottoms, and stalked across the room. It was not appropriate to answer your door half-naked, especially in an upscale estate neighborhood like this one, and as he flung open the door he had the thought, *but what if it's that little girl from down the street, selling Girl Scout cookies?* A neighbor knocking would explain the breeching of the security system that made getting into Calgary's tony Mountain View Villas akin to getting into Fort Knox.

But as it turned out, it wasn't a wide-eyed Girl Scout. It was imminently worse.

"Jacey," he said. Inside he cursed. If there was one person he did not want seeing him like this—disheveled, unshaven, only partially dressed in the middle of the day—it was her.

Or maybe his concern wasn't so much for his appearance, but for that of the house. The outside grounds, of course, were impeccably kept by the community association. The gatehouse, just visible in the distance, was winter-themed, like a dollhouse. In the central man-made lake, which his house fronted, the fountain had been replaced for winter with an extravagant ice sculpture of a mother grizzly bear trailed by two cubs.

No, it wasn't his state of undress, or the state of the house. It was the *day*.

"Trevor," she said.

He let the uncomfortable silence bleed between them.

"The gatehouse didn't call," he said, aware his tone was faintly accusing.

"Interesting," she said, mildly. "I thought maybe your phone was broken, permanently set to off, or at the bottom of that lake."

"You can't order pizza without a phone."

"Does it come by cab? That's probably why we were waved through the gate."

She sidestepped slightly, to squint into the dimness behind him. He thought he detected disapproval in her look. He folded his arms over his naked chest and planted his feet, a *go-away* stance if ever there was one.

She ignored the message. Completely.

"May I come in?"

"No!" There. If she couldn't get the subtle messages of his body posture, he'd have to be forthright.

He didn't want her to see the house. How could she not think his neglect was a desecration of Caitlyn's dream house?

Trevor hated it when this happened—unexpected flashes of memory. And he especially hated it today. But there it was, the image of him and Caitlyn entering this house for the first time. Her wide eyes, her excited laughter, her tears of joy.

This is what he could expect from a visit with Jacey. The very thing he had been running from for two years.

Memories.

People said the first year was the worst, but Trevor was not sure he believed that. People said time healed all wounds, and he didn't believe that, either.

"You should have called," he said, though, in fact, despite the mess the house was in, he could not deny the sense of connection he felt with Jacey Tremblay that he probably would never feel with another human being. They had been through a war together.

"I tried," she said, and lifted her chin at him. "Apparently, your phone is used exclusively for pizza delivery."

It was true. His phone had been set to go straight to voice mail for a couple of days. He hadn't checked them. Still, he wasn't apologizing.

"Maybe you should have taken that as a hint."

Something in the deliberate braveness of her expression faltered, and Trevor felt the smallest niggling of something.

Shame. Jacey lived over three thousand miles away from Calgary in Toronto. She'd obviously made a huge effort—misguided as it was—to be with him for this awful second anniversary.

She had been the one, of all their friends, and all their family, who had never shirked. Who had stayed the course. She'd given up her music clients and abandoned her husband to be there in those final weeks for her best friend—his wife—when she was dying of cancer. Jacey had made it possible for Caitlyn to be here, in the home she had loved, right until the end.

Which had not been pretty, but this woman had not flinched.

Trevor took Jacey in. Even under a trench coat that didn't look warm enough for this cold day and that hid most of her—Caitlyn had always said of her friend she was small and had no idea how mighty she was—she looked even more slender than he remembered.

She had cut her blond hair short, and it was sticking up in spikes all over her head, whether from travel or by design he had no idea. Her ears, exposed by the new haircut, were tiny, like a doll's, and pink from not wearing a hat in the January chill. The haircut also made her eyes look huge and showed her features to be gamine.

She had applied the lightest dusting of makeup. It didn't cover that spattering of freckles across her pert nose, or the shadows under—or in—those green eyes.

Why had Jacey come here?

She was obviously travel rumpled and tired. And yet,

even underneath those things, he recognized something of himself in the expression in those deep green eyes.

Unrelenting sorrow.

So much for time healing all wounds.

His sense of shame at the abruptness of his greeting deepened. He had a sudden awareness of how angry Caitlyn would be with him for this lukewarm—make that as ice-cold as this January day—greeting to her dearest and most loyal friend.

Still, *shame* was a feeling, and as such it felt dangerous.

And anger, more powerful, now battled with it.

If Caitlyn wanted him to be a better man, she should have stuck around to finish the job she had started.

The shame swept forward again. How could he act as if she'd had a choice? She didn't want cancer. She would have done anything to stay in this life they had built together, to have those babies she had been so desperate for.

So it wasn't Caitlyn he was angry at.

And not Jacey, either.

It was the whole world. It was his powerlessness, his fury at himself and his inability to change anything when it had truly mattered.

Really? This world—this dark space he was in, that he tried to shut out with games and multiple television sets—was no world to invite Jacey into, no matter how rude that seemed; no matter how good her intentions in coming.

He ran a hand through his hair. "Look, it's not a good day."

"You think I don't know it's not a good day?" she asked, incredulous and miffed.

And yet, even knowing that, there she stood. She

didn't wait for him to finish his explanation, or for an invitation. She put a hand on his naked chest. It felt as if it burned him. Shouldn't her hand be cold, since she was standing outside on a frosty morning without gloves on?

Before he could come up with a defensive maneuver, Jacey shoved him. Given her size, her strength was shocking, and for the first time he noticed a rather frightening detail. One of those wheeled suitcases followed her like an obedient puppy as she marched right by him and into the deeply shadowed house.

She paused and took it all in. The darkness of pulled shades, the pizza boxes, the rumpled clothes on the floor, the layers of dust, the film of sadness everywhere.

He reluctantly closed the door against the blast of cold air that came in with her and then turned and stared, not at her, but at her suitcase. It wasn't one of those tiny ones that fit in the overhead bin.

He wasn't quite sure what it meant that Jacey Tremblay had arrived with a full-size suitcase.

Though he was pretty sure it wasn't good.

Jacey drew in a deep breath as her eyes adjusted to the murky light inside the house. It did not smell good. Not dirty, exactly, but stale. Stuffy.

She quickly turned her attention from Trevor. She looked beyond his state of undress—difficult as that was—and the lack of warmth in his greeting, to realize he looked haggard, and her heart went out to him.

Now, two years later, it was evident from how Caitlyn's space looked and smelled that he had used up every single ounce of his considerable strength in those last weeks with his wife.

But she had seen this man tested beyond the limits of

what any person should endure, and so she had a sense of *knowing* what this man was capable of.

Bravery.

Depth.

Selflessness.

Despite the current state of the house, Jacey had a sense of homecoming. She had spent so much time here, and the mark of Caitlyn's beautiful spirit remained.

It was really more a mansion than a house, like you might see in a movie or a magazine article.

The architectural style was a sophisticated blend of modern and traditional. The main floor was open concept, the sightline going all the way from the front door to the back of the house. Huge floor-to-ceiling windows were at both ends of the space. Usually, dazzling light spilled in through those front windows that faced the lake. Now they were covered in heavy drapes that were closed against the brilliant midmorning sunlight that danced off the snow outside.

Caitlyn had somehow managed to make the cavernous space homey and welcoming with her unexpected use of color and texture. A turquoise sectional sofa and pink accent chairs—how had she managed those particular colors with Trevor?—had made the soaring Brazilian stone fireplace the focal point of the room.

The living room transitioned seamlessly to a dining room with a ten-foot harvest plank table, rescued from a two-hundred-year-old farmhouse. The table sat twenty people, easily. And had. Often.

Beyond that was the kitchen, its modern lines in sharp and lovely contrast to the old table. It had clean white lower cabinets, no uppers, lots of marble and stainless steel. There was that surprising pop of pink again in the upholstered chairs at the island and more soaring windows that should have looked out to a pool and grilling area.

But today the shutters had been closed on those windows, also.

The space had always been faintly scented of carnations, a flower Caitlyn had adored and Trevor had indulged her with several times a week; more, once she'd gotten ill.

The house had always been so glorious, luxurious but also young and fun and filled with energy, a reflection of Caitlyn's perfect life.

Now it was a testament to how temporary everything was. The front area had been reduced to a messy bachelor pad, full of pizza cartons and socks on the floor. That might even be men's underwear... Jacey carefully averted her eyes.

To the television sets. Three of them! One was on the fireplace, above the mantel, and the other two extended out from either side of it on ugly, obviously adjustable arms. There were also tangles of electrical cords.

The televisions had replaced Caitlyn's collection of gorgeous black-and-white wedding photos that had once been on, and beside, the fireplace, gallery style. Amongst the pizza boxes, on the slab of pure mango that served as a coffee table, were several very dead plants, game sleeves and controllers.

The worn boards of the harvest table were littered with papers, the magnificent Koa wood bowl, brought back from Trevor and Caitlyn's honeymoon in Hawaii, barely visible for the debris that surrounded it. The kitchen island was likewise covered with leaning stacks of dishes and smudged glasses.

Jacey could feel Trevor's presence behind her, and she turned and looked at him. His expression dared her to comment on what day it was, the state of the house, the missing photos, the dead plants, the air of neglect.

As she gazed at him, it seemed impossible that someone could look as horrible as he did, and still look so damn good at the very same time.

Not that she was looking at Trevor like *that*. Of course she wasn't!

She was just noticing the changes in him. The Trevor of two years ago had been impeccably groomed, even on the worst of days, keeping up that illusion that he wasn't falling apart as an act of love for Caitlyn. Trying to make everything easier for her.

Now Trevor's hair, a shade darker than the darkest of chocolates, was too long, the curls gloriously thick and entirely uncombed. Amongst those curls, a wild rooster tail had separated itself and was sticking straight up on the back of the crown of his head. She told herself it was only because she cared about him—the widower of her best friend—that she felt a sudden desire to smooth it down with her fingers.

Black stubble roughened the planes of high cheeks and the perfect cleft of his chin. It made him look roguish, not at all like the ultra-successful businessman he was.

Letter or no letter, Jacey was confused. She probably should not have come. He didn't want her here; that much was obvious.

Well, too bad. She didn't want to be here, either. It all felt too rife with complications, not the least of them being that she found his bristling presence awkwardly attractive.

And if it wasn't for the look in those deep brown eyes—so filled with pain, so hopeless, so empty—she might have backed out; she might have silently told Caitlyn, *I tried.*

But she knew she hadn't yet, not really, so instead of leaving, Jacey took a deep breath and folded her arms over her chest in what she hoped was a stance that portrayed firmness. Someone who did not back down.

Which was kind of laughable, but he didn't have to know that.

"Go put on a shirt," she told him. "You look like one of those guys on those calendars."

He obviously was not accustomed—at all—to being told what to do, particularly by an unexpected and uninvited visitor to his own house. Well, she was not accustomed to telling people what to do, but she was here now.

Still, Trevor's features took on an obstinate look—lowered brows, mouth set in an even firmer line. It could intimidate her, if she let it.

"What calendars?"

His bafflement seemed genuine.

She sighed. "You know. The chest-bared fireman holding the Dalmatian puppy? With the funds from sales going to the Burn Unit at the local hospital?"

He was looking at her way too closely and with faint derision as if he *knew* all about her secret stash of the kind of calendars that made a normally perfectly rational woman feel as if she might melt with longing.

"Look," Trevor said, and moved toward the door as if he intended to hold it open for her. "I know you think you're doing a good thing, and that we can prop each other up for this second anniversary. But you're mistaken. A phone call, like last year, would have sufficed."

There was no point reminding him, again, that he hadn't been answering his phone.

"I'm sorry you came all this way for nothing. I don't want to be with anybody."

And there was Jacey's excuse for the perfect exit.

CHAPTER TWO

THE EXPRESSION ON Trevor's face was steely and immovable. Despite having come a long way, Jacey felt it would be so much easier to waltz back out that door than to stay.

She could get Trevor to call her a cab, go back to the airport, grab something to eat—she realized she was starving, the subliminal message of all those pizza boxes?—and be back in her pajamas on her lovely new sofa by bedtime.

It was really what she did best—retreated, instead of standing her ground.

Except, of course, there was the letter. And her sense of duty to Caitlyn.

The easy thing was not, unfortunately, always the right thing. Was that a quote directly from her father?

Jacey had never been able to do the right thing by him, not even as motivated as she was by her need for his approval.

She shook that off.

"I don't really want to be with anyone, either," Jacey told him, forcing her tone to be brave. "I'm quite capable—as are you—of nursing the pain of my loss, and my bewilderment at the cruel caprice of life, all by myself."

He raised a surprised eyebrow at her agreement with him, and his hand found the doorknob and turned it.

But instead of moving toward it, as tempting as that was, Jacey went farther into this cave, slid a pizza box off the turquoise couch and sank warily onto the seat, avoiding what might have been a grease stain. The aroma was intriguing and not at all repulsive, as she would have expected it to be. Old pizza mingled with pure man.

"It's not that simple," she said, and channeled some assertiveness—probably Caitlyn's because Jacey didn't usually have any. "Go put on a shirt and then we'll talk."

Trevor looked surprised at her tone, but after a moment's consideration, left the room. That should have given Jacey plenty of time to compose herself for his return. Instead, she got up restlessly and went and opened the heavy front curtains. Light, made more brilliant by the mounds of undisturbed snow it reflected off, poured through the windows.

The view was stunning: the lake and the ice sculptures, and beyond that the swell and roll of the snowy foothills bordered by the majestic peaks of the Rocky Mountains. On a sunny day like this, the mountains looked deceptively close, as if a good brisk walk would take you there in an hour or so. On her first visit to Calgary after Caitlyn had become engaged to Trevor and moved there, Jacey had actually suggested a walk to those mountains might make a refreshing start to the day!

She had been shocked to discover that, in fact, those looming peaks were over an hour's drive away. It would take days to walk to them.

Though Jacey knew she shouldn't be so presumptuous and should leave Trevor to his obvious preference of darkness, she could not resist going and opening the back shutters, as well.

The yard was not quite as magazine-photoshoot worthy as it had been the summer the housewarming had been held there.

The pool was covered with snow, the rocky waterfall at one end of it shut off. The hot tub looked as if it had been drained of water. The outdoor kitchen was covered, and the area under the pagoda was empty of the deep, comfy yard furniture that had been there in the past.

Still, she could remember the laughter and how carefree they had all been as that summer day had melted into night. It felt as if it had been a long time since she had either laughed or been carefree.

"What have you done?"

The growl behind her made her whirl.

Trevor had been roguish before. Now, possibly because of the better light, he looked even more fabulous his hair even curlier, damp from the shower he'd obviously just taken, and his face freshly shaved. Sadly, the shirt he now wore did nothing to obliterate the memory of how he had looked shirtless. A pair of worn jeans clung to the muscles of his thighs and an aroma, clean and tingling, swept into the room with him.

She didn't like this *awareness* of him. Of course, she was aware he was attractive—how could any woman not be aware of that?—but her awareness had always been in the hands-off kind of way reserved for your best friend's husband.

And it would stay that way!

It would be easy to react to his disapproval and close the shutters again, but she didn't. Instead, Jacey lifted her chin. "I let some sun in. It's amazing out there and the views are too beautiful to be missed."

"It hurts my eyes," he said, shading his eyes dramatically.

"There's no need to act as if you're a vampire who can be slayed by light."

"I like it dark in here."

"That is obvious."

He looked around, and his mouth turned downward in an aggravated line at how the light illuminated the mess. "It makes it easier to ignore dust. And other, er, debris. It's also better for the television screens."

Okay, so she had probably overstepped herself opening the drapes.

Still, that explanation for the darkness he was living in told her far more than he had intended.

This was why Caitlyn had sent her. This man—Caitlyn's beloved husband—was, even after two years, behaving like a wounded bear, blocking out everything from his life, even the sun. Distracting himself from his pain.

One thing Jacey needed to remember: wounded bears were extremely dangerous. Actually, there were probably two things she needed to remember: wounded bears were extremely dangerous, and she was the least likely person to ever confront one.

"Tell me why you're here," he said, his voice gravelly with menace and pain.

Since he wasn't going to invite her, Jacey gathered her courage and went past him, back into the living room, and took up her seat on the sofa. He followed her, threw himself into one of the pink chairs opposite her, hooked one long leg over the arm of it and gave her a look that was impatient at best and irritated at worst. It was hard to ignore the fact that his masculinity was in no way threatened by the color of the chair.

"Please don't keep me in suspense. Why are you here?"

"Caitlyn wrote me a letter," she said quietly.

The grim lines around his mouth deepened. His brows lowered ferociously as he bit out a few words. "Where Caitlyn is, you don't write letters."

"Believe me, it was an unexpected surprise. I just got it a few days ago. She must have left instructions with a lawyer. To time it for…you know."

Oh, he knew. She saw the shock—and hurt—register in his face.

"She wrote *you* a letter," he said flatly.

"I think she wrote it to me because if she wrote it to you, what are the chances you would be sitting in Toronto on my sofa right now?"

Jacey suddenly wondered if Trevor would like her sofa, which was absolute madness. But of course, the whole mission was absolute madness.

Thanks, Caitlyn.

"How did you react to the pink chairs?" Jacey heard herself asking. "When they first came home?"

Trevor looked bewildered, as well he should, by the unexpected change of subject. It was absurd how badly she, fresh from a relationship where she had never bought a single piece of furniture she liked for fear of disapproval, needed to know.

He looked at the arm of the chair his leg was draped over. Something in his expression softened.

"I hated them," he said, gruffly. "I hated these chairs so much. But I looked at her face when she was showing them to me, and she was just glowing with excitement. She wanted so badly for me to like them. And then it was weird. I just did like them. Not pretending or anything. I just liked them because of what they did to her."

Some emotion clawed horribly at Jacey's throat, his statement making her painfully aware of the deficiencies in her own marriage. This is what she had missed.

Love—wanting the other person's happiness more than your own—trumping the color of furniture.

Trevor looked annoyed with himself then, as if he had revealed a state secret.

"Okay," he said, rolling his shoulders, shaking it off. "So Caitlyn wrote you a letter. Why?"

Jacey took a deep breath. "The letter said she doesn't want us—you and me—to be sitting around moping our lives away."

He winced and looked away.

"She knew us, Trevor," Jacey said quietly, trying to convey the love she had felt in that letter—and had just seen again in the story of the pink chairs. That story made her feel more committed to this rescue than she had been at any moment since she had opened the package.

"She knew we'd just stop living."

"I'm living," he said, but Jacey was heartbroken by the regret she heard in his voice, as if he didn't really care to be alive at all.

"I don't think she meant just going through the motions of living," Jacey said carefully. "I think she guessed we'd be living without joy. Without having fun."

"I'm having fun. Three television sets and a steady diet of pizza. Are you kidding me? I can watch three separate sporting events at once. Livin' the dream here." His tone was flat and he squinted at her, daring her to argue.

"What I'm trying to say," Jacey said, weighing her words even more carefully, "is that Caitlyn knew that, left to our own devices, both of us would just sink into a mess of morass, and without a little push we might just stay there."

"That's ridiculous," Trevor said, but he slid a look around the mess his house was in, now harshly illuminated by the light pouring in the windows. The realization crossed his face that morass probably described his circumstances just about perfectly.

"Anyway," he said, "what does she want us to do? It's been two years and I still don't know how to move on. If I knew how to do that, wouldn't I have done it already?"

His pain was so intense, just as his love for Caitlyn had been.

"Why don't you look at what she sent me?" Jacey suggested.

She got up, deposited the letter on his lap and went and sat back down on the couch, facing him. She watched Trevor's face as he unfolded the piece of paper.

There was unguarded softness as he recognized the handwriting, followed by growing hardness. Once done, he set the letter down and ran a hand through the silk of his still-wet hair. It made that rooster tail pop up. He pulled in a deep breath and then fixed Jacey with a look.

"She knew we might be sad, and get stuck there," Jacey told him, then finished softly, "She just wants us to be okay."

"Well, that's not possible," he said. "To be *okay*."

She passed him the second envelope. "I don't think we need to look at it as moving on," she suggested softly, "so much as somehow rediscovering that joy for life she gave us. That she gave everything she did."

Trevor gave her a dark, pained look, then let the contents of the envelope spill out onto his lap. He filtered through them, picking up one item, glancing at it and casting it away to go on to the next. The entire time his expression darkened.

"No," he finally said.

Really, it was exactly what she had expected. Hadn't that been her initial reaction, as well?

"Okay," Jacey said, mostly relieved, though maybe a teeny-tiny bit disappointed. Like 99 percent to 1 percent.

"A ski excursion?" Trevor snorted derisively. "Moonbeam Peaks for three days? Not even maybe."

"Okay," she said again, conciliatorily.

"Caitlyn and I met on a ski hill."

"I know," Jacey said, and then went on, despite the fierce expression on Trevor's face. "I remember her telling me the worst possible thing had happened. That she'd fallen for a ski bum."

She was rewarded when the most reluctant smile tugged at the firm line of his lips.

"Our first fight," Trevor remembered, "was when she found out I wasn't a ski bum. Imagine that. Angry because I was a gainfully employed engineer."

"That's a bit of an understatement. You weren't just a gainfully employed engineer. You were some kind of fabulously well-known—not to mention rich—tycoon."

"Now, that's a bit of an overstatement. I'd made a name for myself. I am *not*, by any stretch of the imagination, a tycoon."

"Do you prefer *billionaire*?" she asked sweetly.

He scowled at her but made no denial.

"Anyway, Caitlyn wasn't angry with you because you were fabulously rich and famous. She was angry because you lied to her."

He was silent for a moment. "Did you discuss it?"

"Of course!"

He mulled that over, then sighed.

"It was after that fight that I knew I was going to marry her," he said, his tone pensive. "Because she loved me *before* she knew. It was just such a novelty being liked for who I was, not for what I had. I did play the broke ski bum for far too long. But I convinced her to forgive me."

"You did," Jacey said.

"I don't think I can ski. Ever again. Why would she even ask that of me?"

"She knew your greatest joy was on the slopes."

"My greatest joy was her, Jacey."

Jacey tried to hold it together. She really did. But today marked two years since she had lost her best friend. Plus, his words were like a sword that pierced her own sense of failure and disillusionment over the dissolution of her marriage.

To be *that*. Someone's greatest joy.

She was so glad Caitlyn had experienced it. And so, so sad that her best friend and Trevor had not had the happy ending they so richly deserved.

Her lip trembled. She could feel her eyes stinging and her throat aching.

She glanced at Trevor. He looked terrified that she was going to start crying.

Do not cry, she ordered herself. *Do not.*

He swore under his breath. He closed his eyes. He folded his hands over his belly. He opened one eye and slid her a pleading look before closing it again.

"Please don't," he whispered.

"I'm trying not to."

"Good."

She bit down hard on the inside of her cheek and swallowed twice. Thankfully, it worked.

"I'm okay now," she said, her voice only a tiny bit wobbly.

"I'm not going to go spend three days at Moonbeam Peaks," he repeated with careful patience, but steely resolve.

Moonbeam Peaks was a very famous ski village just outside the Rocky Mountain township of Banff, a town at the very entrance to those Rocky Mountains they could see out his front window.

He opened his eyes and glanced at the cards and papers and tickets that had spilled out of the envelope onto his lap.

He picked up one and glared at it. He waved a voucher at her. "I'm especially not going tomorrow. I have a life."

His life—the televisions and game stations laid out in front of them—seemed to mock that statement, a fact of which he seemed aware since he fixed her with a defensive glare.

"I'm not going tomorrow, either," Jacey decided, relieved. "I have a life, too."

CHAPTER THREE

JACEY CONSIDERED THAT. *I have a life, too.* It was almost as bad a lie as Trevor telling Caitlyn he was a ski bum.

Because right now her life consisted of a failed marriage.

And a failed career.

Her life to-do list included getting an application form that could lead her to a bright new career as a checkout cashier at Grab-n-Go. She'd probably make more money.

But she certainly wasn't going to get into all that with Trevor Cooper, billionaire extraordinaire!

And there was absolutely no reason to admit she actually had cleared her "life" schedule—and bought new pajamas—to do exactly as Caitlyn had suspected she would do: wallow in the pit of her despair in the days leading up to, and following, the tragic anniversary.

"I'm not going tomorrow or any other day," Trevor said as if she might have felt he had left himself open to negotiation. "Geez. Two years are up. Did she think there's a magical line on the calendar? One day you feel this way. The next you don't. Let's go skiing."

"I know it's crazy. I knew from the moment I opened the envelope how crazy it was. I mean, I don't even know how to ski," Jacey agreed.

Still, hadn't part of her leaned, just a little bit, toward

Caitlyn's plan? Because it was insane in that delightful Caitlyn way that was the antithesis of the Jacey way. Caitlyn's way was spontaneity, unexpected adventures, pure delight for life.

In her careful world, Jacey missed her friend's influence so much.

It occurred to her that getting on that airplane today had been the first spontaneous thing she had done since Caitlyn had died. Unless the purchase of the love seat counted.

But she would have to concede defeat. Her efforts would have to be good enough. Trevor had read the letter; he'd looked at the trip and activities that Caitlyn had planned, and he'd said *no*.

Caitlyn, of all people, should have known Jacey was not the best person for this job. Convincing Trevor to do something he didn't want to do would require someone more assertive than Jacey knew herself to be. Maybe even pushy.

The silence stretched between them. He broke it.

"Why did you come all this way if you didn't want to go? You must have known I wouldn't go. You could have just called."

"Yes, you've already suggested that. You're not answering your phone," she reminded him.

"Oh, yeah," he said, "there is that."

"The airline ticket, Toronto to Calgary, was in the packet, in my name, with this date on it. I tried to do what I thought she wanted done."

Why *had* she come all this way when she had suspected, from the moment she had looked at the contents of that envelope, that it was pretty much mission impossible? She was not known for being impulsive! She was known for being careful, measured. Maybe even hesitant. No, definitely hesitant.

"I had to," Jacey admitted, puzzling through it as she spoke. "I had to bring her message. I had to know I had done everything I could do to deliver it, to do what she wanted me to do and exactly the way she wanted me to do it."

He grunted as if he got it. Just a little bit. It was a tiny encouragement, but it did help her muster her bravery.

"It *was* her dying wish," Jacey ventured, after a while.

"I think she had to make that wish *before* she died in order to plan it," he said. His voice was like ice, and yet right underneath that, Jacey could hear a veritable mountain of pain.

"I guess *technically* it would have been made before she died," Jacey said, carefully. "She would have had to contact lawyers, tell them what she wanted and when. I'm assuming they looked after the details."

Trevor suddenly fixed her with a look.

"What does your husband think of all this?"

Trevor noticed Jacey was suddenly looking everywhere but at him. There were lots of things for her to look at. Was that a pair of his underwear on the floor? Her eyes skittered past that and she pretended sudden interest in the golf game unfolding on screen number three.

He reached for the remote and shut off all three televisions.

"I'm sorry," he said. "His name escapes me."

"Bruce," she squeaked.

"You're not together, are you?" he asked her softly.

She hesitated, then tilted her chin and held up her empty ring finger. "Divorced," she said. "Finally."

He was not the least bit fooled by her attempt at a cavalier tone. If ever a girl wasn't the *I'm happily divorced* type it was her.

Of course, if ever a man wasn't the *I'm a widower* type it was him. And yet, here he was. Life was full of nasty surprises. Why did that continue to surprise him?

"I'm sorry," Trevor said. The thing was he *really* was.

Jacey lifted a shoulder. While he had showered and dressed, she'd lost the jacket, and he noticed how painfully thin she was. She was dressed practically, for travel, in wrinkle-free dark trousers and a plain white button-up shirt.

This is what he remembered about her, with deep gratitude. That she was practical. Jacey was that quiet force in the background making things happen.

"Wow," he said, "tough couple of years."

It occurred to him, just on the periphery of his being, that he *cared* about her suffering. It was a first. Caring about anything other than his own pain. He was not sure he welcomed it.

"What happened?" he asked. He remembered Jacey's wedding, maybe a year after his and Caitlyn's. Caitlyn had been in Jacey's bridal party, just as Jacey had been in hers.

It had been a small, budget-friendly event. Jacey, who seemed to cultivate an air of the unremarkable, he recalled now, had been the most remarkable thing about that day: her then long, blond hair piled up on her head and threaded with ribbons; her features expertly made up to show how delicate and perfect they were.

He recalled her eyes, huge and green, brimming with joy and hope for the future. It felt like a knife jab remembering those days when they had all been so filled with optimism. They hadn't been particularly young and yet, looking back, it seemed they had been very young. Hopelessly naive.

Planning their house purchases and vacations and career successes—and children, especially children—as if they truly believed nothing bad could ever happen to them.

Jacey hesitated. "Obviously, my relationship with Bruce had a few cracks in it. When pressure was applied…it went *kaboom*."

She flung out her hands with the *kaboom*, signaling a world being blown to smithereens.

"What pressure?" Trevor asked.

She was silent.

"Tell me," Trevor said. Why did he feel like he needed to know so badly what, beyond death, shattered dreams? It felt as if he wanted to know so that he could build the bastions of disillusionment even higher around himself.

"When Caitlyn got sick, I had to come here for her. Bruce didn't get it. We'd just bought a house." She made a strangled sound that might have been an attempt at a laugh. "Probably one we couldn't really afford. We needed both our incomes to make the payment."

Trevor felt stunned to learn of the sacrifice Jacey had made. In all the time she had spent with them leading up to Caitlyn's death, she had never said a single word about it.

"Why wouldn't you tell me that?" he asked sharply. "I could have asked my mom to come more. Or Caitlyn's."

"Oh, Trevor," she said softly, and with faint reprimand that reminded him how hard this had been on the two mothers, his and Caitlyn's, both of them shattered and frail.

"I would have helped you with your payments," he

snapped, with more irritation than he intended. "It's the least I could have done."

She gave him the kind of sad look he remembered sometimes Caitlyn would give him. It meant: *You're not as smart as you think you are.*

"My father used to say that any kind of problem that could be solved with money wasn't really a problem," she told him softly.

Somewhere in the back of his mind, he recalled Caitlyn telling him Jacey had been raised by a single dad. There had been something else his wife had said about the relationship, but he couldn't remember what it was. Was it that they'd been poor? It sounded like the kind of statement someone without money made.

Still, regardless of the motivation for the statement, there was an undeniable truth to it and one he was well aware of. Caitlyn's death being a case in point. All the money in the world could not save her, had left him reeling in the truth that in a world where money was generally regarded as power, a man could still be powerless.

"You never said anything," Trevor said, appalled. What would he have done if he knew she was going to lose her husband and her home to be there with them?

She smiled shakily, her eyes looking huge and suspiciously damp. Was he going to have to beg her not to cry again?

"There was no way I would say anything. Add to your and Caitlyn's burdens?"

"I could have given you the money," he said stubbornly.

"But could you have given me a man that understood the importance of loyalty, the honor of being there for a friend, the absolute grace of serving with love?"

Trevor saw, then, exactly who Jacey was. He was

shaken, not just by the truth he saw in her, but in the truth that was revealed about himself.

It was not a comfortable truth.

"I think maybe Caitlyn knew your marriage was in trouble," Trevor said slowly.

"I hope she didn't. I tried not to let on."

But his wife had become almost spookily intuitive in those last months and especially in the final weeks of her life. He remembered the worried look on her face after Jacey would come in from a phone call with Bruce, the way her eyes followed her friend, soft with sympathy. Even dying, Caitlyn was able to put her own difficulties aside and *see*.

Caitlyn had known what Jacey was giving up for her. No, for *them*.

Trevor was not sure how he would have gotten through those final days without Jacey in the background. Making sure he ate. Giving him clean clothes. Being a calm presence in a chaotic, constantly unfolding situation.

Jacey had been there, loving Caitlyn, when he needed to grab a few hours of sleep, or walk away from the intensity of it all, just for a few minutes or hours.

Jacey had been there, after, for all the difficult phone calls and the hard arrangements.

She had even protected his mother, Jane, and his mother-in-law, Mary, sending them away when she saw it was too much for them, that they were being overwhelmed.

He might not have realized at the time just how much they needed protecting, but a few months ago both had arrived and quietly cleaned his house and cleared away Caitlyn's clothing and personal items. Thinking it would help him.

It had nearly killed them both.

Watching her stuff being boxed up had nearly had the same effect on him.

Trevor saw, suddenly, that Caitlyn's last wish wasn't for him.

It was a way of trying to thank the friend who had given up everything for her. For them. What had Caitlyn said about Jacey?

That she had no idea how mighty she was.

But hadn't he seen her bravery? Hadn't he seen her mightiness on a daily basis? Jacey, who had even protected the two mothers from so much of the burden, who had taken all of it on her slender shoulders.

And even if the last wish wasn't for him, the last message was.

Trevor, be a better man.

He let the feeling of shame come. His defensiveness, his pain, had allowed him to be rude to Jacey, to not welcome her in the way she deserved to be welcomed. So what if today was a hard day?

Be a better man.

He saw he had missed his opportunity to beg her not to cry. She was biting down hard on the plumpness of her lower lip, but a single tear slipped from her eye and slid down her cheek. She wiped it away hastily. But it was followed by another. And then another.

Be a better man.

Trevor got up from his chair. He went and sat beside her. Awkwardly, he took her hand. It was warm and soft in his. She gripped him as if he had thrown her a lifeline. He was acutely aware of how, for two whole years, he had avoided human contact, fraught as it was with the potential for pain.

"I'm sorry," he said again, his voice rough with his own held-in emotions.

Unfortunately, it made the tears come harder and faster. She made a little hiccupping noise. And then, still with her hand gripping his, she turned her face into his chest and just sobbed.

"Two years without her," she whispered. "The world feels so different now. I miss her so much."

It was the way he wanted to sob. The way he had wanted to every single day since he had kissed Caitlyn goodbye for the very last time.

"It's okay," he said awkwardly, patting her back, his clumsiness making him aware he was out of practice at these rituals of human connection. "There, there, it's okay."

It wasn't really. As Jacey's scent, clean and lemony, tickled his nostrils, and her tears pooled into a warm puddle on his chest, he knew that. He knew it never would be okay again.

But he also knew, in the name of being the man his wife had always believed he was, he was going to be going to Moonbeam Peaks for the next few days.

"I can't believe you've never skied," he said to her, putting Jacey away from him, taking his hand from hers and holding her shoulders in what? A nice, brotherly gesture of support?

"You can live without having skied," she said, trying to smile through the tears.

"Not once you've done it, you can't." With someone else, he might have added, jokingly, *like an orgasm*, but he bit his tongue before he said that to Jacey.

He considered the jokingly part. How long since he had joked around?

And just a minute ago he had said he would never ski again. Whether he wanted it to or not, his life seemed to already be changing in subtle ways now that Jacey was here, and Caitlyn's final wish had been revealed.

And yet, with that realization he felt, not defeat, but a sudden unexpected swoop of anticipation at the thought of the slopes, the skis, the snow, introducing someone else to that magical world.

Maybe those slopes would even reveal Jacey's mightiness to her.

For an astounding moment Trevor felt exactly what he had vowed he would never feel again.

Alive.

It was a reminder that his wife's well-meaning wish for her friend—and for him—was putting him on very dangerous ground.

He was aware Caitlyn might have approved of the uneasy feelings her last request was causing in him.

Trevor got up abruptly and moved away from Jacey, trying to clear his head. It was hard to do with her tears still wetting the front of his shirt. He was extraordinarily annoyed with himself. For *feeling.* For giving in.

For that speck of happy anticipation he had felt when he'd given in.

Jacey's suitcase was still in the middle of the floor. It was wildly neon, with a pattern in pinks and greens, as if it was revealing a secret personality that was not in keeping with the Jacey he knew: responsible, reliable, calm, brimming with common sense, low-key.

The suitcase said she was mighty. Bold.

The fact that she had committed to coming across the country on the basis of a letter might also be a hint that there were facets of her he was unaware of. That she hid, even from herself.

"I bought it to come," she said as if she needed to defend herself against the bright choice of the suitcase. "I wanted one that I could pick out easily at the luggage carousel."

"Okay," he said, running a hand through his hair. "Let's figure this thing out. Do you have what you need for a few days in the mountains?"

CHAPTER FOUR

"OH, ABSOLUTELY," JACEY SAID.

Trevor's doubt must have shown in his face.

"Three days, three books."

"For a ski vacation?"

"I figured the ski part of the package was for you. I was thinking a comfy chair by a fireplace and good books for me. But I packed mittens! You know, in case I venture outside."

Mittens, Trevor thought incredulously. Who went to a ski resort and *maybe ventured* outside? Whether Jacey knew it or not, she needed to ski. He saw, suddenly, what a perfect gift this had been to her from her friend.

And being there with her, lending his expertise, was what he was agreeing to take on: an essential part of the being-a-better-man equation.

"Do you have a different coat?" he asked. "A different one from the one you were wearing when you arrived at my door?" *When you turned my whole world upside down in the space of seconds?*

"Well, no, I thought with a sweater I could make do with the one I have. I packed two sweaters," she said brightly.

It was apparent Jacey was hopelessly unprepared for

a mountain excursion, even of the most civilized variety, Trevor thought. He began a mental list: *ski jacket.*

"I guess ski pants are out of the question?" he asked her.

"Ski pants? I told you I won't need those for sipping hot chocolate in the lounge while *you* ski. That's what Caitlyn's wish was. For you to ski."

Trevor, however, was pretty certain his wife's wish was for him to focus on Jacey's enjoyment. And if she had never skied, he was going to make sure she did that.

"Are you familiar at all with Moonbeam?" he asked.

"No."

"Ah."

"Why do you say it like that?"

"There's no road up to the village. There's only one way to arrive at the resort and that's by gondola. There are a few shops at the ski village, but it's probably a good idea to arrive with at least the basics."

"Gondola," she repeated, her eyes wide. She giggled nervously. "I take it you don't mean the nice kind. Like in Italy."

"Italy?"

"Venice? Boats? Man standing? Singing?"

What was she talking about?

She sang a few bars, "Figaro, Figaro."

"Geez, no, not that kind. Obviously. The cable car type. But they're really nice. Completely enclosed from the weather. Comfy. Spectacular views."

"To be honest, I've never been very good at heights."

"It's an experience you really can't miss," he said.

"Like skiing?" she asked.

And orgasms. Where was that coming from? It had to stop. You didn't have thoughts like that anywhere in the vicinity of your wife's best friend. There were unwritten rules about these things.

"It seems maybe I've missed a few of life's essential experiences." Her tone was chipper, but she looked worried.

Step one to uncovering her bold and mighty side, he thought, would be getting her on the gondola. Since the very idea had made her go quite pale, even while she was trying to joke about Venice gondolas, Trevor thought this might be a bigger challenge than his wife had anticipated.

"You can do it," he assured her.

"I guess I have to try," she said uncertainly.

"There will be a rental shop up there for skis," he said, thinking out loud, moving on to try to take her mind off her gondola trepidation.

"I haven't exactly committed to the skiing idea! I'll need to recuperate from the gondola."

"You could try boarding. Whatever you prefer." He read her blank expression. She really wasn't even aware there was a difference between skiing and snowboarding.

"There will be lots to occupy me while you ski."

It occurred to him this excursion was going to be a huge undertaking, probably beginning with convincing her to get on the gondola and then to use the slopes.

"Look," he said, "I'll bring your suitcase upstairs. You might as well plan on staying here tonight and we'll leave first thing in the morning."

It felt familiar to be making a plan.

Taking charge.

Not good, exactly, but edging toward normal.

"You can go through your suitcase and separate anything you think might be useful for a ski holiday—"

"A reading-in-front-of-the-fire holiday," she corrected him. "After surviving a ride in a gondola."

"Millions of other people have survived the gondola. You'll be fine. Then let's assume," he said, and heard the dryness in his own voice, "that you might put your nose outside once in three days."

She beamed at him. "I brought mittens, just to address that very possibility!"

"Well, yippee. Of course, that's assuming they're the right kind."

"The right kind? Of mittens?"

"You don't want anything that absorbs moisture, so cute woolies are out."

He could tell from the disgruntled look on her face exactly the kind of mittens that were tucked inside that suitcase.

"That's if you're planning on getting wet!"

He sighed. "Can we assume you might throw a snowball? Participate in some *snowy* activity at a *mountain resort*?"

"I'm not planning on it," she said with a hint of stubbornness.

"Here's something you and I both know," he told her, softly, sternly. "Life doesn't always go according to plan. Just lay out your stuff for me and I'll decide if it really is useful or not. Meanwhile, I'll go through that envelope and see exactly what Caitlyn had in mind for the next few days so we can be properly prepared."

To cut off any further argument from her, he hauled her suitcase upstairs and put her in the guest room. She was already familiar with it, so he wouldn't need to tell her where anything was.

She followed him up and shut the door behind her with just a little more snap than might have been strictly necessary.

He went back downstairs and heard the shower turn

on as he gathered all the items from the envelope Jacey had brought and took them to his kitchen island.

There was a woman showering in his house. It had been a long, long time since life had surprised him like this, but since the moment Jacey had arrived an element of the unpredictable had shivered in the air.

Focus, he ordered himself. He swept the existing clutter down to one end of the island, and then began to organize the items from the envelope Caitlyn had sent.

Trevor realized, unwanted surprises aside, he was, for the first time in two years, a man with a mission.

That mission, Trevor told himself, was to put the needs of another human being ahead of his own. To take care of Jacey. To help her break out from under the shadow of grief and give her a few moments of fun.

Real fun. Not sitting in front of the fireplace with a book.

His mission was to help her discover her mightiness.

He was suddenly aware he had not offered her a single thing to eat or drink after her long trip. Mightiness probably needed nourishment!

"Are you hungry?" he called up to her when he heard the shower turn off.

"Famished," she called back.

"Why don't I order something? Do you have any preferences?"

"I seem to have a sudden craving for pizza."

He actually laughed. He heard it, rusty in his throat. "A girl after my own heart," he said.

And then wondered if it was okay to say that.

This was a brand-new world, with brand-new rules, that he was navigating with his wife's best friend. It felt oddly complicated.

He called for a pizza and then focused intently on the

contents of that envelope, sorting them into piles that brought order, his favorite thing, not that you would know it right now from the state of his house.

Most of the items were in the form of vouchers.

Hotel accommodations for two nights.

Lesson reservations. For one person.

Ski passes, for two people, for three days. Caitlyn, apparently, was with him on this: Jacey was not to spend three days reading books in front of the fire.

His wife did not want her best friend to be alone this week, and he could dig deep inside himself to make sure that her wishes were carried out.

Jacey arrived downstairs just as he completed making an agenda and a list of basics they would need for her. He folded that and put it in his pocket. He could cross off items if she had brought anything that was appropriate.

Which he highly doubted.

He slid her a look. Considering how hard she seemed to work at appearing unremarkable, he could see she was lovely, in that understated way of true beauty: no makeup, no fussing with her hair, or her wardrobe.

Her hair was spiky from being towel dried. A fragrance, soapy and clean, wafted off her and she had changed into yoga pants and a dark T-shirt.

Her eyes looked huge—possibly because she was so thin. Still, it was her eyes that gave him a glimpse of the real her: that strong spirit, rooted in an old-fashioned ability to be compassionate, to serve, to love deeply and unconditionally.

The mission, he reminded himself sternly, was straightforward. Three days of introducing Jacey to the joy of the mountains, and therefore, to herself.

Three days of being a better man.

It was completely doable.

The pizza arrived and she cleared a space at the dining table. Because she had spent time here, she knew where everything was and she went and got plates and cutlery and napkins. It had been a long time since he had eaten at this table or put out a plate. These were simple things, and yet, it felt again, as if *normal* was crowding at him, and he wasn't ready for it.

He could do it for three days.

He opened the lid of the pizza box and put a piece on her plate for her. They had done this so many times when Caitlyn was ill. Sat at this table, heart-weary and broken, eating takeout, talking in quiet voices about their day, what needed to be done next.

But oddly, sitting here with her again, those didn't feel like bad memories. It just felt right to have Jacey here, in a space that seemed to belong to both of them.

The next morning, predawn, Jacey squinted through the windshield of the SUV. She was terrified.

It was in such sharp contrast to how she had felt last night, back in that familiar bedroom, her tummy filled with pizza, a down comforter over her.

Trevor under the same roof.

She had felt content, somehow. Safe.

How quickly things could change! She tried to pick out elements of a landscape, but they were completely hidden behind a veil of darkness and heavily falling snow.

"This reminds me of a ride I was on once at an amusement park," she said as the white particles of snow caught and glittered in the narrow tunnel of the headlamps, swirled, smashed on the windshield and were swept away.

"Yeah," Trevor said, "it's kind of fun, isn't it?"

Fun? If this was his idea of fun, her plan to sit inside

reading for the next few days was looking like an exceedingly good one!

"That ride was extremely frightening, and so is this," she told him, grimly. "How could this happen? It was such a nice day yesterday."

"They have a saying in Alberta. If you don't like the weather, wait five minutes."

"But I did like the weather! It was gorgeous and sunny. Where did this storm come from?"

"These mountain climates are notoriously unpredictable." He cast her a look. "Are you really frightened?"

"Yes! It's my first experience with a whiteout."

"You have bad weather in Toronto. It's Canada!"

"We have the kind of bad weather in TO that makes you put on your *woolly* mittens, pull your hood over your forehead and wait for the bus *inside* the shelter. Not the kind where you could slide off a road, into the forest and be lost forever."

Did he snicker? Ever so slightly? She sent him a look. His face was impassive.

"Uh, we're not in the forest yet," he said with maddening calm. "Not even close. Rolling hills. Ranch country. The kind of place you can watch your dog run away for three hours. If we go off the road—and we aren't going to—we aren't going to disappear into a wilderness abyss."

"Quit trying to be funny. It's starting to get light out there, and I still can't see anything. It's a bona fide blizzard, isn't it?"

Her voice had a shrill note she would have controlled if she could have.

"I'm not sure I'd call it that." His voice was rich and calm, soothing, if she'd allow herself to be soothed. She considered allowing it.

"It's a bit of a winter squall," he clarified.

"What's the difference between a squall and a blizzard?" she demanded.

He cast her a look and smiled at her. He pushed a button on his dash and asked, "Hey, Jeeves, what's the difference between a squall and a blizzard?"

A robotic voice answered, "A squall is much more dangerous than a blizzard. They involve heavy bursts of snow that can result in whiteout conditions and falling temperatures that freeze road surfaces and create hazardous—"

He hastily shut off the voice.

"More dangerous than a blizzard," Jacey said woodenly.

"Hey!" Trevor said. "On the bright side, we have internet connection. See? We're not exactly heading off in a covered wagon across the uncharted wilderness."

"Just as I suspected," Jacey said, sadly, peering out into a storm that was not made any better for the fact daylight was trying to pierce the murky grayness of it. "The day has plenty of potential for catastrophe."

"As does life," he pointed out, quietly, but then with cheery determination added, "Let's keep it in perspective. It's not a tour of duty in some bug-infested hellhole where everyone is intent on killing you."

She remembered, vaguely, he'd done some time in the military before he had gone on to university, gotten a degree in engineering, become a very wealthy businessman and met Caitlyn. That would explain how damnably relaxed he was.

Yes, her own ability to ferret out catastrophe had been a part of her life ever since she had sat at a grand piano at thirteen, in front of a select audience, about to give her first concert.

She had completely frozen. Completely.

That sense of every day holding the potential for impending doom had taken another giant leap forward when her beautiful, young best friend—a woman with everything to live for—had been diagnosed with a terminal illness.

She suspected this was part of Caitlyn's motive in sending her on this excursion. She would have known that Jacey was going to do a full retreat to safety after losing her friend.

"I was born and raised in Calgary," Trevor told her.

Was his voice naturally soothing or was it deliberate? Either way, she could feel herself leaning into it.

"I've been driving to Banff National Park and the ski resorts there since a week after I got my driver's license. I've made this trip hundreds, maybe even thousands, of times."

"Hmph," she said in defiance of the part of her that wanted to lean in to the calm and strength she heard in his voice.

"You know what the most dangerous thing in the world is?" he asked her solemnly.

Oh, yeah. She knew that one.

CHAPTER FIVE

LOVE, JACEY THOUGHT. Love was the most dangerous thing in the world.

"Your bathroom," Trevor said, sagely.

That was annoying! She was thinking esoteric thoughts, and he was being aggravatingly earthbound. Still, there was a lesson in the difference between men and women, right there.

"Wow. That gives new meaning to *get your mind out of the toilet*," she noted, and then added, "Besides, that's ridiculous."

"It isn't. Slips and falls in bathrooms kill way more people annually than, say, airline crashes."

"I'm also terrified of flying."

"Somehow, I guessed," he said dryly.

"Damn. Who wants people being able to guess something like that?"

"You already told me you were scared of heights."

"Flying is a separate fear entirely." Sheesh. Just as she wanted to come off. *Timid*. But was there any hiding it? "And a legitimate one, I might add."

"Well, except for the bathroom thing."

"How would you know something like that?" Jacey, who wanted to be bold and wasn't, asked him grouchily. "That bathrooms kill more people than airline crashes?"

He nodded sagely at the dashboard. "Jeeves had made me an expert on all kinds of unlikely topics."

"Thanks, Jeeves. I'll probably never look at my bathroom in quite the same way again."

He flashed her a grin and, suddenly, there was that awareness of him again. He looked particularly attractive this morning, dressed casually in a navy blue sweater that showed off the impossible broadness of his shoulders and depth of his chest. He had on matching navy blue ski pants that hugged him in all the right places.

That crazy rooster tail was sticking up out of his chocolate curls, and her fingers itched to reach over and smooth it.

The heater was circulating warm air and his scent, and both pierced her fear like light pierced darkness. Her awareness of how attractive he was was distracting in the nicest way. Her awareness that love, not bathrooms, was the most dangerous thing in the world, felt more threatening than the raging storm.

That just felt *wrong.* To be thinking of Trevor and love in the same sentence. He was Caitlyn's.

Only, what did that mean *now*?

Stop it, Jacey told herself. If anything, Caitlyn's death and his suffering, and her own, just proved her point. Love, not bathrooms, *was* the most dangerous threat of all.

Still, what did it mean to her relationship with Trevor now that Caitlyn was gone? Did it have to mean anything? Did everything have to mean something? Did her whole life have to be a study in the seriousness of unintended consequences? Did she have to ferret out catastrophe because it had visited her in the past?

Of course not. She could consciously decide not to be

timid, couldn't she? Jacey was aware she needed to accept this gift in the spirit it had been given.

Was it not possible to just relax and enjoy the unexpected adventure? Even being caught in a storm with an extremely capable guy could be interpreted as an adventure instead of a harbinger of doom, couldn't it? What was it *other* people said?

Enjoy the moment.

With effort, she forced herself to breathe.

She had taken several yoga classes online, after Caitlyn had died, hoping to find moments not filled with angst, memories, pain, powerlessness. She had taken more after the failure of her marriage and more again after Johnny's horrible, unexpected audition result.

It *had* helped.

She closed her eyes. Deep breath. Through the nose. Out the mouth. She felt the breath move like a cool wave, up through her nostrils, and down her throat. She expelled it gently.

"Are you hyperventilating?" Trevor asked, worried.

"No! I'm practicing Ujjayi."

"Is that a martial art I'm unaware of? Should I brace myself for a karate chop to the throat?"

She refused to open her eyes. "It's a breathing technique. Yoga."

"Ah, yoga," he said. Was there the tiniest hint of amusement in his voice?

"I'm not likely to karate chop you in the throat while my life is in your most capable hands."

She opened her eyes. She looked at his most capable hands, relaxed on the steering wheel. His fingers were long and strong, his wrists square and masculine. There was that *awareness* again. Maybe even something more. A longing.

Not for him—of course not for him!—but for things masculine in her purple-pansy sofa world. She quickly shut her eyes again.

Still, as she breathed, Jacey became aware that while a storm raged outside, warm air blew gently on her. The lovely, masculine, reassuring scent of Trevor was in the air. The poignant notes of a classical guitar embraced them. After a while she remembered there was a coffee in the cup holder beside her.

She opened her eyes and reached for it and took a sip. Caffeine was probably not the best answer to rattled nerves, but it tasted unbelievably good.

To her surprise her fear melted away, replaced with a lovely, languid sense of calm. Of safety. Trevor was handling the conditions with such ease. She suspected it was his confidence, as much as the Ujjayi, that was making her feel like this. Almost catlike: calm and alert at the very same time.

She tried to remember the last time she had felt this way. Peaceful. Connected. Protected, somehow.

She realized she had known Caitlyn and Trevor years, and then lived with them for weeks, and that, really, beyond the fact he had loved her best friend intensely, and that Caitlyn had returned that love, she didn't know very much about him.

"What do engineers do?" she asked. "Caitlyn was always vague about what you did for a living."

He laughed. "There's a reason for that. There are probably twenty different kinds of engineers, only one of them being in any way what most people would consider interesting. I'm a mechanical engineer, which is far more boring than my romantic cousin, the structural engineer."

Well, Jacey thought, thank goodness he wasn't the *romantic* type of engineer.

"Caitlyn's eyes glazed over when I talked about work. In fact so do most people's."

"Perfect! A nice boring topic to keep my eyes off the deepening winter conditions unfolding around us."

He chuckled, considered, gave in. "Basically, I design or improve mechanical systems used for processing and manufacturing."

"You're right," she said with a happy sigh. "Exceedingly dull."

"Ever since I was a kid," Trevor confided, "I was obsessed with taking things apart and seeing how they worked. I was quite nerdy in my formative years."

She glanced at him, felt her mouth fall open—Trevor, nerdy?—and then snapped it closed again before he registered how incredulous the thought made her.

"My mother claimed I'd be the death of her," Trevor went on. "Every new item she brought into the house was taken apart and put back together. I once ramped up and *improved* her new food processor so badly it turned everything she put in it into powder. In two seconds."

Jacey laughed. It felt good to laugh with him. It was nice that he indulged her. In all the time she'd known him and Caitlyn as a couple, he had rarely talked about himself.

"My mother was unimpressed with my suggestion that powder could be *useful*. I was unable to reverse the changes so, to my delight, I inherited the food processor and experimented with pulverizing everything from wood blocks to my cousin's fashion doll."

She laughed again, not unaware of how nice it was to laugh while the storm raged outside the cozy capsule they were in. "I think you were the rotten kid in that movie about toys, weren't you?"

"I only did that to one toy. It was after she ratted me

out for letting the cat in my room. She was over visiting, and she kept chasing that poor cat, who despised her, as cats are known to do to people who want to force themselves upon them."

"The cat wasn't allowed in your room? Because of the food processor on steroids?"

"Nah, I had allergies. See? I told you I was a nerd more than a junior mad scientist. Anyway, my mother proved to be a bit of an investigator herself, because she sifted through that powder and determined doll demise.

"I had to save money from mowing lawns for a long time to replace both the doll and the food processor. Well worth it on the road to scientific investigation, though!"

Jacey was delighted at this unexpected insight into him, and his laughter joined hers.

Far from glazing over, Jacey found herself enjoying this. She liked the way his face looked as he remembered family memories. She had met his mom and dad at his and Caitlyn's wedding, and again at their housewarming.

His mom in particular had been in and out of the house a lot, in those horrible days of Caitlyn's illness.

Trevor came from the solid, good old-fashioned stuff families were made of.

Even though she wouldn't say she *knew* them, Trevor's folks were working-class people just bursting with pride at their son's accomplishments and joy at his happiness.

In sharp contrast, of course, to her own father.

Jacey felt an almost greedy enjoyment of glimpses into Trevor. She could picture him mowing lawns, and she could picture him with those dark curls awry, his tongue caught between his teeth, taking apart his mother's prized possessions, his glee at avenging himself with his cousin's doll.

"So how does one go from taking apart Mom's food

blender and pulverizing the annoying relative's toys to the heady world of the rich and famous?" she asked him, lightly.

"I'd love to tell you my path to good fortune was created by my skill, smarts and savvy, but no. It was blind luck. Like winning a lottery.

"I was called into a plant to troubleshoot a machine they constantly had trouble with. I redesigned a part for it. That single part revolutionized the way that machine operated. And there are millions of those machines around the world.

"I get a royalty every time one of my parts is sold. I'm always astonished when some engineering or business firm wants me to speak at their conference, or some magazine wants me on the cover."

Jacey found his humility endearing.

"Besides, being rich and famous didn't do me one iota of good when I set my sights on Caitlyn," he remembered. "After I came clean that I wasn't really a ski bum, I tried to apologize with an emerald bracelet. The expense suggested it came directly from the tomb of Cleopatra. She handed it back to me and told me that was way too easy. She expected time and energy and creativity be put into winning her, not money. Or baubles. That's what she called that bracelet. A bauble."

The air between them was suddenly saturated with that same feeling as when he had told her about his reaction to Caitlyn's choice of the pink chairs.

Love, the most dangerous thing of all, was in the air between them. They both let the silence go for a while and then he changed the subject.

"Tell me about this fear of flying," he said. "Amazing that you got on a plane to come. In fact, you came every time she asked. The wedding. The housewarming."

He didn't mention the last time Jacey had come.

"Oh, you know," she said. "They make drugs for that."

He laughed, as she had hoped he would. It occurred to her his laughter could very easily become an addiction, something a person wanted more and more and more of.

"Besides, it makes you a better person, facing fear. Even traversing icy roads that lead deep into the unknown could be seen as part of what makes life worth living."

"You know airplanes are safe, right?"

"Of course! You just told me. Safer than my bathroom."

"Well, statistically—"

"Never mind statistics!"

He raised an eyebrow at her. It was very Sean Connery being sexily surprised and amused. "You're talking to an engineer. Statistics are my life."

She lifted a shoulder.

He laughed again. She loved the sound, deep and rich, oblivious to the dangers that swirled around them outside this vehicle.

"Statistics only tell part of the story," she told him. "You can never know everything. Like, what if the pilot is hungover?"

"Airlines have very strict bottle to throttle rules."

"They do?"

"Yeah, a pilot can't fly within eight hours of having a drink. Many airlines have a twelve-hour rule."

"Okay, what if it's something more subtle? A fight with a friend? A sick child? A messy divorce?"

"Has anybody ever told you, you worry too much?"

"Oh. Constantly." It had been a flaw even before Caitlyn's death, before the end of her relationship, before

Johnny's colossal failure. "My catastrophe radar is constantly up and searching."

He glanced pointedly at the coffee in her hand. "You seem pretty relaxed right now. Is that laced with something?"

"Ha-ha, you ordered it from the drive-through window. If it's laced with something, that's on you. I'm not much of a drinker, anyway."

He nodded. "I can tell."

What did that mean? That she looked like a stick-in-the-mud? Didn't know how to let loose?

"If you were any kind of a drinker," he said, "I'm sure you would have turned to it a long time before now." His approval was subtle, but there nonetheless.

Oh! That was better than being thought a stick-in-the-mud: that she had handled the pressure of a friend dying without crutches.

How aware she was that it would be entirely too easy to follow her life pattern and twist herself into a pretzel for the prize of Trevor's approval.

"Besides," he said, sensing they were going somewhere maybe they didn't want to go, "I'd hate to arrive in Banff with a sloppy drunk music teacher under my care."

Despite the terrible conditions outside, there was something so soothing about the way Trevor handled the vehicle, the warmth and the music. Yesterday's traveling, the strain of the storm, a life unexpectedly fraught with emotion and surprises, caught up with her.

Jacey's head felt heavy. Her eyes closed. Twice, she managed to jerk herself awake, aware of the irony. She, who sniffed out the potential for catastrophe, who vibrated with apprehensive tension for what could go wrong next, was totally relaxed.

In the middle of a snowstorm. No, a squall. More dangerous than a blizzard.

Her head nodded again. She surrendered to the sensations.

Of being safe. Of being looked after.

CHAPTER SIX

JACEY WAS NOT sure how long she slept, but the slowing of the vehicle woke her up. In sleep her head had fallen sideways over the center console, until it was resting against his arm. She was appalled to find she had drooled on Trevor's sleeve!

"Where are we?" she asked, snapping her spine straight, blinking, disoriented.

She looked out the window. The snow was still falling extremely heavily. On either side of the vehicle were thick, shadowed stands of enormous evergreens.

Out the front windshield, through the veil of snow, she could see a series of adorable little rock cottages, with pitched roofs and Tudor-style slats on the steep gable ends.

"We're at the entrance to Banff National Park. These are the gatehouses."

Was she really awake?

"This looks like something out of a fairy tale," she said, awed. "It's like we're entering a magical kingdom."

He looked over at her.

"And indeed we are," he said, quietly.

Fairy tales, Trevor reminded himself, had happy endings, something he had lost faith in. Really, Jacey should have, too. Still, he could not harden himself to her wonder, or to his admiration that that quality had survived in her after the challenges of the past couple of years.

They stopped in the parking area just beyond the gatehouses after he had purchased his pass for the park.

She tumbled from the vehicle, her phone out, taking pictures of the gatehouses, tilting back her head to catch snow on her tongue, laughing. She put away her phone and picked up some snow. She made an inexpert snowball and tossed it at him. He dodged easily out of the way.

"You remind me of a puppy who has never seen snow before," he told her, but indulgently.

"Of course, we have snow in Toronto. But not like this! It's so…pristine. Even the air is different. Pure." She took a deep breath.

The mountains were, of course, gorgeous, but the conditions could also be deadly to the naive. Her mittens, the woolen kind, were still packed in her suitcase and she hadn't bothered to retrieve them before getting out of the vehicle.

Trevor felt a surge of responsibility for her.

No, it was more than responsibility. Protectiveness. He contemplated that uneasily.

"Come on," he said, "get back in the vehicle. That jacket isn't right for this weather. And you're going to freeze your hands."

Reluctantly, she obeyed, blowing on her fingertips.

In another half hour, they were on the main street of the world famous Township of Banff.

As it was known to do in these mountains, the weather shifted. The snow lightened and swirled and just as they exited the vehicle the clouds thinned to reveal the craggy magnificence of Cascade Mountain, which towered over Banff Avenue.

Even for him, cynic that he proclaimed himself to be, Trevor could see the early-morning light making an effort to pierce the clouds. Crystals of ice in the air looked like glitter. It was, indeed, like something out of a fairy tale.

But then the cloud thickened again, and the storm resumed unabated. The wind howled down off Cascade, and then the clouds enveloped it, making it invisible.

"Oh," Jacey said, taking it all in and hugging herself against the wind in her inadequate jacket. "It's amazing. The quintessential mountain village. Look at all the people."

It was true. The streets of the village were clogged with people in colorful parkas and various hats.

"You can feel it in the air," Jacey said, that wonder still strong in her.

He could definitely feel something in the air; he just wasn't sure what it was. Until she clarified.

"Happiness," she said, cocking her head as if she could *hear* it as well as see it. And you could hear it: in laughter; in breathless conversations; in the odd exuberant shout.

After all his time in darkness, it felt jarring and vaguely dangerous. As if he might catch it.

"Of course they're happy," he said gruffly. "It's snowing and they're skiers and boarders anticipating fresh powder on the slopes. Let's go get you some, er, mittens. I'm sure you can tell from making your one snowball that the mittens you brought aren't going to cut it."

"I'm afraid you're probably right. And I might take a break from the fireplace to win a snowball fight with you!"

He held open the door of a ski shop he was familiar with.

She stepped in, then looked around, wide-eyed. The shop had a woodsy cabin feel to it, including a fire in a hearth at one end, crossed snowshoes, antique skis and animal mounts hanging from walls that looked like weathered logs.

"Look! There they are!" She went over to a bin, overflowing with mittens, not unlike the ones she already had. Cute, but not particularly practical.

"Let's have a look at these gloves instead," he suggested, guiding her to a rack.

She joined him at the rack. She flipped over a pair of gloves and squinted at the price tag.

"It looks very expensive in here," she said nervously.

"In skiing, you kind of get what you pay for."

"But I'm not skiing," she reminded him. "I might throw a few snowballs. I'm not paying over a hundred dollars to throw snowballs, no matter how warm it keeps my hands. I'll suffer instead!"

He took a deep breath.

"That was Caitlyn's point, I think," he said, softly. "You've suffered enough."

Her mouth worked. She looked as if she might cry. Which, while terrible, he had to look at pragmatically.

She was sensitive right now. It was a good time to hit her with the truth.

"Caitlyn wanted you to go skiing. There are lift passes for both of us. And there's a lesson voucher for you."

"I don't have any of the stuff to go skiing," she said. "I don't even have skis."

"Well, skis are easy. We can rent those. The rest of this stuff we'll have to buy." He fished in his pocket and handed her a list.

She turned her attention to it, and her lips moved as she read: ski pants, jacket, gloves, goggles, toque, neck gator, long underwear, good socks.

The joy she had had at the gates and surveying the

main street disappeared. He could see she was trying not to panic.

"You knew I needed all this. You've made a list."

"Yes."

"Why did you wait until now to tell me?"

"Is it a big deal?"

"Yes!"

"Survival in the elements is not an easy thing."

"I didn't think this all the way through," she said. "I can't—"

She clamped her mouth shut, but he could see the turmoil in her face. She might as well have finished the sentence. *She couldn't afford it.*

"I'm buying," he said.

She headed for the door. "No. I can't. Oh, why did I come? I knew this was a dumb idea. What was I—"

"Now?" he asked, incredulously. He cut her off, maneuvering around her, blocking the door.

"Let me by."

"Now, after you've traveled three thousand miles and convinced me to go along with this? *Now* you decided to have second thoughts?"

"Actually," she said stubbornly, "I was having second thoughts as soon as you mentioned the gondola. But I'll do that. I'll do all the parts we don't need *lists* for. How's that sound?"

"Like I'm negotiating with a terrorist," he said dryly.

"We can go to the resort, without the skiing for me. That's the expensive part, right? Really, Trevor, I'm *happy* with a book."

In her comfort zone. Not taking any chances. Except for the gondola part, which was hardly a concession.

"Look," he said patiently, "the ski lift vouchers were in that package Caitlyn put together. It included a lesson for you. That's the expensive part. And it's all already been paid for. What do you want to do with those?"

He'd hit the right button. The pragmatic part of her didn't want to see all that money wasted. He pressed his advantage.

"It *was* Caitlyn's wish. You honored her by delivering it. You got me to go along when I didn't really want to. Jacey, we've come this far."

She looked flustered. She went over to a rack of jackets and turned over a sleeve of one, looking at the price tag. She went very pale.

"I can't accept this kind of gift. And I certainly can't afford it."

"Well, you can't go skiing in the jacket you have on."

She frowned. "I should have gone to the secondhand store before I came." Then she brightened. "We could find a secondhand store."

"We're not finding a secondhand store!"

"Snob."

"No, I'm being practical. I don't know where one is. And we don't know if they would have what you need in your size."

She contemplated that dubiously.

He took a deep breath. "Jacey, you lost your house and your marriage over us. This is the least I can do."

Her chin tilted up proudly. "I would never accept payment for what I did for you. Never. It wasn't really for you. At least, not just for you. Being there for Caitlyn was for me, too!"

"What is it with people like you?"

"People like me?"

"Yes, people like you," Trevor said, his voice patient but with a deliberately stern note inserted. "You can give endlessly but you can't ever accept anything back. Did you ever consider the fact that other people like to give, too? That it's as much a blessing to accept a gift as to give one?"

"No," she said stubbornly.

"Let someone do something for you," he said. "Let *me* do something for you."

"You don't *owe* me anything just because I came to be with you when my best friend needed me. You're insulting me."

"Maybe you're insulting me," he snapped back. It occurred to him they were having an argument.

And that he wasn't winning it. She was still trying to slide around him, tiny step by tiny step, toward the door. What was she going to do when she got there? Go sit in the vehicle with her nose in the air until he found a secondhand store?

"For God's sake," he said to her, hoping their bickering wasn't entertaining some bored salesclerk hiding behind a rack of jackets, "Let me be nice."

"You already are nice!"

"A minute ago you told me I was a snob."

"Well, besides that—and the pulverizing of your cousin's doll—you seem pretty nice."

"No, I'm not!" he said.

"Caitlyn wouldn't have married you if you weren't!" she crowed as if the argument was won.

The argument. Geez. He was standing in a very public, very expensive, store, arguing.

It felt oddly invigorating.

"Let's get something straight," he told her. "Guys aren't nice. It doesn't come naturally to us. We're self-centered, self-indulgent narcissists for the most part. Don't you see? Caitlyn would have approved of this. Of me being generous and helpful. She was on a mission to make me a better man."

Jacey stopped moving toward the door.

"No," she said, firmly, those green eyes sparking. "She wasn't. She gave you the best gift of all, you numbskull. She loved you exactly as you were."

"Did you just call me a numbskull?" he asked, incredulous.

They stared at each other.

The tension broke when she giggled. He found himself smiling. Thankfully, that friction that had risen between them dissipated as quickly and as furiously as that storm.

"Yes, I did. I'm sorry."

"You don't sound very sincere."

"Because what kind of numbskull would think Caitlyn was trying to remake you into something you weren't?"

"You just called me that again. Okay, maybe she wasn't *trying* to remake me. But I became better, because of her, whether that was her intention or not."

Jacey's mouth worked. She wanted to argue, he could tell. He didn't remember her being this aggravating.

"So," he said, feeling like Beast wanting Belle to have dinner with him, "allow me to make kindness part of Caitlyn's legacy."

He was aware he was practically begging her to let him be nice to her.

Jacey's face softened. Her green eyes swelled up with tenderness. That look felt as if it would slay the very part of him he had guarded so tenaciously since the death of his wife.

"Okay," she agreed.

"There's one other thing. No, two."

"What?" There was that querulous tone of voice again, as if she was already giving up way too much by allowing him to buy her anything, and now he was daring to ask for more. "Now who sounds like a terrorist negotiating?"

"You can't look at any of the price tags."

"Of course I'm looking at price tags. Are you crazy?"

"Apparently," he said dryly. "A crazy numbskull."

"What's the other condition?"

"You have to have fun. Like a kid in a candy store." She looked mutinous.

"Caitlyn's wish," he reminded her. "Have fun."

"I think I could grow to hate you, Trevor Cooper."

"For asking you to have fun?"

"For backing me up against a wall by using Caitlyn's wish. I'll accept your offer to outfit me for the slopes. But reluctantly. The other two things—not looking at price tags and having fun—I have to think about. Spending money is not fun for me. Even someone else's."

He sighed. "What is it with me and women who hate my money?"

"It's a curse," she agreed, but there was a small, rewarding smile playing across her lips as she turned back to that very expensive rack of parkas.

CHAPTER SEVEN

JACEY FINGERED THE jacket and contemplated the task she'd been given. Have fun. Spending someone else's money. Trevor's money, specifically.

Why not? Why was it so hard for her to accept good things?

Well, where was the line between accepting good things and being seen as a charity case?

She moved on from the jacket she knew to be very expensive. It was very difficult not to look around for a sales rack. Places like this probably didn't even have sales racks, particularly since they were in the height of the winter season.

She pulled out a solid battleship-gray jacket that looked puffy and warm, if unexciting. She held it up to Trevor.

"No," Trevor said, with barely a glance at it.

"Why? What's wrong with it? It looks very service-able."

He came and took the jacket from her hand, hanging it firmly back on the rack. It was quite an arrogant thing to do, really.

Why did something sigh inside her at the prospect of someone just making the decisions for her? Someone who was clearly intent on spoiling her?

"I'm guessing you're a size small, right?"

Don't let this man railroad your life. On the other hand, it *would* be interesting to see what he chose for her.

He pushed through the jackets, paused, pulled one from the rack and held it out. It was a collage of possibly the brightest colors Jacey had ever seen.

That was how he saw her?

"It looks very wild." She squeaked a halfhearted protest. Everything in her leaned toward it. The jacket, with its unexpected flamboyant colors, was extraordinary. Mostly white, it looked as if paint—in iridescent peacock-emerald greens and stunning blues—had been splotched on it randomly. Only a very bold person could wear that.

It wasn't her, at all. It was for someone who loved life. Who embraced it. Who knew how to have fun. Did he really see her like that?

"That would be a good jacket for someone who is an expert skier, who *wants* people to look at them."

"That's quite a lot to read into a jacket," he said. "So what if it makes people look at you?"

Oh! To have that kind of confidence!

"You'll look perfectly adorable practicing your snow-plow."

Perfectly adorable. Is that how she wanted Trevor to see her? As perfectly adorable, like a golden retriever puppy? Of course that was how she wanted him to see her!

As a trusted friend, she told herself firmly. Though what woman wouldn't want such a handsome man to see her as an attractive, *sexy* trusted friend?

"They aren't my colors," she said, firmly.

"Really? Tell your suitcase."

Though she'd told him it was a strategic purchase to help her find it easily amongst the other passengers' luggage, that wasn't the whole truth. The suitcase had appealed to her for the very same reason her couch did. It somehow expressed a lightheartedness she longed for.

"This jacket choice is the very same thing!" Trevor insisted.

"I'm not seeing the connection."

"I won't be able to lose you on the slopes any more than you'd be able to lose that luggage at the baggage claim."

Jacey felt dashed at the reason for his choice. It wasn't because he saw her as having the potential to be bold and fun—albeit adorable—instead of timid and retiring. It was practical!

But trepidation squeezed out her disappointment as she registered his reasons for choosing that jacket.

"You can lose someone on the slopes?" she asked, trying to keep her tone casual.

"Sure." He was still sorting through outerwear, now holding up a pair of brightly colored ski slacks that matched the jacket and squinting at them appraisingly.

"Like how lost?" Jacey pressed. "Out of view for a few minutes?"

"It's happened. Skiers get separated. You saw what the weather is like out there. What do you think of these?" He held up the pants for her inspection.

If they reduced her chances of getting lost, she liked them very much! She snatched them from his hands.

"What about *really* lost?" she asked him. "Like wandering through the freezing wilderness *lost*? I've seen that."

"In Toronto?" he asked, raising an amused eyebrow at her.

"On the news!"

"I'm not going to let you be the topic of a news story, Jacey."

"There are things outside of your control, you know."

"Yeah," he said, a hint of bitterness in his voice, "I know."

This, Jacey told herself, was not why Caitlyn had sent her on this mission. It wasn't to remind him things were out of his control, but to coax him, a wounded bear, out of his cave, back into the sunlight.

"Bears!" she said. "Have you ever seen a bear while skiing?"

The change of topic, as absurd as it was, did exactly what she had hoped. The bitterness melted from him as the lovely lines of his mouth quirked upward.

But her enjoyment was short-lived at his answer.

"I have," he said solemnly.

So seeing a bear was not absurd? "Do I need bear spray?"

"They don't like bright colors," he said.

"You're teasing me."

"I am," he agreed.

The thing was she kind of enjoyed being teased by him.

"Though I have, indeed, seen bears while skiing. Just not at this time of year. You'll sometimes see them in the spring."

Note to self: *never* ski in the spring. A possibility so remote, she didn't even have to make a note to herself.

He looked at his watch. "We better make some time if we're going to get in a few runs today. Come on, let's wrap this up."

Together, they chose toques and socks and gloves until she was staggering under the weight of them as she made her way to the change room.

It was only once she was there, her bounty laid out before her like pirate's treasure, that she realized she had had fun.

Just like a kid in a candy store.

"When you find anything you like that fits," he called through the closed door, "just leave it on. Next stop, Moonbeam."

When she emerged from the change room, he grinned at her.

"You look awesome," he said. "As if you've been skiing your whole life. As if you're ready to win your gold medal."

He stepped in very close to her.

For a moment her heart stopped.

Why on earth would she think the warmth in his eyes and the easiness of his smile was going to translate to a kiss?

If he tried to kiss her, she told herself firmly, she wouldn't kiss back. He was Caitlyn's husband!

In fact, she would *hate* him if he tried to kiss her. She might have to slap him. Good grief! They were friends. She couldn't respect him—or herself—if that boundary was crossed!

As it turned out, Jacey's brief and silent debate was akin to debating whether the most dangerous thing was a bathroom or love—pointless. Because Trevor wasn't moving in to kiss her.

He wasn't even moving in to tuck a stray strand of hair under her toque, which, oddly, would have been almost as alarming as being kissed by him.

No, he moved close and with lightning swiftness found each price tag from each item and snapped them off.

"You can wait outside while I pay."

Really? She should have protested. But it was nice that

he wanted to protect her from the shock of the expense of it all and she was so unsettled by her kiss thoughts, she couldn't speak.

When she emerged from the store in her new, splashy, outdoor wear, Jacey discovered an amazing metamorphosis had occurred.

It was still snowing, and hard. But even that felt different. Not threatening. Because she was one of them now, part of this colorful throng, celebrating the snow. As she looked around, she realized she looked *exactly* like all the people on the streets, in their bright jackets and snazzy toques.

But what was more, she felt like them, too.

Happy.

Ready for the next stop. Moonbeam Peaks.

Not just Moonbeam, but three days and two nights at Moonbeam with him. The guy who was, if she was being honest, probably the true source of her happiness.

Except it turned out to be not exactly true, that their next stop was Moonbeam.

Their next stop was the gondola, which was the only route to Moonbeam. An enclosed go-cart arrived at their vehicle when they parked in the spot reserved for hotel guests. All their luggage was loaded and they were chauffeured to a little station at the foot of an absolutely gigantic mountain.

Even the storm could not hide how humungous it was. And rocky. And high.

And moving up it, like ants in a determined line, were steel cages swinging from a cable, that while thick, did not appear to Jacey's amateur eye to be up to the task of holding all that weight.

"How many gondolas do you think there are?" she asked Trevor, subdued.

"I think this gondola is one of the largest in the world at seven kilometers. I'd guess there are maybe a hundred and fifty cars."

"That's a lot of weight."

He reached out and gave her gloved hand a squeeze. "They're still accident-free, after all these years of operation. Imagine that."

Of course, what Jacey imagined was they were about due.

"It seems to go very high," she said. She started reading the "fun fact" sign beside the line they were in but none of the facts seemed particularly fun to her.

Every single item that went to or left Moonbeam was delivered by this apparatus. More weight! They would be two hundred feet off the ground when the car they were in reached its highest point! It traveled at nearly 20 feet a second, which meant they were going to be trapped on it for more than twenty minutes!

Jacey felt her stomach dip. And then that awful, familiar feeling of her palms sweating. She slid off one glove, and then the other, wiping her palms on her new pant leg.

As they edged closer to their turn to get on, the happiness dried up in Jacey as if she'd been turned from a grape to a raisin in the span of three seconds.

She watched as one of the cars loaded, those brightly dressed, happy people disappearing inside it.

Within seconds, as if it had been shot from a catapult, the gondola was up in the air—way up in the air—dangling from that grotesquely thin arm and disappearing into the storm.

Sweat beaded on her brow. Her stomach swirled a little more vigorously.

And then she was that little girl in the concert hall.

Just like now, she had been all dressed up then, ready for her big moment, though that night she'd been in the pretty dress that she and her father had chosen together.

She remembered being led out to the grand piano, all those people watching her, her father beaming with pride as he adjusted the bench for her, opened the music book and placed it in front of her.

Just like now, it had felt momentous, like some kind of turning point, like her life would never be the same.

And therein lay the problem, then as now.

Jacey liked things to stay the same.

Trevor returned the gondola attendant's smile as he waved them forward. Their luggage was loaded on, along with Trevor's skis.

When Jacey didn't move, Trevor nudged her. She still didn't move.

He glanced down at her and noticed her face was very pale. Was there a little bead of sweat over her upper lip?

"I can't," she whispered.

For a horrible moment he thought she might faint. He tugged her out of the line and nodded at the attendant to let the gondola—with their luggage on it—go. The next group gave them a curious look, then shuffled by them.

Trevor took her by the arm and guided her out of the line and around the corner of the gondola station.

The wind whipped at them.

"What's up?" he said, carefully casual.

"I told you. I'm afraid of heights. I thought I could get over it, but I can't. Trevor, did you see how skinny that arm is that's holding the car onto the cable?"

"Yes," he said agreeably, "it's an engineering marvel."

She gave him a baleful look. "It can't possibly be safe."

He knew he could reiterate to her how safe the gondola was. He knew he could check his phone for all the facts in the world and present them to her.

And he knew that it wouldn't help. Not one little bit.

CHAPTER EIGHT

"So that's why we're really here," Trevor said to Jacey. He congratulated himself on the unfamiliar gentle tone in his voice. He was doing it! He was being a better man.

That better man knew exactly what to do next. He pulled her deep into his arms and held her so tight he could feel her heart beating, even through the thick padding of both their ski jackets. Her heart was going way too fast, as if she was a rabbit running from frothing-at-the-mouth dogs.

"What do you mean?" her muffled voice asked him.

"My beautiful, sensitive, intuitive wife knew it wasn't about being you—us—being happy. She set this up on the pretext of having fun, but that's not really what it's about."

"Yes," Jacey said, peeking around him to gaze balefully at the gondola cars going up the wire, "because anyone can see that *thing* is not fun."

"It's about not being scared anymore," he told her. "Terrified that life is just waiting to deliver some new dastardly blow, some horrible surprise."

"Like a gondola falling off a cable," Jacey agreed. She sighed her relief that he *got* it.

"That's why she arranged all of this, Jacey. Caitlyn

knew we can't be happy until we get over the fear that's holding us back."

Jacey pulled her head out of his jacket and scanned his face.

"You're not afraid," she said.

"Yeah, I am," he said softly, amazed to be admitting this thing he had never admitted, not even to himself. "Of everything. Since the day she died."

"I was afraid way before that. It just confirmed—"

"I know," he said softly.

"You do?"

And he felt as if he did know her. Completely. Her every fear and her every insecurity. As well as his own. It made him feel the most frightening tenderness for her.

"This is what happens when you least expect it," he told her, though really he was thinking out loud.

Yes, this is what happened when you forgot to protect yourself. When you said yes instead of no.

He wasn't sure he was ready for this, but it already felt as if it was way too late to try and go back now.

"Life's asking more of us," he said. "Do you hear it? Listen."

She cocked her head and they heard the whir and clunk of the machinery, the cars on the cables, and beyond that, the storm howling down the mountain.

"Life is asking us to be stronger than we were before. And braver than we've ever been. I can't do it without you." Trevor was absolutely stunned by how true this was. He was aware, even though they had not had much contact over the past two years, that he treasured her friendship.

Her eyes were locked on his, searching. She found whatever it was she was looking for.

"Okay," she said, her voice trembling, "I'm ready now."

"Are you sure?"

She nodded and left the protection of his chest. Her hand reached for his, though. He took it, but it wasn't good enough for her.

She took off that brand-new glove, and he knew instantly what she wanted. A touch that would be skin to skin, warmth to warmth, person to person. He took his glove off, too.

When her hand came to be in his, he could feel her heartbeat in the pulse that ran between her thumb and her pointer finger. Her heart was still racing. He could also feel the whole world shift. He had held her hand last night and it hadn't felt like this.

What was changing?

The truth?

Everything.

He was coming back to life, whether he wanted to or not.

The gondolas were designed for four people, or two who had luggage. Since their luggage had gone without them, Trevor and Jacey really should have been put on a gondola with another party of two. But the attendant took one look at them when they came back around the corner of the station and held up his hand to the people who were supposed to get on next.

He gestured Trevor and Jacey forward and they ducked into the gondola and took the seats facing up the mountain, side by side.

The attendant shut the door behind them.

"I think that's what a prison door sounds like when it shuts," she said.

"You can't know that."

"Ha. Movies."

"Well, this is twenty minutes, not twenty to life."

He was rewarded with a stifled giggle, but then Trevor felt every single fiber of Jacey tense as the gondola car trundled forward, the bar caught the cable and they soared.

He moved close to her. He put his hand around her shoulder, and tugged her yet closer, feeling the deep connection of shared experience between them.

All through those days of Caitlyn dying, Jacey had been there for him. Now it was his turn.

"Breathe," he whispered to her.

She seemed to contemplate that.

"Try Ujjayi," he teased gently.

She was silent, and then she said, "Prepare for a karate chop to the throat."

He laughed, and then she laughed, just a little bit. He felt some of the tension drain from her rigid shoulders.

"This is the similarity to prison. We can't get out if we change our minds," she noted.

"Well, technically, you probably could."

"I think we're locked in."

He reached over her, as if he was going to try the door lever and test her theory. She squealed her protest.

"No! Don't touch it."

"We could be the first accident on the gondola," he said. "Death by exit at two hundred feet."

She closed her eyes. "I don't think we're at two hundred feet yet. Don't tease me. It's not funny."

He liked teasing her, and he suspected she liked it, too, because she snuggled closer to him, and he tightened his grip on her shoulders. Her new toque, fuzzy, tickled his nose.

"I can't believe you got me on it!" She tilted her head

and leveled him a look. He saw the deep green of her eyes taking him in, taking him *all* in.

It was unsettling to feel this *known.*

Of course, she did know him. And she'd known him long before now. She had seen him every single day of the battle he had ultimately lost.

It was not news to her that he was afraid. He just wondered why she had gotten on the gondola with him instead of running the other way.

Every word he had spoken to her had been his deepest truth. He felt stripped bare by it.

She leaned back in the chair, closed her eyes, to avoid looking out the window, he suspected.

"My mom died when I was eight," she told him in a low voice.

"Caitlyn told me you were raised by a single dad."

"It was me and my dad against the world. He was a musician, and music provided us both solace. After my mom died, I really lost myself in it. Nothing brought me comfort like sitting at the piano, not just playing music, but becoming music.

"My dad felt I was gifted. I had the best teachers and even they thought I was extraordinarily talented. I think my father found solace from his own pain in my immersion in this new world. I think it allowed him to feel successful as a father when most days he just felt bewildered and in way over his head. My piano became his focus and my escape.

"When I was twelve, my teacher arranged for me to do a solo concert. It was an incredible honor to be asked. The who's-who of the music world were going to be there.

"But I got out in front of the audience, and I froze.

"I could not do it. I could not persuade myself. My father could not persuade me. I was absolutely paralyzed.

"I had the same feeling looking at the gondolas, just now. When I lost my mom, the world changed irrevocably for me. I've hated change ever since then. And some part of me, even though I felt frozen, powerless, like I wanted to play more than anything in the world, knew if I did, things would change again in ways I could not control."

"I'm not sure getting in the gondola has the power to change your life in quite the same way."

"But it does. You said it. It's about facing fear to live fully."

"Where's your father now?" he asked.

"He died of cancer five years ago." Jacey hesitated. "I wish we could have fixed things between us before he died."

"In what way?"

"I don't ever think he got over the sense of being betrayed by me that day."

"That's not reasonable. You said you were twelve!"

"He lost interest in my musical development after that. It was the interest we shared, the thing that glued us together. But no matter where I went musically after that, he would always see it through the lens of my best opportunity having been thrown away."

"I'm sorry," Trevor said. "I'm sorry you didn't have a chance to repair things between you."

"Why couldn't he understand? If I could have done it for him, I would have. You know, I've never, ever played publicly since that day? Not even once. I love teaching. I love playing. But I can't perform. I think it's probably exposed my deepest fears—making a mistake, losing control, being embarrassed."

Jacey considered what she had just revealed to Trevor. There it was: the root fear at the heart of all her other fears. And she had trusted him with it.

When he was silent for a long, long time she thought she had revealed too much of herself. Allowed herself, because she felt so vulnerable, to share more deeply and more personally than their relationship warranted.

"What if," he said finally, slowly, "it wasn't about fear of change at all that night at the concert hall? What if it wasn't any of those things? Fear of making a mistake, or loss of control or being embarrassed?"

Something in her went very still.

She opened her eyes and looked at him, puzzled, and yet she could feel some hope fluttering to life within her, too.

He seemed to be able to see something she had never seen.

"What if," Trevor continued quietly, "you didn't want to share that space, that sacred place that gave you such solace from the pain of losing your mom? What if you didn't want to share that with the world? What if it was yours and yours alone?"

Her mouth fell open. Tears filled her eyes. "I've never once thought of it in any other way except as my greatest failure."

"What if you look at it as if taking tremendous courage to keep your gift to yourself instead of giving it away?"

The tears fell.

"Look," he said. "Look out the window."

Jacey did not want to look out the window. She wanted

to pretend the whole world was the three feet they shared, the feeling she had with his arm around her, and her head nestled into his chest.

Of complete trust.

"Look," he said again. "Jacey, don't miss this."

The thing was she could feel the courage inside herself, like a small green stem, coming out of dirt, breaking through the crust of winter.

She turned her head ever so slightly. Through the blur of her tears, she saw shafts of light were beginning to pierce the snowstorm. Weak at first, and then stronger and stronger, until they burst out above the cloud entirely, and a whole brilliant world of rugged rock, untouched snow, shadowed forests and endless blue skies was revealed to them.

Jacey felt overwhelmed by the beauty.

"You see?" he said, that gorgeous deep voice so gentle. He touched her face, wiped the tears away, one by one.

"Yes," she said. "I see. I've made some kind of breakthrough, and the whole world is a reflection of that."

"I meant do you see we're nearly halfway there and the cable is holding?"

What's the worst danger in the world? Bathrooms? Or love?

They were fated to see the world so differently. Or were they? She took her eyes off the amazing view for one second and looked at him. She wasn't the least bit fooled about what he really meant.

She wanted to run her hand over the line of his jaw, trace his nose with her fingertips, smooth down his rooster tail.

Instead, she tucked that errant hand inside her pocket, ashamed of herself. She could know him deeply without complicating their relationship by touching him!

Still, she could not stop the next words from spilling from her lips. "I see why Caitlyn loved you."

"Because I'm extraordinarily handsome?"

She laughed.

But then he said, softly, ever so softly, "I see why she loved you, too."

CHAPTER NINE

JACEY COULD FEEL something within her lifting up, as if her spirit was reflecting the motion of the cable car as it went up and up and up. She and Trevor were in a place human beings rarely experienced.

Birds experienced this.

This place of suspension and motion, a dance between the earth and the sky.

People on airplanes might know this, but to a lesser extent. The flying experience did not have this immediacy. It did not have this silence that felt oddly and beautifully sacred.

Jacey thought this was likely exactly what Caitlyn had hoped when she had made this elaborate plan for her best friend and her husband.

That her love for both of them could heal what seemed beyond healing.

Of course, Jacey needed to fight the feeling that the exhilaration was in some way because of Trevor. It was *with* him, and that was a very important distinction. Conquering her fear had left her wide-open, and she would have to guard carefully that she was not so open that forbidden feelings for her best friend's husband crept in.

Jacey was actually sorry when the cable car journey

ended. The gondola ride finished right at the center of the Village of Moonbeam. As Trevor helped her from the gondola, she looked around herself, trying to take it all in.

She had thought Banff was quaint and lovely, but Moonbeam Peaks was like a village constructed of gingerbread. Deep snow dripped from the steep roofs of log cottages. Rock-fronted shops and small boutique hotels lined a gently curving, snow-clogged main pathway. The sun was brilliant on all that snow, sparking and glittering with the flashing blue light of diamonds.

Ski racks were the hitching posts of the village. There were several in front of every building, all of them filled with skis and boards. The equipment was like artwork with its graphic, bright designs. Poles stood on their own, planted in the snow.

People in colorful jackets, goggles set up on their toques, walked awkwardly in huge boots, sometimes with skis on their shoulders.

Moonbeam Mountain soared behind the village, mighty and majestic. Its pristine slopes looked like mounds of perfect whipping cream and were dotted with skiers coming down them. And skiers and boarders going up, on chairlifts, their legs attached to their equipment, dangling into air beneath them.

Was she going to use a chairlift? It looked even more terrifying than the cable car! But somehow, shockingly, Jacey realized even though her stomach did a little dipsy-doodle at the thought of riding a chairlift, she wasn't quite sure if it was terror. Could she actually be *excited*?

She was aware of having been dropped into a *world* as foreign and as delightful as visiting a different country.

There were no motorized vehicles in this world, and it made all the other sounds—the humming of the chairlifts, people's voices blending together in many languages, laughter—seem amplified.

"I've never seen anything like this," she said to Trevor. "It's a place unto itself. It exists only to bring joy."

He laughed. "And maybe make some money."

She smacked his arm. "Stop it. You're not nearly as cynical as you want me to believe you are."

An open-aired golf cart whirred up, and she saw their luggage was already on board.

"Do you belong to this luggage? I'm Ozzie. I'm going to deliver you to your accommodations. And then—" he checked a notecard— "Jacey is scheduled for a ski lesson. So if it's okay with you, we'll just drop off your stuff and get you checked in, and then I'll take you to the Snow School."

They hopped on the backseat of the cart, Ozzie in the front. His long, dark hair hung out from under his Moonbeam Mountain staff toque. Except for the historical-romance-novel hair, he reminded Jacey of one of those firemen on the calendars.

"Honeymooners?" he asked them over his broad shoulder.

Jacey shot Trevor a look. An irritating awareness of him shivered along her spine and she sternly crushed it. Was there something between them after that connection that they had made on the cable car that would make Ozzie ask that?

Trevor looked annoyed. "Just friends," he said in a voice that didn't brook further conversation.

Yes, Jacey told herself firmly. Friends.

Ozzie dropped them at the door of Moonbeam Mountain Manor and said he would keep Trevor's skis on the cart and meet them at their room with the rest of their luggage.

The hotel lobby was lodge-like and gorgeous. The walls were constructed of logs, darkened to rich gold with age, and soaring twenty feet up to a timber-vaulted ceiling. A huge stone fireplace was at one end, a fire crackling in it. A baby grand piano was beside it. Deep furniture formed a U-shape around the fireplace and the piano.

"Are you going to play that?" Trevor asked her, nodding at the piano.

"Oh, no," she said, uneasily. "It's kind of out in the open."

"I'd like to hear you, though."

"Someday," she told him insincerely. "I'm more interested in that armchair and the fireplace, though I think for now my plan of retreating to a safe and familiar world of a book and a hot chocolate has been thwarted."

"You're right about that."

And as much as she normally hated the unexpected, she kind of liked that feeling in her tummy of anticipation, not knowing exactly what would happen next.

Her and Trevor's accommodations were at the end of a very long, wide hall.

Ozzie awaited them with their luggage.

"This is our presidential suite," Ozzie said as Trevor swiped the pass on the door. "And presidents have actually stayed here. And a princess once, too." He gave her a look and smiled charmingly. "Maybe twice," he said.

Trevor shot him a look. She giggled. Was Ozzie *flirting* with her? Crazy, but still feeling wide-open from her experience on the gondola, she *loved* it.

"Believe me, I'm no princess. Just a music tutor."

"I love music. I play the guitar."

"Not surprisingly," Trevor muttered.

"I'm thinking of giving up being a music tutor." There. She'd said it out loud. Maybe because of her embracing of this adventure it didn't feel nearly as scary as she thought it would.

"How come?" Ozzie asked. "It sounds like the perfect job."

"Oh, you know what they say. Change is as good as a rest."

Trevor made a noise in his throat that sounded a bit like a growl. She turned and looked at him. He was leveling a look at Ozzie that was anything but friendly.

She frowned. One thing she had never pictured him as was a snob. And yet, he obviously did not appreciate the conversation between her and Ozzie.

"Would you like me to put the luggage away?" Ozzie offered. "Which ones would you like in which bedroom?"

Two bedrooms! It really was a suite. Jacey realized that she and Trevor no doubt looked every bit as platonic as they were; two friends on a ski trip.

But Trevor narrowed his eyes at Ozzie. "You can just leave the luggage there."

"I'll wait outside for you," Ozzie said, wagging his eyebrows at her.

"For God's sake," Trevor said once he had closed the door. "He's quite smitten."

"He's not!"

"He was trying to figure out our sleeping arrangements."

"He only offered to put our luggage away," she said mildly. "I think that's his job."

"Yeah, that's what you'll think until you hear a tapping on your window in the middle of the night."

It was absurd—okay, and a little delightful—that Trevor would read so much into the casual encounter.

"Do you always have that effect on men?"

"Come on! You've known me longer than that." She was sure Caitlyn had filled him in all about her introverted friend, just in case he hadn't figured it out for himself.

"Princess," he said with a scowl. "It's so lame."

She studied him. Was Trevor jealous?

"I feel very protective of you," he said when he saw her look.

Of course he wasn't jealous! That rated right up there with mistakenly thinking he was going to kiss her in the ski shop.

They were friends.

Friends. Friends. Friends.

"I mean, obviously you can do better than a guitar-playing ski bum."

"It would take a ski bum to know a ski bum, I'm sure," she said sweetly.

"I never played the guitar!"

"Perhaps he's really a bazzillionaire?"

"He's not."

"Trevor, the ink is barely dry on my divorce papers. I'm not interested." Honestly, she did not know whether to be annoyed or amused by his protectiveness. Or something else altogether.

Not aware of him as a man. That was off-limits! But rising toward what he was doing, allowing herself to feel cared about. Looked after.

"Speaking of bazzillionaires," she said, changing the subject, "look at this place."

Like the lobby of the lodge, this suite's walls were soaring logs, golden with age, that ended in an open vaulted ceiling. The furniture was mountain-cabin appropriate, but in a very sophisticated take on that theme. It had its own fireplace, and double-glass-paned doors looked out on the mountain. She could see skiers swooshing by, and she went to the doors.

There was a private deck out there.

Off to one side was a hot tub.

Here was the thing: she could not get in a hot tub with Trevor. It would be one of those moments—like taking the stage at a concert hall or getting on a gondola—that had the potential to change life forever.

This was so good the way it was, wasn't it?

They were close, but without complications. He was protective of her. Like a big brother. But when she slid him a look, the thumping of her heart gave something away.

With the slightest push, the feelings she had toward him would not be brotherly, at all! That thought made her feel horribly weak and small. Hadn't she suffered quite enough loss at the hands of love?

Not that she didn't care about him. Of course she cared about him! And deeply, too, but in that nice, safe way that you cared about your best friend's husband.

Friends, she repeated, like a mantra. She turned quickly and grabbed her suitcase. She tried one of the doors off the common area of the suite.

It opened to a room with a huge log bed at the center, plush bedding in sharp contrast to the deliberate rustic vibe of the furniture. It, too, had French doors that opened onto the deck. That hot tub was right in front of those doors!

"Uh, I think this is the master suite. I'll just—"

"No, you take it," he said. He came and glanced over her shoulder. "Fit for a princess," he decided, just a hint of something in his tone.

Not jealousy, obviously.

Sarcasm.

What a relief!

What was wrong with him? Trevor asked himself a few minutes later as they got back in the cart. He gave Ozzie a warning look.

He realized he was inordinately annoyed that Jacey

had told a complete stranger she was considering changing careers, and not once mentioned it to him.

Ozzie was, apparently, oblivious to warning looks.

"What lessons are you taking?" he asked her.

"Beginner. It's my very first time."

"A virgin!" Ozzie crowed.

Trevor had to fight an uncharacteristic desire to punch him, especially when Jacey giggled and blushed as if they were discussing a passage out of the Kama Sutra.

Ozzie, oblivious to the dark look Trevor was leveling at the back of his head, said, "I meant are you going to take a ski lesson or a board lesson?"

To Trevor it felt as if this was a discussion *he* should be having with her.

"I thought I'd take a ski lesson. I mean, Trevor skis, so he can give me tips once I'm let loose on the hill."

Thanks for remembering I'm here, Trevor thought darkly, *though it's likely very unwise to mention being let loose with this guy.*

She was naive and thought Ozzie was just being friendly. But Trevor knew all about *that* look in a guy's eyes. Frank male appreciation. That *worth a try* look.

Well, seeing her through Ozzie's eyes, she did look adorable in the new snowsuit. The pants were hugging her lithe form, and little spikes of her hair were sticking out from under the toque.

But there was something a little more troubling about her than adorable.

And then it occurred to him what it was.

Jacey Tremblay looked kind of sexy.

Plus, there had been something about her that he had noticed as soon as they'd gotten off the cable car.

Shimmering in the air.

It wasn't just that she'd conquered a fear, though she

had; there was something more confident in the way she carried herself.

There was also something more open about her, a veneer of reserve gone.

She probably didn't even know.

But Ozzie did.

That veneer had likely gone a long way to protecting her in the past.

She was more vulnerable than she realized. Trevor realized he was going to have to really watch out for her.

He thought of the hot tub that he had glimpsed out on the deck through the main bedroom balcony door.

He felt something stirring in him. He was aghast. Jacey was super vulnerable, and he felt it was his sworn mission to protect her from making bad choices. He'd lay down his life to do that for her if he had to.

There would be no bad choices from his end of things. None. He was not ready—would possibly never be ready again—for where the wrong choice, one moment of weakness, with Jacey could go.

CHAPTER TEN

TREVOR, IN HIS role as Jacey's protector, was relieved to see the last of Ozzie. With a backward wave of his hand, the ski resort employee drove off after dropping them in front of the ski school chalet. Still, he tried to make himself memorable by giving the little cart so much power the front wheels raised off the ground, like a horse rearing.

"I think that little cowboy maneuver was meant to impress you," Trevor told Jacey.

"I doubt it."

"He was flirting with you all the way here."

Jacey regarded him with surprise. And then amusement. "I'm not sure how a detailed description of how the garbage leaves the resort on a special cable car, painted to look like an elephant and named Dumpo, could be interpreted that way."

"It was the *way* he said it."

The look in her eyes told him he was being ridiculous. He wasn't! Guys like Ozzie would take a nice girl like her, use her up and spit her out before she knew what had happened.

He took his skis, which Ozzie had off-loaded from the cart and planted in the snow, and hoisted them onto his shoulder.

Something flashed through Jacey's eyes. See? She

was giving out signals that she didn't even know about! He told himself it was silly to adjust the skis with a completely unnecessary flex of his muscles—she couldn't even see them through his jacket!

Trevor realized with sudden urgency that these kind of thoughts had to be nipped in the bud. He had to get away from her. He had to clear his head. The morning had been way too intense. Something was going seriously off the rails here.

He deliberately removed his attention from her and turned toward the slopes. Something in him sighed. With utter relief.

Skiing. Nothing cleared a man's head like skiing. The immediacy of it. The required focus and strength. He glanced around and spotted the closest chairlift. He could ski there from where he was.

It was a weakness that he liked the idea of skiing over, showing off just a little for Jacey. He was a really good skier. A few perfect carved S curves would no doubt erase Ozzie's very juvenile cowboy maneuver with the cart from her mind. He set his skis on the ground and stepped into the binding. The click of it locking in place was satisfying.

"The ski instructor's name is Freddy," she said before Trevor even had the second ski on. She was squinting at the piece of paper Ozzie had given her. "I'll go in and find him. He probably needs to help fit me with equipment, right?"

Now some handsome guy was going to be floundering at her feet, helping her with boot fitting? Some stranger was going to be the one who saw her first moments on skis? Some stranger was going to be the one who witnessed her sense of wonder and discovery? Who saw her come alive, glow with inner light?

Reluctantly, he used his pole to release the binding. He stepped out of it.

"I think I'll take a lesson, too."

"What? You're an expert skier!"

"I've always wanted to try boarding."

"Really?"

No, that was a complete fib. He had never had the slightest interest in snowboarding, and yet he was astounded to find himself stepping away from his skis and opening the door to the ski school for her.

"Hi! Are you Jacey? I'm Freddy."

Trevor was inordinately relieved to see Jacey's ski instructor was a woman!

Until Jacey said, "This is my friend Trevor. He's decided he would like a boarding lesson."

"I'm not board certified," Freddy said, and then giggled. "That makes me sound like a doctor, doesn't it? I think Bjorn is available, though."

Trevor should have considered this, that the boarding instructor and the ski instructor would be different people. So he wasn't going to be there with Jacey as she discovered the magic of skiing, after all. And he hadn't needed to protect her from overly zealous male attention.

This was the sad result of making impulsive decisions. If he'd done this in his engineering career, he wouldn't have a career!

He should just cancel, now, and go back to his original plan. Ski off, spend an hour or so alone while Jacey had her lesson, get his head on straight.

But then Jacey would know he'd been lying about wanting a boarding lesson, and he didn't want her to start wondering about his reasons for lying.

A perfect Swede—blond, blue-eyed, tall, muscled—swaggered out. It was exactly the instructor Trevor had dreaded Jacey getting. And so Trevor found himself signed up to do something he'd never had any intention of doing.

He wasn't aware, until he was on the snowboard, and it felt *awful*—like he was a duck trying to be a swan—how much he had planned on using his skill on the ski hill to protect Jacey. To be the one to introduce her to the wonder of the mountain. To maybe impress her just a little bit.

What did impressing her have to do with protecting her?

Maybe, if she was focused on him…

Crazy thinking, he told himself. Trevor was not used to crazy thoughts. At all. Or making a fool of himself.

And yet, here he was, on the bunny slope, entertaining crazy thoughts, and in full view of the whole world, making a complete fool of himself.

And somehow it felt as if it was all Jacey's fault!

But at least he could see her, and even from here, he could see the little furrow in her brow of mixed concentration and anxiety.

"Are you paying attention?" Bjorn asked sternly.

Oh, yeah, just not to Bjorn.

Jacey had low expectations of her ski lesson. She had never been either athletic or bold, and she assumed both qualities would be necessary for this sport.

And yet, she could see Trevor, just a few yards from her, and she had to admit she was glad he had stayed. It felt reassuring to have him close.

Somehow, having him close by also made it so she wouldn't give up if it was too scary or too hard.

What was that about? Why was she trying to win his approval?

She soon found out, though, that she couldn't focus

on Trevor and learn to ski at the same time. She had to be entirely focused on herself.

After going through the rudimentary aspects of skiing, Freddy guided her to a baby lift: kind of like a giant black rubber carpet they could step onto with their skis on, and it transported them up the hill.

While on the *carpet*, the slope they were being transported up had seemed neither high nor steep, but standing at the top of it, it seemed both.

"Remember, beak over bindings," Freddy encouraged her. "A little bend, a little lean. Go!"

Jacey held her breath. She leaned forward and pushed a little with her poles. She thought it would be like being shot from a cannon, but no, it was slow. Still, she was going down the hill! She was skiing!

It lasted all of ten seconds until her tips crossed and she fell, but she was up in a heartbeat, and so ready to experience that *feeling* again.

Swooshing down that hill—even in slow motion— was wonderful.

By the end of her lesson, she could not believe how much fun she had had or how quickly the time had dissolved.

"Okay," Freddy said. "You did awesome. You're a natural."

She was covered in snow and her legs hurt but the sun was bright on her face and on the snow and she felt absolutely exhilarated by that, and by her accomplishments.

"For the rest of today stick to the Orion chair," Freddy said, pointing it out. "You can ski to it from here. It covers all the beginner's slopes. By the end of the day, you'll have a feel for it. And remember what I said about getting on and off the chairlift!"

The chairlift! A feeling tried to pierce her exhilaration, but then Trevor joined her, one foot on his board and the other off, pushing it.

The motion made him look extraordinarily powerful, but his expression was the antithesis of hers—dark, annoyed, frustrated.

"Freddy told me I'm ready for the chair!" she announced.

His frown softened slightly. "You looked like you were really enjoying yourself."

"I did. Didn't you?"

He rolled his shoulders. "It was okay."

"Well, I can't even explain what I'm feeling right now."

"I can see it," he said softly. "It's dancing like a light around you."

Was he leaning toward her? For one breathless moment, she felt as if he was going to touch her face.

Of course he wasn't going to touch her face! She had to quit entertaining these ridiculous notions. But she went very still, anyway, waiting to see what happened next.

What happened next was that the board scooted out from under him, his legs went akimbo and his rump went down into the snow.

"I'm going to change back into my skis," he said after lying there for a minute. Then he found his feet and got up. He did not look pleased about it as he swiped new snow off his jacket and his pants.

"Oh! I wish you wouldn't. I won't feel like such a loser if I have a partner in incompetence." She grinned at his expression when he heard the word *incompetence*.

What she really wanted, but couldn't quite find the words to explain, was for them to experience the *newness* of it together.

"How am I going to take care of you if I can barely stand up?"

"We'll take care of each other."

The statement shimmered in the air between them because wasn't that exactly what they were doing? Taking care of each other in this week so filled with terrible memories?

Caitlyn's little plan for them was evidently working. Because Jacey hadn't felt the weight of despondency since she and Trevor had arrived in Banff.

"Okay," he said reluctantly. "A couple of runs."

With a sigh, he pushed off in front of her. Despite the fact he was clearly more comfortable on skis, it was very easy to see that, unlike her, Trevor was a natural athlete, imbued with grace and power. In fact, by the time they reached the chairlift he seemed to have the rudiments of snowboarding completely conquered.

"You made that look really fun," she said, coming to a careful stop beside him.

"I think I may be starting to get the hang of it."

They moved into the lineup for the chair, and she basked in the sensations of it all: sun on her face, happy people around her, Trevor at her side.

"First time," she announced to the lift attendant when it was their turn to get on the chair.

"Quit saying that!"

The chair came up behind them. It caught her on the back of the knees and she sat with a graceless, sideways *thunk*, leaning into him.

"What? Why?"

"Guys are basically all evil-minded creatures, and I don't want to have to punch him if he asks about your virginal status."

She laughed. He glowered at her.

She debated telling him that getting on this chair was at least as terrifying as that other "first" had been in her life! But in the end, she decided that would be pushing the boundary of what was appropriate between them. She was aware she was blushing, anyway, just as if she'd said it.

The chair was gaining height rapidly. Her skis, dangling at the ends of her feet, felt heavy, as if they might pull her over into the abyss.

"Bar coming down," he said.

She closed her eyes. "Bar? Thank goodness. Make mine a double. Margarita."

He chuckled. "Safety bar," he said and she opened her eyes to see him lowering a T-shaped bar between them. There was a place to rest her skis, and she felt infinitely safer.

"If you've made it this far without propping up your courage with a drink, I wouldn't suggest the ski hill as a great place to change."

"Sloppy drunk music teacher under your care on the ski hill!" she suggested, gleefully.

"No, thanks. How come you never told me you were thinking of giving it up?"

"Drinking?"

"Teaching music."

"It's not as if we've exchanged letters, Trevor."

"You confided your career plans in a complete stranger!"

"It came up!" she said and slid him a look. It was quite hilarious how he thought she was in some sort of danger of being bowled over by a bit of male attention.

"Well, since it came up, what's going on?"

Oh, sure, why not tell him about all her failures? It didn't even seem that important sitting here on the chairlift, high above a snow-covered world.

"I had the world's most promising student, and under

my tutelage he failed the entrance audition to one of Canada's most auspicious music schools. It's shaken my confidence a bit. In the one area where I thought I had lots of confidence!"

"Hmmm."

"What's that mean?"

"Well, not enough confidence to perform in public. Even the lobby of the hotel seems to scare you."

"That's true," she agreed reluctantly. "Maybe Johnny's failure just exposed an insecurity I was already feeling. Anyway, maybe it's time for a break from music."

"But what would you do?"

She wasn't going to admit to Trevor the bazillionaire that she was thinking of getting a job at the corner grocery. He'd probably offer to buy her a company!

CHAPTER ELEVEN

"SOMETHING WILL COME UP," Jacey said, noncommittally.

Trevor looked thoughtful.

"That's why I think you need to think about it," he said. "You've had so much loss. Best friend. Husband. Home."

"It wasn't a home," Jacey corrected him. "It was a house. I didn't even like it that much."

"That's a pretty big investment in something you didn't like that much."

"Huh. Bruce's words, exactly. An investment." Why had she gone along with that huge financial commitment to a house she didn't even like? Oh, that was easy. She had been trying to win the unwinnable: Bruce's approval.

"I'm just saying that maybe it's just not the time to make a decision like that."

Jacey watched from her perch high above as the skiers swooped down the beautiful slopes of Moonbeam Mountain. It was a cold day, but the sun was so brilliant, it felt warm on her cheeks.

She could feel Trevor's shoulder up against hers, solid and providing her with a sense of safety and comfort, and something a little more. A sense of being physically in her body, wide-open to sensation, and there was plenty of that from where their shoulders touched.

Or maybe it was just the brand-new experience of skiing that had made her feel this tingling awareness of the physical.

Whatever it was—his shoulder touching hers or her first day on skis—it was providing her with that *something* that made pursuing a new adventure seem more exciting than terrifying.

Even from way up here, with nothing more than a skinny little barrier preventing her from slipping and falling to certain death. She leaned over the bar, better to see her skis dangling in space.

She sighed, drinking it all in, feeling a wonderful appreciation for the caprice of life. Even a few days ago, could she have ever envisaged this for her life?

A remote mountain ski hill, conquering her fear of heights, a gorgeous man beside her who *cared* about what decision she made next.

In the past, life taking abrupt or unexpected turns had never been a good thing.

And yet, she was aware of just feeling good.

"You're right," she told him.

"The words every man loves to hear," he said dryly.

"I should hold off on making the decision about my career. I'm going to do what I've heard other people talking about, but never quite managed for myself. I'm going to be totally in the moment, and embrace whatever life offers."

"Careful the offer isn't coming from someone like Ozzie. Or Bjorn."

"Who is Bjorn?"

"You didn't notice Bjorn?"

"Huh?"

"The Swedish man-god who taught snowboarding and took pleasure in torturing me on the slopes?"

She laughed. "Sorry, no."

And then she blushed. Because, really, not that she needed to let him know, but she'd barely noticed Ozzie, either.

Ozzie was on the periphery, was just part of the bigger picture, a world that she was excitedly sharing and exploring with Trevor. But even more, because of him. He was bringing out a bolder side of her.

Trevor looked pensive.

She was pretty sure they were both contemplating what it meant that she only had eyes for him.

And what this awareness of him, to the exclusion of all else, would mean to the temptations of trying out that hot tub tonight after an exhilarating—but muscle exhausting—day on the slopes.

Was he wondering that, too?

Still, she had to be careful of linking him too much to how she was feeling. It would be easy, with her life in tatters, to imagine there was the possibility of their friendship evolving into the kind of relationship hot tubs encouraged!

But somehow, even entertaining that thought, however briefly, felt disloyal to Caitlyn.

Thankfully, those thoughts were wiped from her mind as the next challenge presented itself: she had to get off the chairlift!

She managed to exit the lift area without face-planting, but then she and Trevor stood together at what felt like the very top of the mountain. It was gorgeous: an endless, snow-covered slope winding through exposed rocks, down to a place where huge timbers lined both sides of the wide run.

It was gorgeous, but hazardous. What if you lost control and hit one of those rocks? Or trees? Or another skier?

Despite Freddy's assurance that this was the novice run, it was no bunny slope! They couldn't even see the chairlift station at the bottom from here.

"Are you going to go?" he said.

She cast him a terrified look.

"It's kind of like having a baby," she told Trevor. "You get to this point and have the sudden realization there's only one way out."

The faintest cloud passed over Trevor's face. She wished she wouldn't have mentioned babies.

That was how they had found out Caitlyn was sick— when she couldn't get pregnant.

Jacey gathered her strength. Why be afraid? The worst had already happened. She positioned her legs in a firm snowplow and planted her poles. She pushed.

It was steeper than the bunny hill had been. But still, she was in control. She did a careful turn across the hill as Trevor whizzed by her, all easy strength and confidence. She allowed herself to pick up speed.

It was exhilarating: the wind on her cheeks; the skis hissing on the snow underneath her; the sensation of freedom, almost of flying.

But then she realized she was going too fast and picking up speed despite her effort to dig deeper with her edges.

"Stop," she told herself. "Stop."

She realized she was yelling it out loud, and not stopping. She flew by Trevor. But then she heard him coming up behind her, trying to catch her.

She felt his hand on her jacket, grabbing for her, trying to slow her down.

But of course, it was impractical.

He was as new to snowboarding as she was to skiing. With a shout, he lost his balance, and as he let her go she lost her balance, too.

They both tumbled until they came to a stop by crashing into each other. They lay there in the snow in a great tangled pile of limbs and equipment. Somehow, Trevor was on top of her, trying to keep his weight off her by holding himself up on his elbows.

She stared up at him. His curls were escaping from under his toque. She took in the beautiful sweep of his lashes, and the milk-chocolate color of his eyes. She noticed the whisker-shadowed cut of his jaw. She was so aware of the way his breath felt on her face, and how his body felt resting on top of hers. She could feel the strength in him, the warmth penetrating his jacket; she could even feel the steady beat of his heart.

She should have been cold, lying there with the snow at her back.

But instead, she felt as if she was on fire.

He took off his glove and brushed snow from her face. He looked down at her, his expression tender, as though bewildered as to how they had gotten here.

"Um, is that how they taught you to stop at ski school?" he asked, his voice a sensual growl.

"Falling over?"

"No, yelling 'stop' at the top of your lungs?"

She giggled. He chuckled. Her giggle turned to laughter and so did his. Here they were, all tangled together on the hill, doing the one thing it had felt as if they would never do again.

Laughing.

Uproariously.

Giving themselves over to it.

To the pure joy of unexpected and spontaneous moments.

The laughter died as Trevor suddenly seemed to become aware he was still lying on top of her and he rolled off her, then leaped up, held out his hand and pulled her back to standing. But he quickly let her go as soon as she had found her feet.

She guessed he had decided to act as if that close encounter of the best kind had never happened.

But the thing about something like that happening? No matter how much you pretended, it could never be the same again.

And it wasn't; the sizzle between them adding to the sensation of being totally free, as on fire with life as she had ever been. It was as if something in her that had been closed tight burst wide-open.

They never ended up on top of each other again, but that wide-open feeling remained. As she skied, Jacey let go a little and then a little more. She went faster. She fell. He went faster. He fell. But both of them were embracing their new skills, and the complete wonder of being part of the great outdoors, part of the mountain on a sun-drenched, brilliant winter day.

Their laughter and their shouts of exuberance echoed off the rocks and trees as they made their way down the run, and back onto the chair.

They sat, shoulder to shoulder, sharing brand-new things about each other that they had not revealed before, even though they had known each other for years.

He liked dogs. She liked cats. He liked rock and guitar, she liked classical and piano. He liked action movies, she liked drama. He liked traveling, she liked staying at home. She liked live theater, he liked live sports.

They stayed out on the slopes, taking run after run,

until the lift attendant announced it was the last one of the day.

"Good thing it's the last run," Trevor said as she sat beside him on the chair. He threw his arm around her. They were both soaked from so many tumbles in the snow and she was shivering.

"It's funny," she told him. "I'm frozen, and I'm starving, and yet I still wish we had a few more chances to go down the hill."

"There's always tomorrow," he said.

When was the last time she had looked forward to the next day with such lovely anticipation?

"I can't wait," Jacey said. "Skiing is absolutely the most glorious thing I've ever experienced. I feel as if I've been missing out on something my entire life."

The frightening thing was it might have been skiing.

But equally, it could be *him*.

It could be the sensation of rocketing down that mountain hugging the edge of control, or it could just as easily be the sensation of ease mixed with exhilaration, confidence mixed with awkwardness, the feeling of getting to know someone deeply.

Friends, friends, friends, she told herself, but the mantra felt tiresome.

They were able to ski right to their hotel, and they left their equipment on the racks outside and raced each other in. Each of their bedrooms had its own en suite, and after they had showered they met again in the middle.

It felt dangerously intimate to be in this shared space.

"I'm starving," Jacey told him, eager to break the spell of Trevor, fresh from the shower, his hair curling sweetly and smelling like heaven. "Let's grab a hamburger."

"A hamburger? I don't think so. Moonbeam has some

of the finest dining in the world, and we're availing ourselves of that."

She should insist on the hamburger. It would be just
too easy to get used to this. To leading a life where money
didn't matter, where all the best experiences were just
laid out in front of you for the taking. How did you go
back to macaroni and cheese after that?

On the other hand, why anticipate the future? Why
not just surrender and enjoy the present?

"I'm not really dressed for anything fancy," she said,
glancing down at her slim-fitting black yoga pants and
white sweater.

His gaze skimmed her with such white-hot appreciation that she shivered, aware she was not the only one
sensing the growing intimacy between them.

"One of the many joys of a mountain resort," he said.
"You can five-star dine in your blue jeans."

He was wearing blue jeans, and a blue plaid shirt, open
at the throat. It was unfair that a man could look so good
wearing something so ordinary!

Trevor looked at Jacey across the table. They had chosen a small French restaurant and were seated at a window that overlooked the winding, snow-covered path of
the village.

"It looks like a storybook," Jacey said.

Indeed, the village square, lit with gaslights, looked
exactly like that. Golden light splashed out of windows
under snow-laden roofs.

If he would have considered the general ambiance of
French restaurants—the candlelight and roses thing—he
might have opted for that hamburger.

Too late now.

Plus, he wasn't sure a hamburger would have brought

about the same glow of happiness he was seeing now as she sampled the delights of coq au vin.

"I've never had food like this before," she said. "My dad and I kind of just squeaked by. And Bruce was, um, quite thrifty."

Trevor decided he didn't like Bruce, a lot.

CHAPTER TWELVE

"OH MY," JACEY SAID. She leaned back and savored her first bite of the next course. It was what the chef was famous for, boeuf bourguignon, served with homemade crusty bread. The stew was the perfect hearty dish to finish the day with.

Trevor thought the look of pleasure on her face was a look a man could die for. Bruce had missed this to save a few pennies? Men could be so dumb.

"I feel about this food the very same way I feel about skiing," she said. "As if I've missed something my entire life."

He was aware of feeling an urgent—and very dangerous—need to give Jacey every single thing she had ever missed.

Trevor told himself his desire to give Jacey everything she had never had before was motivated strictly by a desire to keep her away from losers like Bruce.

And Ozzie.

Once she'd seen how she should be treated, she would never go back. He was quite pleased with the purity of his motive.

"What should we have for dessert?" Trevor asked Jacey. He was pretty sure every item on the dessert menu was something she had missed.

"I can't possibly have dessert."

He would not be thwarted.

"We can't possibly have a meal like that and not have dessert. We'll share something."

He asked the waiter for a recommendation, and they were brought a donut-shaped pastry filled with cream.

"Paris-Brest," the waiter announced with flourish.

"Why is it called that?" she whispered, and they both stared at it. She laughed first, and there it was between them, again.

The thing he had sworn—was it really less than twenty-four hours ago?—that he would never feel again.

Joy.

He took out his phone and looked up the dessert. "It's named after the region in France that it comes from."

She was blushing over the name of a dessert. He couldn't resist taking it a step further.

"Only the French," he said in a low tone intended only for her ears, "would name a whole region that."

"Get your mind out of the gutter," she said, her tone also low. "It probably doesn't even mean that in French."

"We're talking about the people who named the Grand Tetons."

She laughed again, as he hoped she would. Ever since she had laughed this afternoon, he felt as if he could live for that sound.

He was enjoying their low tones—a couple sharing a secret joke. The gorgeous dessert had been presented with only one fork. Trevor realized sharing a dessert might not have been the best idea.

A dessert that made him think of breasts was an even worse idea, despite how much he'd enjoyed teasing her about it. Now it was making him think of him and Jacey tangled together on that slope, the way she had felt underneath him, tiny but supple.

He had to guard against *that* happening again even as he worked hard to give her great experiences.

Sharing Paris-Brest was obviously not forwarding that goal. They were eating off the same fork. She was holding it out to him; he was leaning into it.

"I think that may be the best thing I've ever tasted," Jacey decided.

She had said that about every dish. He steeled himself against the inevitable moment when she closed her eyes, and that low purr of pure pleasure came from her throat.

It was true, though. It was the best dessert he'd ever eaten. But how much of that was because he imagined the taste of her lips remained on the fork?

He had to, of course, keep this from getting out of hand.

Tomorrow, Trevor decided, as a defensive measure, he'd be on skis. That would put him in a better position to help her, without ending up on top of her. Plus, even while keeping his distance, there was the added benefit of being able to show her exactly what he could do.

How did showing off fit into his defensive plan?

They hadn't had any wine. It must be the food and the long day making him feel less sharp than normal.

Almost under a spell.

"I think I'll try snowboarding tomorrow," she decided halfway through dessert. "I'll take a lesson first thing in the morning."

He tried not to glare at her.

A lesson?

He was not leaving her—a woman who looked like that when she ate Paris-Brest—with a guy named Bjorn who, as competent as he was on a snowboard, obviously fell into the same category as her ex.

And her not so secret admirer, Ozzie.

"I'll take another boarding lesson, too," he said, saying a sad goodbye to the comfort of being on skis and wondering when exactly his life was going to get back on track.

But if the past years had been *on track* then maybe he could just embrace what was happening now.

Except for the hot tub.

He was not sure he had ever wanted anything quite as badly as to get into that hot tub when they got back to their suite. His muscles ached and the stars were out.

But Jacey in a bathing suit?

Had she even brought a bathing suit? He didn't recall seeing one in her suitcase.

It occurred to him this was the first time he'd be alone with a woman since Caitlyn. He realized, bewildered by how it had happened, that the evening had taken on a date feel.

He was pretty sure Caitlyn's plan for him involved him being a better man. Not falling for her friend!

Falling for Jacey?

Those kind of dangerous thoughts had to be nipped in the bud. Both he and Jacey had sustained hard lessons about love and loss. They were here to try and have fun. That was all. That was his entire mission: help Jacey have fun. Be a better man.

In the interest of the better-man part, after they had walked home through a village made more charming by darkness and warm lights burning behind closed windows, he claimed exhaustion and went straight to bed… where he tossed and turned and tried to decide if that look on her face, when he had said his abrupt good-night, had been disappointment or relief. The last time he checked the time it was 3 a.m.

Which probably explained why he felt so grumpy when he found himself outside the ski school the next morning with Bjorn ignoring him and absolutely beaming at Jacey.

"Aren't *you* the nicest surprise?" he asked, wagging those white-blond eyebrows at her and flashing perfect teeth.

Trevor Cooper was not an impulsive man. He was careful and meticulous. But in his defense, he was also exhausted.

That must have been why he put his arm around Jacey. She turned slightly toward him, her brow furrowed. Her look of surprise was going to completely ruin the deterrent effect of his possessiveness, so ever so casually, he planted a kiss on her lips.

Trevor had meant it only as a warning to Bjorn. *She's taken.*

But as soon as his lips touched hers, it felt as if the entire world, Moonbeam and Bjorn included, disappeared. Her lips were soft and inviting. She seemed so conventional, but Jacey tasted of wild things, honey and alpine flowers.

He'd intended the lightest touch to her lips but as she leaned into him and her lips parted, she kissed him back.

The tenderness—and the hunger—in her kiss, made him pull away, suddenly the one who was shocked. He tried to grasp all those noble ideas he'd had last night. It felt as if they were disappearing, fog closing around them, the sweet taste of her lips like sunshine after darkness.

"Honeymooners?" Bjorn asked, with good humor.

Trevor gave himself a mental shake, but his second snowboarding lesson was a disaster. He couldn't concentrate at all.

He'd kissed her strictly for her protection.

Strictly.

But he felt shaken. He had never kissed anyone since Caitlyn. It felt wrong to have enjoyed it so much when it had been a mission-driven kiss, motivated absolutely for the right reasons!

Poor Jacey was naive in a sea where sharks swam. Caitlyn would have wanted him to protect her!

Jacey, who still wouldn't look at him, seemed to be concentrating just fine. In fact, she was doing way better on the snowboard than he was!

As soon as the lesson was over, Trevor headed for the chair without consulting her. He got on it and looked straight ahead as she settled beside him. Only then did he realize he was trapped. He hoped she'd be nice and pretend nothing had happened, but he was not so lucky.

"What was that all about?" she asked, her voice quiet.

"He seemed just a little too interested in you."

"Bjorn?" Her stunned tone told him he'd done the right thing. She didn't have a clue what men, including him, were like.

"You needn't act so surprised. Who else?"

"Let me get this straight," she said, her voice not quite so quiet now. "You kissed me, without my permission, to warn Bjorn away?"

"Exactly," he said, relieved she got his motive so clearly. "Normally, I would have asked your permission. But the circumstances were extenuating."

"They were not!"

"Aren't *you* the nicest surprise," he mimicked darkly. "I saw the look on his face."

"That's just insulting. You were marking me with a kiss, saying to Bjorn, *back off, she's mine*?"

"I might not have put it like that."

"Like what? A dog marking his territory by peeing on a tree?"

"I really wouldn't have put it like *that*."

"That's what it was."

"Okay, okay, I'm sorry. It didn't occur to me you might interpret it like that."

"My interpretation is the problem?"

Yes. He knew better than to say it out loud, though. He slid her a look. She was, unfortunately, really cute when she was mad. The taste of her lips, also unfortunately, seemed to be lingering on his own.

"Oh!" she said. "You saw his wedding ring, right?"

Trevor frowned. He hadn't actually seen that.

She started to laugh, but it wasn't a nice laugh at all.

"I'm afraid I fail to see what's funny."

"He's gay, Trevor."

"What? Bjorn?"

"Yes."

"How could you know something like that?"

"I saw him saying goodbye to his husband. They were standing outside Morning Sun Café, where we had breakfast."

Trevor had no right to feel so happy. The only thing that could make him feel happier than he felt right now was if Bjorn's husband was Ozzie.

He told himself his happiness was *protective* only. At least one of Jacey's unsuitable admirers had been eliminated. His *job* would be easier now.

But his happiness was short-lived.

"You know the real message you gave?" she asked him, her voice shaking with outrage. "That I'm not capable of making my own choices!"

"I said I was sorry."

"It wasn't heartfelt."

"Geez," he said. "Okay. In terms of your choices, there is Bruce to consider."

He pointed this out even though something was warning him now might not be exactly the time for his engineer's pragmatism to insist on backing his concerns for her with evidence.

"Bruce?" The quaver in her voice increased.

"Bruce, that guy you married who didn't support you through a tough time, who bought a house you didn't like and who was too cheap to take you out for a nice dinner. Ever."

Rather than being convinced by this very reasonable argument, her face went very red. It shouldn't have made her look cuter. But it did.

It shouldn't have made him want to kiss her again. Particularly since there was no one here to protect her from. But it did.

"I trusted you with that!" she sputtered.

It was a good thing they arrived at the top of the chairlift then because Trevor had the awful feeling she might have tried to push him off if she had to spend one more second with him.

Instead, Jacey cleared the chair with relative ease and whooshed off down the hill, never once glancing back, as if she had been riding that board her whole life.

Considering the level of confusion he was feeling right now, his motives and his mission weirdly muddy inside his own head, Trevor was glad to see her putting some much needed distance between them.

Why was she so angry? Jacey asked herself. The truth was that the overly protective part of Trevor was kind of endearing.

But the fact that he hadn't meant that kiss—at all— wasn't.

She had, embarrassingly, thrown herself into it! The terrible truth was she had found herself completely help- less against the primitive pull of his lips claiming hers.

And his cool assessment of her poor choice of a life partner hurt, probably even more so because it was true.

There had been warning signs about Bruce even be- fore Caitlyn got sick. There had been the shoestring dates, the tiny ring, the budget wedding, the poor quality fur- niture choices. By the time they got to buying the house, Jacey had been well aware what she wanted placed a poor second—or maybe even third or fourth—in his consid- eration.

It made her so angry that Trevor saw all of that!

Still, the snow and learning the new skill forced her to focus hard on getting down the run in one piece.

That kiss, or maybe the anger—or some combina- tion of both—seemed to heighten this experience. Snow- boarding down the hill she felt an astonishing boldness. She felt extraordinarily aware—of her body and breath, and of how connected she was to the snow and the moun- tain through the vehicle of the snowboard.

It was everything Ujjayi had ever promised!

Intensity seemed to surge through her veins.

It felt as if it was a secret ingredient that had been missing from her life. Even before the death of Caitlyn, the failure of her marriage and Johnny's disastrous au- dition, this had been lacking from her.

This verve.

And then those life events, those disappointments, those heartaches, had dimmed her light even further.

Jacey got to the bottom of the run and glanced over her shoulder. She felt quite gleeful that Trevor was struggling with the snowboard. Even with his natural athleticism, he was obviously having difficulty with transferring a lifetime of doing things one way to a brand-new way of doing them.

She got on the chairlift by herself. Without him! Without anyone. And it felt absolutely awesome!

She did another run by herself, and then another. But it finally occurred to her that Trevor appeared to be avoiding her, too. Was he *glad* they weren't skiing together?

CHAPTER THIRTEEN

Jacey squinted up the mountain. Trevor was a few minutes behind her. She could get on the lift without him. She could board all day without him.

But he was missing her transformation into a person who was powerful and independent. She wanted him to witness that.

So that the next time he kissed her, it would be because he wanted to, not because he had some archaic notion that it was up to him to ride in on a white stallion and save her from a lifetime habit of making bad choices!

The next time?

Oh, yeah. There was going to be a next time, and it was not going to be his choice at all. The next time the decision would be made by the newly empowered Jacey Tremblay!

Reality burst the bubble of her moment of empowerment.

What would Caitlyn think about Jacey's desire to kiss her husband? Was making a plan to kiss Trevor the right thing?

She frowned and thought of that letter.

Two years.

They had been drawn together by Caitlyn's own hand.

Trevor said his wife had suspected Jacey's own marriage was in trouble.

Could her friend have possibly guessed they would both be single? Certainly, she would have known Trevor well enough to know he wouldn't move on easily.

You're being crazy, Jacey told herself, uneasily. Her best friend was not match-making from heaven.

And yet, she remembered, suddenly, lying on the banks of the Bow River the morning after Caitlyn's bridal shower. It had been a beautiful spring day, and coming from out of town, Jacey had stayed with her friend. They had walked down to the nearby river, coffees in hand and, exhausted from all the shower shenanigans, had lain on their backs on the grassy slope, knees up and arms folded over their tummies.

"I love your happiness," Jacey had said to her.

And she had said, so softly, "I wish there were two of him so we both could marry him."

By bringing them together for this trip, had Caitlyn put her stamp of approval on what might unfold? Drawing in a deep breath, Jacey made her decision.

She waited for him to get on the lift with her and didn't move away from the pressure of his shoulder.

"Are you going to be mad all day?" he asked, not realizing she wasn't mad at all anymore, but the enormity of the decision she had just made had rendered her to silence.

"Because you're spoiling it," he said quietly.

"I'm spoiling it?" But she turned her head and looked at him. Really looked at him. He looked exhausted. He'd already said he hadn't slept last night.

If she was going to be a woman worthy of the man who had loved Caitlyn, she could not make it all about herself.

Helping each other—emotional complexities aside—was the reason they were here.

Caitlyn had been bang-on sending them here. They certainly hadn't been wallowing in the sadness of the anniversary that had just passed.

She touched his arm. "Let's not spoil it," she said. "You're right."

"The words every man loves to hear," he reminded her.

And then he smiled. And the sun seemed to shine even more brightly in her world.

With the tension eased between them, they snowboarded all day. They embraced the simple pleasures of new challenges, being outside, exerting themselves. Both of them gained confidence and after lunch they moved off the Orion chair and onto the Big Dipper.

"Last run," the liftie told them as he guided the chair to them.

"I can't believe it's the last run already," Jacey said, leaning into the back of the chair, breathing deeply of the fresh mountain air. "Part of me is glad. My muscles are screaming, *no more*, and part of me is so sad."

"We have tomorrow."

That made her feel even sadder. That only tomorrow was left. Would she be brave enough to kiss him again, to follow her heart where it wanted to go? The time seemed too tiny to explore the feelings building in her like the clouds on top of that mountain.

"We can ski out tomorrow afternoon. I am definitely skiing instead tomorrow."

It was *love vs. bathrooms* again! She was thinking of romantic possibilities; he was planning his ski day.

Maybe they were miles apart. Maybe there was a chasm between them that could not be crossed.

"I like boarding," Trevor said, "but I have a man's natural tendency to show off what I can really do."

He wanted to show off *for her*. Maybe the chasms were not so deep and wide as she thought. She felt herself looking at his lips. She had experienced what he could really do!

"You'll love skiing out," Trevor told her. "Or boarding."

"I don't even know what that means."

"We can send our luggage on the gondola and we can ski down. It's a really long run. I'd have to look it up, but maybe the longest in the world."

"I'm glad it's going to be ending on that note," she said. "Because I'm really sorry it's ending. I have had the best time."

He gazed down at her. "Me, too."

"I'm so glad."

"Caitlyn was right. I should have known she would be. She was always right."

"Women generally are," she said, straight-faced.

"Says the one who took the wrong turn up there on Merak that nearly took us off a cliff."

"Says the one who decided he was ready to take air and I followed him off a jump!"

"You loved it."

"Everyone says that when they survive."

"Anyway, it's not over yet. Let's go find something to eat."

And so they ate. Hamburgers tonight, because they were both too hungry to go back to the hotel and change. And far too hungry to wait for really good food to be prepared.

When they came out of the restaurant, it was dark.

"It feels like it's warming up," Trevor said. He stopped

and sniffed the air. "I wouldn't be surprised if it's snowing by morning."

After that day of chasing each other down Moonbeam Mountain, after the truce, Jacey was aware she was still being consumed by the memory of that kiss.

There was some trembling kind of awareness of him inside her, made sharper by this wolflike sniffing of the air, the prediction of flurries.

He leaned over and scooped up a handful of snow. He made it into a ball. "See? It's getting sticky."

"Like snowball-fight sticky?"

"Grow up," he said, sternly.

Hurt, she marched ahead of him. The snowball hit her in the middle of her back. She turned around and he shouted with laughter and dashed away.

She gathered up some snow and formed it into a missile.

"I have the right gloves for this," she warned him. "I'm not giving up until you surrender."

A childlike joy shimmered in the air between them as they chased each other through the main square of the village, screeching with laughter and tossing snowballs at each other until they were shivering and soaked.

"My hands are freezing despite the gloves," she told him, finally, puffing with exertion and laughter. "And my legs are killing me. They feel as if they're turning to mush."

He came and stood in front of her.

She gazed up at him, at the darkness of his eyes, at the fullness of the lips she had tasted.

"Okay," she whispered, "I surrender."

Without taking his gaze from hers, he reached for her hands, took off her gloves one by one and shoved them into his pockets.

And then he lifted her frozen hands to his lips, and he blew on them.

Maybe she had led a sheltered life—okay, she *had* led a sheltered life—but Jacey was pretty sure that Trevor blowing his warm breath on her cold hands on a starlit night in Moonbeam Village was just about the sexiest thing that had ever happened to her.

She had told herself the next kiss would be her choice. She pulled free of where his hands had cupped hers, and she leaned into him. She took his face in between her hands. She had to stand on her tiptoes.

She kissed him.

She kissed him with all that she had learned about herself that day. She kissed him with boldness, embracing the incredible sensation of giving herself over, completely.

She lost herself in his kiss, in the wash of glory that came from sharing such an incredible intimacy with him.

She lost herself. But found herself, too.

Trevor pulled away from Jacey and took her in.

Moonbeam was living up to its name at the moment; the entire mountain and village bathed in silvery light.

Jacey's face, illuminated by that light, was absolutely gorgeous. All day he'd been noticing something about her, something new, shimmering in the air, electrical.

In the moonlight it became crystal clear to him what that was.

Passion, he realized. She was unleashing the side of herself he'd seen hints of in the color of the suitcase, in the way she'd been drawn to the spectacular jacket she was wearing now.

He realized he really should have thought it through. Before he had opened this door by kissing her this morning.

Had his motivation really been about protecting her? He'd tried to convince himself of that all day. Or had he, as men were apt to do, cloaked a selfish motive in one that seemed more virtuous?

Tasting her so fully now, he felt as if he knew himself, and as if that knowing told him a deep truth.

He had wanted to taste her.

He had wanted this moment when they both surrendered.

Looking back, the moment it had all started to shift was when they had gotten on the gondola together. He had glimpsed it then.

Who she really was, that ability to move past fear, to grow from it, to allow it to change her.

And now, as they had explored the whole mountain, laughing, filled with the spirit of adventure, sat, shoulder to shoulder, discovering different runs and different chairs, and each other; now that they had sampled dessert from a shared fork, who she really was was so apparent he could not believe he had ever missed it.

He should have really thought this through before blowing on her hands on a moonlit night on the mountain.

The temptation of knowing her even more rose in him. He could picture them together in that hot tub.

It was the natural conclusion for this day. The only fitting conclusion.

But where was all this going?

He had to think about that. It was Caitlyn's doing that they were here. She had entrusted him with the well-being of her best friend.

He had to get his head screwed back on straight. He had to remember he and Jacey were both in an altered state up here.

So removed from the real world.

So intensely aware of each other.

He just had to be strong. It was just for one more night. He just had to do the right thing—be the better man—for just one more night.

"I was thinking the hot tub might be nice," she said softly.

It was as though she was reading his mind. Knowing his weakness.

He thought how angry he had made her kissing her this morning. But it hadn't really been anger; it had been hurt.

And he saw how much worse he could hurt her now.

"I'm allergic," he blurted.

She was scanning his face.

"The chemicals," he expanded.

Her look of disappointment was crushing.

"I get a rash."

"Oh. We could watch a movie."

"No, no. I wouldn't deprive you. You go ahead. I'll see you in the morning."

And he raced to his room and shut the door before his nose grew ten inches or his pants caught on fire.

He heard her softly open the patio door a few minutes later; heard her pad through the snow on the deck. Could a man hear a towel whisper off? He could certainly hear the gentle splash as she got in the water.

He wondered what the hell she was wearing. He was pretty sure she didn't have a bathing suit. Her underwear?

Naked?

She wouldn't be that bold, would she? Well, the woman who had arrived at his doorstep a few days ago might not have been.

But the woman who had led the charge down the very

tricky Phecda run would certainly be bold enough to step into a hot tub under a starlit night in the altogether.

He contemplated that with some agitation.

As it turned out, you didn't have to be a liar to have pants on fire!

Even long after she'd abandoned the hot tub and gone to bed, Trevor lay awake, tossing and turning, his second night without sleep.

It was a good thing they were leaving tomorrow because he was not sure he could be held responsible, in close proximity to a hot tub, for what a sleep-deprived man could be capable of.

CHAPTER FOURTEEN

JACEY FELT HER physical aches and pains dissolve into the gorgeous hot water. The emotional aches and pains were not so easy to dissolve.

She leaned back and studied the stars through the veil of steam. She felt deeply mortified.

Was Trevor really allergic?

He had shut down the suggestion of the movie, too. So the embarrassing truth was her newfound boldness had been met with rejection.

He probably thought she was a terrible friend to Caitlyn.

Maybe she *was* a terrible friend to Caitlyn, reading way too much into Caitlyn's last wish for them both.

Jacey had no doubt what would have unfolded if they got in the hot tub together.

The air between them tonight had been electric with sensuality. With *wanting* each other.

But that step between them was a huge one, complicated by their past relationship. By their mutual love of Caitlyn. By their mutual loyalty to her.

Jacey suspected Trevor had once again been casting himself in a protective role. He was putting on the brakes before they did something they both regretted.

But would she regret it?

At the moment it didn't feel as if she would have. She felt she was aching with unfilled need. Still, while it was all well and good to be bold, sometimes there were consequences; sometimes the genie could not be put back in the bottle once it had been allowed out.

And it didn't matter if she didn't regret it if he did! It was possible they were having two entirely different experiences.

It was then Jacey realized it was not just *need* that she was feeling.

It went far deeper than that.

It was true the past few days had allowed her to know Trevor better, and on a different playing field.

But she had known him for a very long time. She realized that she felt as if she now knew Trevor *deeply*.

Some terrible awareness wiggled to life inside her.

The most dangerous thing of all had happened while she was out playing in the snow, letting go, being emboldened by life.

It wasn't just that those things were making her feel so alive, so on fire with life, so intense, so engaged.

Not by a long shot.

She was falling in love with Trevor. Maybe she even had been in love with him for a long, long time.

She had seen him go through the most devastating moments of his life, and how he had not broken—even if he thought he had. She had watched his incredible strength be tested and tried beyond what most men could endure.

He had shown her what real love looked like.

Perhaps it was in those moments—of his courage, of his selflessness—that she had known her own marriage was beyond repair.

"Caitlyn," she asked the inky night, "what do you

think of all this? What if I started to love your husband even before you died?"

Her question was met with the deep silence of the dark mountain night.

She realized she was crying.

"I feel horrible," she whispered, "A horrible friend, a horrible person. Trevor probably knows how horrible I am. I'm so mixed up. I don't know good from bad at the moment."

There was no magic at all in the hot tub or in the mountain night. She got out and felt the sting of cold on her wet skin. The whole world suddenly felt jumbled, confusing, terrifying.

In retrospect, Jacey realized she had done nothing but make mistakes in love her entire life. Craving it so badly. Needing to bask in the unconditional approval only love could bring.

She realized she was glad he had put the brakes on, as humiliating as that was. She didn't want what she was feeling for Trevor to be tested.

She wanted to enshrine it.

And she never, ever wanted him to know.

When Trevor got up in the morning, the first thing he saw was that the snow he had predicted had arrived through the night.

Looking out his window, he realized the snow was coming down so hard he could not see across the village square, let alone to the peak of Moonbeam.

The second thing he noticed was the underwear Jacey had worn in the hot tub last night was draped over the towel bar in the bathroom. Red. And lacy.

Surprising secrets. Something white-hot threatened to sear him.

But when she emerged from her own room she seemed, thankfully, distant. One thing she was not was stupid. She had realized he wasn't really allergic to the hot tub and she would have read that as rejection, which he was sorry for. But he'd already let things get way out of hand. She would thank him for it one day.

But that day wasn't today.

It wasn't that she wasn't polite. Cordial even. But there was something guarded in her—and in him. The connection was gone between them, and he missed it.

They packed their things in silence—her undies disappeared off the towel bar—and put their suitcases by the door to be picked up and brought down to the parking lot for them after they had skied out later in the day.

She looked at her phone through breakfast. It was the first time he'd seen the phone since she had taken photos at the Banff gates. It made him aware of how in the moment she had been—they both had been—that neither of them had used their phones at all in the past two days.

He was a little sorry—and a little relieved—that she was using it now. And that it was doing exactly what those devices did.

Locking him out of her world. Putting distance between them.

"Just checking my flight," she said, glancing up at him. "We'll be back in Calgary in plenty of time to get me to the airport, right? It goes at eight."

"You're leaving tonight?"

He had thought she would spend the night back at his house. He was aware he wanted that, even as he dreaded it.

She glanced up at him.

He realized then that she wasn't checking her flight; she was changing it.

As she withdrew from him, he felt an aching lone-liness open inside him. It shocked him how deeply he yearned for her company, to re-create the feeling of con-nection between them.

But he knew he needed to be strong just a little bit longer.

They were on the mountain all day, despite the storm absolutely buffeting them. He skied rather than trying the snowboard again, but he had lost his desire to show off for her, to draw her further into the dangerous game they had been playing.

When they shared the chair on the lift he noticed, de-spite the fact it would have given them both comfort from the storm, she sat squished against the far edge, avoiding touching his shoulder. Conversation was limited by the howling of the wind.

There were other storms brewing that they needed protecting against.

Finally, it was over. He, coming off another sleepless night, was exhausted by the effort of subduing all the things that had been developing between them.

"Are you ready to ski out?" he asked her.

Are you ready for it to be over?

She nodded, not meeting his eyes.

He took the map of the resort from his zipped jacket pocket. He'd skied out before, but in the storm he thought the entrance to the Galaxy Trail might be tricky to find. The wind nearly tore the map from his hands.

Just as they arrived at the trailhead, an attendant was swinging a huge gate shut. In French and English a sign declared the trail closed.

"I'm supposed to get the word out," the resort em-ployee said. "There's been an emergency. Everyone is supposed to gather in the lobby of Moonbeam Manor. There will be an announcement."

They skied down to the nearest chair, rode back up and made their way through the deepening storm back to Moonbeam.

The huge lobby now had dozens of people milling about. When it seemed not another person could squeeze in, a manager held up his hand and silence fell.

"I'm afraid there's been an avalanche," he said solemnly. "The access road that leads from the highway to the parking lot has been completely covered. We'll have it fixed as soon as possible but meanwhile, we are snowed in."

There was a collective gasp from the gathering.

"No need to worry," he assured them. "We're completely prepared for all the surprises Mother Nature throws at us. This isn't the first time this has happened, and it won't be the last. Those of you who were expecting to leave us today have been put back in your rooms, as guests who should have been arriving will not be coming.

"There will also be a complimentary bar and a buffet dinner set up here—" he glanced at his watch "—in just a few minutes. Thank you for your patience with us and Mother Nature."

Trevor and Jacey went back to their room, then showered and changed and went down to the dinner. They exchanged a few polite words about the turn of events, but Trevor noticed how stilted they were with each other. He longed to knock down the wall around Jacey, at the very same time that he wanted to leave it where it was. He was a man at war with himself.

There was actually quite a festive, almost party atmosphere in the lobby. The buffet was out and the drinks were flowing. A fire roared in the hearth.

Bjorn was there and came over to introduce them to his husband, Jasper.

Trevor noticed that despite the charm and humor of the two men, Jacey still seemed distant.

"You know what we need? A good old sing-along! Can you imagine? The fire roaring, the snow outside, voices raised. Does someone know how to play that piano?" Jasper asked.

Bjorn looked at him indulgently. "Life is not 'White Christmas,'" he chided his partner.

"I know how to play," Jacey said.

Trevor shot her a look. She didn't meet his gaze. Instead, she took Jasper over to the piano and sat at the bench. "What would you like me to play?"

"Let's start with a round song!" Jasper said, delighted. This was obviously his forte. He quickly had the people divided into two groups. After his instructions, he signaled Jacey.

Gamely, she accompanied his "Row Row Row Your Boat."

Trevor watched her, frowning. Jacey did not seem to him like someone facing her greatest fear.

He thought of the way she had been today, withdrawn, cold. He felt stricken. He had caused that. Caused this. Now this woman was facing her greatest fear, not because she had found herself, but because she had risked something, been rejected and now felt as if she had nothing left to lose.

Bjorn had joined Jasper. The pair of them had amazing voices and were natural entertainers.

Jacey could play every single request they threw at her. Casually, as if her fingers flying across that keyboard was without effort. Making music happen was as natural to her as breathing.

Then one of the other staff members came over to Bjorn and said something in his ear. He went very still. He held up his hand and Jacey stopped playing.

"It seems," Bjorn said, addressing the crowd, "that they can't find Ozzie. He left early today. He's recorded as going down on the gondola."

Complete silence replaced joy. Where there had been festiveness, now there were growing whispers of anxiety and worry.

"There are search crews out right now," Bjorn said. "They will find him." He nudged Jacey. "Play something!"

She went very still. She glanced at the people gathered. It was almost as if she came awake in that moment and realized exactly what she was doing.

Trevor saw in her face the moment hope won. That she went from *nothing to lose* to somehow who she really was.

Her spine straightened. Her fingers were poised over the keys.

And then she took a deep breath. She closed her eyes. When she opened them, it was as if she was alone in that crowded room. She began to play.

Slowly, as she played, the anxious whispers faded and silence fell over the room. Trevor had never heard music like that, and from the rapt silence in the room, he was pretty sure no one else ever had, either.

Phones came out, people recording her, understanding what they were hearing was a once-in-a-lifetime—if that—experience.

Jacey, looking so ordinary sitting there in jeans and a sweater, became something that was not ordinary at all.

She became the music.

It was incredible. Every single thing it was to be

human was in every note. All sadness, all joy, all sorrow, all triumph. The music soared and fell and soared again.

He saw this was the gift she was giving them; all of them. Jacey, through her music, was going to a place mere words could never go. She was telling them the story of life.

But she was also telling them the story of herself.

Trevor saw every single thing she was. He could see the same quiet courage and resolve he had seen when she would not leave the side of her dying friend, even when it meant her own life was going to be left in shambles.

You could not hear that music and not know who she was.

Her soul was exposed to all of them.

The music wound down, ending finally on a single note that carried on and on like the sob of a woman who had lost her child.

When the note ended, absolute stillness followed. It stretched, and stretched some more, and then someone began to clap, and then the clapping was thunderous.

Somebody called, "Encore."

And others took up the chant.

It felt as if he, alone, in that entire room, could see that Jacey had nothing left. He saw that she was suddenly aware of having exposed herself, of being wide-open to strangers. People were surging toward her. Asking questions, thanking her, but Trevor moved through the crowd, knowing now was the time, if ever there had been one, that Jacey genuinely needed his protection.

She saw him coming, and for the first time that day, they connected. Her eyes met his, she leaned toward him and her face lit up with relief.

And something else that he couldn't quite put his finger on but that warmed him to his core.

He helped her gently off the bench, and the applause started again. He put her under the protection of his arm and acted as a shield as he quickly got her out of the room.

The door separating the main from the hallway whispered shut, but they could still hear the applause. And then, finally, silence.

He heard someone shout into the new silence, "Ozzie's been located. He's okay."

CHAPTER FIFTEEN

JACEY SAGGED. WITHOUT HESITATING, Trevor put one arm under her knees and the other behind her shoulders and scooped her up against his chest.

She sighed her relief, her breath forming a puddle of warmth that expanded with her every breath, until it seemed to envelop him.

Inside the safety of their suite, he set her down with an exquisite tenderness that he had not known he was capable of.

She was actually shaking, like someone in shock. She looked at him, her face pale, those green eyes, so familiar, resting on him with an expression of trust a man could live for.

"I'm sorry," she whispered. "I feel so emotional."

"Because Ozzie's been found?" He realized that niggle of jealousy was gone, completely erased by the look in her eyes.

"Yes, that, too."

"But?"

"It's that piece of music. I've been working on it for a long time. I've never played it in its entirety before. Even then, I played it by myself. And for myself."

"You composed that?"

She nodded. "I did."

"Wow."

She hesitated. "It's Caitlyn's song."

And then he understood. The life and death he'd heard in every note. Sweetness and sorrow. Love and loss. Residing side by side.

It was the whole story of what it was to be human.

Like a man who had been stumbling through the wilderness and had found a shelter, a welcoming light glowing from within, he came home to her.

He embraced all of it.

He embraced her.

He realized he had used all his strength to postpone a moment that could no more be stopped by such a puny thing as human will than that avalanche that had roared down the mountain.

His lips found hers and told her, as words could not, that he saw her. That he saw her completely.

And that he needed her like that, too.

Completely.

Jacey's bones felt as if they had turned to water, even before Trevor's lips sought hers. Found hers. Claimed hers.

Jacey had never experienced her own music in the way that she just had. Her music had been missing all the things her life had been missing.

The intensity. The passion. She knew, somehow, that piece of music had been waiting for the perfect moment, for that secret ingredient.

And so had she. Jacey had never been more aware of that than when she twined her arms around the strong column of Trevor's neck. It felt as if her whole life had been moving toward this moment.

Wholeness.

Her lips parted under the gentle command of his. She

thought the snowboarding and the mountain had shown her everything there was to know about living with intensity.

But now that assumption felt laughable.

This was intensity. The exquisite taste of Trevor, the rippling sensations that shivered through her as he took the kiss longer and deeper, as his hands tangled in the wisps of her short hair, as he pulled her closer into him. She was so close to him, in fact, she could feel the beat of his heart. She was so close to him it felt as if the heat coming off his skin could singe her.

His body was incredible, hard, taut, muscular. She had seen that in him, always, in the way clothes flattered his masculinity, in the way he carried himself, with the easy confidence of a man who was at home in himself and sure of his own strength.

But today, when Trevor had chosen skis instead of the snowboard, it felt as if every nerve in her body had quivered with even more awareness of him. He skied with a grace that seemed unearthly, his great strength blending with snow and rock, mountain and sky, to create a powerful ballet.

Was it because he had chosen to ski that Jacey's awareness had been so painfully heightened? Or was it because she had acknowledged, finally, to herself, how deeply her feelings ran for him?

It had made her greedy for the sight of him, even as she tried, all day, desperately, to hide that greediness, that *wanting*, from him. Being careful not to touch him, hardly engaging, trying not to look at his eyes or his mouth, or his hands.

But now, here they were. She was being confronted with everything that she had secretly felt and fought as they experienced the storm-enshrouded slopes of Moonbeam—the longing, the need, the hunger.

She was aware she could fight no more. Her strength was gone from her. Used up by a day of fighting herself, whatever remnants that remained, used up by the music.

It seemed like a very long time ago that she had arrived at Trevor's house and he had thrown open that door, aggrieved. Without his shirt on, those pajama bottoms clinging to the jut of his hips. Honestly, if she thought about it, she had been both longing for—and fighting—this moment ever since then.

Maybe even long before then.

Trembling, she reached for the buttons on his shirt. She undid them, one by one, slid her hands inside and touched the heated surface of his skin.

He went very still as she explored him. Again, she was aware that what she had understood to be intensity on the mountain paled in comparison to this. Even that feeling she had when she played the piano—immersed, lost in another world—paled in comparison to this sensation.

She was filled to the top and then to overflowing by the heated warmth of his skin, tight and warm, silky and smooth. Her fingertips played over his ribs and belly, over the hard buttons of his nipples.

With a low moan of both pleasure and pain, he finally stilled her hands, capturing them with his own. Holding her hands to his chest, Trevor retook her lips.

There was nothing left of gentleness in his kiss.

His lips captured. They plundered. They took. They demanded.

When he scooped her up in his arms again and strode across the suite, kicking open his bedroom door, she knew she was his captive.

That she was the maiden and he was the warrior. He

put her down on the bed. He stared down at her, his eyes dark with hunger, with wanting, with appreciation, with *knowing.*

And Jacey was certain that there had never, in the entire history of the world, been a captive as willing as her.

He took off his shirt with tantalizing slowness. And then his slacks dropped to the floor, and he stood before her, gloriously male, so beautiful it hurt to look at him without touching him.

She opened her arms to him and he came and laid himself tenderly on top of her, the sensation of his naked chest burning her through her blouse. The trail of fire continued as his lips touched her cheeks, her chin, her neck, and then dipped lower.

Without taking his lips from her, adding to the sensation by flicking her skin with his tongue, his hands dispensed buttons, removed her arms from sleeves. And then, with a snap of his wrist, her bra was open and then gone. They were heated flesh to heated flesh. The fire was now like a volcanic lake, so intense it felt as if it could consume everything around it.

He backed off from that consuming intensity, gazing at her with wonder and delight. And then he surged forward. He teased her. She tormented him. He nipped. She nibbled.

They were captive, not just to each other but also to something bigger than them both.

A force of nature that put the storm outside to shame, that commanded them both to finally, finally, finally surrender.

The sweetest surrender of all, a climb to the very top of a mountain, a moment balanced on the precipice.

And then the leap.

Not to fall.

No, to fly.

And then to find earth, to climb the mountain and to fly again.

All night they explored and experimented; they discovered and delighted in each other. Finally, beyond exhausted, their bodies tangled together, they slept the deep sleep of the utterly satiated.

And yet, in the morning, the hunger—the desire to climb to the top of the mountain—was back, as if it had never been slaked at all. And they began again.

The storm lifted at noon, about the same time they came up for air.

When they went and found a place to eat, they discovered the access road remained closed.

The resort had seemed a place separate from the world even before it had been cut off completely. But now it felt like their private playground. As the sun broke through the clouds, they decided to tackle the slopes for the afternoon.

Jacey was not sure she had ever felt the kind of exhilaration that coursed through her veins as she followed Trevor down Man in the Moon, her first black diamond, the ski run that required the most skill.

With the wind in her hair, the sun on her face and her *lover* leading the way, she was aware her body had never felt so exquisitely and completely alive.

And when she made it to the bottom without a single fall, and he threw his arm around her and kissed her on the mouth, it was bliss.

Pure bliss.

He lifted his head from hers. "Do you hear that?"

"No. What?"

"I think the gondola is running."

She cocked her head toward the sound.

"It means the access road had reopened."

She considered this with a sinking heart. Somehow, she had thought maybe they had days to investigate each other completely, not hours. Bliss notwithstanding, it felt as if they had wasted time skiing!

"Race you back to our room," she challenged him.

And with the mountains ringing with their laughter and shouts, they found their way back to privacy, back to each other's arms one more time before they had to leave their magical kingdom behind.

With a fire in the hearth and darkness falling, they made slow, soft, beautiful love on the floor in front of it.

Poised above him, after the loving, looking at his face, made more gorgeous by the flickering light of the fire, Jacey felt everything within her go still.

She realized it wasn't intensity that had allowed her to give birth to Caitlyn's song after such a long period of gestation.

Intensity had only been one element of a larger truth.

The truth she had been trying so desperately to distance herself from when an avalanche had forced her hand.

Love was the secret ingredient.

Love.

"Love."

She said it out loud this time, consciously. The word felt glorious, rich and full.

"I love you," she said, her voice low, brimming with the truth she was revealing to him.

She wanted to say more—so much more—that maybe she had loved him for a long time. That maybe Caitlyn had *wanted* this for them. That they should love again. That he was everything she could have ever hoped for in a lover: strong, considerate, passionate, beautiful—

But it pierced her euphoria that his expression had changed and she clamped her mouth shut before *all* of it spilled out of her.

If there was one look a woman did not want to see on a man's face after she had uttered her declaration of love to him, it was *that* one.

Regret.

Even before he spoke, she knew what he was going to say.

"I can't."

Slowly, regally, she untangled herself from him.

"You can't?" she asked him, and heard the leashed fury in her tone. "You can't what?"

He was silent.

"You can't what?" she insisted. "Say it back? Love me as much as I love you? Go forward? Have me in your life?"

Just barely, she managed to bite her tongue before she added, "You can't get over Caitlyn? Love me as much as you loved her?"

Looking at him, her fury grew.

"You don't mean *can't*," she accused him, jumping from the bed. "What you really mean is *won't*."

"That's not—"

She held up her hand. "Save it. You know what I just realized? I gave you everything. I trusted you with my every single fear and vulnerability. I trusted you with *me*. And what did I get from you? Nothing!"

She stormed into the shower. But then the fury died as quickly as it had come, and the power of it was replaced with something much worse.

She could feel her heart shattering, breaking into a billion pieces with the helpless realization that Trevor was not in the same place as she was.

He was not feeling the same things she was.

It was that devastatingly simple.

When she came out of the shower, he was in his room, behind closed doors. She could hear the hiss of his shower running; picture the water on his skin. Her mind slid there, tormented.

Revisited the pure sensuality of steam and heat and skin made slippery by soap, by lips tasting, touching *everywhere*.

The thoughts made her so weak with longing she wondered if it was possible to survive.

Of course it was possible to survive! She had an intimate knowledge of surviving disappointment.

Her whole life had really been preparing her for *this*.

Somehow, she managed to leave the hotel with him, to sit beside him in embarrassed silence as the go-cart delivered them to the gondola. It was full dark as they rode it down, but even if it had been light, all the enchantment of the first time—of overcoming her fear—was now overshadowed by the humiliation of not being loved back.

To his credit, he didn't try to say anything. Not. One. Single. Word.

But his expression of guilt—as if he was ashamed of himself—only made everything so much worse.

His vehicle was covered by a mountain of fresh snow.

Only yesterday she would have helped him clean it off. They would have been a team. A snowball fight might have broken out. Or a spate of cold-lip kisses.

Today she got in when he opened the door.

He got in his side and started the engine so that she would be warm while he swept away snow and scraped at icy windows.

She hated it that he was being chivalrous. It would be so much easier if he was a jerk.

Finally, they were ready to go. They got a short distance down the access road when they came to the place the avalanche had come down across it.

One lane had been plowed clear through a debris field, huge walls of snow rising on either side of it.

The headlights of the vehicle starkly illuminated the destruction. The absolute and furious power of the avalanche was so apparent. What had once been a solid road was churned up into the snow. It was as gray and wet-looking as freshly poured concrete.

Huge trees had been violently snapped in half and were embedded in the wall of snow, and a little farther down a root ball from what must have been a gigantic tree stuck out, the roots bare and tangled.

The avalanche felt like the perfect metaphor for Jacey falling in love with Trevor. It, too, had been a force of nature. It, too, had seemed pure, like the snow that had fallen and covered Moonbeam Mountain in seemingly innocent drifts.

But this was what she needed to remember about nature.

It could be beautiful and compelling.

And in the blink of an eye it could turn into a devastating, ugly surge of energy that wrecked everything in its path.

Jacey closed her eyes.

"Can you take me straight to the airport?" she said wearily.

"When's your flight?"

She made a great show of looking at her phone. "In a few hours."

This was a complete lie. The truth was worse, though. She had been so lost in love she had not done anything so practical as rebook her flight when their original exit from Moonbeam had been blocked.

She pretended to look at her phone for a while longer. She actually opened a game app on it—had this silliness actually given her pleasure once? Now she could not even concentrate on it, though she pretended to play. And then she gave up on that and opened her emails.

It was probably costing her the earth, using up data like this, and it was ultimately a waste, since she couldn't focus on one single email.

All that pretense added to her sense of being weighed down with weariness. She closed her eyes. And then she slept with the exhaustion of one who has been through a natural disaster. And who has survived.

But just barely.

CHAPTER SIXTEEN

JACEY'S WORDS PLAYED over and over again in Trevor's head.

And what did I get from you? Nothing.

That wasn't precisely true, but he was wise enough to know it was true in all the ways that mattered.

Trevor took the Stony Trail exit and looped around the city, so that he could come at the Calgary International Airport without heavy traffic and the kind of stops and starts that were sure to wake Jacey.

He glanced over at her.

Unlike the first time she had fallen asleep in his vehicle, her head coming to rest against his arm, she was deliberately avoiding contact with him. Her head was up against the passenger-side window, her neck crooked at an uncomfortable-looking angle. But he knew she would prefer that to touching him, and who could blame her?

Her face in sleep was troubled, but no less beautiful for it.

Jacey Tremblay loved him.

And there was not a doubt in his mind that he loved her. She was right; she had given him everything, shown him all of who she was: sweetly strong, loyal, fun loving, adventurous.

Then why was he letting her go?

Not for any of the reasons she thought.

Not because of Caitlyn, or not directly, anyway. Caitlyn would have wanted him to move on. He even wondered if she might have had a plan, two years ago, when she set the wheels in motion for this time for him and Jacey to be together.

But indirectly, it was because of Caitlyn. She had given him an intimate relationship with pain. Here was *his* truth. Time did not heal all wounds.

Time, if anything, sharpened awareness.

And this was his awareness: he had given his beautiful wife every single thing any woman could ever have wanted. He had given her 100 percent of himself and every material desire she had ever had had been fulfilled. He had given with a glad heart and a sense of pride all that his worldly accomplishments allowed him to give to her.

And yet, in the end, he had not been able to give her the child her soul yearned for. He had lived with her daily heartbreak until they had found out the awful truth. The awful truth—the other thing he could not protect her from.

So he was not letting Jacey go because he did not love her. The exact opposite was true. He was letting her go because he did.

He was letting her go because he knew a secret most men were blissfully unaware of: men were powerless over the caprice of life.

He was damaged—irreparably—by that knowledge. The thought of ever trying for another baby—and didn't Jacey deserve a house full of chubby, laughing babies?—filled him with a nameless terror.

Trevor would prefer Jacey didn't know that about him. That she be left thinking of him as they had been allowed to be for those precious days at Moonbeam. Carefree. Fun loving. Fearless.

She never needed to know what it had cost him to say those words.

I can't.

As soon as he slowed at the airport turnoff, she woke up, just as she had when he slowed at the Banff gates.

With an ache, he remembered her wonder that day.

But now was not the time to remember how going through those gates into Banff National Park had been symbolic of all the doors that had opened in her, revealing her great capacity for life, for bravery, for discovery, for sensuality.

For love.

He steeled himself against the memories that had begun when they had braved driving through that first squall to enter a brand-new world. A world of laughter, of playfulness, of connection. A world that made him so achingly aware of how empty his world had been.

And that was the world he was returning to.

He could change it all. Right now. He wanted to. He wanted to be with her; *don't go.*

But this time the only force of nature he could blame for being weak when he so badly needed to be strong, would be the one raging within him.

Wanting her.

Wanting every single thing about her. Her laughter. Her warmth. Her bravery. But in the end, wasn't every single one of those things about what she could give him?

What could he give her? Brokenness. Cynicism. An awareness that could never go away, not now, of the potential of life—of love—to devastate and destroy.

He forced himself not to look at her again, though even

not looking at her, he drank in the sound of her breathing as if it were water, and he would never have it again.

As he approached the airport, he thankfully needed to focus on the road, on the signage, the lights, the traffic.

And not the fact that goodbye was coming.

He took the loop that pointed to short-term parking. Now was the time to remember only one thing: the trust in her eyes. Jacey trusted him to do the right thing.

He hadn't done the right thing. Chasing her around the mountain, around their suite, holding her, loving her... he'd been weak when he wanted to be strong. He had to fix that now. It felt as if Humpty Dumpty had fallen off the wall and he had to try and put the pieces back the way they were before.

"I'll just park here and—"

"No," she snapped. "Just leave me in the drop-off zone."

She was so angry.

No, hurt. And it was coming out as anger.

"If I park, I can help you with your bag," he said, trying for a reasonable, even tone. He looked in the rearview mirror at the suitcase on the backseat, the one that should have warned him, right from the start, Jacey was not as she appeared.

She was as bold and as adventurous as that bag had hinted. But she was also talented and brilliant, deep and sensitive. The past few days at Moonbeam had proven that beyond the shadow of a doubt.

"I don't need your help." And then in a smaller voice, "Please, don't."

And he got it then. He was trying to hold off that moment when he said goodbye to her, and she wanted the exact opposite: *Please don't drag it out. Please don't make it worse.*

Trevor was not sure he had ever despised himself as much as he did in this moment. He'd seen her so completely over the past few days. How could he have not known taking her as a lover would destroy her?

He'd nearly made it. He'd nearly managed to be the better man his wife had always hoped he would be.

Damn avalanche.

He pulled over in the drop-off zone. Despite her protest, he got out. She was trying to wrestle her bag out of the backseat, but it was too big for her, and stuck at an awkward angle in the door.

He reached over her, took it with one hand, yanked and set it in front of her.

She glared at him for the ease with which he'd accomplished that.

"Jacey," he said, "it isn't about you. It's about me."

She looked as if she was considering slapping him. He almost wished she would. He deserved it. It would let the pain they were both feeling out, given it physical weight.

But she didn't slap him. As he'd suspected, her careful control hurt him worse than the slap ever could.

"Thank you," she said, pulling the handle up on her suitcase, her voice icy with sarcasm. "*It isn't about you. It's about me.* The worst and least original brush-off in history."

Trevor wanted to take her and hold her, to taste her lips one last time, to put his finger under her chin and force her to look in his eyes.

She would see the truth if she looked in his eyes.

It *really* wasn't about her. It was about him *knowing*, as only one who had loved and lost could know, that the goodbye was inevitable between them.

If they felt so strongly after just a few days that the

word *love* had whispered off her lips, what would it be like to say goodbye after a year? Five years? A lifetime?

This was his gift of love returned to her, though she must never see it.

That he *knew* the terrible price of love and could not ask her to pay it.

"Goodbye," he said softly. She didn't answer. When he got back in his vehicle, Trevor could not resist one glance back at her.

She was walking away, her chin high, her spine straight, that crazily colored suitcase trailing along behind her.

And though he waited and waited, some part of him hoping for one last glimpse of her so- familiar face, she never looked back.

A word whispered through him.

Beloved.

She would not sulk, Jacey told herself firmly, fitting her key in the door of her apartment the next morning, and shoving the mail that had gathered in with her foot.

She'd had to wait to get on a flight, stand-by. She'd spent a very uncomfortable evening in the Calgary International Airport.

She would not indulge in that ice cream she knew was in the freezer. Nor would she put on her pajamas and while away days watching movies.

She would not be pathetic.

Having vowed that, she stepped over the mound of mail and entered her apartment. It was tiny. After Trevor's house and the suite at Moonbeam Manor, it looked particularly humble. She could see the whole thing from the doorway. Morning light was battling past the apartment next door to create a meager sliver across the sofa.

She looked at that piece of furniture with the affection one might reserve for the boy they had had a crush on in grade two. She realized how silly it was that, once upon a time—a different lifetime ago—she had thought you could make a statement about who you were with a sofa. She picked up her mail and threw it on the kitchen table.

She went through to the sofa and hoisted her suitcase up on it. She glared at that, too.

A luggage choice did not make you bold! Though possibly, it and the sofa, hinted at something…

"Oh, to hell with it," she said. She was tired and crabby and she did not want to decipher secret messages from past choices. She went and got the ice cream from the freezer and didn't bother with a bowl.

Squishing in beside the luggage on her silly statement-piece couch, she opened the container. She dug straight into it with a spoon.

She only ate a few bites before she burst into tears. There was not enough ice cream in the world to fill the hole in her that needed to be filled.

Nor was a sofa or a daring luggage choice going to fill that place inside her.

Tears streaming, she remembered. She remembered four days of feeling filled to the top. Of feeling as whole as she had ever felt in her entire life.

Four days of exquisite joy. Four days of the exhilarating discovery of what it meant to be brave. Four days of living life flat out. Four days of being so awake, the very spark of life surging through her veins as essential blood.

Now what?

She thought of the days stretching ahead of her. They seemed endless and uninteresting. She got up off the couch and wandered into her bedroom.

There were the new pajamas with kittens frolicking.

Pathetic pajamas for a grown woman. Not the pajamas of a woman who had loved so passionately, so intensely, it had felt as if the love could burn down the whole world around her.

Which was exactly what it had done!

She put on the pajamas as resignation set in. She had, for a few days, tried on a different personality. That didn't make it real.

Trevor had probably seen right through her. And known all that boldness would wear off, and underneath it would be a dull music teacher who wore cat pajamas that were a pretty accurate reflection of who and what she really was.

A scaredy-cat.

She pulled back her covers, exhausted, but she couldn't sleep. She realized she felt really, really angry at Caitlyn.

Why had her friend done this to her? To them?

And worse, had she betrayed her friend by sleeping with her husband? Not just sleeping with him. Devouring him. Letting him be the sun that her whole world circled around.

When Caitlyn was writing that letter, she had only wanted them to return to normal, to have fun. Couldn't she see the danger involved in putting them together? Maybe she hadn't. Maybe she had thought Jacey was just not the type Trevor would *ever* go for. The mousy little music teacher.

Jacey frowned, thinking of that.

That might be how Jacey had seen herself, but the fact was, Caitlyn had *never* seen her like that. As best friends do, it had often seemed to Jacey as if Caitlyn held a vision for her that she did not see for herself.

Mighty, Caitlyn used to say to and of her.

And usually in a moment when Jacey wasn't seeing

herself as mighty at all! Like the time they'd gone to the climbing wall and Jacey had only ascended a quarter of the wall before she had backed off, gone back down trembling.

She had seen it as failure, but Caitlyn hadn't. "Don't you see it's more of a win for you to go a quarter of the way up, than for me to go to the top and back a dozen times?"

Or like that time they'd been walking on a path and that dog had come out of nowhere, snarling and baring its teeth at them, and Jacey had held Caitlyn when she tried to turn and run, stamped her foot, said in a voice not her own, *Get! Or you'll be dealing with me.*

She had practically had post-traumatic stress over it afterward, but Caitlyn had looked at her with that sweet smile that said, *I see you.*

That was what she missed most about her friend.

That sense that somebody saw her. That sense that someone held tight to who she really was, even when she had lost it.

She remembered, suddenly, something Caitlyn had said to her on her and Trevor's wedding day, before the ceremony.

Caitlyn had been trembling with love and excitement.

And yet, even on that day—a day that could have been all about the bride—Caitlyn had not been like that. The comfort of her guests had come first. She had chosen dresses that her wedding party *liked.* In lieu of gifts, she had asked people to make donations to a camp for disabled children.

As they had stood in that room, making the final adjustments to her dress, she had taken Jacey by both her hands and looked deep into her eyes.

"I'm the luckiest woman on earth," she had whispered. "Oh, Jacey, I wish you could feel this way, too."

Caitlyn had loved her so much she had wanted Jacey to find what she had found.

Was there a hidden motive in that dying wish that Caitlyn had bestowed on them? Had she hoped that bringing Jacey and Trevor together would lead to something? Had Caitlyn, always so spookily intuitive, even more so in the last days and week of her life, wondered about *possibility*?

Hadn't the past few days felt as if Trevor *had* seen her in the same way Caitlyn had? Not just seen Jacey's potential, but drawn it out of her, made her into the very person Caitlyn had always insisted was there?

No, that was craziness.

Wasn't it?

Or was that what love did?

Over the next few days Jacey canceled her classes and her students. She sat around in her pajamas and ate ice cream. She watched movies.

Caitlyn's letter had only postponed the misery, and now it felt as if Jacey was grieving two losses.

But even as she went through the motions of despair, Jacey slowly arrived at the awareness she was not the same person she had been before she had gone to Banff with Trevor.

She was changed from the person she had been when she left this apartment just a few short days ago.

She was completely and irrevocably changed.

It might be a tired metaphor, and yet she felt like the caterpillar who had broken out of the cocoon; she felt as if that struggle had made her stronger and better than she had ever been before.

Once upon a time, when she was a different person,

she had naively believed that buying a couch or picking a suitcase could change who you were, could fill some gaping hole within you.

Now, slowly, Jacey came to a new conclusion.

You didn't go to a man like Trevor with holes that needed to be filled. You went to a man like that already filled to the top, and you gave him that gift that overflowed out of you.

She saw her life in a raw, new light.

She saw herself as constantly waiting for the approval that never came. She had been like a storybook damsel in distress waiting for a rescue. Why had she never looked for ways to rescue herself?

She had wanted her father and Bruce to love her.

As if, as a result of their love, she would feel lovable.

But if she first didn't love herself, if she didn't see herself as valuable, how could she possibly expect others to see that?

Trevor's rejection wasn't an excuse to lose herself in ice cream and movies! It was a reason to grow! To become…to become the person Moonbeam Mountain had hinted she could be. To become the person she had always seen reflected back at her in Caitlyn's steady gaze.

A little voice in the back of her mind whispered, *someone who is worthy.*

It didn't even sound like her own voice. It sounded like Caitlyn's.

Worthy of love.

And it seemed to defeat the purpose of her discovery to even ask where Trevor fit into that equation, or if he did at all.

Maybe Trevor was lost to her, but she did not want to lose the lessons she had learned on that mountain; lessons it felt as if her friend Caitlyn, defying death, had given her.

And given Trevor, too, even if he chose to reject it. But Jacey did not want to lose—ever—the gift that loving him, even so very briefly, had given her.

She didn't ever want to lose the intensity with which she had lived those few days. She didn't want to live in a state of being constantly vigilant, watching for and waiting for the next inevitable catastrophe.

Living like that hadn't kept her safe! It had made her a prisoner.

She had been held prisoner by the insecurities that felt as if they had dogged her all the days of her life, since she had sat in front of that audience, as a twelve-year-old, and not met a single expectation, not even her own.

Failure.

The reoccurring theme of her life.

Had she inadvertently passed that on to her most promising student? It seemed like as good a place as any to begin addressing her issues.

She called Johnny. His phone rang for a very long time. She reached the conclusion he was not going to speak to her—the one responsible for his shattered dream—and rehearsed a compelling message that would make him call her back. Then, he answered, breathless.

"Miss T! Hi! I almost didn't answer and then I saw it was you."

He sounded *happy* to hear from her; it sounded as if he'd answered because it was her. The engineer of his defeat, she told herself, before she made too much of his enthusiastic greeting.

"I've been thinking of you," Jacey told him. "How are you?"

"I'm doing great!" he said.

This was so far from the brooding-in-the-basement-nursing-his-wounds picture she had formed, that she actually laughed.

"It's nice to hear you laugh," he said. "I wondered what it sounded like."

"I never laughed in the two years we worked together?"

"Well, not like that. Sometimes when I hit a sour note you'd kind of bray."

Bray?

"You were always so serious. I mean, I liked you, but it was as if I was getting ready to play at a funeral. Which the CABA audition sort of was."

He was right about the audition for the Canadian Academy for the Betterment of the Arts. It had been the death of his career. Though she was shocked that she'd come across as so humorless.

"That's what I phoned about. I've been thinking about the audition," she said.

"Oh, I try not to think about that. At all."

Of course he wouldn't. He was young! Who sat around contemplating the death of their dreams?

She had.

Since she was twelve years old she had thought about that failure almost every day.

But now that she thought about it, had it really been the death of her dream? Or the death of her father's dreams? The death of his hopes for her?

In the same way her marriage had been the death of her most dearly held fantasy: happily ever after.

"Look, I know where we went wrong," she told Johnny.

She was met with silence, except for a loud banging

noise in his background that made her jump. Were people yelling?

"Where we went wrong?" he asked, likely distracted by all that noise.

"Technically, Johnny, you're a superb pianist, but I feel as if I failed to allow you to imbue that Chopin piece with the intensity—the passion—it deserved."

There were those noises again. Banging. Shouting.

"Miss Tremblay, it's not like that."

She rushed on. "I failed you. But I'm sure I can make it right. I'll work with you for free if you want to try again."

"Miss Tremblay," he said, "you've got this all wrong."

CHAPTER SEVENTEEN

"I DON'T UNDERSTAND," Jacey said slowly.

"It wasn't about you," Johnny said.

Hadn't she heard those very words quite recently?

"I blew the audition. I blew it on purpose."

"What?" She thought of all those hours. All that work. Sometimes her back actually hurt at the end of a session, from leaning over the piano for so long, forgetting time. "You can't mean that."

He was just trying to let her, the humorless, laughter-deprived piano teacher, off the hook. He was being noble, the poor kid.

She was changed! And she could change his music. "Let's try again."

"I don't want to try again," Johnny told her, the firmness of his tone very grown-up, and letting Jacey know he wasn't letting her off the hook, because he didn't see her as being responsible for his failure in the first place.

"But—"

"It was never what I wanted."

Now that she thought about it, Johnny Jordan didn't really seem like a kid anymore, either.

"It wasn't?"

"Not even close. It's what everyone else wanted for

me. But I just wanted to be a regular guy. I'm playing hockey."

Those were the sounds she could hear in the background: hard pucks hitting side boards, skates scraping on ice, young men shouting.

"My parents wouldn't let me play hockey," he told her, "because of my hands. They were worried about me hurting my hands. But I've wanted to play all my life. I'm late to it. Most of these guys have been playing since they were five. I'm the worst one on the team, but I'm getting better every day. And I love it."

In that quiet statement, Jacey heard the very intensity—the passion—in his voice that she had mistakenly thought she had failed to give him.

"I gotta go. My line is on. Hey! I'm glad you phoned." He hung up without saying goodbye.

She looked thoughtfully at her phone for a long time before sliding it into her pocket.

It was the second time in a very short period that she had been given the same message.

It's not about you. It's about me.

The first time, delivered by Trevor, Jacey had dismissed it as the least original brush-off line ever.

But what if it was true?

And what if it was true, not just about Trevor, but about all the things that she had taken responsibility for—the list of failures she had allowed to shape her?

The list of failures that she had allowed to make her timid instead of bold. That had made her afraid to try new things in case she failed yet again.

There was a world waiting for her to discover it! A world waiting to show her what made her passionate. A world that would put that enthusiasm in her voice, the way she had just heard it in Johnny's.

She wanted to feel the way she had felt at Moonbeam. Intensely alive. On fire with life. It couldn't just be because of the way Trevor made her feel, even though just thinking about the way Trevor made her feel made her tingle.

But in the end, it had to be about the way she felt about herself.

"The world awaits you," she said out loud, and then louder.

She noticed a catalog peeking out from under the mail she had deposited on her kitchen table. She went over to the table and slid it out.

It was a list of winter activities and courses being offered within the community.

Beat the Winter Doldrums.

She flicked open the first page. The activities were listed alphabetically. Bread making. Calligraphy. Crochet. Doughnut Basics. Doll making.

She flicked ahead a few pages.

Her heart began to pound in her throat.

Skydiving.

Jacey tried to turn the page, but her hand seemed to be frozen.

She read: *You'll never feel as alive as you do when you and your tandem instructor leap into the big blue and let gravity do the rest!*

She was afraid of heights!

It was not a good idea, part of her insisted primly, to get that *never so alive* thrill from tempting death.

Or from taking on lovers.

If she looked at it rationally, trying to get a sense of herself from skydiving wasn't that different than trying to get a sense of herself from buying a sofa.

Except buying a sofa didn't challenge fear.

It made a bold statement, without being bold at all.

Before she could talk herself out of it, before she could come up with a zillion excuses to find a different way to live fully and boldly, she picked up her phone again.

"Go away," Trevor called from his prone position on the couch. It was the Masters at Augustus. Who would have the unmitigated gall to interrupt this event?

He hunkered down. The new kid looked like he might birdie—

The knock came again, persistent.

He got up, resigned, and went to the door. He threw it open.

And *she* was there. Jacey. The one he thought of, longed for, fought his feelings for every single day. For the second time in his life, he was desolate over loss.

He drank her in, aware it felt like a miracle to see her again, when he had resigned himself to that never happening. Her hair was longer. It looked good. Unreasonably sexy. She had put on a bit of weight, but in a good way. It made her look, what? Satisfied?

It felt like a knife going through him to wonder if someone else was *satisfying* her. What was it about Jacey that brought out the jealous teen boy in him?

Her unreasonable sexiness, he decided, that men spotted long before she had discovered it herself.

Though she did have the look of a woman who had discovered herself now. How dare she look so happy and alive when he was in worse shape than when she'd arrived here the first time?

Not that she could know that. Ever.

"Trevor! You're still in your pajamas."

"It's Saturday."

"I meant the *same* pajamas as last time I saw you in them."

Did it mean something that Jacey had noticed they were the same pajamas as the ones he'd worn two months ago? Of course it meant something! The awareness had been there all along. And it was still there. The danger between them had not died.

If anything, that look of breezy confidence about her was making it worse!

Despite her light tone, her eyes drifted to the nakedness of his chest. There were memories in her gaze, and hunger. She touched her lips with her tongue.

It made him want to grab her, drag her in the house and kiss her until they were both breathless, until the entire world became just the two of them, nothing existing outside the boundaries of what they could make each other feel.

She had done this once before, he reminded himself sternly, made reality evaporate, made him weak when he wanted to be strong.

"What are you doing here?" he growled.

"I've come to rescue you," she said.

Rescue? *Him?*

"Annoying," he said. "The Augustus is on."

But his heart, the heart that had felt like a stone within his chest, came back to life with a hard thump.

"What is that? A movie?"

"The Masters?"

Some heat sparked in her eyes, turning the green to emerald. "Is that kinky?"

Trevor felt the shock of her asking *that*. The shock and unwanted heat.

"Golf," he managed to sputter.

"Oh, golf." She wrinkled her nose. She looked really

cute when she did that, not at all like someone who would inquire about his kinkiness without blushing.

He thought he might be blushing. If he was wearing a shirt, he had a feeling he'd be tugging the collar away from his throat, giving himself some breathing room.

She was looking at him way too closely. As if she saw everything. The emptiness. The months of pain. The regret. The questions. The doubts. The four thousand times he had nearly reached for the phone.

Please. Save me.

Trevor said, hastily rebutting the thought as if he'd said it out loud, "I don't need rescuing."

She peered in behind him at his house. "It looks like you might."

"It's socks on the floor, not a fire-breathing dragon." But the heat rising as he looked at her, as he remembered her, made it feel as if there *was* a fire-breathing dragon inside him.

"Quite a few socks."

"Look, it's a long way to come to talk about socks." On the television behind him, he heard the crowd roar. "You made me miss the putt."

"Boo-hoo," she said.

There was something so different about her. That was part of what was stoking the fire within him.

It wasn't just the new hairstyle. It was the way she was carrying herself. The light in her eyes. That little smile tickling across the lushness of her lips.

He realized what it was. Confidence.

Even the way she was dressed seemed different than what he remembered. Except for her wedding day, Jacey Tremblay had always seemed subdued, the woman who least wanted to draw attention to herself.

But now spring sunshine spilled around her, and she'd

worn a dress in celebration of the season, apparently. He squinted at it while trying not to appear too interested.

It was the same color as the banks of daffodils the community association had planted. It hugged the parts of her that had filled out and showed quite a bit of the length of her legs. He knew how strong those legs were, and not just from watching her snowboard, either.

Something clawed at the inside of him. It was more than hunger. Hunger didn't feel as if it could consume you, did it?

Maybe if you hadn't had anything to eat for two months, it did.

But no, it wasn't hunger. It was fire.

"What's with the suitcase?" he asked her, trying for an unfriendly tone, one that would chase her away. For good.

Even as part of him sighed its welcome.

It wasn't just a suitcase. It was *that* suitcase, the one that should have warned him there was a wild side to her that she kept carefully hidden from the unsuspecting.

Now, he noticed, leaning against the suitcase was a snowboard. The design and colors on that were *way* crazier than the design and patterns on the suitcase.

No, no and no.

He frowned at her. He pointed at the snowboard. "What's that for?"

"Uh, isn't it obvious? I bought my own. I found out that the rental ones aren't all that good."

"You've been snowboarding?" He nearly added *since* but managed to bite his tongue. No need bringing either of their attention back to *that*. The logical question wasn't whether or not she'd been snowboarding; it was why she had arrived here, on his doorstep, with her snowboard. And her suitcase.

That was the logical question. Engineers relied on logical questions.

Logical questions kept the world from going crazy, kept it running according to irrefutable and predictable rules.

"I've been snowboarding lots," she said. "There's a hill outside Toronto. I mean, compared to Moonbeam, it's pathetic, of course. But still, it was okay to practice stuff."

"Huh." She'd gone snowboarding without him. He had no right to feel faintly miffed, as if somehow he had thought that would be *their* thing.

They were not *they*.

He hoped she hadn't been practicing anything else since he wasn't there to protect her from the Ozzies of the world.

"Why are you here?" he asked gruffly, asking the logical question. He drew in a deep breath. "Please don't tell me you got another letter from Caitlyn."

Jacey actually cocked her head at him. For God's sake, it looked as if she felt sorry for him.

"No, no letters from Caitlyn," she said. "Unlike you, I got the message the first time."

Unlike him? He glared at her. "Oh, yeah, and what was that?"

"It was that time can be short. Shorter than we think," she said softly. "The message was to live every minute."

He supposed that explained her snowboarding without him.

"The message," she continued softly, "was to accept every single gift life offers."

He warned himself not to say it to her. But the words came out, anyway.

"I got a message, too," he said. "It's different than

yours. You know how we've talked about things that have the potential to be dangerous?"

"Airplanes, bathrooms," she said.

"You know what's the most dangerous thing of all?" he asked her.

"Love?" she guessed, softly. She had no right to be looking at him like that. As if she *saw* him. Completely.

"Hope," he whispered, his voice hoarse. "We hoped for a baby. And instead we got a diagnosis. And then we hoped for a cure."

Tears were slipping down Jacey's cheeks. See? This is exactly what he hadn't wanted. To drag her into his world of disillusionment.

He wanted to stop speaking. But he didn't.

He said, "Right until her very last breath, I hoped. I hoped for a miracle."

The tears kept coming. Strangely, it did not feel as if her tears were hurting her. It felt as though they were healing him.

Then she spoke. "Maybe this is our miracle. Love rising out of the ashes of all that despair. I know it's not the one we asked for. Or hoped for. But maybe this is the miracle we needed. The miracle of believing love can win."

Trevor was thunderstruck. He could feel everything in him that wanted to be strong, that wanted to stubbornly hold on, that wanted to protect her, beginning to tremble, a structure warning of collapse.

"Look what I have," she said.

He was not sure he would have been surprised if she pulled a toy poodle from that oversize bag. She held something in front of him, right under his nose.

Lift tickets. Moonbeam.

"Plus a couple days at the hotel."

He could actually feel a little bead of sweat breaking

out over his upper lip as his heart, foolish thing it was, leaned toward what Jacey was holding out.

Not lift tickets.

No.

The most dangerous thing of all.

Hope.

CHAPTER EIGHTEEN

Hope that Jacey was holding, not tickets, but a key. To the way out of his life, layered now, discontent on top of his grief.

He'd felt flat, out of sorts since he'd dropped Jacey at the airport. His life had seemed like a yawning cavern of emptiness.

He'd asked himself a thousand times, maybe more, if it had been the right thing to do, to let her go.

He'd beaten himself up at least that many times for the affair.

Though he wasn't sure if it was an affair, and he sometimes got lost in debates over the semantics of it.

Intimacy.

Event.

Fling.

Hookup.

What he'd discovered was beating himself up, and inner debates kept it all at an intellectual level. It kept it in his head, where he could cope with it. It kept the physical longing for her at bay. Slightly.

The facts: he'd had a hookup, fling, intimate event, affair, with one of the best people he had ever met.

He was in a prison of absolute loneliness and self-loathing.

Jacey didn't have the good sense to be holding it against him, apparently. In fact, she was waving a reprieve in front of him.

Hope.

Trevor leaned his shoulder against the door, just to make it clear he was not inviting Jacey in. He thought it was probably a pretty good impression of a man who could have a casual fling and walk away after.

Without her ever knowing it was for her own protection. Without her knowing about the fire-breathing dragon that was taking in her lips and her curves and burning him up.

"A plane ticket," he said as she held up items for him to see, one by one, "a snowboard, extra luggage fees for the snowboard, a couple of days at Moonbeam. Did you win a lottery or something?"

"In the weirdest way, I did. Remember when I played Caitlyn's song?"

A moment in his life he would never ever forget, but it felt as if an admission would tell her the awful truth. That he'd been unable to forget her, or one single thing about that time they had on the mountain. He lifted a shoulder instead of answering.

"I guess people were videoing it on their phones."

"They were," he confirmed. "I remember that. Everyone was taking out their phones." Except him. He had been so lost in that moment, it had never occurred to him that he could have recorded it.

Could have tortured himself with it all these months.

"I'm not sure I could say it went viral, but it's certainly all over social media."

He contemplated that. He could have been watching her, the way she had looked that night they had learned of the avalanche? That night he had seen her so fully and completely herself? That night that he had seen her soul? It would have been torture, but torture of the love-liest kind.

"Anyway, long story short, a woman saw it who is kind of a big deal executive in the music world. I've got this contract to record it. And some of my other compositions. They gave me an advance. It's a ridiculous sum of money."

He tried to say something sarcastic. *Don't spend it all in one place.* But he couldn't. That earthquake-about-to-happen sensation increased as he felt a brick in the wall that made up his defenses loosen.

"Not that I'm rich or anything," she said, "but I knew right away what I wanted to do with it."

No matter how much he wanted to protect her from the destructive caprice of love, even as his barriers were showing signs of weakening, he needed her to know. That he was happy for her.

"Jacey, that's incredible." He meant it. He could see her flying far and high. He hoped she was ready for it. "I'm glad you didn't give up music."

"I actually talked to that boy who didn't pass the audition I trained him for. Remember my sense of failure? It turned out it wasn't my fault. He failed the audition on purpose. It's not what he wanted."

He looked at the light on her face.

Oh, she was ready for whatever came next. The fact she had stopped taking responsibility for the whole world was written all over her. She didn't need him.

"It *has* been incredible. It seems the more I've opened myself up to life, the more good things have happened to me. Anyway, I have money. And I decided I had to use a bit of it to try snowboarding in the spring."

"I thought you were scared of bears," he reminded her. He heard something morose in his tone.

"Oh, I am. Terrified. But that's why I'm here. Part of why I'm here." She blushed, and her eyes skittered to his chest and then away. "I remembered you said that. About bears in the spring."

"So you're hoping to bump into a bear while snowboarding?"

"Not exactly. But I need to face the possibility."

He wondered if he lived to be a hundred, and if he saw her every single day, if she would ever stop surprising him.

Delighting him, really.

But no, he could not think of that. Of a life that had her in it, every single day.

"Here's the thing," Jacey said, solemnly. "I try to do something I'm scared of. Every. Single. Day."

He was terrified himself at the moment. Of her.

Of this new Jacey.

Only it wasn't really new. It was just as Caitlyn had said. Jacey was small and had no idea how mighty she was.

Except that now, apparently, she did.

"I went skydiving," she said, beaming at him.

He'd given up a chance at happiness to protect her from all the unpredictable vagaries of life and she'd thrown it away? Gone skydiving?

"I want you to come with me," she said softly.

"Skydiving?"

"Don't be silly."

As if he'd be *afraid* to skydive. Come to think of it, he would be, as would any sensible person.

"I'd like you to come with me. To Moonbeam. Right

now. I have reservations for tonight. For the next three days."

"No." He thought he said it formidably, in a way that brooked no argument.

"That's what scares me today."

So he was an *exercise* in fully unwrapping the new her. *Terrifying.*

"Asking you to come with me is what scares me," Jacey said softly. "Leaving myself wide-open to rejection."

She was deliberately attacking him at his weakest point. He didn't want to hurt her. But if he could just be strong for one more minute. One more second. The time it took to say—

"No."

Jacey didn't look rejected. In the least. She didn't look scared, either. She looked like she knew how hard that single word had been for Trevor to utter.

She stepped into him, not the least bit intimidated. He had plenty of time to back away from her, but he didn't. There was no sense in her thinking he wouldn't stand his ground.

She laid her hand on his naked chest, right above his heart.

Her scent tickled his nostrils and her touch made him remember things he shouldn't remember right now, not when he needed so desperately to be strong.

She looked up at him, those wide green eyes wise on his own, and he knew he wasn't hiding one single thing from her. Jacey saw him. She knew he was terrified. And she probably knew he was on fire for her, too.

"Thank you," she said softly. "Thank you for trying to protect me."

"From? Not skydiving, apparently," he snapped, still

trying, but feeling the mortar crumble and a single brick fall with a *thunk* from the wall of his defenses.

"That's what you do, isn't it, Trevor? Protect? When I think back on it, it's in *everything*. Starting with really tiny things like the mittens."

He didn't say anything.

"When I told you I loved you, it sent you into overdrive, didn't it? To protect me from the most fearsome thing of all. And it's not death by bathroom."

Her gaze was absolutely stripping. She saw to his soul.

"You were trying to protect me from love."

"From hoping for too much," he heard himself say. He felt another brick fall, and then another, until his whole wall lay at his feet and at hers.

He felt naked, transparent before her. He felt as if her fingertips were drawing his freed heart to her.

He yanked himself away from her hand on his chest, but it didn't matter. It was too late.

"You see, Trevor," Jacey said firmly, "Caitlyn's legacy to us wasn't to instill in us the belief that love hurts. The lesson wasn't to avoid it at all costs. She would hate that message. She loved with every fiber of her being until her very last breath.

"This is her message to those of us who remain—to embrace every single opportunity life gives us. And especially this one. Love," she continued softly. "I think we should give it a chance."

Jacey felt as if she had stopped breathing, as if her heart had stopped beating. Waiting for Trevor's answer.

Waiting.

Waiting.

Waiting.

Her whole lifetime it felt as if she had been waiting

to know whether Trevor would say yes or no to giving love a second chance.

With her.

This time she knew it wasn't about her. Not at all. It was about him. So wounded on the battlefield of the heart. It would be the gravest act of bravery for him to say yes to this journey when it had nearly destroyed him once already.

She would not do anything to coerce him. To change his mind if it did not go the way she hoped. This had to come from him.

This single act of courage had to be his.

To say yes instead of no.

He looked away. He ran his hand through the tangle of his dark hair. He shifted from one foot to the other.

And then, his voice low in his throat, like a warrior on one knee, surrendering his weapons after a hard fought battle, he answered.

"I think we should," Trevor said, his eyes meeting hers. "I think we should give love a chance."

Every single thing within Jacey sighed with relief and gratitude. She stepped back into him, twined her arms around his neck, pulled his lips to hers.

Homecoming.

She had missed him so much. She was starving for him. The Jacey she had become over the past few months did not hold back.

Her lips sought his, her hands explored the familiar surfaces of his face, his neck, his chest. She demanded an answer, and answer he did, every bit as hungry as she was.

"I've missed you so much," he said, in between nips and kisses. He was a man who had been dying of thirst and she was a long, cool drink of water.

"I want you," she whispered. "I've never wanted anything as much as I want you."

Trevor broke the contact. He took a step back from her. When she tried to move back into the circle of his arms, he held up his hand.

Stop? Seriously?

"It's not going to be like this."

"Like what? Glorious?"

He smiled, with annoying patience, as if he was explaining a complex math formula to someone who wasn't very smart.

"We aren't going to jump in as lovers and see if a friendship develops."

"I think we've already jumped in! We've been friends for years!"

"Let's jump back out. And no, we haven't been friends for years. We had a mutual friend. A mutual love. It's not the same. We have to get to know each other in a different way, on brand-new ground."

She frowned. "I liked the ground we were on just fine."

"Humor me."

Jacey realized she felt distinctly pouty about the way this was going. "I pictured something a little different for our reunion."

She saw heat flash through his eyes—in fact, she was fairly certain he was burning up—but then resolve strengthened in his features, reminding her what she was dealing with.

A strong man. And a principled one.

"We need to back up a few steps," Trevor said. "We need to know if what we felt on the mountain can translate to real life. We need to go slow."

CHAPTER NINETEEN

"I'VE BEEN GOING slow my whole life! What we had on the mountain was the most real thing I've ever had."

"Was it? Or was it an amazing distraction? Did we put the cart before the horse? Did entering a physical relationship get in the way of our getting to know each other?"

She glared at him.

"Jacey, the next time I make love to you, I want it to be deliberate. I want it to be intentional. I don't want it to be an impulse. Something we fall into by accident."

She felt the shiver of his words go up and down her spine. *The next time.*

Still, she didn't want to just give in to him. She didn't want to be the people-pleaser she had been her entire life.

"I'm trying to learn to be *more* impulsive."

"And look where that got you."

"Here?"

"Jumping out of an airplane at five thousand feet!"

"Ten thousand!"

He laughed.

Oh, the sound of his laughter!

But then he became very, very serious. "I want to honor you, Jacey. I want to romance you. I want to cherish you. I want to treat you with honor and old-fashioned respect."

"It practically sounds as if you want a chaperone appointed. And I thought I've always been the dull one!"

"Does that sound dull to you?"

"Yes!"

"Then," he said, "you've never been romanced by me."

She felt the tingle of that promise go through her whole body, from her toes to her fingertips to the tips of her hair.

"What would being romanced by you involve, exactly?" she asked.

"I think it should have an element of surprise to it."

"Huh. I bet that means you don't even have a plan. You have no idea how to romance me!"

"I do. I have all kinds of ideas. I have so many ideas it's hard to pick just one."

"Hmmm," she said skeptically. "Name a few."

"Okay. We could go to Paris and drink hot chocolate at a café on the banks of the Seine. Or I could take you to *Phantom of the Opera* in New York, and have you hold my hand so hard it hurts. I could feed you She Crab Soup in Charleston, South Carolina."

"Not bad," she said, pretending thoughtfulness, even though the thought of that—exploring the world with him—made her feel as if the fire she sensed burning in him was leaping to her.

Both of them, on fire with life.

"Not bad?" he sputtered. "How about this? A gondola ride in Venice."

"You forgot the most important one."

"Which is?"

"Well," she said, "you've never been romanced by me, either. And the first rule?"

"Rules," he said. "Perimeters. Boundaries. I like it."

"The first rule is that you don't make all the rules. Because, really, hot chocolate in Paris, and gondola rides and the Phantom in New York doesn't exactly sound like real life, either."

"Huh," Trevor said, pretending he was irritated. "What's your idea of being romanced in real life, then?"

Jacey loved this teasing between them, the back and forth banter. It felt so right and so good to be with him.

"You win me a stuffed bear at the carnival. We go on-line and look up a complicated recipe and try to make it together. We volunteer to walk dogs at the animal shelter. On a whim, you go by a market and buy me the odd posy of flowers. We build a snowman together."

He cocked his head at her. "See? It's a good thing we're doing this. We're already learning we're miles apart in the romance department."

"Is it hopeless?" she teased him.

"I don't know. Meeting halfway could be all right. Should we go to Moonbeam and think about it?"

"Absolutely."

Ozzie was running the gondola when they arrived late in the afternoon. He was so happy to see them he was extra friendly, even for Ozzie. He kept letting people go ahead of them as he caught them up on what had happened in his life in the two months since they had last seen him.

Apparently, he and Freddy were now a number.

Jacey glanced at Trevor, surprised at his patience—no, his *interest*—in Ozzie's life. He was encouraging him!

Finally, Ozzie gestured them onto a gondola.

Jacey ducked through the door, and then gasped, and tried to back out again. "There's someone—"

But Trevor pushed her gently from behind, and she heard Ozzie's shout of satisfied laughter.

It wasn't, after all, "someone" already in the gondola car. It was a huge stuffed bear, with a bow on it.

And a tag that said, *To Jacey, love from Trevor.*

She took the bear. It was brown and dressed in a toque and a sweater and just about the softest thing she had ever touched. She could hardly lift it, it was so big, but she settled it on her lap and hugged it tight.

"You said you wanted to see a bear on the mountain," Trevor said. "And you said you wanted a stuffed bear. Two birds—make that bears—with one stone."

She thought of all the trouble he would have had to go to, to make this happen. The secret phone calls, the money. It was possibly one of the most romantic things that had ever happened to her.

She decided not to tell him that, after all the trouble he'd gone through, the best thing about the bear was the tag.

Love from Trevor.

"Hmmm," she said, tapping her chin as if she was evaluating his effort. "You didn't win him for me at the carnival."

"It's harder than you think to find a carnival at this time of year."

"I know you'll do better next time," she said sternly. And then, she couldn't keep it up anymore. She kissed the bear all over, and then she kissed Trevor.

"Hey!" he said. "I thought we were going to—"

"Shush. I told you. You don't make all the rules."

"So unfair. I can't escape."

She took his lips again. She made sure he didn't want to.

"I think there's cameras."

She moved the bear in front of them and kissed him and kissed him and kissed him.

They emerged from the gondola, breathless and lugging the bear.

They were at the same hotel, but Jacey found out he'd changed her arrangements. Now they were in separate rooms. She went to put the bear away and change into her ski gear. They were hoping to get in one or two runs before the day was over.

When she opened the door to her room, the scent of flowers hit her.

She walked in, and her mouth fell open. The room probably had two dozen little posies scattered throughout it.

She sank down on the bed with her bear and thought about how she was feeling. She felt listened to, but it went deeper than that.

Cherished.

Moonbeam proved to be the counterpoint to the physical sizzle between them. The mountain was a mistress and her challenges required full focus and attention.

But she was a magical mistress. That afternoon they were above the clouds just as they had been in the winter, and just like then, the sun was brilliant on the snow.

But the difference now was the warmth in the sun. Jackets could be left behind. There were actually people skiing and boarding in shorts!

Jacey and Trevor slathered on the sunscreen to prevent sunburn as they lifted their faces to the promise of the coming days.

Jacey soon discovered her vision of herself flying down the mountain—impressing Trevor with all her new skill—was to be thwarted.

The snow, fast melting now, was sticky and could be devilishly hard to navigate.

Halfway down the run, she pulled off toward the trees and lay down in the snow, defeated.

"What are you doing?" Trevor asked, coming down behind her. He did one of those stops that sprayed her with snow.

Heavy, wet snow.

"Hey!" she said, wiping the snow from her face. "My legs are tired. I need to rest."

He flopped down beside her, and they stared up at the endless blue sky; let the sun touch their faces.

She noticed how comfortable the silence was between them.

"You know what this snow is perfect for?"

"Not snowboarding?"

"Snowmen!"

She cast him a glance. Despite his assertion they needed to get to know each other, she had a feeling Trevor was working through that list with lightning speed!

He kicked off his skis and leaned them up against a nearby tree. Then he came and sprang the bindings on her snowboard.

He held out his hand and pulled her to her feet. She looked at his lips.

She thought, *to heck with snowmen.*

But he let go of her and scooped up a handful of snow. He formed it into a careful ball. The engineer was coming out in him!

He began to push the ball, and the snow was perfect. Each push more snow clung to it, and it began to leave a wide snow-denuded pathway behind it.

She joined him, their shoulders together, gasping, slipping, laughing.

"It's way too big," she told him, when it felt as if they couldn't push it another inch.

"It's never too big," he insisted.

And it turned out he was right, because soon two teenagers who had been snowboarding had kicked off their boards, too, and were pushing that huge ball of snow.

Then, as they started the second ball, a family joined them.

Jacey recognized that, somehow, she and Trevor were at the center of it all, their glow drawing people to them like nectar drew bees. Soon, the crowd of people had created an epic snowman. They stood back, admiring their work only briefly, and then they created a snowwoman, now children and a snow house for them all to live in.

It was amazing to her how that community had leaped up around them, orbiting their joie de vivre.

It began like that. A magic between them overflowing into everything as they enjoyed the mountain and all its amenities.

Jacey found she quite enjoyed tormenting him—laying her hand on his shoulder, touching his tush when no one was looking, kissing him and coaxing him to kiss her back.

She was tormenting herself, too, of course. Still, this playful teasing sharpened their awareness of each other to that point where it was hard to tell whether it was pleasure or pain.

She took the greatest chance of all. She said the word to him that had chased him away the first time.

Only this time she added two words to it. *I love you.*

CHAPTER TWENTY

TREVOR LET THOSE words sink in.

I love you.

Without a doubt, the most powerful and the most meaningful words in the universe. To receive.

And to give.

And so he said them back.

He was stunned by how the words rolled off his tongue with the taste and effervescence of the finest champagne.

He was amazed and gratified at how alive he felt.

And shocked and dismayed by how quickly the time at Moonbeam dissolved. Their journey to the airport this time was completely different than the last time he had dropped her off there.

He went in with her.

They said goodbye as if they might never see each other again. He'd never been publicly demonstrative. He was pretty sure Jacey never had been, either. But her getting on the airplane made him kiss her without the reservation he had inserted—with super human effort—into their time on Moonbeam.

She had named the bear Moonie, and as she went through to the secured area, she was clutching it as if it was a life support.

He was surprised that security didn't try to take it.

But no, they indulged her, sending Moonie through the X-ray machine on its own, the whole world bowing to what was so evident in the way she carried herself, the look in her eyes, the glow around her.

Love.

And he was humbled that he was the recipient of that.

But also the slave of it. He could no more stay away from her than the tides could disobey the command of the moon.

He was on a plane, Toronto-bound, the next day.

When Jacey opened her door she was shocked, but only for a second. Then she flew into his arms.

"What are you doing? What are you doing here?"

"There's two things left on your list," he said.

She took him in, and then laughed. "Trevor! You said you wanted to go slow."

"To hell with that. Where's the nearest animal shelter?"

They walked three dogs in Trinity Bellwoods Park. The dogs were terribly misbehaved, pulling on the leads, getting tangled up with each other, lunging at other dogs and barking incessantly.

The park was quite lovely in the spring with some trees in blossom and the grass turning a vibrant green. Trevor was not sure he had ever been so *aware*. Of the way the air felt on his skin, the way the sunlight looked in her hair, the way the slender column of her throat begged for the touch of his lips, the way she laughed at those misbehaving dogs as if they were adorable.

"No wonder they aren't adopted," he muttered when they returned them.

"I thought Casey had potential."

"Yeah, the potential to eat your sofa in one serving."

"You'd probably be happy if he ate that sofa."

"Why would I be? I *love* your sofa."

And for some reason, she looked at him as if he had drawn down the moon and given it to her as a gift.

"Okay," he said, "let's figure out what we're making for dinner. Do you have something in mind, or do you just want me to search for *complicated recipes*?"

"You can't just put in *complicated recipes* and expect something to pop up."

He took that as a challenge. He put the words *complicated recipes* into the search engine on his phone.

"You want gnocchi with burnt butter and walnuts?"

"Sure," she said.

As it turned out, the only part of making gnocchi they were good at was shopping for the ingredients.

"It looks like a flour bomb went off in here," he told her several hours later as they sat side by side on her couch. "Sorry."

"Love means never having to be sorry about flour bombs."

"We went wrong at trying to make the gnocchi from scratch." He deliberately mispronounced it, just to make her laugh.

"It was supposed to be complicated. Besides, I think we've got burning butter down to an art."

"Agreed. And we know your smoke detector works."

"And that you're a man who can be counted on to flap a towel wildly at it to make it stop."

They chuckled, but Trevor suddenly seemed somber. "I can't do it, Jacey."

She looked stunned. "I remember the last time you said that to me," she said, her voice choked. "I thought this time—"

"Jacey." He touched her face tenderly, looked down

into her eyes. "I don't mean I can't be with you. I mean I can't finish the list."

"What?"

"Paris. New York. Charleston. Vienna. They'll have to wait. Because I can't wait any longer."

"What do you mean?"

"If you don't know somebody completely after you've burnt butter together, you're never going to know them."

"Agreed," she said softly.

"I realized I'm being ridiculous with my lists and rules. It's the engineer in me, trying to come up with the perfect formula. But the truth is, I've always known you, Jacey. I knew you as Caitlyn's friend, and I loved you for who you were to her. And then I knew you as the friend, above all the others, who was there when I needed you, when I needed a true friend, more than I ever had at any point in my whole life.

"I know you, Jacey."

"Yes, you do," she whispered.

"I know your heart. I know it's so strong, and so good and so brave. Maybe what I needed more time for, really, was to know myself."

"And do you?"

"I know I can't live without you. That I don't want to. That you have brought the color back into a life that had gone black-and-white."

"Just promise me one thing."

"What promise do you want me to make?" he asked her softly, a man who would give her the world if that was what she asked.

"Don't ever make gnocchi again."

She deliberately mispronounced it.

He took his thumb and wiped the flour from her nose.

And then her cheek. And then he put his thumb on her lip and felt the full plump sensuality of it.

She nibbled.

This was going to be his life. He did not know what he had ever done to deserve to be loved so richly, not once, but twice.

He planned to be a man who deserved the grace that had been bestowed on him. He drew Jacey into his arms and picked her up, carried her through to the bedroom.

"I promise," he said. "Next time we cook something complicated together we're doing pork, fennel and sage ragu with polenta."

He deliberately mispronounced *polenta*.

And her laughter was more essential to him than the air he breathed.

"Let's do something complicated together right now," she whispered, and stole the laughter from his lips with her kiss.

EPILOGUE

Three Years Later

TREVOR STOOD AT the very top of Moonbeam Mountain. An eagle danced with the same fresh, pure breeze that lifted his hair.

The mountain was so totally different in the summertime. Like life itself, it had its seasons. And this was its season of joy and abundance, the huckleberries, like gorgeous purple jewels, were thick on the stunted mountain shrubs. The lush grass of the meadow was sewn through with a breathtaking array of arctic lupines, alpine daisies, mountain heather, glacier lilies.

The Big Dipper Chairlift had been opened just for this.

For a wedding on top of the mountain.

For the past hour it had been bringing their guests up, many of them their Moonbeam family. Since Trevor had purchased a condo on the mountain, he and Jacey had become super close to several other couples including Bjorn and Jasper and Ozzie and Freddy, who were expecting a baby.

A baby.

The thought of a baby, of other people having babies, no longer filled him with sadness, with a terror of hoping for too much. Instead, when he thought of that possibility, he felt a wonderful anticipation of the future, and the surprises life had in store for him and Jacey.

The guests were assembled now, in chairs that had been brought up on the lift yesterday. Not like the grand piano—they'd had to use a helicopter to bring that in.

It had cost the earth to get it up here, but Trevor couldn't think of a better use for money. Why have it if you didn't use it for moments like this? If you didn't use it to bring joy? To share your joy with others? His intention was to make this gathering, this celebration of love, as memorable, as perfect, as joyous as possible.

He could feel his heart beginning to thud harder as he waited, watching as empty chair after empty chair reached the top of the lift, paused, and then completed the circle and went back down, swaying gently.

Finally, he could see a chair coming that had people on it.

She was coming.

His light. His love. His strength. His spirit.

His soul.

As the chair trundled up the mountain, he could see her. Jacey, who had once been so terrified of heights, was leaning over the safety bar and looking at the meadows, her own bouquet of wildflowers dangling casually from one hand. Underneath the yards of silk, her legs swung like an exuberant child on a swing.

His mother sat on one side of her.

And Caitlyn's on the other.

They wore lovely spring dresses. His mother had had her hair "done" and was trying to pat it back into place as the mountain breezes messed with it.

Both looked a little nervous, Caitlyn's mother gripping the safety bar tightly. Trevor had offered to have them brought up in the helicopter, but both mothers had refused.

She didn't have a father or a mother, but she had inherited two families, his and Caitlyn's and those mothers, Mary and Jane, had insisted they be with Jacey the whole way, standing with her, and not just symbolically.

As he watched, Jacey said something that made both the moms laugh. She kissed one cheek and then the other, too, taking Mary's hand with the hand that did not have the bouquet in it.

This was his Jacey. It was her day. She could have been entirely focused on herself, and her nerves, but no. She was bringing comfort to the nervous moms.

His father, and Caitlyn's, stood beside him, the very best of men.

"Wow," his dad said, and when Trevor glanced at him, he saw he was not looking at Jacey at all, but his wife of over forty years.

Family.

In the absence of Jacey's father, Trevor had gone to Caitlyn's family and asked their permission to marry her.

He had worried that Caitlyn's parents might think he was moving on too soon. Or that they might believe that he was replacing their daughter with someone else.

He should have known better.

The well of love that had created Caitlyn ran deep and pure.

Caitlyn's parents told him that his love of Jacey—and hers for him—did not replace the love he'd had for Caitlyn, but honored it.

Honored that magnificent entity called love that would not be slayed, ever, not even by death.

Well-meaning people had told him throughout his journey of grief that time healed all wounds.

This was not his truth.

His truth was that love was the balm for wounds. It didn't heal wounds so much as weave them into the tapestry of a life, making it stronger, more intricate, more real, more beautiful.

Love stood as a testament.

It was the one thing that could defeat all the sorrow, all the pain, all the sadness. Love triumphed, like those meadows full of wildflowers that had lain silent under the snow all through the cold, dark winter. Waiting for spring, faithful in their inherent knowledge, the sacred knowing that lived inside every seed.

The chair paused and Jacey and the mothers got off. If ever there was a bride who didn't look the least bit nervous, it was her. She laughed as the wind caught her hair. It was now long again, and she wore a ring of wildflowers as a crown.

The dress was stunning. Trevor had not been allowed to see it, and now he could feel his eyes smarting at the beauty. In sharp contrast to the mountain's masculine ruggedness, it was a celebration of feminine softness. Jacey was no longer so painfully thin. As she'd come into herself, she had filled out, becoming the woman she was always meant to be before his very eyes.

Her shoulders were bare, her hair touching them, and the beaded bodice hugged her fullness, showed off her beautiful curves. At her waist the fabric pinched in and then flared out dramatically.

The wind caught those folds of silk and the dress billowed out in a cloud of white around her. Laughing, she tried to capture the wayward dress, reminding him of that very famous photo of a movie star standing over a grate.

He knew Jacey had debated the dress, not at all sure

if she should go so traditional. After all, she'd told him solemnly, she had been married before.

But Trevor had suggested she—the woman who had leaped from airplanes and soared down the slopes of Moonbeam—make her own rules.

He saw that she had. And that this time she was accepting—embracing—every single thing she deserved.

As he watched her playfully trying to pin the dress down, he considered the age-old vows he was about to take with her. For better, for worse, for richer, for poorer, in sickness and in health.

He thought, perhaps, most people who took those vows misinterpreted them as some kind of endurance test, a promise to grit your teeth and stick with it, no matter what.

But Trevor saw the vows on a deeper level. He saw that love was not diminished by the many challenges that would be thrown at it. Indeed, it was made stronger as people found themselves, and found who they really were, discovered what they were made of. A smooth life, a life without bumps and obstacles, a life without mountains to climb, rarely showed people that. But a strong relationship that survived storms did.

The wind died then, as if on cue, and Jacey's dress settled around her.

Johnny Jordan began to play. It was Trevor's gift to Jacey, his surprise for her. The mountaintop grand piano, Johnny here to play. Caitlyn's song spilled out over the gathering, over the meadows, over the mountaintops.

Though it had become one of the most played and well-known compositions in the world, right now, in this moment, it felt deeply personal, as if it was only for them, as if it had been created to bring Caitlyn—whose love had made all this happen—into this moment with them.

Even the eagle seemed to celebrate that there were elements of mystery to this that were beyond the comprehension of all living things. He circled the gathering with spread-wide wings, effortlessly gliding on the air currents, throwing his shadow over the bride, like a blessing.

Jacey went very still. She tilted her head to look at the eagle, and then she closed her eyes and listened until the last note sobbed, haunting and beautiful, over the mountains and the valleys.

Only then did she open her eyes, take a breath, smooth the dress one last time and, finally, give her full attention to him. She moved toward him, Mary on one elbow and Jane on the other.

She had tears, but *that* smile was on her face and *that* light was in her eyes.

That smile and that light held every truth he cared to know.

After the cold came the warmth.

After the darkness came the light.

After death came new life.

Love was that seed that waited.

* * * * *

COMING SOON!

We really hope you enjoyed reading this book.
If you're looking for more romance, be sure to
head to the shops when new books are
available on

Thursday 5th January

To see which titles are coming soon, please visit
millsandboon.co.uk/nextmonth

MILLS & BOON®

Coming next month

CONSEQUENCE OF THEIR DUBAI NIGHT
Nina Milne

Perhaps he should refuse to see her, but that would be rude. Stella must have some reason for being here. Only one way to find out. 'Send her in,' he said.

To his own irritation he could feel the thump of his heart against his ribs, as anticipation churned inside him. Then there was a perfunctory knock on the door, Mariella pushed the door open and ushered Stella in, nodded at Max and retreated.

He rose to his feet, actually glad that his desk separated them, gave him a barrier to absorb the impact of seeing her.

She tugged the scarf off her head and pushed the sunglasses atop her blonde hair in an impatient gesture and for a long moment they stood staring at each other. Stella looked different, every bit as beautiful but there was something he couldn't put his finger on, a subtle change. Her blue eyes held a certain something he couldn't decipher, the gloss of her hair held an extra lustre. But what hadn't changed was the instant charge, the magnetic pull of attraction, the urge to take up where they left off.

Her blonde hair was pulled back and then caught in a clip, tendrils escaping to frame her face. Blue eyes studied his face, as if she too was drinking him in, eyes that were shadowed with a trepidation that had been absent in Dubai.

'Stella. This is unexpected.'

'Yes.' Her lips twisted up into a smile that held wryness. 'I saw the article about your first date.' The article had come out two days ago, headlined with 'Spotted in the Wild – CEO Max Durante and heiress Dora Fitzgerald. Is it a date? The notoriously single CEO of InScreen certainly looked smitten as the possible couple … blah blah.'

'And I'm not here to make trouble.'

'Then why are you here?' He saw her hands curl into fists as though she were digging her nails into her palms, saw her shoulders pull back as she took a step backwards as if in preparation to turn and run and a sense of foreboding trickled through him.

'I'm pregnant.' There was a moment where the penny failed to drop where he could only look at her in bewilderment and she continued. 'With your baby.'

Continue reading
CONSEQUENCE OF THEIR DUBAI NIGHT
Nina Milne

Available next month
www.millsandboon.co.uk